A PACK of VOWS and TEARS

OLIVIA WILDENSTEIN

A PACK OF VOWS AND TEARS
Book 2 of *THE BOULDER WOLVES* series

Cover design by *Ampersand Book Covers*
Art of Ness & August by *@elionhardt*
Editing by *Krystal Dehaba*

RUN A LITTLE WILD.

PROLOGUE

The first time I shifted, I was eleven. I still remember the matching looks of shock on my parents' faces. Where my mother's gaze had remained wide, my father's had crinkled with a smile. He'd crouched with his arms wide open to corral me. Disoriented and unsteady, catching me had been a swift affair. Dad had pinned me against his chest until my wolf quieted, until I morphed back into a naked child made of flesh and tears instead of fur and claws. And then he'd wrapped me up in a fleece blanket, whispering, "It's okay, Ness. Everything will be okay."

He was wrong.

After that day, nothing had ever been okay.

What are you thinking about, babe? Liam's voice resonated inside my skull, making me jump. I could morph into a furry beast, yet communication without sound was still bewildering.

I wasn't sure I would ever get used to hearing my Alpha speak to me through the pack's mind link.

My Alpha . . .

With blood pledges, Liam had been sworn in mere minutes ago as the Boulder Pack's new Alpha. His dream had come true. And mine along with it, because I'd gotten to swear my allegiance to him. I was now part of the pack who'd shunned me because of my gender. Take that, Heath Kolane.

How Heath had birthed a son as fair and good as Liam was almost as mystifying as an Alpha's ability to speak into minds.

Smiling up at Liam, I threaded my fingers through the soft, black swoop of hair that fell into his reddish-brown eyes and pushed it off his forehead. "Nothing. Nothing's on my mind, besides how proud I am of you."

Tonight was his night. I wouldn't spoil it with my glum thoughts.

His gaze hunted my expression. Although Alphas could speak into minds, they couldn't read what crowded them. "Ten more minutes, and we'll head out."

I looked around the large stone-walled room of Headquarters where the pledging ceremony had taken place. Outside, the world was going to sleep. Inside, the party was just beginning. The animated chatter and the tinny scent of blood drying on the pledges' wrists made my head spin.

"We can stay longer, Liam. I'm not in any rush." It wasn't as though I had anywhere to go . . . anyone to see.

No, that wasn't completely true. I'd made a friend in Colorado: Sarah Matz. She was a deejay on Thursdays and Saturdays at a place called The Den, and a Pine wolf the rest of the time. Technically, she should've been my enemy—the Boulders and the Pines despised each other—but since we'd met at her brother's engagement party, she'd been nothing but friendly. Actually, Sarah was only pleasant *after* her first cup of coffee. Before that, she was a major grouch.

Still, her personality beat the fake pertness of the Boulder wolves' girlfriends who all seemed to resent me because I possessed something they didn't—the werewolf gene—and because I'd defied Liam Kolane, the boy reared to become Alpha.

As I watched Liam talk animatedly with the pack, my stomach throbbed. Hunger, I supposed—I'd had a sandwich, but that was hours ago. Unless the throbbing was emanating from my nervousness. Liam had asked me to go home with him once the evening concluded. I'd never gone home with a man before.

I pressed my palm against my abdomen that was hardening by the second and walked toward one of the walls where drinks, cold cuts, and energy bars had been laid out on a long wooden table. I fished out a peanut butter bar from a glass salad bowl and was about to peel off the wrapper when headlights flashed over the window, blinding me in the process.

My first thoughts were that my traitorous cousin, Everest, had come to right the wrongs he'd caused by blackmailing me into believing I'd killed Liam's father.

But then the driver got out.

The energy bar slid from my fingers and toppled back into the bowl.

I could almost feel the earth shake as his boots hit the ground.

After pledging himself to Liam, August Watt had stalked out of Headquarters. And yet, here he was again, minutes later. I hoped he'd returned to apologize for his odd behavior, but his rough stride and narrowed eyes told me that was most definitely not his intent.

CHAPTER 1

As August approached Headquarters, my entire body tightened. I felt as though someone were winding me up and up, like one of those tiny ballerinas in jewelry boxes. Crossing my arms, I watched him approach and, like those ballerinas, I whirled as he rounded the square building toward the heavy door. Had he returned to apologize for acting so distant toward me earlier or had he forgotten something?

I willed it to be the former. I willed *him* to walk toward me and say he was sorry, because I'd done nothing to deserve his aloofness. August had always been one of my favorite people in Colorado. And I wanted it to stay that way, in spite of the miles of land and ocean that would soon separate us when he returned to active duty.

The second he stepped inside, his green gaze pummeled into mine, before roving over the room toward the white-haired elder bent over my gaunt-faced uncle.

Liam intercepted August as he made his way toward Frank. Something must've been said through the mind link because August's expression became thunderous.

He brushed past Liam. "I need a word with Frank."

Liam squared his shoulders, eyes flaring with annoyance. At least I wasn't the only recipient of August's moodiness.

Frank straightened out slowly, leaving my catatonic uncle to stare at his tan loafers. Finding out his son was a traitor would haunt him for a long time.

Why did you do it, Everest? Why did you make me fight Liam? Were you hoping I would die or were you hoping he would? I yearned to get answers because a part of me couldn't believe the boy I'd grown up with could backstab me and his pack so guilelessly.

I tried to make out August's hissed whisper to Frank, but the lively banter in the glass and stone room drowned out my friend's deep timbre. Unable to leave well-enough alone, I strode through the small clusters of men chugging celebratory beers, uncrossed my arms, and poked August in the bicep. He didn't brush away my finger, but he squeezed his eyes shut a moment.

"What the hell, August? What did I do to you that merited—"

He opened his eyes, and the force of his gaze made me stop talking.

Frank sighed. "I was worried it had happened."

"That *what* had happened?" I asked, scowling at August.

"Both of you, follow me." Frank started toward the back of the building.

Neither August nor I moved.

"Now," Frank said.

August lowered his eyes.

"I don't understand," I said.

"I don't either, Ness." August's voice was infinitesimally softer, which wasn't to say soft. It was still as strained as the cream-colored Henley on his back.

"What do you mean, you don't understand?" I kept my voice low. "You're the one who snubbed me. Not the other way around."

"Ness, now." Frank's voice brooked no argument.

Stomach writhing with nerves, I started across the room that had fallen way too quiet. Lucas and Matt stared at me as I passed by them, and then they stared at August, who was a step behind me.

Ness? I felt Liam's voice inside my head, looked for him through the fence of enormous male bodies. He wasn't hard to spot. It wasn't so much that he was taller than all the others—he wasn't—but because he emitted something the others didn't, this intractable pull . . . an *Alphaness.*

6

"I'll be right back," I told him as August went around me.

Liam's eyes had shifted to amber, as though the wolf in him was trying to surface. He was protective and possessive of the people he liked. Since he'd climbed onto my balcony and we'd shared our first kiss, I'd become one of those people.

I pasted on a smile to reassure him that everything was all right. But was anything all right? Why did Frank want to talk to me? And why was August acting like someone had wronged him? He hadn't coveted the title of Alpha, so it couldn't be jealousy. Before he'd left Boulder, he'd even urged me not to fight Liam for it.

I walked toward one of the two small rooms in the back of the building. August was already inside. As I treaded past him, he shut the door, then planted his boot against the wood and leaned back.

I dropped down onto the black leather couch, folded one leg over the other, and laced my fingers around my knee, which had started bobbing with crackling anticipation. "Why did you need to see the both of us?"

Frank removed a wicker chair from a short stack and propped it on the stone floor. The chair groaned as he took a seat. He looked from August to me and then back at August, who'd crossed his arms, tendons pinching underneath his burnished skin. He'd never disclosed the location of where he'd been stationed these past few weeks, but I suspected he'd acquired his deeper-brown hue some-where in the Middle East. Few regions were as contentious. Well, besides Colorado. Our state was chock-full of contention thanks to feuding packs.

At the elder's sigh, my stomach cramped again. Maybe it wasn't hunger. Maybe it *was* stress. Stress brought on by August's strange behavior.

"Your abdomen is spasming, isn't it, Ness?" Frank asked.

Blinking at Frank, I whipped my hand off my middle and clasped my knee.

"It's normal."

"Normal?" I croaked.

"A symptom of what you've *contracted*."

"What I've contracted? What have I contracted?"

Frank's gaze slid toward August. "How's your stomach, son?"

"Fine," he replied gruffly.

"What did I contract, Frank?" I was scared now. I wasn't in pain but definitely in discomfort.

"A mating bond," Frank said. "That's what."

"What?" My brain felt as though it were pirouetting inside my skull. "A what?" I looked toward August.

The color had leached from his skin, and his full lips parted with an inaudible gasp. "No . . . "

"Yes," Frank said. "I'm sorry, son. I imagine this isn't what you or Ness want to hear, but your wolves decided they were meant for each other."

Our wolves?

A mating bond?

I sucked in a breath. "What?" I whispered, not because I was dumb or dense—I'd gotten what Frank had just thrown at us—but because I was shocked. Beyond shocked. I was probably experiencing what my mother had felt the night I'd barreled out of my bedroom on four paws and white fur.

While Frank explained the technicalities of a mating bond, I zoned out. I didn't want a preordained fate. I wanted the freedom to fall in love with the person of my choice. And that person wasn't August. I mean, I loved August, but as an older brother.

I didn't love him as more.

I could never love him as more.

"This has nothing to do with love," Frank said.

Had he heard my thoughts? Had I spoken them out loud?

I scrutinized the beige grout between the slabs of gray stones on the floor. The lines blurred and intersected at wrong angles. This couldn't be happening . . . I'd just become part of the pack. I'd just kissed Liam Kolane. I didn't want a mating bond.

"Mating bonds are evolutionary—"

I cut Frank off. "Like eradicating females?" I was still bitter about this. I think I would always be bitter about my pack ingesting a fossilized tree root to ensure only boys were born to the pack.

"No, Ness."

A hush fell over the room. Since Frank wasn't launching into an explanation, and August wasn't asking any questions, I deduced he'd been brought up to speed about the Boulder Wolves' selection tool.

"Not to sound pedantic, but let me give you a little history lesson. As you may already know, werewolves began existing when men and women settled around these parts. To survive, our ancestors were given the gift of claws and fur. They used their gifts to protect those who walked the earth only in skin." Frank scraped in a breath. "To make sure our species endured the test of time, each one of our ancestors was drawn to a particular mate, someone who complemented their skillset, whose genes would ensure the making of a better, stronger wolf.

"Now, with the advent of modernity, the world became less hostile to the settlers, and so our numbers dwindled, but thanks to generations of mating, we never stopped existing. Sadly, with our people being killed off by hunters—"

"Or by tree roots," I interjected, my gaze wandering over the tiny clumps of earth left behind by dirty boots, clumps that led all the way to a padlocked fridge.

What could possibly be kept in there that merited a lock and chain? The pack artifact? I hoped Liam would destroy it tonight.

"Or by tree roots," Frank conceded, "mates have become rarer. It still happens, though. Some werewolves will even experience this with humans, a rare occurrence, but still an occurrence."

"Can we . . . " I loosed a rough sigh. This situation was so unfair. "Can we break it?"

"Break it?" Frank rasped.

My navel felt as though it had been filled with gasoline and set on fire. Was that a result of our link? I didn't press my palm against my abdomen, afraid to bring attention to my duplicitous body.

"Why would you want to break it, Ness?" Frank asked.

I looked at August, who was studying the humming refrigerator in the corner with such intensity that if he'd been a warlock instead of a werewolf, I was pretty sure the fridge would've melted into a puddle of steel.

"So few of us are bequeathed such a gift—"

"Gift?" I yelped, cutting off Frank. "The theft of our freewill isn't a gift. If anything, it's a curse! Clearly, neither August nor I want this."

August's gaze zipped off the fridge and landed on me.

My pulse throbbed everywhere. "Right, August?"

After a beat, he said, "Right."

Frank's bushy white eyebrows knit on his forehead. "August hasn't been back for a day. Maybe if you give yourselves some time."

I shook my head, and my long blonde hair unraveled from the knot I'd wound it in and slipped over my bare arms. "Frank, with all due respect, August and I know each other, but it's not like that between us. It can never be like that between us."

"Why not?" the elder asked.

I startled. Why was Frank being so pigheaded about this? Because pack traditions were sacred to him? Well, they weren't sacred to me.

"What if I left long enough? Will it fade?" August asked.

"Distance dims the strength of the tether, but it won't make it magically snap. This isn't like an Alpha bond, children."

"So only death will stop it?" I mused. "I'm not contemplating dying or killing August," I added, so they wouldn't lock me up. I couldn't lose all my freewill in one night.

"Good to know." August shot me a rueful smile that dimmed the insistent pounding inside my belly.

Great. My stomach was now endowed with an emotional barometer that broadcast August's mood. My gaze drifted to his stomach. He'd never once clutched it. Did my emotions not register the same way with him?

His smile waned, and his jaw hardened again. "Is there a way, besides death, to break this bond, Frank?"

"Yes." Frank leaned back in his chair and shook his head like a teacher facing two petulant children.

"How?" I asked.

"You shouldn't want to—"

"How?" August asked, voice firm.

"If mating bonds aren't consummated—"

"Consummated?" I asked.

"The bond snaps into place through sexual relations."

My cheeks lit up like brake lights. *Oh . . .*

"As I was saying, if they aren't consummated by the next solstice, the bond disintegrates."

Rolling the hem of my sky-blue camisole between my cold fingers, I said, "You'd just have to stay away for six months, August. You were planning on deploying for that long, right?"

Slow seconds passed before he answered, "Right."

Frank's features were scrunched in disapproval. "You'd be destroying something sacred."

Pounding on the door made me jump.

"Frank?" *Liam.*

Oh, crap. I wanted Liam to come in as much as I wanted to share another meal with the vile hunter who'd killed my father, Aidan Michaels.

I pressed my clammy palms against the nape of my neck, trying to lower my body temperature.

August cocked an eyebrow, as though waiting for my approval to open the door.

I reasoned that Liam deserved to hear what was happening. And yet, I abhorred the thought of him finding out. I was afraid of what it would do to him . . . *to us.*

I finger-combed my hair so that it draped around my cheeks and nodded.

August stepped away from the door at the same time as it flew open. And then Liam was standing there, crowding the entire space, slashed, bloodied T-shirt flapping. Although the cut over his heart had sealed shut, the remnants of the pledging ceremony had left behind a razor-thin pale mark and reddish smears. Like Liam's chest, my wrist had also sealed shut, yet the place I'd sliced still smarted.

He shut the door behind him with a bang. "I waited. I'm done waiting. What the hell's going on?" he demanded, a brittleness to his tone.

I rubbed the thin streaks of dried blood on the inside of my wrist, careful not to skim the knit skin.

Silence.

The sound of it was so hostile that I almost explained everything, but the words kept jamming in my throat.

Slowly, Frank said, "I was explaining to August and Ness the dynamics of mating bonds."

"Mating bonds?" Liam's eyes flared. "Is that why—why they smelled like they'd—"

I cringed. "Please don't say it. Please."

"Like we what?" August asked.

Maybe *I* would leave. Race away from Boulder until I didn't feel like I was about to die of embarrassment.

No one spoke for a long second. At least, not out loud. From the surprise rippling over August's features, I suspected Liam had finished his sentence through the mind-link.

I couldn't sit here any longer. "I need to go home," I said, shooting up.

"Home?" Liam lifted one of his dark eyebrows.

Right. He expected me to go to *his home.* "To the inn."

There was a tiny hitch in his breathing. ***This doesn't change anything, Ness.*** His voice stroked my harried brain.

"Doesn't it?" I whispered hoarsely.

Not to me.

Frank had gotten up too. He clapped a hand on Liam's shoulder. "It's not wise to get between mates."

Liam shrugged off Frank's hand. "With all due respect, Frank, it's not wise to tell your Alpha what to do."

Frank let his hand drop. "You're right. I apologize."

"Besides, we both know firsthand that mates don't always end up together," Liam added.

Did Frank have a mate? Or did Liam have one? No. If he'd had one, he would've known why August and I smelled like we'd . . . like we'd—*Ugh.* I couldn't even think it without growing embarrassed.

"When do you deploy, August?" Liam asked.

A vein throbbed in August's neck. Even though his expression didn't betray his annoyance, I felt the insistent pop-pop of it deep in my belly. I didn't understand the reason for it since the choice to leave was his. Liam wasn't chasing him away.

"In the morning." August's gaze hadn't moved off my overheated face.

"If you're going back to the inn, Ness," Frank said, "can you take

Jeb with you? Eric got him here, but he needs to hang around a while longer."

"I don't have a car . . . " Or a license. First thing tomorrow, I'd stop by the DMV.

"I'll give you and Jeb a lift. Let me say goodnight to everyone," Liam said.

"Liam, the elders and I need to go over many things with you," Frank said.

"I'll just drop her off and then——"

"I can drive them. I was leaving anyway," August said.

Liam narrowed his eyes. The friction between the two males was so heavy that if I stuck out my finger there would probably be static.

"That'd be great. Thank you, August," Frank said.

I clasped Liam's hand, spread his fingers with mine, because his jagged expression told me he didn't find this arrangement *great*.

"And, Ness, Evelyn's at my house. Just so you don't worry when you get back to the inn."

Thinking about Evelyn, the woman who'd taken care of me during the six years I was living in LA with my mother, stole my thoughts away from Liam and August for a welcomed moment. Did that mean she and Frank were rekindling what they'd had at the time she was still married to the werewolf-hating hunter who'd shot my father? I still couldn't wrap my mind around the fact that Evelyn had once been a woman named Gloria Michaels, wife of Aidan, lover of Frank, citizen of Boulder, Colorado. I wondered if I would ever come to terms with that.

"Tell her I'll come by to see her tomorrow."

Frank nodded as he slipped between August and Liam.

Liam let go of my hand and wound his arm around my waist, pulling me against him possessively.

"I'll get Jeb and wait for you in the car." August backed out of the room.

Like a spool of thread, I felt him retreat. But then I felt something else, a hand travel up my spine, settle on the nape of my neck, tip my face up.

"It's just a car ride. And like he said, he's leaving tomorrow."

"I'm aware of all that, but I'd rather be the one taking you home."

I kissed the puckered spot between his eyebrows.

Finally he sighed and caressed my cheek, nails scraping gently over the pale scars left behind by his claws during our last trial. I could tell that, although unintentional, hurting me still tormented him.

He hovered his mouth over mine. "You are still mine."

Was he reminding me or himself? "I am."

His tongue skimmed the seam of my lips, prodding them open, while his deft fingers massaged the back of my head, eliciting a groan from me. The sound had him deepening the kiss, deepening the kneading. After a delicious minute, our mouths came apart.

"I'll stop by as soon as I'm done here. Leave your balcony door open."

"'Kay," I breathed.

He lowered his hand to the base of my spine and guided me back into the main room. Although people were still chatting boisterously, I felt gazes dart our way, saw pupils pulse with intrigue, caught nostrils flaring.

"Everything'll be okay, Ness," Liam murmured.

I glanced up at him, wishing he hadn't uttered those words, because they felt like a curse. If fated mates were real, then curses were too, right?

CHAPTER 2

When I walked out of Headquarters, August was closing the door to the backseat of the pickup. He must've secured the seatbelt across my grief-stricken uncle's chest, because Jeb was wearing it and looked in no state to have put it on himself.

I slid into the passenger seat and clipped in my own belt. "Thanks for the ride."

August kept his gaze on the windshield, on the dark slope of pines bathed in white moonlight. Yesterday, the moon had been full and all of the wolves, young and old, had run wild through the forest. August hadn't been among them. At least not when I'd been with the pack.

After turning the key in the ignition, he drove down the dirt road, past the rusted fence and the large wooden sign emblazoned with the words *Private Property*.

"Will you go for a run before you leave?" I asked.

"Yeah."

Old August, the one who'd looked upon me like a little sister, would surely have asked me if I wanted to run with him. This new August . . . he didn't ask me to join him. Not that I would've gone. I hadn't left the party early to go for a run. Besides, what would Liam think if he showed up on my balcony and I wasn't home?

I reached over and touched August's knuckles before realizing that I probably shouldn't touch him at all. What if it somehow strengthened our bond? I removed my fingers, feeling my navel pulse as wildly as my heart.

"I'm really sorry about . . . about all this, August."

"Not your fault, Ness," he said in a rough voice. "No one's fucking fault."

I winced.

After a beat, he said, "I'll have to add a penny in Mom's curse jar now. Closer to a quarter actually."

For the first time since August had driven back to Headquarters, I smiled. "She still has it?"

"Oh, yes. She calls it her retirement fund."

I smiled wider. "I miss your mom." Preoccupied with making a place for myself in Boulder, I hadn't paid Isobel a visit yet.

"She misses you too. You should go see her once I'm gone. It'll make her happy."

I nodded. "Good thing I'm signing up to get my driver's permit tomorrow."

August glanced at me, his face much more relaxed than earlier. "You don't have your license?"

"I didn't really need one back in LA. Besides, we didn't have a car, so it wouldn't have served much of a purpose."

Jeb made a little sound, between a wheeze and a sob, which had me spinning in my seat. His lids were shut, though, and his neck craned at an awkward angle—he was asleep.

"Still can't tell me where you're going?" I asked August, turning back toward him.

"It's classified."

"But I'm your mate."

He almost swerved off the road.

"Sorry. That was supposed to be funny; it wasn't." I wrung my fingers in my lap, wondering what had gotten into me to even joke about our new bond. "I can't believe I just said that. Can you just delete it from your memory?"

August didn't say anything. Instead, he turned on the radio, tuning into a jazz station. August had always been a great fan of jazz. I used to tease him about it, telling him he had the taste of an old man. Unfortunately, I didn't consider him such an old man anymore. Would've been a heck of a lot easier if I did.

Speaking of old men . . . "Did Frank have a mate?"

"Not to my knowledge."

"Does anyone else in the pack have a mate?"

"Eric. He and his wife are going on fifty years."

"That's a long time."

"My parents are celebrating thirty next month."

I appreciated his reminder that true love existed outside of mating bonds. Not that I'd doubted it. After all, my parents had loved each other, and they hadn't been fated mates. "That's crazy."

"Yeah." He studied the dusky road ahead. "So what are your plans for the big eighteen?"

I rubbed my palms against my jeans to stop myself from fidgeting. "That's still a long time from now."

"Five weeks isn't that long."

I moistened my lips. "I'm not much of a birthday person."

"You used to love birthdays. You used to request fireworks. I almost set myself on fire lighting one up for you. Remember?"

"I remember." The bottom of his jeans were still smoking when he'd jogged back to us. "You cursed so much your mom joked she would go on a huge shopping spree thanks to all those pennies you owed her."

The memory made me smile, but it also made my eyes heat up and my lips wobble. This year would be the first birthday I'd spend without Mom.

He must've sensed my sudden sorrow, because he touched the top of my hand. "How about we don't talk about birthdays?"

"Yeah," I croaked.

"Tell me more about LA."

I discreetly wiped my wet lashes before feeding him tidbits of the years we'd spent apart.

"It wasn't all bad," I said, flipping my phone over and over. Its screen suddenly lit up with a message.

LIAM: *Don't worry, but don't leave your patio door unlocked, okay? I'll be there in an hour.*

How was I supposed to *not* worry?

ME: *You think Everest will ambush me?*
LIAM: *Just lock up OK?*
My nerves churned. *OK*, I typed back.

August glanced my way, and the car swerved a little. "What?"

I stuck my elbow on the armrest and cradled my head. "It's nothing."

"You forget I have an internal lie detector. You're scared. Why are you scared?"

"I'm not scared." I shook my head because my words didn't seem to convince him. "Annoyed, but not scared."

"Why are you annoyed?"

I sighed. "Liam seems to think Everest didn't flee Boulder."

August side-eyed me.

"You know what he did to me, right?"

"I heard pieces of the story. How about you start from the beginning?"

I glanced over at my uncle, who had drool leaking from his mouth. Even though he was asleep, I kept my voice low as I recounted how Everest convinced me I'd killed Liam's father with the three anti-shifting pills I slipped him the night I'd paid him a visit. Which led me to tell August about the escort agency, about my alliance with the Pine Pack Alpha, about Evelyn's kidnapping, and my cousin's blackmail.

I scratched a fleck of dried blood off the inside of my wrist. "I can't figure out if Everest was wishing I would die or if he was hoping I would kill Liam."

Although splashed with moonlight, August's face was too dark to read. "Your cousin was always shifty."

"The shifty shifter."

August didn't smile at my little play on words.

"I know you two never really got along, August, but he and I did. I'm holding out hope he wasn't rooting for my death. I'm holding out hope he wasn't hoping for Liam's either . . . That he did this to test my loyalty to Liam."

After a long beat, August said, "You should stay at my parents' house tonight. Every night for that matter. At least Dad can keep you safe."

I shot him a smile. "I'm not going to hide. If anything, I plan on hunting my cousin down."

He gripped the steering wheel tighter.

"I'd rather be the hunter than the hunted."

"No," August barked.

Jeb released a loud snore.

"I'm not scared," I said, dropping my voice.

"Let the pack bring him in. Liam's the Alpha now, and that's what Alphas do. They exact justice in the name of the pack."

"He'll rip out Everest's throat before hearing him out. I want answers, August. I *need* answers."

"Maybe I *should* stay . . . "

"What? No." I winced at how fast the word whipped out of my mouth. The strange tether in my stomach writhed like a snake. However petty, August couldn't stay. I had enough to contend with without our weird fated-mate connection. "Don't change your plans on my account. Everything'll be fine."

"I know you want me gone because of Liam, but do you really think I could live with myself if I left and something happened to you?"

"Nothing'll happen. I made it out of the trials alive, didn't I?"

He grunted.

"Look, I'll promise you something. If at any point I'm worried about my safety, I'll go to your parents' house."

His hazel eyes were murky with doubt.

"I promise."

"I want this in writing."

"August Watt"—I slapped a palm against my chest—"you don't trust me?"

"You've been known to backpedal on promises."

The playfulness I'd gone for withered away. "What do you mean? What promises didn't I keep?"

"When you left for LA, you said you would write."

I nibbled on my bottom lip. "Mom didn't want me to make contact with anyone from Boulder. She said cutting my ties with everyone here would help me move on, but in retrospect, I wonder if she did this so Heath wouldn't find out where we'd gone. She was scared of him . . . after what he did to her."

"What did he do to her?"

Right . . . Only a select handful of people were privy to this. Not once did I regret that Everest killed Heath. Liam's father deserved what he got.

"He raped her, August," I whispered, as though saying it softly could somehow dim the horror.

August's eyes rounded. "Shit . . . " he whispered, voice as rough as sandpaper.

We didn't talk after that.

The tight coil of mountain roads lengthened and straightened as we approached the glowing inn. I was thankful there were guests. I wouldn't have wanted to go back to a silent, dark place. I had enough silence and darkness inside of me.

After parking in front of the revolving glass doors, August draped my uncle's limp arm over his broad shoulder and heaved him into the lobby. I grabbed the master key from the small office behind the bell desk and led the way up to my uncle's private apartment on the first floor. Jeb's place wasn't as grand as Everest's attic dwelling, but it was still vast—my uncle and aunt's closet alone was the size of my entire bedroom.

After August laid my uncle in bed, I pulled off Jeb's shoes, tucked a blanket around him, and then turned off the lights. My nostrils itched with the scent of Lucy's prized potpourri. How could Jeb stand it? I'd had to put mine out on the patio, which angered my already pissy aunt.

I wondered briefly what sort of accommodations Eric had given her in his basement. Did it make me a terrible person to hope she was lying on the cold, hard floor? The image of her standing over Evelyn tied to a chair made me ball my fists. How I hated Lucy . . .

"You can talk to me, you know." August's voice made me look away from the mason jars filled with desiccated rose petals adorning the stone chimney mantle.

I wasn't going to ruin August's one night with his parents. "You should go." I started leading the way back toward the door.

"Ness—"

"Please, August. I don't want to talk anymore. I just want to watch TV until my eyes bleed."

He exited the bedroom, and I closed the door and pocketed the key. We walked back down the flight of wooden stairs decorated with an evergreen-colored runner.

At the foot of the stairs, I stood on my tiptoes and pressed a kiss against August's stubble. "Have a safe trip. And call me from time to time, okay?" I smiled at him before hurrying toward my bedroom, feeling the invisible rope thin out.

"Ness," August called out again, but I didn't stop.

The tether weakened some more, becoming as insubstantial as a spider web filament.

I took it August was gone.

A pang of sadness hit me as I realized I wouldn't see him again for months. But it was better this way. Better for everyone.

CHAPTER 3

L iam arrived at one in the morning. I'd been just about to drift off when I heard him knock and call out my name.

The second I let him in, his arms came around me, his head dipped to the curve of my neck, and he inhaled me. "You smell like him. I hate that you smell like him."

I was startled to hear him say this considering I'd soaked in a scalding bubble bath until the water grew cold. I'd even washed my hair. I guessed soap couldn't remedy the magical mating scent. Come tomorrow, it would no longer be a problem, though. I couldn't smell like someone who was thousands of miles away.

Liam licked the spot he was nuzzling and then dragged his tongue up the column of my neck, making me shiver. Was he trying to layer his scent over August's?

He backed me into the room, lips crashing down against mine, hard and demanding. Even though I was worn out, I answered with as much fervor as I could muster.

When my calves hit the side of the bed, I pressed my hands against his chest and unglued my lips from his. "I might smell like August, but you smell like every male in our pack."

He glanced down at his bloodied shirt, tore it off, chucked it on the floor by my flannel armchair, kicked off his jeans, and finally dropped his underwear. Naked, he turned and headed toward my bathroom.

Water gushed, and the rings on my shower curtain clinked against the rod. I didn't move. Barely dared breathe. Even my heart held perfectly still. Liam was naked—not for the first time—and taking a shower in my bathroom.

I still hadn't moved when he came back out, a towel wrapped around his carved waist. He smiled brazenly as he observed my perplexed expression. And then he cradled my face in his hands and kissed me deeply, sweetly, thoroughly.

His hands left my face and raked up and down my arms that were hanging limply at my sides. I should probably have gripped his waist or clawed his back or done something with my fingers, but I couldn't get them to move. I'd never been intimate with a man and was feeling a ton of conflicting feelings from edginess to fear to excitement to guilt.

All of them made sense, except the guilt. August's face flashed through my mind, and my stomach tightened. I squeezed my lids shut, willing his face to vanish, willing the tension in my gut to recede.

"I can't do it, Liam," I said, breathless.

"Can't do what?"

My cheeks burned. "Have sex. I can't. Not tonight." My breaths were coming out in short spurts. I was having a full-fledged anxiety attack.

"Shh." He rubbed my arms. Up and down. Up and down. "We don't have to do anything, Ness. Shh."

His arms went around me, and he pulled me against him, where he held me until my chest stopped pumping with fevered breaths.

"Can I stay the night, or do you want me to leave?"

I swallowed. "You can stay." I raked my hair back. "I want you to stay."

"Good. Because I want to stay too." He kissed the tip of my nose.

I climbed into my bed and scooted over to make room for him. He clicked off the lamp on my nightstand, then molded his body around mine.

"How did it go . . . with the elders?" I asked him as he played with my hair.

"I now know everything there is to know about being an Alpha."

"I can't believe you're Alpha. *My* Alpha."

"I like the sound of that." He slid his nose down the nape of my neck.

I shivered. "Do they know where Everest went?"

"They located his car in Denver."

I turned to face Liam. "Denver? What would he be doing in Denver?"

"Don't know."

Did my cousin know someone in Denver? Maybe Megan, that last girl he'd cozied up with, the one he'd met at the music festival and then kissed at Tracy's Bar and Grille, maybe she was from Denver? She was a student at UCB—the only thing I knew about her besides that she was a shapely blonde. Maybe there was a way to check the college's directory?

Liam's eyes were smudged with exhaustion. He needed sleep, not a cross-examination, but I couldn't help but ask about the hateful gender selection tool.

"Did you destroy the stick, Liam?"

"The stick?"

"The fossilized root."

His mouth solidified into a straight line. "I'm not going to destroy it."

I added space between our bodies. "Why not?"

"Because it has value, and valuable things are worth holding on to."

"Value?" I squeaked. "It's just vile, smelly, and criminal."

"Ness"—there was an edge of exasperation to his tone—"please, let's not fight about it. Not tonight. I'll never use it, I promise." He rolled onto his back and scrubbed both his hands down the length of his face.

"But someone else might." I propped myself up.

"Ness," he growled.

"Did you ever stop to consider that if your dad's generation hadn't used it, more girls would've been born, and maybe one of them would've been your mate?"

Liam's eyes glowed as bright as a Harvest moon. "Then I'm happy it was used, because I don't want a mate. I want *you*. Temper and all, I want you."

He pushed on the elbow propping me up until I collapsed back onto the mattress. Then he threw one of his legs over my lower body and settled on top, bracing himself on his forearms. As he dipped his face toward mine, I forgot all about the Boulder relic, all about Everest, all about breathing.

"I don't have *that* much of a temper," I murmured.

He smiled as he gazed down at me. "Just like a thunderstorm doesn't have that much rain."

"I'm not sure that's a compliment."

He slanted his mouth over mine, but before breaching the distance, he whispered, "From a man who loves storms, it is the greatest compliment." And then he kissed me until our bodies became as exhausted as our minds.

CHAPTER 4

When I awoke the following morning, Liam was already gone and the bedsheets were cold. I checked the time on my phone: six-thirty. The meager hours of sleep I'd gotten would have to do. There was an inn to run and an uncle to check up on.

I ran a brush through my hair, then applied the tiniest bit of concealer to hide the circles beneath my eyes. I had my mother's eyes —cornflower blue—but where hers had always glittered, mine seemed as dull as smudged glass these days.

After tying up my hair in a ponytail, donning jeans and a black V-neck, I fluffed my pillows, straightened my sheets with military precision, and tucked my comforter. I hoped no guests had come down for breakfast yet. I was sure we had the basics, but without Evelyn, the offerings would be modest: toast, jam, butter. Evelyn and Mom had taught me how to cook, but I wasn't especially good at it. I'd mastered the basics though.

I quickened my pace toward the kitchen, expecting it to be empty and dark, but light leaked from under the door, and the scent of caramelizing onions clung to the air. Was my uncle making himself a snack? I pushed my shoulder into the swinging door and froze at the sight of Evelyn bent over the stovetop.

Her merlot-tinted lips arched up. "Morning, *querida*."

The door smacked my back—not hard, but hard enough to make

me stumble forward. I caught myself on the steel island. "I thought—"

"That I would leave you to run this place on your own? I made Frank drop me off an hour ago." She shook her head, and her bottle-black hair danced over the apron protecting her jeans and red top. She seemed happy. Happier than I'd ever seen her. Blissful. "Can you fetch the warming trays?"

As I went to retrieve them from the shelving in the back of the kitchen, I checked over my shoulder a few times to make sure Evelyn was real.

"Liam spent the night?"

I dropped one of the tray lids, and it clattered loudly against the tiled floor.

As I crouched to retrieve the fallen lid, she added, "I am not judging. I am simply enquiring."

I cleared my throat. "He—but nothing . . . "

Evelyn laid the tongs she was flipping the thick slabs of bacon with on the spoon rest and walked over to me. She grabbed both my hands. "*Querida*, you are almost eighteen. You are allowed to have sleepovers with boys. Just promise me that you will not settle for a man who is anything but kind to you. You deserve kindness and respect."

The memory of last night flashed through my mind, and then another memory, an unwelcome one settled over it like tracing paper —the night of the engagement party when I'd stopped by his place and he'd let his bestial nature override his human one. Was I being naïve to place the blame on the wolf inside him? Were our wolf natures so different from our two-legged ones?

Evelyn's black gaze tracked over my face. "Ness? You are worrying me."

I shook my head. "You don't need to worry about me."

"I will always worry about you. I love you too much not to worry."

The image of her tied to a chair flashed behind my lids. I gritted my teeth, trying to stop my canines from sharpening. I longed to visit Eric's basement and sink my teeth into Lucy's fleshy, pale throat.

My aunt hadn't hurt Evelyn, or so Evelyn had claimed, but she was the type to bear her pain in silence. She'd never complained about the arthritis that locked up her joints or the old bullet wound in her legs that still made her limp.

BREAKFAST WENT OFF WITHOUT A HITCH.

Emmy, one of the women who worked at the inn, arrived shortly after me and insisted on handling the service. She asked where Lucy was, and I mentioned she'd gone after her heartbroken son. Emmy shot me a pained smile. She'd worked long enough at the inn to be up to date on Clark family gossip. What she didn't know—or at least I didn't think she knew—was the dual nature of her employers.

While Emmy took care of the early risers, I prepped a tray of food that I brought up to my uncle. I drew his drapes open and tried to coax him out of bed to eat, but he didn't move. I checked his pulse to make sure he was alive. He was. After my third failed attempt at getting him up, I let myself out.

As I went back downstairs, it dawned on me that I'd be in charge of the inn today. The responsibility tightened my stomach so abruptly that I pressed my palm against it.

It'd be okay.

I could manage.

Besides, it was temporary. A day. Maybe two. Right?

The cramping didn't ease up. I tried spacing out my breaths, but that didn't help.

The revolving doors of the inn spun, and I realized that working on my breaths wouldn't loosen the knot in my abdomen.

What I was feeling wasn't stress; it was August.

And his mother.

"Isobel?" I exclaimed.

She hadn't changed much—her hair was still a lustrous deep brown, and her complexion pale as ever—but she seemed thinner, slighter. She opened her arms, and I descended the stairs more quickly, walking into her embrace.

"Oh, sweet girl, I've missed you." She squeezed me tight before pressing me away to look me over. "By God, you are Maggie's"—her voice caught on my mother's name—"spitting image."

I tried to smile, but Mom's name had my heart twisting. She'd died in January, yet it felt like she'd left me yesterday. Sometimes, I still reached for my phone to call her.

"What are you two doing here so early?" I asked, breathing through the ache in my heart.

Isobel gestured to the bell desk. "I've always dreamed of manning one of these."

"Um. Really?"

"I heard the position opened up." Her gaze swept back over to me, vivid green like the pines hedging the inn's driveway.

I blinked.

"I'll get myself set up . . . if that's all right with you?"

"Are you sure you want—"

"Yes."

As she walked over to the bell desk, I glanced up at August. Had he asked his mother to fill in for Lucy?

"Anything need fixing?" he asked.

"What?"

"Lightbulbs? Chipped paint?" He gestured toward the inn. When I frowned, he said, "I imagine Jeb won't be much help in the coming days, what with everything going on."

Oh. Gratitude curled through me.

"You can't do this on your own. Well, maybe you can, but you shouldn't have to." He pushed up the long sleeves of his thermal top that clung to his torso like a second skin. "I'm good at manual labor, but don't stick me in the kitchen unless you want to poison the guests." His lips quirked up.

"Aren't you supposed to be on a plane or a submarine right now?"

Gaze roaming over the lobby, he said, "I've delayed my departure."

Relief warred with worry. "You did?"

I prayed he hadn't done this because he was worried for me. I didn't dare ask.

"I need to be at a construction site in an hour, so you have me for sixty minutes."

I had him for longer than sixty minutes if he wasn't deploying. "Um, the deck might need some rearranging."

He nodded and walked toward the double-storied living room.

"Hey, sweet girl, can you walk me through a typical day here?" Isobel stood in the doorjamb between the bell desk and the back office.

Although I'd never manned the bell desk, I'd observed my aunt and uncle enough to have an idea of what they did. I explained what I knew to Isobel, then started for the stairs that led to the laundry room in the basement when Matt walked through the revolving doors arm in arm with a blonde who looked uncannily like him.

"Hey, Ness. Don't know if you remember my mom?" He tipped his head toward the woman beside him.

I didn't remember her. She must've attended the pack gathering though. Then again, Isobel hadn't been there. Maybe Matt's mother hadn't either.

I doubled back and extended my hand. "Pleasure to meet you, ma'am."

She latched onto my extended fingers. "Kasie. And the pleasure's all mine, Ness."

After she freed my hand, I slipped it into the back pocket of my jeans. When neither supplied the reason for showing up, I asked, "Did you two want some breakfast?"

"Oh, we've eaten already," Kasie chirped.

I glanced at Matt, not really understanding what else they could want. "Coffee? Tea?"

"We're here because—"

Kasie interrupted her son. "Because I love to cook. And I remember from the pack reunion that Evelyn was a fantastic chef, so I've come to train with her."

Oh.

"Why don't I show myself to the kitchen?" She stopped by the bell desk to kiss Isobel's cheek, before crossing the lobby and vanishing into the dining room.

I turned back toward Matt. Whatever he'd just told Isobel had her grinning wide.

"Such a smooth talker, that one," she told me, shaking her head at him.

The revolving doors spun again, and Lucas walked in, a gym bag slung across his chest. "I need a room," he announced, strolling up to the bell desk and sticking one forearm on the counter. "Hey, Mrs. W."

Isobel smiled. "Hi, Lucas."

I raised an eyebrow. "Why do you need a room?"

"My place got flooded. Fucking neighbors."

My eyebrow came crashing back into place. "Wow. I'm sorry about that."

He ran a hand through his shaggy black hair that curled around his ears. "Why are you sorry? Did you make them leave their tap running all night?"

I let out a small grunt. "You know what, I'm not sorry."

Lucas's light-blue eyes shone with delight. I bet he'd been crowned Boulder's Most Annoying Person back in high school. "What's your room number, Ness? 105, right?"

I crossed my arms. "Why?"

"Just want to avoid bunking in the same room." He winked at me. "Liam would have my balls in a vice. Shit. Sorry, Mrs. W."

Isobel smiled. "I've heard worse, son."

Lucas leaned forward to see the computer monitor. "Room 106 free by any chance?"

"It is. Let me get you the key." Isobel disappeared into the back office.

I crossed my arms. "Did your apartment really get flooded?"

He shot me a cocky grin.

That answered my question. "You're here to babysit me, aren't you?"

"Babysit you?" Lucas snorted. "What an idea."

"Oh my God, you are!"

He waggled his eyebrows.

"Did Liam put you up to this?"

Metal clinked in the office as Isobel sorted through the rows of keys.

"No one put me up to this. I'm doing it out of the kindness of my heart."

"Your heart isn't kind," I volleyed back.

Matt snickered whereas Lucas scowled.

I wheeled on Matt. "Your mother's not here for cooking lessons, I suppose?"

He slung a big arm around my shoulder. "The pack takes care of their own, Ness."

My wide gaze ping-ponged between the two males crowding the lobby.

"Are you crying?" Matt asked.

I touched my cheek. Sure enough, my fingertips came back damp.

"Is it that time of the month . . . *again?*" Lucas offered, sporting a smile that made me want to punch his throat.

I flipped him off a second before August's mother popped out of the office, jingling a key. I dropped my hand back to my side, praying she hadn't caught my vulgar gesture.

Lucas's lips quirked in a taunting grin as he pocketed the key, but then fell flat as his gaze landed on a spot over my head. I sensed August stood behind me, sensed it in the pit of my stomach which writhed as though the invisible rope that connected us had been cranked.

"On your way to off all the baddies?" Lucas asked.

"I've postponed my trip." August slowly wiped his palms on a pair of jeans blemished with grease smears and wood stain. "Two of the lightbulbs on the living room chandelier need changing. You know where I can find some, Ness?"

"Yeah." I ushered him toward the supply closet. The room smelled of laundry detergent, cool metal, and dusty cardboard. "Lightbulbs are over there." I pointed to the shelf that sat underneath a hatch window, and he walked over and riffled through the rows of bulbs until he located the ones he needed.

"I'll get those screwed in before I leave."

Something occurred to me then. "Does Liam know you've postponed your trip?"

He stopped in front of me. "Not yet."

"So your mom coming over to help, that was your idea?"

"Not just mine. My parents didn't want you to be alone. So Mom called Kasie. I suppose Matt called Lucas."

"Going to go unpack, roomie," Lucas said to me while staring at August, who stood inches from me.

I backed up until the base of my spine hit the doorframe. "We're not roomies, Lucas."

"Almost. Hey . . . you got an extra pair of ear plugs in there? Wouldn't want to overhear any moaning."

My body went completely rigid.

Glass broke. I shot my gaze down to the boxes of lightbulbs clutched in August's fist. Without saying a word, he went to grab new ones, staying next to the shelving a minute, surveying the piece of sky visible through the hatch window.

"Anyway, if you find me a pair, slide them under my door, will ya?" Lucas said, starting down the hallway, humming some chirpy tune. Before turning the corner, he called out, "Hey, August, you should stop by Tracy's. There's a certain waitress who's going to freak the fuck out when she learns you're single."

The muscles in August's back bunched up.

"I have to go check on"—I swallowed—"on the laundry. Thanks for all your help."

And with that, I hurried away from the supply closet, feeling my navel throb as the distance between August and me grew and grew.

CHAPTER 5

I stayed in the laundry room a long time, sorting through dirty sheets and towels, and also through my emotions. After three loads of washing and drying, and two hours' worth of ironing, only the inn sheets were neat. My insides were still a complete mess.

I wanted to drop everything and head to the gym to punch my way to a clearer mind, but there was still too much that needed to be done before I could clock out. I returned upstairs to check on Isobel, praying I wouldn't run into anyone else.

"Everything okay up here?" I asked August's mom.

"Everything's great, sweetie. We got a couple reservations for the weekend and a birthday dinner on Friday for a party of twenty. I checked in with Evelyn and placed a grocery order, and I was just now updating the wine list. Oh, and someone left a hotel bike out front. I found it when I greeted some new arrivals. I didn't know where to put it, so I wheeled it inside the office." She gestured behind her while clicking through an excel spreadsheet—I supposed, the inn's wine list.

When I entered the office, my body went as stiff and cold as a block of marble. A nametag tied around the handlebar flapped in the cool air blasting from the revolving fan in the corner. Spit jamming up my throat, I snagged the tag and popped it off its string, hoping beyond hope Isobel had tied it.

In dark marker was written: **So you can stop by again.**

A chill crawled up my already icy spine.

"Did you see who dropped it off?" I asked, hoping my voice didn't betray my nerves.

"No. I just found it at the bottom of the driveway."

Had Aidan delivered it? Considering the injuries Lucas had inflicted to the bastard's neck the night he'd shot Liam, I doubted the hunter was strolling around Boulder, transporting bikes. He'd probably had his driver bring it over.

I crumpled the tag and tossed it into the bin.

Like hell I would pay the creep a visit.

I guided the bike out the inn doors and down the driveway toward the stockroom where Lucy and Jeb stowed the hiking gear, kayaks, fishing poles, and other paraphernalia they made available to guests.

As I walked back up, I squinted down the driveway into the bright sunlight, looking for Aidan's chauffeured limo, but if it had been here, it was long gone.

Meeting at eight tonight at the inn to discuss Everest Clark's fate. Every pack member convened.

Liam's voice was so sharp and clear I swiveled my head, expecting to see him, but not a soul stood next to me. After I got over the shock of hearing him, I focused on what he'd just said: *Everest Clark's fate.* My pulse picked up, thumping against my eardrums. I peeked at the first floor. Behind one of the windows lay my uncle. Had he heard Liam's call too, or had Liam excluded him?

I went back inside the inn, grabbed the master key, then climbed up the stairs, taking them two at a time. I knocked before entering my uncle's room.

"Jeb?" I called out. When I saw the comforter shake and heard a muted sniffle, I hurried to his side.

"Liam will . . . he will . . . *kill* my son." Jeb's voice was as thick as the syrup I'd ladled over his pancakes. "My only child."

So he had heard Liam. "He said *discuss*. Maybe—"

"You don't know the ways of the pack, Ness. You've been part of it for what? Twenty-four hours? Wolves have no mercy."

I bristled from his condescending tone. "I may not know as much as you do, Jeb, but they didn't avenge my father's death. Maybe they won't kill Everest."

"He strangled Heath and left him floating in his pool. You think Liam will forgive my son? Oh, dear girl, you have so much to learn . . . "

I pressed my lips together. Even though my urge to walk out was strong, I stifled it. "Can I get you anything, Jeb?" I asked stiffly.

Without glancing away from the Flatirons beyond his bay window, he whispered, "Why did he have to go and kill him? Did you ask him to do it?"

My vertebrae locked up. "How could you even think that?"

"Because of what he did to Maggie."

"In case you forgot, Heath also raped Becca. Maybe *she* asked Everest to kill Heath."

"She was in a coma."

My throat locked up like my spine. I swallowed. "Before she tried to take her life and fell into a coma."

My uncle's reddened gaze drifted toward me before returning to the panorama of mountains. In a way—unknowingly—I'd been an accomplice to Heath's murder, but if I'd meant to kill him, I would've done it. I would never have asked someone to do my dirty business. How could my uncle think so poorly of me?

"Call me," I whispered, backing away from his bedside. "If you need anything, call me." I wheeled around and clambered back down the stairs.

Isobel looked up from the computer monitor she was checking. "Is everything okay?"

I nodded. "Concerned about Jeb, that's all."

Isobel didn't respond, but I could feel her studying me.

I went out onto the wrap-around deck to clear my mind. Instead, the dense forest reminded me of Aidan and of the strange note he'd sent. I tried phoning Liam to tell him about it, but my call went to voicemail.

The pack meeting was in a few hours. Informing him could surely wait until then. It wasn't as though it was a threat. You didn't threaten people with invitations. Then again, Aidan Michaels was a crafty man. Maybe it was an underhanded threat. A reminder that he knew how to get to me . . . how to get under my skin.

I pushed away from the knotted wood railing my father and the Watts had crafted. I wanted someone else's opinion on the matter and since Liam wasn't answering, I decided to seek out my "roommate."

CHAPTER 6

I knocked on Lucas's bedroom door and didn't stop until he drew it open.

"Geez. Give a man a minute." Lucas stood there barefoot, sporting a pair of low-riding sweatpants that displayed too much boxers and a wifebeater that showed off too much biceps. Although I wanted to tell him to pull up his pants, I hadn't come to police his poor taste in fashion.

I strode into the room, kicking the door shut.

"I usually don't turn down booty calls, but—"

"Oh my God, get over yourself." I rolled my eyes. "If you were the last man on Earth, I would still never get with you."

He smiled. "That's cold, Clark."

"I'm here because I got a strange delivery."

His smile vanished. "I'm listening."

"The night I went to Aidan Michaels's house, the night he shot Liam, well, I used one of the inn bikes to get there, and it was returned to me just now with a note saying, *So you can stop by again.*" I said this all in one breath.

Lucas's eyes darkened. "Who returned it?"

"I don't know. Isobel found it in the driveway."

"How do you know it was the same bike?"

"I don't, but—"

"Maybe the note was meant for someone else."

I growled in frustration. "Fine. Don't take this seriously."

His jaw ticked. "Have you called Liam?"

"I tried. He didn't answer."

For a long minute, Lucas stared at me as though trying to decide whether to trust me.

I rubbed my clammy palms against my jeans, then looked around the room that was almost identical to mine: same beige drapes, flannel-covered armchair, copper light fixtures, white sheeting. Only the landscape painting on the wall was different.

"Look, I came to you because I thought you could help me figure out if I should be worried about Aidan—"

"You should always worry about people who have too much money and influence, but we've got a bigger problem than that bedridden asshole right now."

My extremities turned bone-chilling cold.

Lucas dropped into the armchair, then leaned forward, elbows planted on knees, fingers slotted together. He watched me as though contemplating whether to tell me. Finally, he said, "This morning Liam found out something was stolen from HQ."

I frowned. What did the Boulders keep in Headquarters that—"The selection stick?"

Lucas snorted. "You wish."

I did wish.

"The pack's entire supply of Sillin is missing."

"Sillin? You mean the anti-shifting pills?"

He nodded.

My mother had made me ingest Sillin for three weeks when I'd moved to LA to prevent my body from shifting and to dim my scent in case other werewolves were in the area. She didn't want anyone sniffing me out. Lone wolves were deemed loose cannons and, thus, were hunted down by packs. Eventually, distance from the Boulders caused my body's werewolf gene to become dormant, and I no longer needed the drug.

"Why would someone steal them?" I asked.

"According to Greg"—it took my brain a second to remember he was the pack doctor—"they don't make them anymore."

"So?"

"So there's a market for them."

I couldn't believe I was having an actual conversation with Lucas without wanting to throttle him. "Who do you think stole them?"

"We don't think; we know. Cole checked the surveillance feed as soon as Liam called him."

"Who took them?"

"Who do you think?"

I gritted my molars. "Seriously, Lucas? You're going to make me guess?"

"Everest. Everest fucking took them. And guess when? At the exact time you showed up at the Watts' warehouse to duel Liam. And the only reason we didn't catch him earlier is because when there's a duel, the whole fucking pack has to be present, which meant the person in charge of watching the surveillance feed of the inn and of HQ was at the fucking duel."

I bristled. "Are you insinuating it was my fault?"

He let out a ragged breath, running his palms the length of his face. "You didn't know what he was up to, right?"

"How could you even ask me that, Lucas?"

"I'm sorry. We're just trying to figure out what his endgame is, that's all."

"Are they worth money?"

"You think Everest stole them for monetary gain?"

"You said they were rare. Maybe he took them to buy himself alliances with other packs."

Lucas perked up at that theory.

"Or maybe he's planning on using it on us?" Like I'd used it on Heath, which had been Everest's idea.

Lucas's pupils became pin-sized.

"You hadn't considered that?" I asked.

He slapped his hands against his knees, and the loud clap startled me. "Fuck me."

"Never." The word popped out before I even realized I'd uttered it.

Lucas smirked, but then the effect of my humor was lost as we both mulled over my suggestion.

"We have to call Liam," Lucas finally said.

And so we did, and this time our Alpha answered.

CHAPTER 7

L iam stormed into Lucas's bedroom about fifteen minutes after our phone call, arrowing straight for me. Once he reached my side, he cupped my cheeks and swept his gaze over every inch of my face as though to ascertain I was unscathed. I wasn't sure why he imagined I was hurt, but who was I to complain someone cared enough to worry about me? One of his hands drifted down my arm to my fingers, while the other drifted over the faint white scars he'd inadvertently clawed into my cheek during the last trial.

Lucas updated him on our theories and told him about the bike. In the grand scheme of things, the bike seemed futile.

"He doesn't know about the meeting today, does he?" I asked.

"He didn't pledge himself to me, so no, he didn't hear." Liam stabbed his hand through his tousled hair as he paced the small room. "If the bastard plans on poisoning us with Sillin, he has another think coming."

"At least Sillin can't kill us," I ventured, but regretted my words when both Liam and Lucas slanted looks at me. Sure, I'd given some to Heath, but it was the silver cord Everest had wound around the Alpha's neck that had snipped his life.

"Sillin might not kill us," Liam said gently, stopping his mad prowl, "but it'll steal our edge."

I swallowed back the overwhelming guilt. Even though Liam

hadn't been a fan of his father, Heath had been his only remaining parent, and I'd had a hand in his demise.

Liam ran his thumb over my furrowed brow. "Stop blaming yourself."

I whispered, "I'll never stop blaming myself."

Liam gathered me to him and stroked my hair. His minty musk scent swirled around me, soothing my fried nerves.

"What are you thinking, Liam?" Lucas asked after a beat of silence.

"I'm thinking I should pay Aidan Michaels a little visit like he asked."

I pressed away. "No. The man's a psychopath! You can't go back there."

Liam shot me a smile that was all at once rueful and dangerous. "Ness, he won't shoot me again."

"How do you know that?"

"Because one, we'll show up prepared; and two, he's at the hospital."

"Liam—no."

"What would you have me do? Sit back and wait for him to *reach out* to you again?" Liam stroked the edge of my quivering jaw. His touch just made me shiver harder. "No one threatens one of my wolves. No one."

"Then I'll go with you," I said.

"Absolutely not."

"Liam—"

"Out of the question, Ness."

"But—"

Liam shot Lucas a loaded look, probably gave him a silent order, too, because Lucas said, "On her like spandex."

Gross, and so not fair. I told them so. Not the gross part, but the not-fair one. I even squared my shoulders and gave both men my fiercest look, or what I hoped was a fierce look.

"What's not fair?" Liam asked. "Trying to keep you away from danger?"

"Isn't the pack motto to protect the Alpha at all costs?" I asked.

Liam narrowed his dark eyes. "You would be protecting my sanity by staying safe. If anything happened to you, I'd go feral, Ness. I'd go feral and maul whoever got in my way. Preserve my sanity, please." He scraped a knuckle against my cheek.

I pouted, angry to be benched. "I hope it's not because I'm a girl and you think I'm too delicate, because I'm n—"

"It's because you're *my* girl," he said.

"I'll just wait outside," Lucas mumbled.

A second later, the door snicked shut.

"Mine, Ness."

"And how do you think I'll deal if anything happened to you?"

"The pack will protect you."

My eyes heated up.

A deep emotion rushed over his face, and he pressed his mouth against my forehead, then against each one of my eyelids, my nose, my jaw, my scar. He didn't leave a single millimeter on my face untouched. No, that wasn't true. He hadn't kissed my mouth yet. But his kiss came, and along with it, waves of intense sensations. They pummeled and filled me like the Pacific Ocean had pounded and foamed against the sandy shores of Venice Beach.

Our kiss tasted of thunder and lightning and need.

So much need.

A need to keep each other safe, but also a need to hold each other, to fill each other.

As he deepened the kiss, as his hands coasted down my spine, cupped my ass, my stomach hardened like a fist. I reeled back as though someone had punched me.

Swollen lips parted and panting, Liam cast me an apologetic look. Did he think I'd detached myself from him because he was going too fast? I forced my fingers into fists to stop them from clutching my still knotted abdomen. I blamed the stupid mating link for the sudden pain. It wasn't fair.

So much wasn't fair.

Liam rubbed the back of his neck. "I'm sorry, Ness. I didn't mean to rush you—"

"You didn't."

"Then why'd you pull away from me?"

I couldn't keep this a secret from him. Not if the knee-jerk reaction happened each time Liam and I made out. I touched two fingers to my stomach. He frowned, and then he didn't. Then he understood. And the understanding steeped his face in shadows.

"But he's gone," Liam said.

"No. He's not."

The look that stained his eyes scared me. Liam backed away and exited the room. A moment later, Lucas came back inside.

I sank onto my bed and hung my head in my hands.

I hadn't thought this day could get any worse, but apparently it could.

CHAPTER 8

"He's going to force him to leave, isn't he?" I asked Lucas.

"Hopefully he'll concentrate on Everest and Aidan and deal with your *bond* later." His cheek dimpled. Unlike me, he didn't have dimples, so I guessed he was worrying the inside of his mouth. "This makes me glad Taryn and I aren't together. You girls screw with our focus."

"You and Taryn broke up? When did that happen?"

"A couple days ago."

I didn't like Taryn, but I didn't like Lucas much either, so I'd found them well-suited. "Were you together a long time?"

A fly buzzed around my desk before landing on the landscape painting behind Lucas's head.

"Long enough for it to hurt."

I sensed she'd done the breaking up, but I didn't pry. I got up and rubbed my hands on my jeans. "I need to go work."

"You're not planning on visiting Aidan, are you now?"

"No." I snorted softy. "I'm vindictive but not suicidal."

"Then I don't have to trail your ass through the inn?"

"You can try, but I know the place better than you, so good luck with that." I shot him a smile. "If you're bored, though, I can fetch you a feather duster."

"Hard pass. I was going to hit the gym."

"Don't you have a job?"

"You are my job."

I jerked my head up so fast the pen I'd stabbed through my makeshift bun poked my skull. "You can't be serious."

"As a heart attack. Until Everest is ki—*caught*."

"Killed?" I croaked.

"Caught."

My heart held as still as the fly perched on the painted stream. "But you were going to say killed . . . "

"Does it matter?"

"It does."

"Don't you want him to die?"

"I want Aidan Michaels to die."

"Not Everest?"

"I don't know how I feel about my traitorous cousin right now. I don't understand his motivations for any of this. I thought it was Becca, but he got with this other girl while Becca was in a coma, so I don't know . . . " I toed the corner of the plush beige rug. "Speaking of the other girl: is a college directory open to the public?"

"No, but Cole can probably hack it. Why?"

"Because I wanted to see if that other girl Everest was with came from Denver."

"What's her name?"

"Megan."

"Megan what?"

"I don't know."

"How do you spell Megan?"

"I'm not sure."

"Are you fucking kidding me, Ness?"

I stuck my hands on my hips. "Don't hiss at me."

"I'm not a fucking cat."

"Fine." I huffed out a little breath. "Don't *bark* at me. Better?"

He snorted. "Do you know which college she goes to at least?"

"She's a freshman at UCB."

He typed something in his phone. "So she'll be a sophomore in the fall?"

Right . . . This was summer.

He growl-grumbled. "You don't know, do you? UCB has 24,000

47

undergrads." I hadn't known it was that big. "She's not Everest's Snapchat buddy by any chance? Would make things a hell of a lot easier . . . "

"I wouldn't know. I don't do social media."

Shaking his head, he brought his phone up to his ear. "Yo, Cole. I need deets on a chick called Megan, who's a freshman or sophomore at UCB . . . No, this isn't for a hookup, you tool."

I smirked.

Lucas peeled lint off the arm of the flannel armchair. His nails were ragged, chipped and roughened by stone and earth. Mine had been the same after my full-moon run with the pack. I'd filed them down to the quick after, but three days later, white crescents had already grown back.

"What color hair? Skin? Eyes?" Lucas volleyed at me.

"Fair-skinned. Blonde, shoulder-length hair. I never saw her eye color."

Lucas related the info. "Cole asks if she was fat? Thin? Any distinctive markings?"

"I saw her from afar at the music festival—she was sitting on a bench—and then again at Tracy's—sitting again. She was pretty. Does that help?"

"Girls' versions of pretty aren't usually a dude's version," Lucas muttered.

"She had a heart-shaped face."

Lucas cocked the eyebrow that was slashed with a white scar—a remnant of the car accident that snuffed out the lives of both his parents. "What does that even mean?"

I drew an air-heart with my two index fingers.

"According to Ness, she's got a massive forehead and a pointy-ass chin." While he switched his phone to the other ear, he muttered, "And you said she was pretty."

I rolled my eyes. "Her forehead wasn't freakishly wide or anything."

While Cole searched on his end, Lucas told him about the awry footage of the inn. Considering Lucas didn't break into song and dance, I imagined Matt's brother hadn't yet fixed the problem.

"Okay . . . I'll show her. Thanks, dude."

Two minutes later, Lucas's phone chirped. He tapped on the screen before passing it over to me. I scrolled through the email Cole had sent full of screenshots of Megans spelled five different ways.

I handed the phone back over, shaking my head. None of them were Everest's Megan.

Lucas scanned the screenshots. "Becca was an escort. Maybe Megan is too?"

"Everest said she wasn't."

"He also said you murdered Heath."

The fine blonde hairs on my arms stood up straight. "You're right." Then under my breath, I added, "Never thought I'd say that."

Lucas's lips quirked into a lopsided grin. "Hot men are always underestimated."

I snorted. "Oh my God. Shut. Up."

He chuckled. "What's the name of the website?"

"RedCreekEscorts.com."

"Hate the name creek," he said as he typed.

"Got something against small bodies of water?"

"I got something against large bodies of fur." He flicked his gaze up to me. "Don't tell me you've never heard of the Creek Pack?"

I frowned.

He kneaded his chin that was in dire need of a shave. "You haven't, have you? The smallest pack that became the largest . . . Ring a bell?"

I shook my head.

He leaned back in the armchair. "I'll tell you the sob story after we finish up with the escort agency." His fingers flew over his phone's screen. Without looking up, he said, "Their website's down. Do you still have a contact there?"

My skin crawled at the mere idea of calling Sandra, the pimp—or whatever running an escort service made her—Everest had introduced me to. Even though she'd always been pleasant and chirpy over the phone, I'd hoped never to speak with her after my "date" with Aidan Michaels. I shuddered from the memory.

"Give me the number."

So I did. And Lucas called the agency over loudspeaker.

An automated message for Red Creek Escorts came on,

prompting us to leave a message. When the beep sounded, I shook my head so vehemently that the tendrils of hair that had escaped my bun during my earlier make-out session fluttered around my face.

"Hiya, Red Creek Escorts, I was looking for some female company for a buddy's party this weekend. I'd appreciate if you could tell me about the available girls." Lucas left his phone number before ending the call, jaw a smoky red.

"You're blushing," I said, mostly to annoy him.

He flipped me the finger, which just made me smile.

"So, tell me about the Creeks now."

He tapped his phone against the padded arm of his seat. "Four years ago, a pack we all thought was off the map seized the largest pack of the Rockies."

"That's why I didn't hear about them. Four years ago, I was in LA."

"Ever heard of the Aspens?"

"Of course. They were a pacific pack. Dad used to call them hippies."

He twirled his phone between his fingers. "Sort of. They lived in a compound—more of a small town than a compound—and barely interacted with humans. Anyway 'bout ten years back, there was a pack summit, the first in almost a century. Boulders, Pines, Aspens, and a few of the Eastern packs signed a truce of non-invasion. No Creeks came. The Aspens who were geographically closest to the Creeks reported they hadn't heard from their neighbors in years, thus we marked them as extinct."

Boulders didn't go around sticking daisies into each other's hair. And although Pines were on the civilized side, some—Justin's face flashed through my mind—were brutish and egotistical.

"How do packs become extinct?" I inquired.

"Too many of the young renege on our way of life. They move to big cities and lose touch with their true nature, and then they die sooner, because not shifting is unnatural for our bodies."

I wondered how many years of life I'd lost by being away from Boulder.

He scratched his chin. "The worst part, though, is when those who leave reproduce."

"Why is that the worst part?"

"Because, if their offspring isn't born close to the pack, the gene becomes defective and results in kids who can't fully shift. We call them *halfwolves*." His expression turned so bleak that it made me wonder if he'd ever witnessed a shifting *halfwolf*. "Creatures of nightmares." Lucas flexed his knuckles. "Anyway, turns out the Creeks weren't extinct . . . just in hiding. One winter night, the Creek Alpha walked right onto the Aspen compound with her handful of wolves and challenged the Aspen Alpha to a duel. The fight was gory as hell apparently, and the Aspens—Creeks now—mentioned foul-play, although no one was able to prove—"

"*Her?* The Creek Alpha is female?"

Lucas snorted. "Of course that's the part that sticks with you."

I crossed my arms. "Just because she won a fight doesn't mean there was foul-play, Lucas. Why would anyone jump to that conclusion? Because she was female, and females are supposed to be inferior to males?"

Lucas sandwiched his lips together. I'd obviously hit a sore nerve. "How do you explain that each high-ranking Aspen, who challenged her after the duel, lost their lives too, huh?"

I shrugged. "She's exceptionally strong."

Lucas shot me a withering look. He didn't even think this was a possibility! Sexist pig.

I squeezed my arms harder. "Have you met her?"

"No. And I never intend to meet the crazy bitch."

"You are *so* sexist."

"*Sexist?* I'd keep the judginess in check. You know nothing about me."

"Judginess isn't even a word."

Anger and something else flashed across his face. "Do you think you're superior to everyone or just me?"

I halted. "I don't think I'm superior to anyone."

"You certainly act like it."

My breastbone prickled from his comment. "I just want to be considered an equal."

He stared at the rug with such intensity I expected to see flames curl from the long fibers.

"There are forty of you. One of me, Lucas." My eyelids stung. "You try being the odd one out." I hated how my voice broke.

I spun around and left, attempting to rein in my emotions. As I tidied rooms, I thought about the Creek Alpha. Lucas might not want to meet her, but I did. Did my curiosity make me disloyal? It wasn't as though I could pledge myself to her pack—Boulder blood ran through my veins, and unless she beat our Alpha in a duel and stole his connection to us, I'd remain a Boulder.

Besides, I didn't want a new Alpha. I trusted Liam, and I didn't trust many people. But how was I supposed to prove I was their equal when he'd stuck me with a freaking guard dog?

Maybe if I found Everest first . . .

As I readied the conference room with refreshments for the meeting and tidied up the living room, I racked my brain for reasons Everest could be in Denver.

"What's in Denver, Everest?" I murmured to myself, watching the sky outside the inn's bay windows darken to a glittery periwinkle.

I felt there was something I was forgetting, but what was it?

CHAPTER 9

At 7:45 p.m., the men started trickling into the inn. First, Nelson arrived. He embraced his wife as though he hadn't seen her in days instead of hours. I couldn't help but stare at them, remembering a time when my parents would stand that way, cheek to cheek, heart to heart, whispering to each other. Because I didn't want to pry, I averted my gaze, rearranging the green apples in the wooden bowl I'd added on the corner of the bell desk.

I heard Nelson ask Isobel if she wasn't too tired. From the corner of my eye, I caught her shaking her head no. After kissing her on the forehead, Nelson moved toward me in those fluid, long strides of his. Like his son, he was long-limbed, but where August's legs and arms teemed with muscle, Nelson was on the slender side.

He touched my shoulder, making the apple I was trying to place on top of my artful pyramid skid down.

He caught the fruit before it rolled off the counter and popped it back on top. "How are you holding up, Ness?"

"Great. Thanks to Isobel and Mrs. Rogers."

Isobel smiled at me. "By the way, I asked Skylar to man the bell desk after I go home. She said it shouldn't be a problem and that her wife could cover the dining area. I hope that's all right with you."

"It's more than all right." I hadn't even thought about finding a night manager. I would hunt Skylar down after the meeting to ask how long she could cover the night shift—hopefully, until my uncle felt "better." Would he ever feel better, though?

The revolving door spun again, carrying in the crisp, blue scent of evening and the musky smell of male bodies. Liam was among those arriving males. At the sight of him, my hearing dimmed to a faint buzzing. He walked straight to me. After greeting Nelson, Liam threaded his fingers through mine and pulled me away from August's father.

How was the rest of your day? he whispered inside my head.

I lifted my gaze to his. "Never-ending. And yours?"

What I really wanted to know was what Aidan had said.

I heard Lucas gave you a history lesson.

"He did." Had Lucas also told Liam how the lesson ended?

Passing a couple guests on their way to dinner, we turned toward the staircase that led down to the conference room. He didn't let go of my hand until we reached the head of the oval table. As he took his seat, he tipped his head at the chair next to his.

"Maybe an elder should sit here, Liam." Or someone higher up on the pack pyramid.

His dark eyes held mine. *Your place is next to me now.*

Worrying my lip, I slid into the seat. Dating the Alpha meant something; sitting next to him meant something more.

As wheels rolled over the hardwood floor and jeans whispered against the smooth leather seats, I drummed my fingers on the tabletop, studying the row of shiny glasses I'd aligned in the center of the table.

The chair next to mine stayed vacant for so long that I began to think no one would sit next to me. But Matt took pity and dropped into the seat. I exhaled a quiet breath.

A knot formed in my abdomen. *Stress* . . . I was feeling stressed. And nervous. Or was it—

I lifted my eyes to the doorway just as August strode into the room. He took a seat next to his father and scanned the room, his gaze hopping right over me.

My heart pinched from that tiny action. What had Liam said to him? I lowered my gaze back to the row of glasses, finding solace in the quiet study of inanimate objects.

"Where's Jeb?" Liam asked.

I blinked up at him, then whisked my gaze around the table. My uncle was the only person missing.

"Hasn't left his bedroom all day," Lucas said.

"He needs to be here," Liam said. "Lucas, Matt."

Both boys rose and marched out of the room.

My heart was beating double-time. I wanted to ask Liam if dragging my uncle down to this meeting was truly necessary, but bit my tongue. I didn't think it judicious to challenge the Alpha before the meeting even started.

Frank tipped his head toward Liam. Where the Alpha wasn't speaking out loud, Frank was answering with nods and *yes*es, so a conversation was happening.

Muted grunts and heavy footfalls sounded just outside the room, and then Lucas and Matt were back, my uncle wedged between them. They released him in the last free chair before returning to their respective seats.

Jeb slumped forward, complexion as gray as his salt-and-pepper scruff, and forehead as puckered as a raisin. He seemed to have aged years in the space of a couple days.

"Close the door, Little J," Liam told one of the youngest members of the pack, a boy with acne and shoulder-length copper hair.

The boy reminded me of Everest the year I left Boulder. Everest, too, had worn his red hair long, and he, too, had had a bad bout of acne. I remembered wondering how he could stand the chemical smell of the cream he'd rub into his face every day to clear it up.

"Thank you all for coming." Liam's voice rang clearly in the low-ceilinged room, echoing against the clay-colored stone walls. "We have two matters to discuss tonight. Let's begin with Everest Clark, my father's killer."

Frowns pleated foreheads, and gazes narrowed on me. My pulse spiked as I realized people still saw me as Everest's willing accomplice.

"Unless you can live without eyeballs, I urge you all to stop looking at Ness that way," Liam growled.

The men averted their gazes.

"The pack's custom has always been to avenge a death with a death."

I'd been wringing my fingers together in my lap but stopped when Liam spoke of avenging deaths. I crossed my arms and leaned against the springy backrest. *Not always*, I thought but didn't say out loud. Everyone around this table knew my father's death hadn't been avenged.

"All those in favor of Everest Clark's death, please raise your hands."

Jeb made this squeaking sound that prompted Nelson to put a hand on my uncle's slouched shoulder. Although August's dad didn't say anything, his pinched expression told me he, too, thought having Jeb sit in on this meeting was cruel.

Many hands shot up; not mine. I didn't want Everest dead; I did want him punished, though. I counted hands, looked at the faces of the men who voted for Everest's execution. Thirty-four hands out of forty. Jeb squinted at the hands too, pallid lips wobbling. Nelson hadn't raised his hand, but August had.

Liam didn't have a gavel, but he banged his fist against the table. "The majority has decided."

And just like that—a fist against a table sealed my cousin's fate. Blood beat against my skin that suddenly felt too tight for my body. I rubbed my bare arms, trying to ease the sudden strain. The dusting of hairs began to thicken underneath my palms. I was shifting! I couldn't shift here. I closed my eyes, and my nostrils flared as I pushed against my rising wolf.

I would let her out later.

Later, I promised her. *Please not now.*

I couldn't lose control in front of all these men.

I pressed harder against her. Repressed her. Slowly, like thawing ice, her hold melted away. When I felt in command of my body, I raised my lids and glanced around, praying no one had witnessed my struggle.

Thankfully, the pack was discussing some other matter. Or maybe they were still discussing Everest. Whatever they were talking about, it captivated all of their focus.

No, that wasn't true.

August was watching me, and from the concern smudging his expression, I deduced he'd witnessed my little tussle. I was about to offer him a reassuring smile but remembered his raised hand—his vote. I stared at the revolving ceiling fan, at its blades that blurred as they sliced the tension-filled air.

Liam tapped his fist against the table again to garner everyone's attention. "Now onto the second matter at hand." Liam dug an aluminum-foil tablet out of his jeans pocket and held the thing out between his middle and index fingers. "Is everyone familiar with these?"

CHAPTER 10

L iam wiggled the tablet, and the aluminum wrapping crinkled in the quiet conference room. "It's called Sillin. We ingest it when we need to avoid shifting. In other words, if you ever travel out of state, break a bone, or get silver poisoning, this is what we'll give you."

Silver poisoning? I didn't know Sillin countered that effect.

"Over the years, we've amassed a large stock of these. Last time my father asked Greg to procure some from the hospital, the pack doctor was told the formula had been discontinued." Liam tossed the tablet to one of the younger boys so he could take a look at it, sniff it.

Sillin didn't have an odor, which was why Heath hadn't detected it in his drink.

"Those who've taken these pills can tell you that the effect wears off fast and causes no lasting harm."

"That's the drug Ness gave Heath, isn't it?" Little J asked.

"It is," Liam said calmly, narrowing his gaze on the boy.

Little J flinched and concentrated on the tablet again before passing it along. Cheeks the color of rare beef, he leaned forward, grasped a water carafe that almost slipped out of his shaky hold, and poured himself a glass.

"This morning, the elders and I discovered the pack's entire stock of Sillin was stolen from HQ."

"Did Ness steal them?" someone asked.

"What?" I whipped toward the interlocutor.

The man was in his early thirties with a gold hoop speared through his right earlobe, and chest hair spilling out of a purple button-down shirt. For the life of me, I couldn't remember his name.

"I didn't steal anything!" I exclaimed.

"Rodrigo"—Liam's clipped tone had the man thumbing his earring—"*Everest* stole the pills."

The man next to Rodrigo placed a soothing hand on the dark shifter's forearm.

"We have footage of him cutting the lock off the fridge and taking everything inside."

The lock on the fridge . . . "It didn't look broken on Monday night," I said.

Frank sighed. "That's because he replaced it with an identical one. We realized what had happened when we tried to open it and it didn't work. When we asked Cole for the feed—"

"Bastard didn't even try to avoid the camera." Shaking his head, Cole slid the cigarette he'd wedged behind his ear and tapped it on the table.

Rodrigo lowered his fingers from his earring. "What's he planning on doing with all the Sillin he took?"

"We think he'll either try to sell it to other packs," Liam said, "or use it on us."

Rodrigo snorted. "How the hell could he swing that?"

"He could spike our drinks or mix it into our food," Liam said. "Sillin is tasteless, so it's not like any of us would notice."

When the hairy-chested wolf ogled the carafes I'd set in the middle of the table, Little J spit out the gulp of water he'd just taken, then stuck his arm in front of his face and watched his limb until the strawberry-blond hairs thickened and turned into tawny fur.

"I didn't contaminate the water," I gritted out.

"But did you stay next to it all day?" Rodrigo asked.

"Everest isn't in Boulder," I said.

"Really?" The man linked his fingers together. "And how do you know that? Did he text you?"

"Enough!" August's voice detonated like a gunshot in the room.

"Ness isn't Everest's ally. He used her, made her feel guilty for something she didn't do, so cut her some fucking slack!"

Ping. A penny for his mom's jar.

Liam's lips tightened, but he didn't reprimand August for his outburst. At least not out loud. My stomach clenched from my heightened nerves, or from our bond, I wasn't sure. I laid my palm over my abdomen, hoping heat and pressure could undo the tension.

A second later, Liam stole my hand away from my stomach, laced our fingers, and tugged. My chair rolled and bumped into his.

I frowned at him, but his eyes were fixed on August. August who'd seized one of the glass carafes and poured himself water. Half of the contents sloshed over the rim. He mopped it up with the sleeve of his long-sleeved Henley, then lifted the glass to his mouth and drank long and hard. Realizing Liam was trying to make a statement, I stole my hand out of his.

The man who'd placed his palm on Rodrigo's arm earlier quirked a dark-blond eyebrow. "Maybe Lucy knows what her son is up to."

Jeb made a deep keening sound that was more animal than human.

Eric leaned his forearms on the table. "I interrogated Lucy again this morning, James. She said she didn't know."

"Then why was she helping him in the first place?" someone asked.

My uncle's Adam's apple jostled repeatedly in his unshaven throat, and his puffy eyes misted over as he shook his head from side to side.

Eric's gaze glided over to me. "Everest told her"—he rubbed his bald head—"that Ness killed Heath but was trying to frame him for it."

"He did what?" My claws came out so suddenly that I scraped the table, leaving curls of wood. No wonder my aunt hated me.

Shh. Liam's voice bounced around in my skull.

I dragged air that felt like fire into my lungs until my wolf relinquished her hold on me. Once I felt calmer, I said, "Someone had eyes on me at the warehouse."

"Lucy was monitoring you remotely," Eric said. "Everest planted a cell phone on one of the shelves and linked it to hers. We recovered the phone in question."

"She *claims* Everest put it there, and I hope she isn't lying. I hope no one else was involved in the con." Liam leaned back into his chair. "I'm feeling merciful tonight, but my mercy will be off the table come morning. So if anyone has something to confess, I strongly suggest you do it now."

No one spoke.

I highly doubted anyone would come forward, but maybe Liam wasn't seeking verbal responses . . . Maybe he was checking his pack's body language, looking for tells.

After scrutinizing his men, Liam said, "Okay then . . . "

"Do we have any leads on Everest's whereabouts?" Little J asked, his voice sounding almost squeaky.

Liam's gaze surfed over the heads of his pack members without ever settling, as though still on the lookout for a conspirator. "We do," he said slowly without offering any further details.

"Can we join the search party?" Little J asked.

Frank smoothed a hand over his thick white hair. "Your enthusiasm is commendable, Joseph, but Liam has everything under control."

"Oh, come on, Grandpa . . . "

So Little J, i.e. Joseph, was Frank's grandson? I felt a twinge more sympathy toward the boy, because like me, he'd lost his father. And I liked Frank.

"No, Joseph," Frank said. "You're too young."

Joseph crossed his freckled arms and pouted.

"The most important thing right now is that we stay united and alert. Open your own bottles and prepare your own food, and if anyone has trouble shifting, report to me immediately." Liam squared his broad shoulders, pushed away from the table, and stood. "Thank you all for coming."

Chairs rolled back, and men rose, chattering in low tones. I didn't get up. At least, not right away. Liam hadn't mentioned the bike, nor his meeting with Aidan Michaels. I wondered if it was because he didn't want to cause more alarm or because he thought there might be a mole in the pack. I glanced around me. Only August stared back, lips alternatively parting a little and pressing tightly, as though he wanted to say something.

A hand settled on my shoulder, kneaded it. "Are you ready?" Liam asked.

I craned my neck. "Ready? To go find Everest?"

Liam shook his head as he kept massaging my shoulder. "I'm taking you home." I almost purred from how good his fingers felt against my knotted muscles. "I think you could use a full-body rubdown."

I wasn't a blusher, yet heat scalded my cheeks. I wished he hadn't said that last bit quite as loud. He could've used his Alpha link—

It hit me then. Like earlier, he was making a statement, because he felt threatened by August. I sighed and let Liam make his statement, let him claim me. When I looked around the room, only Matt and Lucas remained. I rolled my chair back, clasped Liam's fingers, and rose.

On the way out of the room, I stopped next to Lucas. Setting my annoyance aside, I asked, "Did they call you back?"

Liam frowned while Lucas's eyes turned a stormy blue. I sensed he was pissed I'd brought up the escort agency in front of his friends. What I didn't understand was why. It wasn't as though he actually wanted to hire an escort.

"Did *who* call him back?" Liam asked.

"The escort agency," I said.

Matt waggled his eyebrows. "Trying to get over Taryn, huh?"

Pink-cheeked, Lucas slugged him. "No, you douchebag. Ness thought Everest's last girlfriend might be working for Red Creek Escorts. And yeah, they phoned me back. They don't know any Megans."

My heart contracted with surprise. *So Everest hadn't lied.* I toyed with my mother's wedding band which hung from a leather cord around my neck. Slid it on my finger, then off, then on again.

"Why were you looking into her?" Liam asked.

"She thought the chick might be Everest's link to Denver," Lucas grumbled.

Liam and Matt exchanged a look. When Liam nodded toward the door, the blond giant closed it.

"We found your cousin's link to Denver," Liam said, voice low.

I let go of my ring, and it bounced over my T-shirt a few times before settling. "You did?"

"Thanks to you."

"To me?"

Liam scrubbed his thumb over my knuckles. "You know that visit we paid Aidan Michaels? It was very . . . *edifying*."

Matt cracked his knuckles. "Don't know if you're aware of this, Little Wolf, but Michaels has a hotel in Denver."

That's why Denver sounded familiar! Sandra had sent me information about Aidan before I'd met him. He owned a hotel in Denver, Las Vegas, and . . . what was the third location again? It didn't much matter, I supposed. Unless Everest fled the Denver hotel. Then it might matter.

"So Everest traded the Sillin against shelter?" I asked.

Liam shook his head. "No."

"No?" I cocked a dubious eyebrow.

"Your cousin sold Aidan something else."

"His soul?" Lucas quipped.

Matt snorted. "I doubt he had one to sell."

"His land," Liam said. "Effective upon his death."

"His land?" What land did my cousin own?

Matt gestured to the room.

"The *inn*? He sold Aidan Michaels the inn?" I shrilled.

Liam nodded heavily.

"Good thing we never set up Headquarters here, huh?" Matt continued.

Something dawned on me. "That's why Everest struck the deal . . . Even though the inn's not Headquarters, this place is central to the pack's territory."

"Maybe that was his reasoning, but it doesn't change the outcome," Liam said.

My throat closed and opened.

Liam let go of my hand but not of my body. He cupped my cheeks and spoke to me gently. "We don't need this property, Ness. The pack has a lot of land. *I* have a lot of land."

"But it's—" I wanted to say my family's, but my dad had sold his share to buy the plot where he'd built our house. The inn and the rolling hill on which it stood wasn't *my* anything. "Can the pack really afford to part with this property?" I swallowed, blinking back the heat building behind my lids. "Your father sold Aidan Michaels so much land . . . Wasn't it enough?" I whispered. "Did he really need this place too?"

Every line on Liam's face seemed to sharpen, and his grip turned almost bruising. After a minute of complete silence, he said, "Aidan Michaels is a greedy son-of-a-bitch."

I placed my hands over his and pried his fingers off. I shouldn't have reminded Liam of the deal his father had struck with the devil.

"At least the Sillin isn't in Aidan's hands," I mused, mostly to ease Liam's lingering tension. "Can't believe that the man who hates were-wolves wasn't interested in buying pills that can make us weaker."

Matt crossed his arms. "My guess is he doesn't know about them."

"He hates us, Matt. Has entire files on us. The man surely knows about Sillin."

"What I meant was maybe your cousin didn't tell him about the *stolen* ones."

I raised my eyebrows. *Oh.* After a beat, I said, "Can't believe Aidan Michaels sold Everest out that quick."

Lucas grunted. "The man has no fucking scruples."

"Everest dying is in Aidan's best interest." Liam's expression had gentled again. "The quicker it happens, the quicker he gets the deed to this place. That's why he sent you the bike. He wanted to lead *you*, or one of us, back to him, so he could boast about his clever little deal."

"How are we even sure he's telling the truth? Maybe it's a trap."

Liam stroked a finger along my neck, leaving a trail of heat. "I left the bastard in the hands of Greg and two Boulders. They have orders to *slow* his healing process if he lied. So again, it's in Aidan's best interest that we find your cousin."

I sighed. This was so many shades of messed up, but at least I'd gotten answers. "We should set out tonight."

Liam frowned.

So I elaborated, "To recover Everest. We should head to Denver now."

"I already told you. You're not coming with us."

I jerked back. "But I want—"

"No."

"Liam—"

"No."

Lucas drew the door open. "I could use a beer right 'bout now. Matty?"

"Lead the way." Before trotting up the stairs, Matt glanced at me, then at Liam. Wisely, the blond giant decided to stay out of our *discussion*.

I crossed my arms. "He's my cousin, Liam."

"Which is precisely why you're not coming."

"I won't get in the way."

"Ness, unless memory fails me, your hand wasn't up earlier."

"Just because I don't want him dead doesn't mean I'd interfere with a pack decision."

"I'm still not taking you along. I don't want you to witness this. Even if the person deserves death, it isn't a pretty act."

A sour taste filled my mouth as I remembered the smell of gunpowder, the gaping black hole in my father's brown fur, the taste of metal as I tried to lick his blood away. Even though I'd thrown up the silver-laced blood, I'd had to get my stomach pumped. Had I been given Sillin then? Everything after the gunshot was such a blur.

I squeezed my eyes shut and shuddered.

Arms wound around me and reeled me in. "Let me spare you this, Ness," Liam said gently, propping his chin on the top of my head. "As a wolf, you'll see enough terrible things during your lifetime. Let me spare you one of them. Plus, I'd rather you don't watch *me* exact justice."

For a long moment, neither of us spoke. Memories of Everest crashed through me. Like the time he and I snuck around the inn, collecting pillows and comforters to construct a fort of epic proportion inside his bedroom. When Mom had found us hiding behind our fluffy cotton walls, she lay down with us and told us the story of two little wolves that went on adventures instead of going to school. I wasn't yet a wolf, so I didn't think the story was about me, but her tale had allowed me to dream that I might become one. After that day, Everest and I discussed at great lengths the adventures we'd go on if I were able to shift.

I bit my trembling lip as I realized there would be no adventures for us. A tear escaped, and then another, soaking the thin fabric of Liam's navy V-neck. He was right. I shouldn't accompany him. I might put myself between Everest and the weapon used to end his life.

"I can't believe Jeb didn't even fight to save his son's life." My words trembled like the rest of my body.

"Jeb knows the rules of the pack."

"This will *kill* him," I croaked, my voice barely louder than the whirring fan.

I waited for Liam to tell me that I was wrong, that my uncle was strong, that he'd get over it, but Liam didn't say any of these things. He just held me, stroking my spine up and down, up and down, until my body calmed.

Come home with me tonight.

I peered up at him through watery eyes and swallowed. "Okay."

CHAPTER 11

As we drove over to his house, I realized the inn would soon belong to Aidan Michaels. Which meant I would need to find a new place to live. Maybe I could bunk with Sarah. She'd said she didn't want a roommate, but I'd make myself tiny and burrow in a corner of her palatial apartment. Or Evelyn. Maybe I could move in with her and Frank. Or would I have to continue living with Jeb, my legal guardian? What if Jeb didn't survive Everest's death? What then? Would I be entrusted to Lucy . . . if Eric ever released her from his basement? Would social services come for me, or could Evelyn finally become my guardian?

In five weeks, I'd be eighteen. Until then, my life belonged to people who were in no way fit to care for me.

"What are you thinking about?" Liam's voice made me look away from the star-strewn sky.

"Everest." I lied because I didn't want to burden him with my problems. Besides, my cousin wasn't far from my mind.

Liam squeezed the steering wheel. "I'm sorry, Ness."

"About what?"

"About the decision that was voted tonight." Starlight made his chiseled profile gleam white.

I bit my lip, then released it along with a ragged breath. "I appreciate you saying that."

After he parked in front of his modern wood-and-glass cabin, which was as dark as the sky outside the windshield, he picked up my cold hand and rubbed the pad of his thumb over my knuckles.

"Don't think for a second I'll enjoy ending his life."

I swallowed. Hard. It did nothing to dislodge the boulder-sized lump inside my throat.

He cupped my cheek and leaned over the center console of his car, ghosting a kiss across my mouth. The contact sent a shiver straight down my spine.

"Liam?"

His lips were tracing the edge of my jaw. "Yeah, babe?"

"Ask him why he did it. Before . . . " The rest of my sentence dangled silently between us.

"I will."

"And promise to make it quick. Don't torture him, okay?" I inhaled, and his potent scent swirled through me, the familiarity of it soothing.

"I promise."

Before cracking my lids open, I sighed, wondering if he'd keep his promise come morning.

He lifted my hand, flipped it over, then placed a chaste kiss against my palm. Lowering it, he asked, "Have you eaten?"

Food was the furthest thing from my mind right now. "No."

"Are you hungry?"

"Not really."

He tapped his finger against my cool skin. "Maybe once you see the contents of my fridge, it'll inspire you."

"Maybe." I doubted it, though. My stomach was one giant knot.

Clutching my crossbody bag to me, I pumped my door handle and hopped out. Once inside the house, he kicked off his boots. I followed suit, lining my sneakers up next to his shoes. As I stood back up, a nervousness—that had nothing to do with my cousin's fate —overwhelmed me. I'd never stayed at someone's house before— well, besides Evelyn's apartment.

When Mom would work late, I'd stay with Evelyn. She'd fill my belly with her delicious cooking, then fit a mug brimming with stove-top-warmed milk into my hands and read to me until I fell asleep with my head on her lap and her fingers in my hair. The month following my mother's last breath, I'd stayed with Evelyn almost every night. She'd tried to feed me, tried to make me sip milk, tried to distract me with one of her books. All I'd managed was to sleep, and even that had come in fitful bursts.

Liam propped my chin on his fingers and crooked my face up toward his. "You just checked out on me again."

"Sorry." I slid my chin off his fingers and swept my gaze over the clean, sharp décor that seemed simple but had probably cost him a small fortune.

He sighed as he wrapped his hand around mine and pulled me toward a large door. Behind it stood a bachelor's kitchen: beige-veined chocolate marble with copper fixings and smoky-mirrored cupboards that rose with the press of a finger. I'd come to his house before, but hadn't ventured into the kitchen then.

Liam seized plastic containers from the fridge and set them on the marble island, popping the lids off.

"Did you cook all of this?" I asked as I climbed onto one of the leather stools, admiring how clean and shiny the kitchen was.

"Since Dad died, Matt's mom's been sending food over religiously."

"That's really sweet of her."

"She's a good woman. I heard she came to help out at the inn." He took out two plates and silverware.

"She did. Isobel too."

"The pack takes care of their own."

A warm, fluttery feeling swept through me. I would never tire of hearing I was part of the pack.

He tipped his chin toward the offerings.

Realizing we still knew very little about each other, I asked, "What's your favorite food?"

"Steak." He spooned something that looked like polenta onto his plate before adding a bunch of green beans and a thick piece of browned meat. "Original, huh?" He shot me a brazen smile as he slid his plate into the microwave and pressed a couple buttons that filled the quiet kitchen with a soft whirring noise. "What about you?"

"I pretty much love everything. But I have a soft spot for

Mexican cuisine. Evelyn"—I dragged my hand through my hair—"she made a lot of our meals back in LA."

After I prepped myself a plate, Liam set it in the microwave.

"Want anything to drink?"

"Water would be great."

He pulled open his fridge and took out a bottle of water and a beer.

"This feels like a first date," I said.

He uncapped his beer, then took a deep drink and swallowed before leaning over to kiss me. "I don't want this to be our first date. I want to take you out. Tomorrow night, you and me."

My heart rate accelerated, but then it dipped when I remembered that tomorrow night I would be deleting my cousin's contact from my phone forever. A sharp spike in my breathing had Liam tipping his head to the side.

"You don't want to be seen out with me?" he asked.

"What?" I tried to iron out my erratic pulse. "No, it's not that." I ran my index finger along the sweaty sides of my bottle. "I do want to go out with you, but not tomorrow."

His eyes shrouded with contrition. I wasn't sure—and didn't ask for fear of the answer—if the remorse was for my cousin or for postponing our dinner.

The microwave beeped then. He handed me my plate before propping himself on the stool beside mine. We didn't speak again after that, both of us tucking into our food, lost in our respective musings.

I didn't taste anything. It was just fuel for my depleted body and a means to avoid deliberating about Everest.

I took my plate over to the sink when I was done and scrubbed it clean.

"You don't have to do that, Ness. I have someone who comes over every couple days to clean."

"Been cleaning after myself and others for so long it's ingrained in my DNA." I smiled at him as I dried my hands on the kitchen towel tucked over the handle of the oven door.

"Was that really your job back in LA?"

"That, and waitressing, but I hated waitressing." I wrinkled my nose. "What's the cleaning company you use?"

Liam sipped the dregs of his beer. "Why?"

"Because I'll be out of a job soon."

"You're not seriously entertaining the idea of cleaning houses?"

I frowned. "It's what I know how to do, Liam."

"You're pack now, Ness."

"And what?" I crossed my arms in front of my chest. "Housekeeping is beneath werewolves?"

"I'll help you get a real job."

"Housekeeping *is* a real job."

"But you can do better."

"I have a high school education, Liam."

"Tomorrow, we'll stop by UCB and enroll you."

"You mean, after you off my cousin?" I snapped, voice as tight as the rest of my body.

Liam rose from his stool and rounded the island toward me. "Ness . . . "

I mashed my lips shut.

"You're angry."

I was. I was angry about Everest's fate. Angry about Liam's belittling view on my job. Angry I hadn't taken the next step in my education.

He set his palms on my sharp shoulders. "I get it, but don't be angry with me."

I glared at the dip of his midnight-colored V-neck, unwilling to look into his eyes.

"An Alpha protects his pack, Ness. Everest is a threat to you . . . to all of us." He hooked my chin and raised it until our eyes met. "As for your future, I think it would be best for you to go to college. I'm sure it's what your parents would've wanted."

My anger dissipated at the mention of my parents. In the last month of her life, Mom had hounded me to fill out college applications.

"I'll need to apply for financial aid first," I finally mumbled.

"The pack has resources. If you want to go to UCB in the fall, you'll have a spot there. All expenses paid."

"Even a dorm room?"

"Even a dorm room."

So I'd only need to figure out where to live for the next month . . . This felt too good to be true. "What's the catch?"

Liam smiled. "No catch. You're part of the pack. Education is one of the perks. We like our wolves to be equipped to conquer the world. Or at least, Boulder."

I was still going to need a job to pay back the four and a half grand I owed the bank for past rents and miscellaneous expenses, but I didn't want to bring that up again.

Liam wrapped his hands around my wrists and dragged down the bony blockade that separated our bodies. "Don't fence me out. I know you've been taking care of yourself for years, but I'm here now. And countless others are here for you too. Let us in. *Trust* us."

"I'm trying."

He pressed his mouth to mine, soft as silk, but then his kiss grew harder. It took me a few seconds to relax, but finally I sighed—more of a moan than a sigh—and hooked my hands around his waist. As though my heart had migrated into my stomach, my abdomen began to thud. I tried to squelch the offensive sensation, but it soon took over all the others.

I pulled away from Liam so quickly I half expected pieces of my lips to have stayed glued to his. His dark eyes raked over my expression, then over my body, pausing on the palm I'd pressed against my stomach. I lowered my hand, balling my fingers. The throbbing was already receding.

"Eric warned me about this, but I thought—" His Adam's apple worked in his throat. "I hoped it would be different."

"What did Eric warn you about?"

"He said your body would reject any advance that didn't come from its natural mate."

Horror filtered through me.

"The only way to void this is distance, but August isn't leaving." Liam sighed, and his muscular chest deflated the tiniest bit. "I don't know if you heard, but his mom had breast cancer a while back."

The word cancer soured my blood.

"They thought she'd beat it, but it's back. And more aggressive this time. Anyway, she's scheduled for a double mastectomy next week, and—"

I let out a shrill whimper before slamming the back of my hand against my mouth.

"Fuck." He gathered me against him. "I forgot cancer was how your mom . . . " He didn't finish his sentence. Didn't have to. He smoothed his hand over the back of my head.

I reeled from the news that hit too close to home. At least now I understood why Isobel's husband had fretted over her back at the inn, why she'd looked so wan beside her healthy son.

"August said the doctors were confident they'd get it this time, but he wants to stay until after the surgery. He promised he'd leave after."

I shook with anguish for Isobel, Nelson, and August, and with shame at how selfish I'd been. Not only had I believed that August had stayed for me, but I'd been ready to beg him to leave so I could be intimate with Liam. *Ugh.*

Liam tangled his hand in my hair. "He didn't want me to tell you, so please keep this between us."

I nodded, still pressing my knuckles against my mouth to stifle the dread brought on by Liam's news. "It's not fair," I murmured.

"Life's rarely fair." Even though I couldn't see into his mind, I sensed he was thinking of his own mother taken from him when he was only eight, by his abusive father no less.

"Speaking of unfair, I know you hate Everest, and I know you want to uphold the pack's"—I wet my lips—"*traditions*, but my cousin did you a favor. He killed your mother's murderer." I hoped phrasing it that way would sway him a little. "Won't you reconsider his sentence?"

Liam's fingers wrung my T-shirt as though it were Everest's neck. "My mother wasn't pack."

"So what?" Anger struck me in violent strokes. "Her life wasn't worth as much?"

"Don't mistake forgiveness for integrity." His eyes were so black his pupils seemed to have devoured his irises. "My father was a mean bastard, but he was still my father. If I let your cousin walk away from this, what sort of Alpha would that make me?"

"A merciful one."

"Mercy doesn't inspire respect."

"That's not true. Compassion is a laudable trait in a leader. I'd respect you for showing compassion to someone who didn't deserve it."

His gaze set on the shiny chocolate marble. "Don't, Ness."

"Don't what?"

"Don't tell me how to rule the pack. I'm the Alpha, not you."

His words grated against me, made my spine snap straight. "You might win the pack's respect with those words, but not mine." I backed away from him and walked into the living room. "Not mine."

"Where are you going?" He strode behind me.

"Outside."

He captured my wrist and wheeled me toward him. "I'm sorry. I shouldn't have said that. I'm just tired and on edge, and with all that's going on with you"—he gestured to my abdomen—"it came out wrong."

I stared at his fingers still clasping my wrist.

"I want your respect"—he tucked a piece of hair behind my ear—"but I can't change pack laws for as much. Not yet. In time—"

"You accepted me—a girl—into the pack and you didn't taint the new pledges' drinks with the stupid fossil, so you *can* change things! When you want to, you can. Which just proves you want my cousin dead or you'd have forgiven him." I flipped my hand up to loosen his grip, then yanked my arm toward me to break his hold. His fingers hadn't hurt me, yet I nursed my wrist against my chest.

His eyes widened as they fastened to the spot of skin they'd manhandled. He palmed the back of his head. And then he fell to his knees in front of me and pressed his face against my stomach, arms hooking around me.

"I'm sorry, Ness. Please don't leave."

I watched him for a long moment, watched how his apology made his big body quiver. It brought me back to the night on the inn's terrace when he'd cried in my arms. He wasn't crying now, but he was shaking.

Liam might've acted strong and brave, but so much inside him was broken, and although I was good with messes, I didn't know where to start on the one his parents had left behind. Could *I* even fix it? I was such a mess myself. Orphaned. Almost homeless. Penniless. Mated.

I rested a hand on top of his head. "I won't leave you, Liam."

He tipped his head up and inspected my face as though to make sure I was speaking the truth, and then he climbed up the length of my body. For a long minute, he just stood there, looking down at me instead of up, and I saw the solid man inside him rise again, push back the wrecked child.

Then he cupped my cheeks and tilted my head up, and he slammed his mouth against mine. Even though my stomach began to churn, I pried my lips open and tangled my tongue with his.

I didn't delude myself into thinking that this was the end of our argument, but it was a ceasefire. I wished it would last, but how could it when tomorrow he'd leave to perform a vile act? I pushed my cousin's face out of my mind while Liam demolished my mouth. I tasted blood even though none had yet been spilled.

Liam groaned and kissed me harder. The taste of blood thickened in my mouth to the point where I gagged. I dug my palms into his chest and pushed him away.

Liam's mouth and chin were smeared red.

CHAPTER 12

"Oh my God, you're bleeding!" I yelped.

"You did bite me." There was a lilt in his tone. *Amusement?*

How could this amuse him?

I swiped my tongue against my teeth, and sure enough, my canines had lengthened. I touched my mouth. My fingertips came away red. Absolute revulsion seized me.

Liam's smile widened as he grabbed a tissue from the leather box atop the console next to the front door. He dabbed his lips, dabbed mine. Blood still trickled from the puncture wound.

"Damn if that wasn't the hottest kiss I've ever had."

I blinked at him. How could *that* have been pleasurable?

He pressed the tissue to his mouth a while longer before balling it up and tossing it on the console.

"I *hurt* you," I said, my voice as raw as his broken lip.

He frowned. "Babe, getting bitten only increases the pleasure. Or so I've been told . . . since I've never been with a she-wolf."

I momentarily forgot about having bit him. However silly, I liked the fact that I was different from his past girlfriends.

His eyes flashed yellow—wolf eyes. "Do you trust me?"

I nodded.

He nudged my jaw up with his nose, dragged his teeth that had sharpened to points down my neck, then sank them into a patch of skin right above my collarbone.

I gasped, but not in pain.

The skin he'd pierced tingled, and then shockwaves of pleasure radiated from that one spot into the rest of my body. He released my skin and laved the spot he'd bitten with his tongue.

"Fuck, you taste sweet." Once he was done lapping up all the blood, he peered into my stunned face with a satisfied smirk. "I'm happy I've found one way to pleasure you. Even though I'm not giving up on finding more."

Heat engulfed my cheeks, my entire body for that matter. "I thought only vampires did *that*."

"Vampires don't exist."

Yet we do . . .

He licked his lust-swollen lips, eyes gleaming but no longer yellow. "Have you ever heard the legend of the bite that saved a life?"

I shook my head.

"It's a good story. One of my favorites. My grandfather used to tell it to me."

I rubbed the spot Liam had bitten.

"Apparently, during a terrible forest fire, an Alpha was hit by a blazing fallen tree. The blow was so violent that while his pack worked to roll the crackling trunk off him, they felt his link to them unravel. His second-in-command"—I frowned, so he explained—"large packs have *betas*. Well, he urged the wolves to make their way home to prevent any more casualties, but the Alpha's mate, she refused to leave him. She dug a trench in the ground to reach him, and then she grabbed him by the neck and dragged his asphyxiated body out. Legend says that when her fangs pierced his skin, her love for him leaked into his bloodstream and jumpstarted his heart." He shrugged. "Story's probably embellished, but I like to think our magic has the power to save lives." He moved my fingers off the spot I was still rubbing and kissed it.

I shivered. I hadn't lost much blood, yet felt as lightheaded as when I'd extracted a whole pint from my veins to try and save my mother. She'd insisted that injecting herself with my blood wouldn't magically defeat her ovarian cancer, but I'd tried one gray afternoon.

While I'd slid the needle in her catheter-bruised arm, I'd begged for a miracle.

Unlike the Alpha's mate from Liam's legend, I never got my miracle, so I didn't put much stock in our magic saving a life.

Liam tugged me out of my dreary memory by leading me into the bedroom. He flicked on the lamp on his nightstand, then let go of my hand and walked to his connecting bathroom. "Give me a sec."

He vanished into his en suite, leaving me to stand on the edge of the electric-violet rug that stretched from one wood-paneled wall to the other. Alone in the bedroom, my thoughts whirred like the microwave, continuously spinning images of my cousin.

How I wished I could save his life.

Over my shoulder, I spied my bag on the couch. My phone was in there. I could text Everest. I could warn him. He could run and stay away forever. Glancing at the bedroom door, I took my phone out and hovered my finger over the text messaging icon.

With a few little words, I could change the course of his fate. I almost went through with it, but then I thought about how he'd toyed with my life, how he'd strangled Heath, and realized I couldn't betray the pack for the sake of a blood-tie.

As I lowered my phone, it vibrated, and a message appeared on my screen.

SARAH: *Hey, friend, want to hang tomorrow?*

Even though I was feeling rather glum, Sarah's message managed to make me smile.

ME: *Would love to.*

SARAH: *Lunch at Tracy's at 3?*

ME: *No one has lunch at 3.*

SARAH: *We do.*

I shook my head. *Fine. See you tomorrow.*

The floorboards creaked, and I jumped.

Liam leaned against the doorframe of his bedroom, jeans slung low on his hips—and shirtless. My throat went a little dry at the sight of his honed chest and the indents at his waist, and the thickening trail of dark hair. Liam was so incredibly perfect. Why did I have to imprint on August?

"Who you texting?" There was a hint of something in Liam's tone —suspicion or jealousy?

"Sarah. We're meeting up tomorrow."

He uncrossed his arms and strolled over to me. "Can you be careful with her? I know she's your friend, but she's a Pine. I don't trust Pines. Same way I don't trust Creeks, or any of the Eastern packs."

"And you say I'm the one with trust issues?"

He flashed me an almost predatorial smile as he plucked the phone from my fingers and tossed it on his leather couch. "You're wearing too many clothes. Arms up."

I looked around me at the walls of glass and the night-soaked landscape beyond them.

"No one's out there," he promised. Sensing my enduring anguish, he walked over to the wall and hit a switch that brought down metal blinds before returning to me.

"Are you sure?"

"Close your eyes."

I frowned but did as I was told.

"Now, listen."

Still frowning, I strained to listen. It took a second for me to hear anything over my quick breathing and the droning of the descending metal curtain, but then I made out the steady thump of Liam's heart, the plink of insects against the windows, the rush of a breeze over the swaying wild grass, the scratch of pine needles, the hoot of owls, the flutter of insect wings, and the shallow beat of hearts too tiny to be human or wolf.

"I know you're still growing attuned to your senses, but never forget to use them. Being human allows us to live in the world. Being a wolf allows us to survive in it."

Delicately, he gathered my wrists in one hand and raised them toward the ceiling. With his other hand, he dragged my T-shirt up and over my head and arms.

Goose bumps pebbled my skin as desire spread through me. Even though my body wasn't meant for Liam's, it still desired his. After he unhooked my bra, he dipped his face to my breasts and breathed against my sensitive skin.

"Does this hurt?" His voice was low and husky.

"No," I said, a little breathily.

His fingers skimmed down my stomach, unbuttoned my jeans, and slowly rolled them off. He was on his knees again, but this time, it wasn't to implore me. His gaze turned hooded as his face leveled off on a part of me that no man had ever been near.

He hooked a finger in the side of black lace. Cold sweat slicked over my brow as he roamed nearer to my core. When a bolt of pain shot up to my navel, I batted his hand away.

"I'm sorry. I'm sorry," I croaked. "This sucks."

Liam rose to his feet, wrapped his arms around my body that had begun to tremble, and tucked my head underneath his chin. "It does, but it's just temporary."

I rested my cheek against his thumping chest, wondering why my wolf had to go and choose August as a mate.

CHAPTER 13

I awoke with a start. Disoriented, I took in the room that was streaked with dull sunlight. My gaze landed on the peacock feather painting over the stone fireplace. I was in Liam's room. In his bed.

I twisted around and touched his pillow. It was cold. I tore the sheets off my legs and leaped out of bed.

"Liam," I called out, padding about the bedroom.

The door to the bathroom was cracked open, but no one was inside. I picked up my phone and checked the time, reeling when I made out the digital readout: 10:30 a.m. I couldn't remember the last time I'd slept in this late.

My phone's screen was riddled with messages from Evelyn asking me where I was and if I was okay. I dispatched a quick text to inform her I was fine and on my way to the inn.

Liam had also sent me a text message: *On the road to Denver. I already miss you.*

My heart began jackknifing my throat, making breathing a feat.

I checked the time stamp on Liam's text: 7:30 a.m. That meant he was already in Denver. Had been for more than two hours. The fact that I hadn't gotten a message from him made me queasy as hell. Did that mean they were out looking for Everest? Or did it mean they'd already gotten to him and were on their way back? Images of what they could be doing to him wafted through my mind like sticky chimney smoke.

I quieted my imagination. I needed to corral my mind, keep it from crafting scenarios. I looked for my clothes but remembered they were in the living room. In my underwear, I padded toward the door.

When I opened it, Lucas looked up from his magazine. "She finally awakens."

I shut the door with such force that the hinges rattled. *Crap. Crap. Crap.* I cupped my hands over my bare breasts as though he could somehow see them through the door.

"Would it help if I got naked too?"

Help? How did Lucas think that would help?

"I take your silence as a negative."

I hunted down a towel and wrapped it around myself. Pulling in great big gulps of air, I trudged back to the door and yanked it open.

Lucas smirked. "You do know you're pack now, Ness. You're going to have to get used to getting naked in front of us. It'll help you bond with your people."

"You and your bonding . . . " I muttered, trudging to the couch.

"Paintball was fun, eh? We should do it again."

"I'd rather eat a rotten squirrel."

He chucked his magazine on the wrought-iron coffee table before readjusting the royal-blue baseball cap he wore backward. "So cold, Clark."

"What part of paintballing was fun? Getting shot by my own teammates?" I plucked my bra off the couch before grabbing my jeans and T-shirt. "You guys were awful to me."

"It's called hazing. Everyone goes through it."

"Really? Who else in the pack got to experience the same *fun* treatment as me?"

Lucas shot me a sheepish grin.

"That's what I thought."

"Did you ever hear that holding onto resentment is like drinking poison? Only hurts you."

I gritted my teeth. "What are you doing here, anyway? Come to play guard dog again?"

He puffed air out of the corner of his lips. "First off, I'm a wolf, not a dog. Secondly, even though spending the day with you is as exciting as clipping my toenails, I take my job seriously."

Did he have to give me a visual of his feet? *Yuck.*

He got up and rubbed his hands against his black mesh shorts. "Besides, if all goes well, you'll be rid of me by tonight."

His words echoed through me. *If all goes well* . . . In other words, if Everest was found and killed.

I clamped my fingers around my clothes. "Do you have any news?"

"No." He studied me for a long second. "So, what's the plan?" His voice was a tad less cocky, as though he felt pity for me instead of annoyance. He must've figured out that my sullen mood was more due to what was happening in Denver than what was going down in Boulder.

"Do you have a car?" I asked.

"I have access to one." He gestured to the window. Even though the sky was overcast, Liam's black SUV gleamed.

However much I wanted to get rid of Lucas, I couldn't deny how practical it was that he could drive. "You have a license, right?"

He cocked the eyebrow slashed by the white scar. "Since I was sixteen. Why? You don't?"

I pressed my lips together. "No, I don't."

"Seriously?" His eyebrow seemed to rise a couple more millimeters.

"I never had time to get it. But that's what I wanted to do today. After I stop by the inn to see Evelyn and Isobel." I started for the bedroom door, holding my clothes against me, but paused and turned back to Lucas. For the first time since I'd woken up, I smiled. "Oh, and then I'm having lunch with Sarah at three at Tracy's. Or should I say, *we're* having lunch with her?"

His lips puckered as though he'd swallowed something sour. As I entered the bedroom, I heard him grumble something that sounded like, "*I'm not being paid enough for that.*"

I smirked as I donned yesterday's outfit. When I returned to the living room, tying my hair up in a ponytail, Lucas was gone. I spied him outside, crouched with his nose low to the ground. Heart pounding in time with my feet, I treaded to him, surveying the dirt road and the gently swaying pines.

"Is something wrong?" My low words were snatched up by the blustery breeze.

"I got a whiff of some wolves."

"From the pack?"

"No."

"Pines?"

His nostrils flared one more time before he unfurled his long body back to standing. "No."

"Real ones, then?"

"Smell." He nodded to the grass.

I crouched and inhaled. Mixed among the earthy, green aroma of the slick blades was the woolly scent of wolf edged with the distinctive musky scent of humans.

Werewolves.

CHAPTER 14

"How can you tell they're not Boulders?" I rose from my crouch, morning dew seeping into the fabric of my tight jeans.

"I'm a tracker, Ness."

"Meaning?"

"Meaning while you studied calc, I sniffed scraps of fabric belonging to various bodies before going after them."

"You didn't go to school?"

"Oh, I went to school." He flashed me a smug grin. "I just had more interesting after-school activities than most."

As we walked toward the car, I said, "I have a lot to learn."

"What?" He slapped a palm over his chest. "The great Ness Clark doesn't know *everything*?"

I slugged his bicep, and it was like hitting solid rock. "Shut up."

He chuckled, which was strange, because Lucas was a sulky bastard, not a chuckler. He jutted his chin toward the house. "You locked up?"

"I don't have a key."

"Liam didn't give you a key?"

I frowned. "Why would he?"

As he pulled out a keyring from the pocket of his mesh shorts, he cast me a sideways glance. I didn't ask what his look meant. While

Lucas locked up, I climbed into the SUV and strapped myself in. A minute later, he sprang behind the wheel and revved up the engine.

As he pulled out of the driveway, I examined the forest again. "Is there another pack in these parts?"

"Not that I know of."

"So loners?"

"Possibly. But they're playing with fire by running around here. If they value their lives, they better have been passing through."

The landscape was cloaked in a gray light that turned everything flatter, duller. I was glad there was no sun. I didn't feel like sunshine. I checked my phone for updates on the Everest hunt. Having none, I stuffed my phone into my bag.

"Nervous?" Lucas asked as we headed up the inn's long driveway.

I chewed on my thumbnail. "Aren't you?"

"Nah. I have total faith in my Alpha." He side-eyed me. "Unless he's not the person you're nervous for."

The golden log façade of the inn rose beyond the windshield. Soon it would belong to a detestable man. Aidan would probably strip it of its hominess and transform it into another impersonal, multi-million dollar venture.

"He's my flesh and blood, Lucas."

"He used you, then tried to have you killed, yet you hope he gets away with his life? I don't get it, Clark."

I twirled the ends of my ponytail. "What if there's more to it? What if he didn't mean to do any of that? What if Aidan Michaels coerced him to do it? Or blackmailed him?"

"And what if Aidan Michaels didn't?"

My skin prickled from his sharp answer. Then that would make my cousin truly heartless. "I guess we'll never know since Everest won't get a trial."

I gripped my door handle.

"We're not animals. They'll interrogate him before putting him down."

Sucking in a sticky lungful of air, I gritted out, "He's not a dog."

"You know what I mean."

I did, but it still bothered me. "You don't have to come inside."

"Until it's over, I'm shadowing your ass."

I heaved an annoyed breath and hopped out.

While Lucas went to park, I pushed through the revolving doors. The inn was bright and warm and smelled faintly of potpourri and varnished pine, scents I'd come to associate with Boulder. It wasn't home, and it wasn't a safe haven, but for a while it had been the closest place to a home I'd had. I stopped by the bell desk where Isobel was answering a call. She raised her index finger. I waited, studying her face. She was pale, but not sickly so. And although her cheekbones pressed against her skin and her shoulders jutted through her cream blouse, she wasn't emaciated. For a moment, I superimposed the image of my mother over Isobel, and my heartbeats slowed.

After she hung up, she smiled. "Hey, sweet girl."

"Hi. How . . . " I'd been about to ask how she was feeling, but I wasn't supposed to know. "How's everything going this morning?" I jerked a hand toward the inn.

"All's fine. Quiet night. Quiet morning. I've rescheduled a couple outings for some of the guests because of the weather, and I reorganized the cleaning staff schedules."

"Thank you."

"You have nothing to thank me for." She squeezed my hand. Her skin was clammy, the same way my mother's had been on the worst of days. "I also went to check on Jeb. He's been sleeping most of the morning. I dropped off some food. Perhaps you should stop by to see him. He might appreciate some company."

I wondered if she knew what was happening. Wives weren't kept in the dark, but were they informed of the Alpha's every move?

"After I stop by to see Evelyn, I'll go sit with him."

I also needed a shower and fresh clothes. Could she smell Liam on me? She wasn't a wolf, but she'd seen me walk in, so she knew I'd spent the night somewhere other than my own bed. If she sensed where I'd been, there was no judgment on her face. Just a sweet smile. Why did disease have to attack the good people? Why couldn't it strike down people like Aidan Michaels?

I started in the direction of the kitchen when Isobel's voice stopped me. "Do you have any plans for dinner tonight?"

I turned around just as Lucas came through the doors. I longed to say no, but in what state would I be tonight? In what state would Liam be? Plus going to dinner at the Watts' probably meant August would be there, and even though I'd spent my childhood having dinner with him and his family, things were different now.

"I can't tonight," I ended up saying, at the same time as Lucas said, "Morning, Mrs. W."

"Good morning, Lucas." She smiled at him before looking back at me. "Okay. Let me know when you have a free night. I'd love to catch up."

"I . . . I will. I promise. Maybe this weekend?"

"You just let me know. Or you just show up. Our house is your house."

Her words squeezed my heart. I gave a jerky nod before resuming my walk toward the kitchen. The large space was riddled with delicious smells that had my empty stomach rumbling.

"Ness!" Evelyn handed Kasie the tongs before hobbling toward me.

The change in air pressure always made her arthritis flare up, and considering how she limped this morning, I sensed her body ached. I met her halfway. The menthol balm she religiously rubbed into her sore joints soothed my frayed nerves.

She kissed both my cheeks, surely leaving bright lipstick smears behind. "Kasie, do you have everything under control? I need to speak to Ness."

"Take your time, Evelyn. I've got our vegetables *provençal* covered."

Evelyn tucked my hand in the crook of her arm and pulled me toward the door. "Come. Let's have some tea, *querida*."

I grabbed a teapot from a high shelf in the pantry, when Skylar popped in carrying a laden breakfast tray. "Hey! How are you, hun?"

She set down the tray next to the sink, then pushed a piece of peroxided hair off her forehead and seized the teapot from me. "Here, let me do that. Black, green, herbal?"

"Earl Grey," I said. Evelyn only liked dark teas. "But I can do it—"

She shooed us away. "Out of my pantry."

"Thank you, Skylar," Evelyn said. "We will be on the terrace. It is not raining yet, is it?"

Reaching up to grab the tin box of loose-leaf tea, Skylar said, "Not yet, but I suspect it'll come down any minute."

"We will take our chances," Evelyn said, guiding me through the dining room and out onto the deck.

Only Lucas was out here. He'd taken a seat on one of the many Adirondacks and was checking out something on his phone. Had Liam sent a message? I was tempted to pull out my phone, but it could wait until after my visit with Evelyn.

The sky was tiled with mauve clouds that reminded me of the quilt Mom had sewn for me when I was a kid, the one I'd given to the army vet on our street corner one unseasonably cold winter day. While the man's dog growled at me—I assumed because I still smelled like a wolf—his master smiled, raising the bottle of liquor that seemed forever grafted to his palm, and gathered the cover around himself and his pet.

Eyeing Lucas, Evelyn walked toward the farthermost edge of the terrace. We took our seats at a square teak table.

In a low voice, she said, "Frank informed me that my ex-husband has purchased the inn from your family."

I darted a glance toward the enormous glass sliding doors, making sure that Skylar hadn't emerged from the entrails of the inn. I didn't want to alarm the loyal staff before alarm needed to be sounded. Perhaps Aidan Michaels would safeguard their jobs. I didn't know his intentions for the place. Was it simply a strategic location to keep the packs in check, or was this a business transaction to grow his real estate portfolio?

"Evelyn, do you think he bought it to insult . . . *us*?"

By us, I meant werewolves, although I didn't doubt for a second that Aidan was the type of man who'd take great pleasure in thwarting his ex-wife's happiness. Since the man was a snoop with too many connections, I didn't doubt for a second he knew she was back in Boulder.

"Or do you think he bought it as an investment?"

She scratched at a piece of citronella candlewax that had melted onto the teak. "He does not need more money or more land, *querida*."

In other words, this was no commercial endeavor.

"Here y'all go," Skylar said chirpily, depositing a wooden tray loaded with two mugs, a teapot, a bowl of sugar, a tiny pitcher of milk, and a plate of bite-sized jam cookies—one of Evelyn's specialties.

Since Evelyn had gotten access to a larger kitchen and a limitless quantity of fresh produce, she'd been making the jam herself, and the already delicious cookies had become downright sinful.

"Can I get you anything else?" Skylar asked, eyeballing the sky.

"No thank you," Evelyn said. "You have already spoiled us."

I smiled up at Skylar, who returned my smile, but her lips kept bending and straightening, as though she wanted to ask me what was wrong. Even though we'd only known each other for two months, I sensed she understood me; perhaps it was because we'd both lost our mothers. Skylar had once told me that she was a good listener in case I needed to talk.

I hadn't wanted to talk about Mom then. I still didn't want to talk about her. Her absence remained too fresh. Although I no longer cried when someone brought her up, it still abraded my heart.

"I haven't seen Emmy yet, but can you thank your wife for covering last night's shift, please? Jeb and . . . and Lucy, they really appreciate it."

She grinned. "Will do. Anyway, let me know if you need anything else."

Evelyn poured two cups of piping hot tea while I pilfered a cookie from the plate.

"Frank has an extra bedroom, which I readied for you last night. I want you to come and live with us. I know Jeb is your legal guardian, but he is incapable of caring for you, and I am not too fond of the men who prowl around you." She flicked her gaze toward Lucas, which had my nose wrinkling. I hoped she didn't assume he was a suitor, because . . . *gross*.

"Are you sure Frank won't mind?"

She placed her calloused hand over mine. "Frank does not mind. His house is . . . it is big. On weekends, his grandson Joseph visits, but otherwise, he lives there alone."

"Not anymore."

Her lips curled into a demure smile.

How I loved the glimmer Frank had put in her obsidian eyes and the rosiness he'd brought to her foundation-caked complexion. I loved that she'd gotten her happy ending. If anyone deserved happiness, it was Evelyn.

"Meet me in the kitchen tonight. We will leave together after I finish making dinner."

"Okay."

We drank our tea quietly after that, both of us enjoying each other's easy company. Almost an hour later, we both stood to leave. She leaned toward me as though to kiss my cheek, but instead she asked, "Why does the boy over there keep looking in your direction?"

"He's just helping me out with some errands today. You know, driving me around."

If I told Evelyn the truth, that Liam was afraid Everest might try to hurt me, she'd fret, and I didn't want her to fret more than she already did.

She kissed my cheeks and then rubbed them. "There. I've added some color to that pale face of yours."

In spite of my summer tan, I could feel I was pasty, the same way I could feel the first drops of rain needling my bare arms. I closed my lids and lifted my face skyward, welcoming the downpour.

CHAPTER 15

O nce I was showered and changed, I dropped by Jeb's room, Lucas in tow. It took a lot of convincing on my part, but I managed to get him to stay outside while I visited with my uncle. My intentions for stopping by weren't only selfless, though. I'd printed all the forms for my permit, for which I needed my guardian's signature.

Isobel must've drawn the curtains open, because the muted light splashed his bedroom.

"Hi, Jeb. It's Ness," I said as I approached him. I didn't want to spook him.

"Is it done?" His voice was jaded, just like his expression.

"I don't know." I pulled a chair up to the bed. "Have you eaten?" The laden tray on his nightstand told me he hadn't, but I was hoping my question might stir his interest in food.

"And Lucy?"

"Lucy?"

He fastened his pale-blue gaze flecked by burst blood vessels to my face. "I thought you might have some news."

I shook my head. "But I can call Eric. Do you want me to phone him?" I didn't have Eric's number, but Lucas probably did. I could get it from him.

"No," Jeb said quietly. For a long moment, neither of us spoke.

Then my uncle's insubstantial voice gusted through the quiet bedroom. "What do I have to live for now, Ness?"

I could've lied to him and said the inn, but he didn't even have that anymore. Who was going to take him in?

"You heard Everest sold the inn to Aidan Michaels?"

His pupils contracted with surprise, and his pale lips fell open. He hadn't known.

"He sold it in exchange for his help in"—I toyed with my mother's ring, weaving my fingers in and out of it—"tampering with the pack's security monitors and getting out of Boulder."

My uncle gaped at me, confirming he hadn't known any of this. Talk about being the harbinger of crap news. I released the ring and set both my palms on my knees.

"I should never have put it in his name. Lucy, she said—" His voice broke. "Doesn't matter anymore what she said." He sealed his lips, as though to prevent himself from badmouthing the mother of his child. After another long stretch of silence, he said, "I own a few apartments in downtown Boulder."

I frowned.

"I'll have one readied for us."

I squeezed my knees. "*Us?*"

"You and me."

So he wasn't planning on ending his life. "You don't have to worry about me, Jeb. Frank said he could take me in—"

"You're my ward, not his," he snapped. That was the most energy I'd heard permeate his tone since the day of the last trial when he'd found his wife holding Evelyn hostage.

I wanted to live with Evelyn, but I couldn't abandon my uncle. "Okay."

Suddenly, he sat up in bed. "Can you hand me my cell?"

I got up to retrieve his phone from where I'd put it to charge days ago and then I stood watch as he dialed a number and barked at the unfortunate soul on the other end.

After disconnecting, he said, "Have one of the housekeepers stop by this address. The place probably needs a good cleaning." He filched a pad of paper embossed with the inn's logo and a pen from the drawer of his nightstand table, scribbled an address, then tore off the paper.

I took it reluctantly, but then pushed away my reluctance. Although my uncle had been the one to drag me back to Boulder the second he found out I was living in LA motherless, he wasn't to blame for the fiasco that had ensued. If anything, I should have been relieved that he cared enough for me that he wasn't skirting his responsibilities. I folded the note with the address, deciding I would take care of the cleaning myself.

He got out of bed so suddenly I stepped back so he wouldn't bump into me and send me flying backward. Anger flushed his features and sparked in his eyes.

"I can't believe he struck a deal with your father's killer," he muttered under his breath, grabbing the frame of a watercolor painting and tugging on it hard.

I braced for chaos by hunching a little, but Jeb didn't toss the canvas across the room. Instead, the frame folded like a book page. Behind it was a safe. He entered a six-digit number, and the safe beeped. He rifled inside, rustling papers, knocking over jewelry boxes until he found what he was looking for: an envelope. He peered inside, extracted two keys hooked to the same ring. He slid one off and tossed me the keyring. It landed at my feet.

"The key to our new home. Good thing I didn't entrust it to my son. Can't believe he sold Aidan Michaels our inn." Jeb was so red I worried he would give himself an aneurism. Not that wolves could die of aneurisms.

I crouched to retrieve the keyring. "What happens once Lucy is released?"

My uncle stopped muttering and peered up at me.

I stared at the small silver key nestled in the palm of my hand. "I don't want to live with her, Jeb. I can't," I said raising my gaze back to my uncle.

"I'm filing for divorce."

Oh.

Jeb walked over to me and gripped my shoulders. "We'll get through this, Ness."

His renewed desire to live restored my hope that we could heal from the deepest of wounds. Changed and scarred, but we survived. Even though I sensed Evelyn would put up a fight, I was touched that my uncle hadn't abandoned me.

"You know, Callum was always trying to give me pointers about how to raise my son. It drove me insane, but now, I wish I'd listened to him." He gave my shoulders a squeeze before letting go. "You're a good kid, Ness."

I pressed my lips together to drive back the emotion rising in my throat.

"Now, go pack your bags."

I nodded and started walking toward the door but remembered the papers I needed him to sign. I took them out, and he signed them, telling me not to schedule driving lessons, that he'd give them to me himself.

Another wave of emotion surged within me. Jeb could never replace my father, the same way Evelyn had never taken my mother's place, but I was glad for his support and his presence in my life, and hopeful that it would take some weight off my shoulders. I would never get to be a kid again—I didn't even desire it—but I wouldn't mind splitting some of my responsibilities with an adult.

CHAPTER 16

By the time Lucas and I reached Tracy's, Sarah was already there.

I'd packed my bags and swung by the new apartment to drop them off and make a list of cleaning products to purchase. Jeb's investment was on the top floor of a two-story house, about ten blocks away from Tracy's. The bedrooms were small, but they had their own bathrooms, and the living area had an open kitchen and an obstructed view of the mountains. In spite of the musty smell and the bare furnishings, I decided I didn't hate it.

What would've been the point in hating it? It was to be my new home. Besides, I'd hopefully be moving into a dorm room soon. I was glad all my stuff fit in two blue Ikea bags. If I'd owned more things, relocating would've been a much bigger hassle. Besides, I adhered to my mother's philosophy that *things* and the desire to always amass more stripped people of happiness and freedom. *"The lighter you travel, the farther you'll go,"* she used to tell me. Back then, it had frustrated me not to be able to get a new backpack at the start of the school year or the Adidas sneakers everyone else was sporting, but I'd learned to stop wanting *things*. It had taken years. To be honest, it had taken my mother falling ill. Nothing else but finding a cure to keep her alive had mattered then.

I walked past the bar toward the wooden table Sarah was sitting at, drumming her perfectly manicured fingernails in time with the rain battering the windowed façade. She smiled when she caught sight of me, but then her smile wilted when she caught sight of my *bodyguard*.

Instead of sitting at another table like he'd done at the inn, Lucas plopped down on the seat beside Sarah. "If it isn't my favorite Pine."

"You don't have a favorite Pine," Sarah shot back. Then to me, she asked, "Why is the Neanderthal here?"

Lucas smirked, twisting the cap on his head. "Still at it with the name-calling, I see."

Sarah glared at him, eyes a condemning shade of brown.

I sighed. "Long story."

"I'm listening." Sarah leaned back in her chair and folded her arms, making her extremely generous cleavage pop. I caught Lucas checking her out, and not just for a second or discreetly. He stared at her chest almost a full minute. *Sleazeball.*

Once I was done giving her the highlights, she uncrossed her arms. "Shit, Ness. That fuckin' sucks."

"Tell me about it."

"I hope they get your cousin today. If only so you're no longer stuck with this one." She tipped her head toward Lucas who stole another lengthy look at her chest. "Eyes up, Mason. Didn't your father ever teach you manners?"

Lucas's gaze slid up to her face. "My father died before I started noticing anatomical differences between girls and boys."

Sarah surely knew that Lucas had lost his parents—unlike me, she'd had a thorough werewolf and pack education. When a breathy gasp stumbled out of her mouth, I frowned.

"Forgot about that," she said, a tad more gently.

"Was a long time ago." Lucas removed his cap, dragged his fingers through his black hair, then screwed the hat back on. "Look who's staring now?" Lucas said, one corner of his mouth tilting up.

Sarah spun back toward me.

Lucas flexed his arm. "Want to cop a feel?"

"Seriously?" She wrinkled her nose, seizing the laminated menu, which I was pretty certain she knew by heart. "I'd rather pet a rattlesnake than your bicep."

"You like snakes, huh?"

"Leave her alone, Lucas," I warned.

He flashed me a cocky grin before raising his eyes to the TV broadcasting a tennis game.

A waitress with thick bangs, a perky smile, and an even perkier voice arrived to take our order. While I asked for a BLT and water, Sarah and Lucas ordered cheeseburgers and Cokes. I wondered if Miss Perky had been the girl Lucas had alluded to the day August had helped fix stuff up in the inn, the one who'd be really glad that he'd stayed in town. I was tempted to ask, but feared it would make me sound jealous instead of what I truly was: curious.

As though thinking of August activated the link, my stomach tightened. I rubbed it while Lucas and Sarah bickered about the music she'd played at The Den last Saturday, and the waitress returned with a pitcher. As she poured water into my glass, the door of Tracy's opened.

The water overflowed from my glass, spilling onto the table and dribbling onto my lap. I backed away from the table so fast my chair legs scraped against the worn wooden slats. She righted the pitcher, then apologizing profusely, she grabbed a handful of paper napkins from the dispenser on the table to clean up the mess.

"It's okay," I said, following her line of sight, which had returned to the entrance of the place.

To Cole and August.

August was absentmindedly rubbing his abdomen. When he spotted me behind the blushing waitress, his hand froze and then lowered, fingers balling into a fist.

Yep, it sucked.

For both of us.

Cole elbowed August and pointed to our table. From August's reluctant strides, I sensed he wanted to go anywhere but near me.

"Hey, Ness." Cole smiled, then nodded at Sarah and Lucas before greeting the waitress by her first name: *Kelly*.

Kelly barely registered his greeting, her entire focus on August. "I thought you'd left."

He scratched the back of his neck. "I've had to delay my departure." His face was all tensed up, which I imagined had more to do with our bothersome link than with Kelly's attention.

"Heard you and Sienna broke up." She said this very softly, so softly that if I'd been human, I would probably have missed it.

August's fingers stilled, and his eyebrows drew together. His expression, coupled with the relentless throbbing in my navel, screamed of discomfort.

I caught Sarah sniffing the air. A frown ghosted over her face. Could she smell our link? I remembered Liam saying that August had smelled like me or me like him . . . or something along those lines, but I assumed the smell had faded.

Thankfully, Sarah shattered the awkward silence. "Don't any of you have jobs?"

The three boys glanced at each other.

"Ness *is* my job," Lucas said, which made August swing the full force of his gaze from Kelly to the shaggy-haired shifter.

"And we're taking a break. Weather's way too brutal," Cole said.

Unlike my jeans that were sticking to my skin, neither his nor August's clothes were drenched, so they must've changed before coming in here. Or maybe their bodies heated at a higher temperature than mine and had already made the moisture evaporate.

Cole gestured to the pool tables in the back. "Want to join us for a game of cutthroat?"

"Thought you'd never ask." Lucas all but bounded out of his seat.

"Ness?" Cole didn't say Sarah's name, but he looked at her, which surely meant he was extending the invitation to my friend.

I shook my head. "I want to catch up with Sarah."

"We still have *so much* to catch up on," she added.

Once the boys were out of earshot and the waitress had scampered away, Sarah hissed, "Why does August Watt smell like you?"

I winced. "Do we really smell alike?" I whispered.

"Unless August and you have been swapping body lotions, then yeah. Usually dudes smell like"—she waved a hand toward the seat Lucas had just vacated—"the inside of a locker room."

"Is it really obvious?"

"To a person who knows you and your smell, yeah."

I wrinkled my nose at her wording. I figured she didn't mean it derogatively.

"Did you guys imprint on each other?"

I bit my lower lip.

"Shit." Her chair creaked as she leaned forward. "So you and Liam are already over, huh?"

"No. Why would you jump to that conclusion?"

She pressed slightly away from the table. "Babe, you do understand the purpose of mating links, right?"

"I understand their *purpose*, but I have no plans on dumping my boyfriend to jump into another man's bed."

"It's sort of unavoidable. Your body must've shut out all other males. My brother and Margaux are mates. He tried to resist her at first. He had a girlfriend. It lasted all of a week. You can't resist mating links. You just can't. It would be like trying to starve yourself and expecting to survive."

My skin prickled with annoyance. "There are lots of mates who don't end up together."

"Really? Name one pair?"

"I don't know names. I just heard about this from Frank McNamara. He mentioned someone in our pack had a mate but didn't end up with her."

Sarah tutted. "Well, I've never heard of mates who didn't end up together. It's biological or chemical or whatever. Plus, it's a good thing. It doesn't happen to everyone. I sort of wished it would happen to me." She thankfully lowered her voice to add, "Apparently, the sex is explosive." She waggled her eyebrows.

I shushed her with a forbidding look. "Besides, he's leaving soon," I added under my breath. "Distance will suppress the link."

"Why would he leave?" She glanced over at the pool table. "Is Liam making him so he can have his dirty way with you?"

Heat snaked up my neck.

She leaned in, her long, kinky blonde curls draping over her shoulders. "Oh my gosh, that's it, isn't it? That's real fucked up, Ness. No one should ever come between mates."

"I don't want a mate all right!" I unfortunately said this so loudly that even the rain pounding against the windowed façade couldn't camouflage my words.

Sure enough, the boys had stopped playing to cop a look, as well as two of the men slugging down beers at the sticky bar. Not that they knew what I was talking about, but August knew, and from the shadows that fell over his strong brow, I could tell my comment had made an impact.

I didn't think he was hurt that I didn't want to be with him, after all, he considered me like his sister . . . people didn't want to get with their sisters because that was all shades of unnatural and wrong, but he probably hadn't appreciated me voicing my disgust quite this brashly. I slid the elastic out of my hair to busy my suddenly shaky hands and to curtain off my face.

"Didn't mean to piss you off," Sarah apologized.

I rested my elbows on the table and cupped my forehead with my palms. "It's not you, Sarah. It's this whole stupid situation."

She sighed just as Kelly brought over our food. She deposited the plates a little heavily, gaze trained toward the boys.

"The other burger goes over there." Sarah pointed to Lucas.

They'd all gone back to playing. Including August. He had his back to me, as though to avoid facing me. More than ever, I hated our link because suddenly I feared it might erase our years of shared history and render us both bitter strangers.

I felt Sarah eyeing me. Whatever she was thinking, she kept it to herself.

Between greasy, ketchup-laden bites, she said, "I'm going to be an aunt soon. My brother and Margaux are expecting."

I blinked at her.

"Twins. They're having twins. A girl and a boy." She took a big bite of her burger.

"The wedding was last week. She didn't even look pregnant."

"She was. Just not showing yet. It's early though—like six weeks or something—so they're not really telling people yet."

"Six weeks! And she already knows the gender?"

Sarah cocked up one of her dark eyebrows. "We don't need ultra-sounds to know these things." She wiped her fingers on her check-ered paper napkin before tapping her nose with her index.

"We can smell the gender of the baby?"

"No. We can smell pregnancies. The gender's purely maternal instinct. She could be wrong, but shifter mamas are rarely wrong."

So if my mom had been a werewolf, she would've known I was a girl before I came into this world. My parents had never done an ultrasound, so convinced I would be a boy. Why would a baby born to the Boulder pack be anything else? I wondered what would have happened if someone had found out I was the wrong gender before being born. Then I stopped wondering because it was an answer I never wanted to find out.

"Did you ever date someone in your pack?" I asked.

"Yeah. Back in high school, I went out with this dude called Channing. Then I picked guys who weren't in the pack, mostly kids from UCB." She swallowed a long gulp of her soda. "My mom will probably force me to marry a wolf, so I'm getting my fix of human boys. They're less conceited than pack boys."

"UCB? Do you attend UCB?"

"Starting year two in a couple weeks. Why? Are you considering enrolling?"

"Apparently I can."

"What do you mean, *you can*?"

"Liam told me the pack sets money aside to cover tuition."

Her eyes lit up. "So you're applying?"

I nodded.

She squealed, which made everyone look our way again. "Oh my God, that's *so* exciting! I'll finally have a friend."

"Oh, come on. *You* don't have any friends there?"

"Hun, I'm opinionated. Most people don't like opinionated girls. Most people like them submissive and pleasant. Mom's always on my case about being more pleasant." She smirked. "You're, like, my first friend."

I peeled a strip of bacon off my mayo-soaked bread roll. "Does that mean I get full access to your closet?"

She tossed her head back and laughed, but then shot me a *nice-try* look.

I grinned. Even though it was thundering outside, and I was nervous as hell about what was happening within my pack, I felt momentarily happy. "You're my first *girl*-friend too."

She raised her glass and held it up, waiting for me to clink it with hers. "To firsts."

I tipped my glass into hers just as Lucas slid his empty plate onto the table and reached out between us to grab a handful of napkins.

"Didn't strike me as a virgin, Sarah," he said.

"If you're trying to get under my fur, Mason, it's not working."

He leveled his eyes on her chest, then raised them slowly. "I'm sorry, but I don't do Pines."

Her grin faltered. "That wasn't me propositioning you, you prick."

Cocking one side of his mouth up, he filched a fry from the plastic basket next to her plate, his forearm brushing against her chest. She jerked backward. His eyes flashed with undisguised amusement that heightened when Sarah glared at him.

She relocated her basket, shoving it to the farthest most edge of the table. "Hands off my fries."

"Possessive, aren't we?" Lucas wiped his fingers slowly on his wadded-up napkin, as though buying himself more time. "You deejaying tomorrow night, blondie?"

"Like every Thursday night." Her skin tone had returned to normal, but her earlier glee was gone. "Don't forget your earplugs. Or better yet, don't come at all." She turned back toward me. "Will you go, Ness?"

I was about to say maybe when the front door of Tracy's flapped open, dragging in the scent of summer rain and male perspiration. My heart stuttered when I laid eyes on Liam. His dark hair was slicked back, and his body was wound so tightly it looked like he was about to pounce on someone.

Pissed.

He looked pissed.

All the more terrifying was that he looked pissed at *me*.

CHAPTER 17

I stood up so fast my knees bumped into the table, sending bolts of pain through my shins. The last time Liam had looked at me with so much scorn was when I'd come out of Julian Matz's maze brandishing the Boulder relic.

Aside from the low drone of the sports commentator and the unrelenting rain niggling the windows, the bar had become eerily quiet. When a cue stick hit a resin ball, I jumped.

For a long moment, Liam didn't move. Neither did Matt who flanked him.

Lucas's thick eyebrows dipped as he watched his Alpha, the slant deepening when Liam stalked over to me, boots pounding the worn flooring.

"You ratted us out?" Lucas asked, voice low. So very low.

Sarah, who'd spun around in her chair, whirled toward me.

Combined with Liam's lethal gaze, Lucas's accusation chilled the blood racing through my veins. "Wh-what?"

He ran!

Liam's voice resonated so shrilly inside my skull that I gripped my forehead, digging my fingertips into my temples. "Wh-who?" I stammered.

Your cousin! Rainwater mixed with sweat dripped from his matted hair into the collar of his black V-neck.

"Why are you screaming at me?"

"Because it's your fault," Liam growled.

Matt folded his arms in front of his huge chest. "Everest left Aidan a voicemail telling him what a prick he was to have sold him out."

I sensed two large bodies coming up behind me. I could smell August. I assumed the other one was Cole. Were they cornering me?

I squared my shoulders, trying to inject bravado into my posture. Bravado I wasn't feeling. "What does Everest's voicemail have to do with me?" I asked, voice faltering.

"He said you texted him that we were coming," Matt said.

I reeled, but then I grabbed my phone, unlocked it, and shoved it in front of Liam's face. "Check it. Check my messages. I never sent Everest a thing."

He stared at the bobbing phone.

"Check. It. Liam!"

He grabbed it, fingers moving deftly over the screen. I waited. Waited for him to see that he had it all wrong. But then . . . then his eyes blazed, and my heart stopped.

He snorted, the sound so ungentle. "Your message is right there, Ness." He flipped my phone around and leveled it in front of my face. "Right . . . fucking . . . there."

My gaze raced over the bright screen, soaked up the black letters: *Liam is coming for you. Aidan told him where you were hiding. Run!*

The words smeared together. "I didn't—" I looked over my phone at Liam. "I didn't write that. Someone—I didn't—" Tears rolled down my cheeks.

Nostrils flaring, he shook his head and thrust the phone into my numb fingers. "Don't lie to me, Ness." His labored breaths punched my throbbing forehead.

"I'm *not* lying."

"Hey, could you guys take this outside?" Kelly asked, darting wary glances at her customers.

Is that why you were with me? To get insider information? His words were ringed with a mixture of bitterness and dejection.

"No." Each one of my breaths snagged in my throat. "No!

Someone hacked my phone and sent him that message." I wheeled around toward Cole. "That's easy to do, right?"

"It is," Cole said, but his narrowed eyes told me that, like the others, he believed I was trying to cover up my tracks by pinning it on a hacker.

"If I'd sent him a message, you really think I would've kept a trace of it on my phone? You really think I would've shown it to you? How dumb do you all think I am exactly?" I croaked, looking at Liam, then at Matt, then at Lucas. I didn't bother turning around to check if Cole and August, too, were glaring. I sensed the weight of their stares on my back.

"You didn't raise your hand yesterday," Lucas said.

Wariness spread over Matt's face like ink.

"So that automatically makes me a traitor?" My voice shook with tremors. My entire body shook with tremors. "Liam?" I didn't care what the others thought. As long as he—

He lowered his gaze to the floor. "You've backstabbed the pack before, Ness."

Overwhelmed by anger and disappointment, I pursed my lips and backed up but collided into a body. Hands set on my shoulders, tried to pin me in place. I brushed them off as though they were cobwebs, then grabbed my bag, dug out my wallet, and tossed a bill on the table to cover my half-eaten lunch.

"For the record, I'm glad Everest got away," I spat out as I elbowed my way past Liam and Matt.

"Ness!" Sarah called, but I didn't stop.

I dove into the crashing rain, slamming the door of Tracy's behind me, and sprinted across streets without looking for cars. Humorlessly, I felt like if a car hit me, I'd inflict more damage to it than it would to me.

You've backstabbed the pack before.

Liam's words played on a loop inside my head.

Like cement, disgust poured through me, drying between my ribs until their cage became a solid wall. My eyesight sharpened. My wolf was coming out. I raced faster down the drab streets, zigzagging through bobbing umbrellas and shoving past hooded passersby. I didn't apologize. I couldn't apologize. My teeth had extended into fangs. I was shifting, and I was still in the middle of town.

I waded through the storm-soaked streets faster, slowing only when I came upon an alley. I couldn't repress the need to shift. Didn't care to. I ran past corroded metal bins overflowing with the sour reek of food waste, relief flooding me when I noted that the alley spilled onto a parking lot edged with pines. Behind one of the bins, I pulled off my necklace and stashed it inside my bag before stripping out of my clothes. They were so waterlogged that peeling them off was a feat. Especially when my fingers began receding into stumps. I managed to kick off my jeans just as my knee joints snapped inward and forced me onto all fours.

I gritted my jaw as my wolf magic swept through me in fierce, raw waves, transforming my feeble human body into a resilient mound of white fur and taut muscles. When the change was complete, I sprang out from behind the bin, ducking behind parked cars, checking for humans.

I could hear their hearts beat in the buildings surrounding me; I could hear the timbre of their voices vibrate behind the lit windows; I could hear toilets flush, a baby wail, a young girl hum a slow tune, car tires squeal, raindrops ping off car hoods. The world turned so cacophonous and sharp it transmuted my lupine body into a livewire.

I dashed and zigzagged until my paws hit soft earth. And then I increased my speed. For a moment I was disoriented, but did it matter? I wasn't running toward something; I was running away from someone.

Away from Liam.

My fur rippled with a full-body shiver. I'd thought a Kolane could be a decent and unprejudiced man, but he'd trusted Aidan Michaels over me. Hadn't even given me the benefit of the doubt.

Thank God my body had locked Liam's out last night. If I'd lost my virginity to him— I couldn't even finish that terrible thought, so I shoved it out of my mind and focused on not losing my footing on the dicey mud and slick grass. I let the awareness of my surroundings flood me, fill me.

Alone, I ran until the sky turned the deepest shade of night, until my lungs contracted so violently I had to stop to catch my breath. I found shelter under a stone ledge. The rain fell so fiercely it curtained off the forest. Even with my heightened senses, I could barely see three feet in front of me. I didn't care, though.

I lay down with my head in between my forepaws and watched the ruined world fall apart around me.

Again . . .

CHAPTER 18

I must've fallen asleep because the next thing I knew, something was prodding my ribs. I jerked awake and bounced onto my paws, spine snapping into alignment and teeth gnashing in a menacing growl.

A mountain of chocolate-brown fur stood inches from me. *It's me, Ness.*

The flash of green around the wolf's pin-sized pupils made my defensive stance slacken.

August?

I still kept my distance, swinging my head toward the lip of the stone ledge that had shielded my fur from the rain. Although my underbelly and legs were caked in mud, I was no longer wet. The storm had quieted while I slept. The storm outside. The one inside still raged as Liam's accusation slotted into my mind. I expected to see the black wolf materialize between the fence of trunks.

What were you thinking, going off on your own like that?

I didn't bother answering August, but I did ask, *Are you alone?*

Yes. He wrung out his body, splattering mine with warm raindrops.

Even though I wanted to trust August, I couldn't help but flick my ears around to pick up on every sound within a one-mile radius. I didn't think I had it in me to trust anyone ever again. Besides Evelyn.

Evelyn . . . She was expecting me. *What time is it?*

He tossed his head back, his slick brown fur rippling. *What time is it? That's what you're concerned about?*

I narrowed my eyes. *What else should I be concerned about? Has the pack voted for my demise?*

Your demise? What are you talking about?

What do you mean what am I talking about? You were there! Liam called me a traitor. My words blustered out of me in a single, heated breath. *Just because I didn't put my hand up yesterday doesn't mean I would betray the pack!*

Tears tracked down my muzzle, over my rubbery lips, glided between my sharp teeth. The darkness would hide them from August. Or maybe he saw them. What did I care? I might've been a wolf, but I was also a human. Underneath the pelt and mud, I possessed a heart, and it had been broken. And broken hearts bled tears. I shouldn't be ashamed of them. What I should have been ashamed of was caring what others thought I had done. I knew I hadn't sent that message, and that was all that mattered.

Or all that should've mattered.

Do you believe me, August?

What do you think? He tried to approach me, but I backed up.

Yes or no?

Of course I believe you.

He said this with so little hesitation that skepticism poked through my relief. *Why?*

Green eyes steady on mine, he said, *Because I can feel you. If you'd done it, you wouldn't have been racked by anguish. You would've been racked by guilt. I told Liam, but he's a stubborn ass. He'll come around, though.*

I can't believe I pledged myself to him. I wish I could take it back. There was so much I wished I could take back: the kisses, the caresses, the trust. Again, I shuddered.

I suddenly wished I hadn't stopped running, wished I'd crossed a state line or vanished into the Rockies. I could've stayed away from Boulder until I was eighteen, until I was free of this damned place.

I stared at the woods longingly.

I felt August's muzzle push against my neck. *Don't even think about leaving.*

I turned on August. *Why not? I hate it here. I hate it so goddamn much.*

He sighed, his breath ruffling the fur around my ears. *That's how you feel tonight, but tomorrow—*

That's how I've felt almost every single day I've been back. I can count the days I've been happy on the claws of one paw.

He puffed a consolatory breath against my neck.

I'm not saying it to garner your pity. I'm just telling you because I don't want you to think I'm being hotheaded. That I feel like leaving because of what happened back at Tracy's. I twisted around and peered up at the veiled moon.

Can't let you run away.

Why not?

'Cause my mother would never forgive me for letting you go off on your own.

I let out a bitter sound that could've been a laugh, except wolves didn't laugh. We cried, but we didn't laugh. *You don't have to tell her.*

He grunted. *I wouldn't have to tell her. My mother's all-knowing.*

I drew my gaze off the sky and onto the soft ground.

Besides, have you thought about what it would do to Evelyn? From what I've heard, she cares about you a lot. How do you think she'd take your disappearance?

She has Frank now.

You think he's replaced you? People can love more than one person.

I pawed a patch of squishy earth, watching how the mud rose and molded around my claws. *I really don't want to go back.*

August leaned forward and drove his muzzle into my shoulder to get my attention. *He'll never attack you like that again. I promise.*

Don't make promises you can't keep.

Why do you think I wouldn't be able to keep it?

Because once your mom— I stopped talking abruptly. I wasn't supposed to know this.

Once my mom what?

When I didn't say anything for a full minute, he sighed. *Liam told you, didn't he?*

I nodded. *Why didn't you tell me?* I didn't want to sound petty, but I wished I'd heard it from him.

I didn't want to worry you any more than you already were. Especially after your own mother passed away from cancer.

My body sagged as though it was being crushed beneath tumbling rocks again. *She never had a chance. Your mom . . . her odds are good. Aren't they?*

He gave a slow nod. *If you don't stick around for anyone else, stick around for her sake.*

I eyed August, and then I eyed the dark woods. *I have no idea where I am anymore, August.* In the woods, but also in my life, I was so incredibly lost.

I'll show you the way back. He started walking but stopped when I didn't follow.

How did you even find me?

I can sense you, Ness. It's pretty much all I can sense these days. The damp breeze rushed his words to my ears.

I'm sorry. I wasn't sure why I was apologizing for something I had no control over.

He rolled one of his shoulders in a shrug, then faced away from me and started up again. *I'm sure it'll get more manageable.*

I was no longer the small pup he'd run alongside six years ago, but I still had to lengthen my strides to match his own. He must've noticed, because at some point he slowed his brisk pace. Silence grew and grew between us, but there was nothing awkward about it. If anything, it was like a balm, healing the deep cuts Liam had gouged in me.

I'm glad you're home, I whispered.

August looked at me in that quiet, all-seeing way of his. *Once you get back with Liam, you'll probably change your mind about that.*

I bristled, horrified he thought I would go back to Liam. *I might be all over the place, but I do have some self-love. Liam and I, we're not getting back together.* I thought about the time he'd sniffed me. *I forgave him once before.*

Although cloaked in fur, his limbs seemed to grow harder. *What did you forgive him for?*

August's green eyes bore into mine, but I didn't explain. I would take what had happened between Liam and me to the grave.

Even though the sky was mottled with pale puffs of clouds, I could still make out the glittery pinpricks of stars. They made me think of my father, of the night we'd star-gazed from our rooftop. He'd been such a gentle and righteous man.

A man who would *never* have lashed out at someone so bitterly and so publicly.

There were some lines that shouldn't be crossed. I'd rearranged those lines to allow Liam closer, but after today, I would paint new ones around myself and wouldn't let anyone undeserving past them.

CHAPTER 19

Augyst had parked his pickup in the lot where I'd morphed from human to wolf. He'd tracked my scent from Tracy's to the metal bins behind which I'd taken cover to strip.

Boulder was quiet and dark when our claws clicked onto the lot's pavement. When we reached the pickup, August's spine heaved, and then his brown fur receded into his dark, bronzed skin. When he unfurled, all his joints and muscles elongated and thickened until his backside was entirely man and no longer wolf. I noticed a line of puckered skin at the base of his spine. I wondered how he'd gotten that scar. When he began pivoting, I averted my gaze, taking great interest in the scratched rim of his back wheel.

A car door clicked, and then fabric rustled and a zipper purred shut. Only then did I let my gaze drift back to August. Lucas said I needed to get used to nudity, but it was easy for the males of the pack. They'd grown up walking naked around each other; I hadn't.

Barefoot and shirtless, August extended a cream flannel button-down to me. "Your clothes are still damp."

The shirt dangled between us. Was he expecting me to shift in front of him? When I didn't make any move to snatch the shirt, he draped it over the side of the cargo bed and turned. I was thankful he'd understood my mute plea. Closing my eyes, I arched my back and allowed the magic to pulse through my limbs and drag away the fur, the claws, the fangs, and every other part of my lupine constitution. My ears migrated back to the sides of my face, my jaw flattened, my lips reshaped.

Back in skin, I pressed my hands into the damp gravel and rose, bones clicking as I stretched to my full human height of five-seven. Glancing sideway to make sure August was still turned, I plucked the shirt from the bed and speared my arms through. I fastened the buttons quickly, leaving smudges of mud on the soft material that smelled so strongly of August it made my head spin. Or maybe it was the miles I'd traveled at breakneck speed that was making my head spin.

Pushing my stringy hair back, I said, "You can turn around now." My voice sounded raucous, as though it, too, had been dragged across the rough terrain.

As August turned, I tugged on the hem of the shirt, thankful he was an entire head taller. Otherwise, the shirt would've exposed a lot more of me.

"Thanks," I said, nodding to the shirt. I pinched the hem to prevent the material from flapping open.

He palmed his close-cropped hair. I'd never known him with any other haircut, but I remembered Isobel showing me pictures of him as a toddler where his face had been haloed by a mane of soft curls that couldn't seem to decide which way to bend. Only two things remained of the little boy from those pictures: the spray of dark freckles over his nose and cheekbones, and the penetrating green eyes flecked by sable and gold. But where the boy had had a soft jaw, the man's jaw could saw through wood.

"Feeling better, Dimples?"

The nickname startled me. I'd spent my childhood hearing it, responding to it, but I wasn't sure I liked it anymore. It made me feel juvenile. I didn't say anything, though. To August, I supposed I would always be the little pigtailed girl he'd ferry to and from school on his way to work.

"Ness?"

"Hmm." I released the lip I was reflexively sliding through my teeth.

"Are you feeling better?"

"Yeah." I wasn't.

When he cocked an eyebrow, I added a meek smile.

"I promise. Running cleared my head."

Although he still didn't seem convinced, he tipped his head to the truck. "Get in. I'll give you a lift back to the inn."

He pulled the door open. Clutching the shirt closed, I heaved myself onto the bench seat and slid all the way to the passenger side door. The scraped leather was rough and cold against the backs of my thighs.

"I need to stop by my new place first." If only I'd had the presence of mind to run toward it instead of—I looked around the lot—wherever it was I'd ended up.

"New place?"

"Yeah. Jeb and I. We're going to be living in town. In an apartment on 13th Street."

He slowed at a traffic light. "You are? Why?"

"Because my cousin sold the inn to Aidan Michaels."

August turned toward me, his stomach muscles rippling in the faint moonlight. For someone who'd sprinted through a drenched forest, he looked incredibly clean, barely flecked with mud.

Unlike myself . . .

My thighs were smeared brown, and my hair felt like dreads. A glimpse at myself in the side mirror confirmed the dreads part. I rolled my hardened hair into a larger rope, coiled it, and threaded the ends through to make it hold.

"You're kidding me?" August whispered.

"Afraid not."

August shook his head as though trying to drive the new information into it.

"Effective upon Everest's death. I bet that's why Liam believes I saved my cousin's life," I grumbled. "To make sure the inn didn't switch hands."

The word *backstab* shrilled in my brain again. I pressed my fingertips against my temple and massaged it. "Actually, can you drop me off at the inn? I need to grab a couple things. The apartment isn't exactly move-in ready."

There were mattresses, but no sheets, no pillows, no cleaning products, and no food.

"Sure."

While we drove, I took my phone out of the bag. My screen was full of messages. Mostly from Evelyn and Sarah, but one of them—a missed call and a voicemail—was from Everest. I dropped my phone onto my lap, then fumbled to grab it before August could see the name in the notification bubbles.

"Is everything okay?"

I blinked at him like a deer in headlights; I hoped I didn't look like one. "Yeah. Just Evelyn worrying. I was supposed to go sleep at Frank's place tonight."

I called her to prevent August from asking me anymore questions.

"*Querida!*" she exclaimed, ridding me of a couple decibels of hearing. "You are alive! *Dios mio*, I thought . . . I thought. Do not do this to my poor *corazón* or I will not make old bones!"

I smiled at the butchered expression, at the love that seeped out of all the Spanish interjections. "I'm so sorry. I had dinner with a friend and lost track of time. Are you still at the inn?"

"I waited forever, but Frank insisted on taking me home. He said you went out for a run with a friend. I do not like you running around the woods at night."

I tightened my hold on the hem of the flannel shirt. "I was in . . . in my other form. It's safer for us at night than during the day. Besides, like Frank said, I was not alone."

"Are you coming over now? I made your bed."

A made bed in a house with Evelyn sounded like heaven. I checked the clock on my phone and cringed when I noticed it was almost ten-thirty. I still needed to grab stuff from the inn, drop it off at my new place, shower, and change.

"I can be there in an hour. Is that too late?"

"What sort of question is that?" She sounded insulted. "You don't think I would wait all night for you?"

Her words filled me with affection. "Okay. I'll be there in an hour then." I added a whisper-soft, "I love you."

Not for the first time, I silently thanked Frank for having placed Evelyn in my life. What would I have done without her?

"Not as much as I love you," she answered.

After I disconnected, I drove the heel of my palm into one eye and then into the other. Even though I'd napped in the woods, I felt exhausted. Surely an accumulation of too many short nights and too many high-stress days.

When the pickup slowed in the inn's circular driveway, I balled up my clothes and bag.

"Thanks for coming to find me, August." I smiled at him before hopping out of the car and shutting the door.

As I started toward the entrance, another car door clicked shut.

I spun around to find August ambling toward me. "What are you doing?"

He frowned. "What do you mean, what am I doing?"

I looked at his parked car, then at him. "You can go home."

"If I go home, how will you get to your new apartment? And then to Frank's?" A gust of cool wind stole the sandalwood scent off his skin and batted it toward me.

How could he smell so good after running through the woods? I didn't dare sniff myself. I bet I reeked of dried perspiration and dank mud.

"I can cab it," I finally said.

A crooked smile turned up one corner of his mouth. "Surprisingly, I have no other engagements this evening."

"Aww. You canceled all your hot dates?"

"Wouldn't be the first time, now would it?"

I grinned. "Whatever are you talking about?"

I knew exactly what he was talking about, though. When I was still living in Boulder, I'd beg him to take me to a movie or bowling or build a campfire to grill s'mores without enquiring if he had other plans.

I hadn't wanted to share August with his girlfriends *or* friends.

I'd wanted him all to myself.

The awareness of how greedy I'd been dimmed my smile. "I'm sorry."

His eyebrows bent. "For what?"

"For having been such a demanding and selfish kid."

"You weren't."

"I took advantage of you. Of your kindness."

"Dimples—"

"Same way I'm doing right now." The heat of his half-naked body wrapped so thickly around me that I stepped away from him and then pushed through the revolving doors.

Emmy, who was manning the bell desk, clapped her chest. "Holy mother of God, you just gave me a heart attack."

I knew I looked awful, but that awful?

"Sorry," I said sheepishly.

She didn't seem to hear my apology, too fixated on the body behind mine. Her face lit up with a smirk that was almost as bright as the row of silver hoops lining the shell of her ear.

"What have you two been up to? Mud-wrestling?"

"Um. I was helping him fix a leak at the warehouse." The lie came out way too easily. To drive it home, I brandished my wet clothes. "I wasn't much help."

"Must've been a real bad leak." Her smile told me that not only did she not buy my stupid story, but that she'd also added a ton of dirty extrapolations to it.

"Her plumbing skills need some improvement," August added.

Emmy shot him a pointed look. "Never belittle a woman's *plumbing* skills."

Although I appreciated her coming to my defense, this was getting weird. "I need to shower and grab some stuff. Is everything okay here?"

"Yes. Well, except—" She flicked her gaze up to the first-floor landing. "Your uncle finally came out of his room this afternoon. He was in a strange mood. A tad manic. He must've looked through every ledger and dossier in the back office. It was like a bomb detonated in there. We tidied up with Isobel, but we weren't sure where things were supposed to be put away, so we just made a big pile."

I glanced at the staircase. "Lucy and him are . . . " I hesitated a second before adding, "divorcing." It was an easier explanation than the truth. "He and I are actually moving out."

Her mouth gaped.

"Please don't tell anyone yet. I mean you can tell Skylar, but no one else. I don't want the staff to worry how the divorce will affect the inn."

She shook her head. "I won't blab, but *wow*. I'm in shock. Poor Everest."

I clasped my phone tighter, desperate to listen to his voicemail. "I'll just head down and stick these in the wash and grab a shower. I won't be long."

August nodded even though he didn't seem too excited to be left behind with Emmy, especially when she said, "Wait. I just connected the dots. You're Isobel's boy, aren't you? She showed me a picture of you."

As she roped him into a conversation, I bounded down the stairs to the laundry room, unearthed a clean towel, tossed my clothes and August's shirt into one of the industrial machines, wrapped the towel snugly around myself, and set the washing machine to the quickest cycle. After I rinsed the rubber soles of my white sneakers, I headed to the locker rooms that connected the indoor pool to the gym.

Only then did I listen to Everest's message.

"Hey, Ness. I'm on my way back to Boulder. Thank you for having my back. I didn't deserve your help. Not after what I did. Everything's such a fucking mess. Such a fucking mess," he repeated slower, lower. I could imagine him pulling at his dark-red hair like he used to do when things didn't go his way as a kid. "In case anything happens to me, I left"—the word he uttered was garbled, as though he'd passed through a tunnel—"in your room"—static filled the receiver again—"under the fl—*Fuck!*" Air whooshed through the phone followed by a muffled thud, as though the phone had clattered out of his hand and onto the floormat. From far away, I heard him hiss, "Son-of-a-bitch found me."

The screech of metal had me yanking the phone away from my ear, and then . . . *nothing*.

Nothing.

With stiff fingers, I jabbed my screen to call him back. The dial tone sounded and sounded. And then I was prompted to leave a message.

I hung up.

I shivered but then whispered to myself, "He must've run out of battery." I prayed that was why the line had gone dead. Unless the *son-of-a-bitch* had caught up with him.

No, I couldn't go there.

Everest was all right. He was on his way back. I checked the time-stamp of the voicemail. He'd phoned about an hour ago. He was probably already in Boulder.

I typed: *I'm at the inn. Where are you?*

My thumb hovered over the send icon as I read the incriminating text above the still unsent one. I searched the wording, trying to find something about it that would prove my innocence. But it sounded like me, which meant the hacker was familiar with my speech. My pulse skittered wildly at that realization.

Or maybe the hacker had perused my phone's contents. That was a possibility, right?

For a long moment, I hesitated to send Everest the message I'd just composed, afraid it would make me the traitor my Alpha already believed me to be. *Screw it.* I'd already tried phoning Everest anyway. Besides, he and I needed to talk. I deserved answers. I didn't care what that made me. I hit send, then stepped into the shower stall and turned the water on scalding to ward away the frostiness enveloping my bones.

I spent a long time lathering away the dirt from my body; I spent an even longer time trying to untangle my hair. When I accomplished both tasks, I turned off the spray and towel-dried myself, but not before checking my phone. I was hoping Everest had messaged me back.

He hadn't.

As I plucked a disposable comb from a tray of amenities and dragged the teeth through my wet hair, I wondered where he would go in Boulder. There were too many cameras here. He was probably hiding in a motel.

I listened to his message again. "In your room. Under the fl . . . " What had he left in my room? And under what? Which word started with an *fl*-sound and could be found in a bedroom?

Fl . . .

Flowers?

Did he mean his mother's desiccated flower-filled mason jar?

As I made my way back to the laundry room, I ran everything there was in my bedroom through my head, but nothing else started with a *fl*. The washing cycle had finished, so I tossed the clothes in the dryer and sat on the countertop to wait, toying with the soft terry towel as I dwelled some more on Everest's enigmatic message.

My mind kept looping back to the flower jar, but I'd gotten rid of it sometime ago because the smell of Lucy's dried roses had felt toxic.

I dialed Everest's number again. The phone rang and rang inside my ear. I was about to play back his voicemail when a dusky figure darkened the doorway. The phone slid out of my fingers and clattered against the white tiles.

CHAPTER 20

August crouched to retrieve my phone. "Didn't mean to startle you. You just left me up there a long time." As he rose, he tendered the small apparatus, his eyes roving over the screen.

I blanched, afraid he'd see Everest's name, afraid he'd think me a traitor, afraid—

"It's not cracked," he said.

Pulse battering my neck, I tightened the towel around myself and reached an unsteady hand to retrieve my phone.

August hitched up an eyebrow. "Dimples, you're worrying me."

"I'm fine now. Just tired."

His eyes lowered to my swinging bare legs, or maybe he was looking at the machine tumbling our clothes.

There was no way they'd be dry yet, but hopefully they wouldn't be too wet. I hopped down, and he backed up, and then I leaned over and opened the front hatch.

As I stuck my hand inside the drum, he cleared his throat. "Why aren't you dressed?"

I pulled out his shirt first. "My entire wardrobe's in the new apartment."

For some reason, he flicked his gaze toward the entrance of the laundry room so fast I checked to make sure my cousin hadn't materialized there.

Empty.

"It's not completely dry yet," I said, wiggling my fingers to get his attention.

His sharp Adam's apple bobbed as he took the shirt.

I gathered up my clothes. "Give me one more second."

Back in the changing rooms, I yanked my humid jeans up my legs —horrible sensation—then clipped on my bra that was so damp my nipples pebbled. I plugged in the hairdryer and ran it for a full minute over my chest, hoping the hot air would warm me up.

It helped some.

When I returned to the laundry room, August had put on his shirt. I stuck my feet into my shoes, omitting the socks. I set them out to dry on the rack, then slung my handbag over my shoulder. I hesitated to fill a basket with sheets and towels, but since I was dressed and heading to Frank's for the night, gathering supplies could wait until morning.

"I need to stop by my bedroom before I go. If you need to—"

"I told you. There's nowhere I need to be."

"Okay." As we climbed the steps, I said, "You can wait for me in the car, if you prefer."

"Whatever you want."

What *did* I want?

I didn't even know what I was looking for . . . a flash drive, money, the stolen Sillin? *Oh my God.* What if it was the Sillin? What if Everest had planted it in my room to make me look guilty again? What if he'd popped each pill from the foil packets and hid them among the dried rose petals? My stomach began to cramp with a sudden upsurge of nerves. I was going to be sick. I reached for the banister to steady my swaying gait.

"What's going on?" August stared at my face, then at my abdomen.

Had I paled, or had he felt my jarring stress through the tether? I didn't want to carry the burden of Everest's voicemail alone, however unfair it was to push it upon someone else. I swallowed, my throat feeling as dry as Lucy's potpourri.

"Dimples?"

I closed my eyes, then opened them. "Everest left me a message."

He didn't say anything for so long that I began to tremble.

I gulped my saliva, trying to wet my throat. "He left me a message thanking me, and then he said some other things, and—"

"Why don't you play me his message?" August's eyes gleamed in the semi-obscurity of the staircase.

I nodded and dug out my phone. With shaky fingers, I located the message and pressed play. I watched August's features shift and realign, first in a frown, then in suspicion, then in shock.

"I swear I didn't warn him the pack was coming," I murmured after it ended.

His gaze hadn't moved off my phone. "What could he have left you?"

"I don't know. I don't even know what *fl-* could be. I was thinking flowers. Lucy leaves these jars filled with potpourri in the bedrooms, but I got rid of the one I had."

He dipped his chin into his neck.

"Please tell me you believe me."

He sighed.

"August, I swear—"

He finally raised his eyes back to mine. "I believe you."

Relief gushed through me.

In silence, we went to retrieve my key from the back office. I told Emmy I needed to grab something from my bedroom even though she hadn't asked for an explanation. Concern made her kind eyes crinkle.

As we made our way down the deathly quiet hallway, I asked August, "Do you have any other ideas?"

"I'm thinking."

The tether that linked us was as taut as a bowstring. I tried not to wonder why that was.

I pushed open the door and flicked on the lights, then walked down the short vestibule. I scanned my room for flowers—any flowers—but there wasn't even a jar. August knelt down and peered under the bed before lifting the mattress and checking under it. While I clanged open every drawer in my room and dismantled the flannel-covered armchair, he caught the edge of the area rug and tugged it free from the bedframe, spraying the air with flickering dust motes.

"Nothing here," he said.

I checked my closet next while he went into the bathroom and banged open the cupboards. I heard the distinct clang of porcelain— probably the toilet tank.

"Did you find any—" My skull throbbed so suddenly with a voice that I lost my balance, and my head bumped into something cold and hard, but the rest of my body landed on something warm and soft.

"Ness!" My name vibrated inside my ears.

I rolled my head back. August was gaping worriedly down at me, my limp body clutched in his arms.

Had I imagined the word *Boulders* screamed into my head? "Did you hear someone—"

"It's Liam."

The voice boomed again, and I clutched my forehead. ***Rodrigo and his team just located Everest's car in a ditch off Beek Ridge. I'm on my way there.***

August's rounded green eyes came in and out of focus.

"Oh my God," I murmured.

August's face swam back into focus. He unwound one arm from around me. Suddenly, his phone was pressed against his ear, and he was speaking into it.

"Fuck," he rumbled. "Fuck."

Two pennies for Isobel's jar, I thought.

Such a silly thought.

I stared at the small buzzing spotlight above my head. Or maybe my head was buzzing.

Everest's car was in a ditch.

Was Everest in the car?

I must've asked this out loud, because August said, "He was."

Tears curved around my cheeks, disappeared into my still-wet hair.

"Is he—" I couldn't push the last word out.

"He didn't make it." August brushed his thumbs over my cheeks, but the tears fell faster than he could wipe.

"T-Take me to . . . to *him.*"

"I don't think that's a good idea."

"Please," I wheezed. "Please, August."

"Ness—"

I touched his cheek, beseeching him with my wet eyes.

He sighed and finally relented.

CHAPTER 21

As we drove to the scene of the accident, neither of us spoke. August had turned the heater up, but that didn't stop me from trembling.

"Dimples, come closer." He patted the seat between us.

I was too numb to move, so he clicked off my seatbelt, dragged me toward him, then draped his arm around my shoulders, rubbing my pebbled skin, trying to deliver warmth into it. Tears still streamed down my cheeks and around my trembling lips, seeping into his flannel sleeve. I closed my eyes and let the scent of laundry detergent and sandalwood lull me.

Every part of my body felt anesthetized. Except my arm.

I felt my arm . . . felt the gentle strokes of August's fingers.

"We're here," he whispered after what felt like an hour. He eased the pickup to a stop dangerously close to the lip of the mountainside and clicked on his hazard lights, streaking the row of other vehicles with orange flashes.

A fire truck topped with a huge beam and two other SUVs were parked behind us. I pressed away from August, scraped the heels of my hands over my cheeks, then took a fortifying breath and got out slowly. When the balls of my feet met the ground, I teetered. I flung out my palm, catching myself on the car door. My head spun like a top. I breathed in and out slowly, each breath raking up my chest like claws.

A hand curved around my waist and another around my elbow. "Are you sure you want to go down there?"

"Yes." I inhaled again. "My bag. You have my bag?"

"It's in the car."

Everest's last message was on my phone.

My phone was in my bag.

"Can you give it to me?"

August grabbed it, then hooked the long strap over my shoulder. After closing the door, he gripped my elbow again and guided me toward the illuminated ditch. The first thing I saw was the overturned vehicle.

Everest's Jeep.

The second thing I saw was Liam's deep glare.

"What the fuck were you thinking bringing her here, Watt?" he barked.

The firefighter beside Liam peered up. The truck's beam made a small hoop gleam in his ear. In spite of his helmet, I recognized Rodrigo, the dark shifter who'd spent most of the meeting scowling at me.

"I made him bring me," I said.

Car doors slammed, and two more people approached: Frank and Eric. Frank did a double take when he spotted me. Obviously no one had expected me to come.

Eric grabbed onto the bent guardrail and hopped down the vertiginous shoulder. He slipped but didn't fall. Putting his weight in his heels, he took careful steps toward the remains of my cousin's car.

Of my cousin.

Frank exchanged a loaded look with August. The elder was probably trying to get August to keep me from going closer. Before he could heed the unspoken instruction, I shrugged him off and made my way to the ripped metal railing, brushing past it. I eased myself down the side of the rocky knoll.

Liam stepped in front of me, blocking my view of the car.

"You shouldn't be here," he growled.

"Don't tell me what to do," I snapped, my voice all at once tight and toneless.

"What happened?" Eric asked, and I thought he was asking between Liam and me, but the bald elder was staring at Rodrigo.

"Looks like he either missed the turn or went over on purpose."

He thinks Everest committed suicide? I opened my mouth wide but regretted it, because the air was laced with the acrid reek of death.

"Cause of death?" Frank asked, traipsing down the steep flank beside August. The elder almost fell, but August caught his arm and steadied him.

"A piece of metal went through his windpipe," Lucas said. He was crouched as though searching for debris among the rock and tufts of dust-flecked grass, but I saw his nostrils flare. He was trying to catch scents.

Bile lurched up my throat. I pressed my knuckles against my lips to keep them locked. Once I had my nausea under control, I said, "He didn't kill himself."

All the men looked at me.

"And you would know this how? Did you *chat* with him again?" Lucas asked.

"Bite me, Lucas," I growled at the same time as Rodrigo said, "Again?"

Liam crossed his arms. "Why do you assume it wasn't suicide?"

More car doors slammed shut, and then two beefy blonds stepped in the beam of the truck and surfed down toward us.

"Hey," Matt called out, his voice gruff. When his gaze landed on me, his honeyed eyebrows quirked in bewilderment. He quickly moved his eyes toward the Jeep. I watched his expression, waited for it to turn pained, but there was no pain. Had he not cared about Everest? Had anyone cared about my cousin?

No wonder Everest hated the pack.

No wonder he screwed them over.

Matt circled the capsized car, stopping next to the driver's side. When he winced, a fresh wave of nausea softened my bones.

Was Everest's body still in there?

"So you were telling us why Rodrigo was wrong about it being a suicide." Liam's voice blazed with cageyness.

"He left me a voicemail about an hour ago." I dug my phone out. "It sounds incriminating . . . Then again, you all think I'm a criminal already, so why am I even trying to defend myself?" I tapped on my phone's screen with my fingers that seemed to have transformed into thumbs. It took me three attempts to get my passcode right.

No one spoke.

Scraping in another breath of death-tainted air, I held out my phone and played back the voicemail over speakerphone. Hearing Everest speak and knowing that he was gone was eerie.

When the message ended, Matt said, "Someone was following him."

Lucas rose from his crouch. "It would explain the pieces of plastic we found on the road." He turned to Rodrigo. "I know you said the taillight could've come off the Jeep when it went over, but it *is* more likely another car rammed into Everest's."

Liam's jaw clenched, unclenched, clenched again. "Check the road for skid marks, Matt."

Matt climbed back, sidestepping the two firefighters who were heaving the Jaws of Life down to the scene.

"What did Everest put in your room?" Liam's voice dragged my attention off the serrated tool.

Lucas, who was still crouched, alternately scanned the tufts of dusty grass and my expression.

"I don't know. August and I turned it upside down, but didn't find anything."

Liam's already dark gaze blackened.

While Rodrigo and one of his men cut open the driver's door, the heat of a body spilled over my back, and then an arm went around my shoulders and twisted me around.

"Don't look," August said.

I didn't fight him.

"Why were you together, and why are your clothes and hair wet?" Liam growled.

"I went for a run. A long run." My words hit August's solid chest. "I wasn't planning on coming back. I might not have if August hadn't retrieved me." I wondered for a moment whether Liam would've even cared if I'd vanished forever. Keeping my eyes locked on one of the buttons on August's shirt, I added, "Frank, Evelyn called. She said I could stay with you tonight."

Frank rubbed his hands against his jeans. "Yes. She's waiting for you."

"I know you probably need to be here, but can you please take me to her?"

"Sure." He exchanged some quiet words with Eric before starting back up the steep incline.

I disentangled myself from August and went after Frank, desirous to distance myself from this dark mountain that smacked of death and distrust.

"I got something," I heard Lucas bark over the sound of an approaching siren.

Both Frank and I paused and glanced back down into the ditch. Something flat and black gleamed in his hands. A phone.

"Is it Everest's?" Frank called down.

"It's not turning on."

"Give it to Cole," Liam said, his gaze rising to mine. "If there's anything to retrieve on it, he'll find it."

His accusation was so palpable that my expression turned to stone.

Did Liam think I'd exchanged other messages with Everest? Did he think I'd colluded with him in stealing the Sillin?

I shook my head and turned away.

CHAPTER 22

My elbow was propped on the armrest in Frank's car, and my head rested on my palm. "Was Jeb—was he informed that Everest . . . " I couldn't finish my sentence.

"He called me for news. Said he was coming, but I told him to stay put. That I'd go to him."

Jeb had been doing so much better. Granted the improvement in his mood had been fueled by anger, but still.

"You honestly didn't send Everest that text message?" Frank asked after a beat.

I hated that he didn't trust me. Then again, it seemed like no one besides August trusted me. "I swear I didn't. Whoever texted him did it remotely."

Frank sighed. "Did anyone have access to your phone last night?"

"Liam did." However angry I was with Liam, I knew he wouldn't have sent a message from my phone.

Frank knew it too. After a stretch of silence, he said, "You are your mother's daughter."

I picked my head off my palm. Well, *that* came out of nowhere.

"Maggie had so much spunk. Drove your dad crazy." He returned his gaze to the road beyond the windshield, an emotion I couldn't quite put my finger on eddying over his face. "Drove a lot of men crazy."

A lot of men? Geez, I hoped he hadn't had a crush on her.

He didn't say a word the rest of the way to his secluded, two-story log cabin a couple miles away from Headquarters. I vaguely remembered going to Frank's house with my parents when I was much younger—a lifetime ago.

Before getting out of the car, he said, "Be patient with Liam. This is an adjustment period, not only for you, but for him too. Between the stolen Sillin and learning what it means to be an Alpha, he's under a lot of stress."

I bristled. I couldn't believe he was asking *me* to be patient.

I was about to shut the door when he added, "And, Ness, be careful about pitting Liam against August. Boys, especially wolves, they're territorial *and* jealous, and well, I've seen this pattern before, and even though the mated pair didn't end up together, it caused a serious rift in the pack."

Whoa. Talk about another abrupt subject change. I took the opportunity to ask, "Who were they?"

"It doesn't matter anymore. They're all dead now."

"All of them?" And here I was certain he'd been part of the unfortunate love triangle.

Frank set his gaze on the gloomy forest dipping beyond his house. "I should head to the inn. Jeb's waiting."

Just as he said this, a voice I knew oh-so-well rang out in the night. "*Querida?*" Evelyn was standing by the front door, backlit by the soft glow of Frank's living room. Her plush robe was knotted tightly around her, and her black hair fluttered around her pale face.

I shut the car door and strode into her open arms.

When Frank drove away, she cocked an eyebrow. "Where is he going at this hour?"

I sighed. "I don't even know where to start."

She pulled me into the house, sat me at the wooden kitchen counter, and warmed water on the stovetop, but then she must've decided against making tea, because she dumped the contents, grabbed the carton of milk from the fridge door, and poured some inside the deep sauce pan. While it warmed, she wrapped her hands around my clammy ones.

"Tell me everything."

And so I did. Well, almost everything. I didn't tell her about the confrontation back at Tracy's. It would just make her resent the pack. When I was done with my account, the milk had bubbled over the sides of the pan and hit the flames, making them sizzle. She jolted toward the stove, spun off the gas, and stood there, lips mashed together. After a while, she plucked a wooden spoon from a terracotta jug and skimmed the skin off the warmed milk before dividing it between two mugs.

As she set them on the counter, she took her seat next to me again. I cupped the warm ceramic and lifted it to my mouth, singeing my lips and tongue. I plopped the mug back down, and milk splashed over the rim. Instead of cleaning it up, I dragged my fingertip through the spilled liquid and drew circles over the wood.

"You think Aidan is behind all of this?" Her black eyes glazed over as though she were remembering another time—probably the time when she was married to the man.

"He's the only one who benefits from Everest's death." Unless my cousin was wanted dead for what he'd hidden in my room.

Blinking away the haze, she got up to get a kitchen towel to clean the spilled milk. "Someone needs to put an end to that man's life."

"If he dies, his lawyers will release information about the pack to the public."

"I heard. Frank told me." She dabbed the sides of my mug until no trace of the overflow remained. "I have never hated anyone like I hate this man. He is a cancer. Do you know how many times I have dreamed of ending his life?" Her breathing increased in tempo, and her cheeks flooded with color.

I caught her hand, the one clutching the towel with which she kept wiping down the countertop even though it was clean. "Promise me you won't get involved."

She lifted her gaze to my face.

The resolve in her expression quickened my pulse. "Promise me."

After a long moment, she exhaled a slow breath. "He should not be allowed to live."

"I agree. Now agree that you will stay away from him. Because if anything happens to you . . . " My voice broke then, and in turn, it broke her doggedness.

The same way her features had hardened, they softened. And

then she was pulling me against her. "I promise you, *querida*, that I will not put myself in harm's way, but you promise me the same thing."

I swallowed. I didn't want to make Evelyn a promise I had no desire to keep.

"Ness . . ."

"Fine. I'll stay away from him."

For now.

CHAPTER 23

T he following morning, after a brief night of sleep in one of the two twin beds set up in Frank's guest room—I suspected it was the room his grandson used when he visited because it smelled like boy and was plastered with superhero movie posters—I dressed in yesterday's clothes and went out into the kitchen for coffee.

Frank and Evelyn were already up, sitting on the couch, talking in hushed tones. The deep circles beneath Frank's eyes told me his night had been longer than mine.

"There is coffee in the kitchen, *querida*," Evelyn said.

I went to serve myself, watching as they resumed their quiet conversation.

"How's Jeb?" I ventured after a bit.

Frank rubbed his jaw that was coated in white stubble. "Not too good. Eric took your uncle back to his place last night so he and Lucy could talk. There was a lot of yelling apparently. And a lot of crying."

I took a careful sip of coffee. "What's going to happen now?"

"We'll bury Everest on pack Headquarters tonight."

I stared into the murky depths of my coffee feeling a familiar burn beneath my lids. No tears fell, though.

"They found yellow paint on one of the Jeep's side mirrors."

My gaze bounded onto the elder.

"Probably transferred from the car that pushed his off the road.

It's a solid lead, because it's not a common color." He studied the vase full of wildflowers on his wooden coffee table.

"Does Aidan own a yellow car?" I asked, wending my way around the kitchen countertop toward the open living room with its peaked timber ceiling and swooping antler chandelier. I wondered if Frank had crafted the light fixture himself from collected stag horns.

"Aidan Michaels is in the hospital."

"Doesn't mean he didn't pay someone to do it."

"Perhaps, but Lucas picked up on a foreign smell out there." Frank raised his wary eyes to mine. "I think we might be dealing with Creeks."

His admission hit my ears like shattered ceramic. I actually looked down to check I hadn't dropped the mug. It was still clutched in my white-knuckled fingers. "Lucas scented foreign wolves on Liam's property yesterday. Were they Creeks too?"

"Creeks?" Evelyn asked.

Frank scraped both his hands down the length of his face and sighed, setting his gaze on the bow window across from me. For a long moment, he looked at the rolling hill dappled in long blades of sun-burnished grass and wildflowers that matched the ones in the vase.

"The Creek Pack," Frank explained, "was once the smallest pack, and then in one bloody night, they brought the largest pack to their knees."

Evelyn tightened her grip on the couch's armrest. "*Dios mío*," she murmured.

My body had turned so cold that I was afraid to move, afraid my limbs might just chip away like icicles. "Did you warn Julian?"

Frank looked back at me. "Liam's meeting with him later today. He'll try to negotiate a firm alliance."

Considering how much both packs antagonized each other, I sensed this outcome was momentous. Had the Pines and Boulders ever worked together?

"Why would the Creeks murder Everest?" I asked after a long moment.

"Liam believes it has to do with the Sillin," Frank said. "We did another sweep of your bedroom. We didn't find anything, and we're hoping no one—no Creek—got to it before us."

While Evelyn asked what Sillin was, and Frank explained it to her, I tried to puzzle out under what my cousin could've hidden the pills. If it was the pills we were talking about.

LATER IN THE MORNING, EVELYN AND I STOPPED BY THE NEW apartment I was supposed to call home from now on. We cleaned the place, made up the beds, and unpacked my clothes. All the while she repeated that she wasn't happy about the arrangement, that my uncle was unfit to care for me, that I should stay with Frank and her. Her unhappiness increased when my uncle dropped by the apartment with a mammoth suitcase and several cardboard boxes close to bursting.

While he unpacked, he talked almost manically, never once mentioning Everest's name. It was as though he hadn't processed his son's death. I asked how Lucy was doing, which won me a pointed look followed by a sour retort.

"She killed our son by covering up for him. I don't give a rat's ass how she's doing."

When Frank drove Evelyn and me to Headquarters that evening, there were so many parked cars that they spilled onto the road. Every Boulder and their family had come. As we approached the body wrapped in a white sheet, my heart tripped. I felt like I was seeing my father's body all over again. He, also, had been enveloped in white. Werewolves weren't buried in caskets; they were placed in the ground with nothing but a sheet around them, so the earth could reclaim them.

For a moment, I wondered if the sheet that cocooned my cousin came from the inn, and then I drove that inane thought out of my mind.

A raucous whimper pierced the still air—Lucy.

I hadn't seen her since the day she'd held Evelyn hostage.

My senses sharpened at the sight of my aunt's kneeling figure. I could hear the tears tracking down her milky-white cheeks, the beats of her heart pumping blood through her organs, the sweat dripping into the waistband of her black slacks.

Evelyn squeezed my arm, which drove back my sudden urge to sink my fangs into my aunt's throat. And then Isobel and Nelson were suddenly in front of me. Where he simply nodded, face tight with grief, Isobel palmed my cheek and caught the fingers I'd balled into a fist at my side.

On the other side of the shallow hole stood Liam, flanked by Lucas and Matt. All three had their hands linked solemnly in front of them and their heads bent. I watched Liam although he didn't watch me. He stared at the hole.

Did it remind him of his father's burial?

Would he have afforded Everest a funeral had my cousin died at the Alpha's hands?

Liam must've felt the weight of my stare because he lifted his eyes to mine. They were so very dark and rimmed with red. Had he cried or was it just the mark of fatigue? Probably fatigue. Why would Liam cry over someone he'd loathed?

Ness? His unwelcome voice prickled my skull.

I lowered my gaze to my uncle, who was pressing his palm against the swathed remains of his son.

Please look at me.

I didn't.

Please, baby. Look at me.

Baby? That got my attention. I glared at him.

I deserve that.

He deserved so much worse than a glare.

I deduced from his apologetic demeanor that Cole had uncovered something from Everest's phone.

Eric started with the ritualistic singing that accompanied our people's departure from this world, so Liam didn't try to communicate with me again. I didn't shed a single tear as Everest was lowered into the dug-out hole. I didn't whimper as his remains were filmed with soil. I didn't make a single sound while the dirt rained down on the pale linen. I watched with dry eyes and a dry throat until the very last scoop fell over him, and then I watched as Jeb patted the soft mound as though tucking his son in for the very last time.

When people headed into Headquarters for the wake, I stepped away from the women holding me up and approached the one who'd always pushed me down.

"I'm sorry he died." My voice was toneless.

Lucy stopped heaving and turned her reddened hazel eyes on mine.

"I always liked Everest. Even after he double-crossed me, I wanted him to live."

She stared at me for a long moment without speaking, and then she started yelling. "It's because of you that he's dead! *You!* You ruined our lives!" She jumped to her feet and began pummeling her fists into my chest, her bangles clinking furiously. "We should've left you to rot in that foul apartment. We should *never* have brought you back!"

Her blows didn't hurt. My chest was too numb to hurt. Besides, it wasn't my fault that Everest had died; it was his own fault. I didn't bat her hands away. I didn't much care for the blows she rained on me. August and Nelson must've cared though, because they each grabbed a freckled arm. And then Jeb was shrieking at her, spittle smacking his wife's nose.

She sneered at him. "I hope you die! All of you. Your species is unnatural and should be eradicated." She spit on Jeb.

August and Nelson hauled Lucy back and then dragged her around the building. Would they lock her up underneath the silver grate? I didn't care what happened to my aunt. She was too miserable a woman.

Ness? Liam's minty scent wafted over my shoulder and snaked into me, burying deep.

Slowly, I turned and faced my Alpha. The pain on his face didn't soften my resolve to keep him away.

"What?" I asked jadedly.

I'm sorry for not believing you.

I pressed my lips tight.

Cole managed to track where the message was sent from through the Wi-Fi that was used, and it wasn't from your phone. Wasn't even from Boulder.

I was relieved to have been cleared, but the pain of the hasty condemnation remained. "Why is it, Liam, that I am I not allowed the trust you give others in the pack so freely? Because I'm new? Because I haven't *earned* it? What exactly must I do to earn it?" Breaths broke like waves around my clenched teeth. "I would never have undermined you, Liam. And not because of any exchange of blood, but because when I give my word to someone, I uphold it. I have a lot of flaws. I'm the first person to admit how stubborn and argumentative I can be, and I've spoken my fair share of lies. I'm far from being an angel."

Liam's black pupils pulsed and pulsed.

"But I've always prided myself on being a good person—a reliable and loyal one. I have *never* betrayed anyone in my entire life. And I wouldn't have started with the pack I've coveted for so long, or the boy"—my voice broke—"or the boy who . . . who . . . " I couldn't finish my sentence. It hurt too damn much.

Liam winced.

The tears that hadn't come for Everest finally surfaced. I scrubbed them away, but they wouldn't stop dripping. I took a step back, and then another. Liam didn't move. He just stayed there, legs planted like tree trunks into the earth.

I spun around. Instead of heading toward Headquarters, I headed for the road and started walking.

And walking.

Evelyn called my name, but I didn't stop.

I walked until the sky grew so dark that all the stars came out. And under this shower of light, upon blistered feet, I made my way down the miles and miles of sinuous dirt road.

I was like a hermit crab when I grieved, balled up tight within my shell. I wasn't even sure if I was grieving for my cousin or for my broken heart.

It was the first time a guy had broken it. Mom used to say that I needed my heart to be broken to know when the right man came along. She said the right one would fit all the pieces together and would fill all the fissures with his love to make sure it never cracked again.

Who's going to put your heart back together now that Daddy's gone? I'd asked her.

Her blue eyes gentled, and she gathered me against her side on our ratty denim couch that had been patched many times over. *Your dad didn't break my heart, Ness. He left with half of it.*

Car tires crunched on the road next to me, spraying tiny rocks into my ankles. "Ness, get in the car."

I stared at the luminous shapes the twin beams cast on the shrubs lining the road.

"It'll take you hours to reach town."

"I'm not in any rush, August."

For the first time in years, my agenda was empty. Sure, I'd need to look for a job, but I wouldn't have to do that tomorrow.

Tomorrow I could sleep in.

I could stare at my ceiling.

Or watch TV.

Or lunch with Sarah in the middle of the afternoon.

After the grief and stress of the last few days, I felt like I could finally breathe again. Which was strange considering Creeks might be in Boulder and a man who deserved to perish was still alive and Everest was dead.

"By God, Dimples, you're as stubborn as when you were a kid."

I smirked, flicking my gaze to August. It felt good to sport an expression that wasn't incensed or weepy. "Were you expecting me to have changed?"

August's eyes flashed in the darkness of his car. "To have matured. I'd expected you to have matured."

"If the mark of maturity is becoming biddable, then I hope I never mature, August Watt."

He shook his head. "You're really going to walk eleven more miles in the dark in heels?"

"You're right." I slid off my heels, hooking them onto my fingertips, then proceeded to the thin strip of grass edging the road to cushion my footfalls. "It's easier without heels."

He growled. "Ness, come on. I'm being serious here."

"You're always so serious. You should lighten up. Maybe take up barefoot promenades under the stars. They're very soothing." I looked at the sky and tried to find the constellations he'd taught me to find so many years ago. "Is that Andromeda or Cassiopeia? I can never tell between the two."

When he didn't answer my question, I turned toward him. Instead of looking at the sky, he was staring at me.

"Not interested in constellations anymore?" I asked.

"I'll tell you which one it is if you get in the car."

I tipped him a crooked smile. "Nice try, but it would take way more to get me off this road and into that truck."

"Ness, this isn't a joke. Creeks are running amok in our woods. They *killed* your cousin."

And he'd just *killed* my mood. "So what, August? I should live my life in fear now? I'm not invincible. I know that. If anything, Everest's death has really brought this home, but I'm also not going to hide. They killed my cousin for a reason, and I doubt that reason was because he was a Boulder wolf."

August loosed another exasperated growl. "Negotiating with terrorists is easier than with you."

And just like that, my smile was back. "So? Andromeda?"

"Yes," he huffed.

I pointed to another assortment of stars. Even though I could sense I was tugging at August's patience, he told me each one of their names. For eleven miles, he fed me information about stars and nebulas and planets.

When we reached my new home, the bottom of my feet ached, but I felt as vaporous as the stars jewelling the heavens.

I folded my arms on the open passenger window. "So this was fun."

August grunted in response.

"Okay then, Caveman Watt." I tapped the window frame. "You have yourself a good night."

I smiled at him, and it thawed some of the tightness around his eyes. As I walked toward the flight of stairs that led to my new front door, I heard him call out, "I'm glad you haven't changed, even though I sense you're going to drive me insane."

I grinned at the door. "A little insanity will do you good."

I stepped inside the tiny foyer, trailing blood and dirt across the clean oak floors, marking my new territory.

CHAPTER 24

I woke up to the brightest and whitest sunshine. It streamed through my window, splashing warmth against my rumpled sheets and the bare patches of skin poking out of those sheets. I stretched, and bones cracked delightfully along my spine.

For a moment, I watched the unobstructed view of the mountains bathed in blue sky. It didn't compare to the view from the inn, but this was still a damn good view. One I could get used to.

What a dangerous thought that was.

Getting used to something.

Just because I wouldn't let myself get attached didn't mean I couldn't enjoy it until I was uprooted and tossed between another set of walls. I rolled out of bed and stood up, but the minute the soles of my feet made contact with the cool floorboards, I winced and fell back.

Maybe I'd overdone it last night.

Walking a dozen or so miles barefoot was probably not the wisest thing I'd done, and God only knew how many *unwise* things I'd already done. I could just imagine August wagging his finger at me and saying, *I told you so.* He probably wouldn't wag his finger, but he would definitely say I told you so. Good thing he wasn't here.

Keeping one hand on the bare walls of my bedroom, I limped to my bathroom. The tiles were still speckled in blood and dirt. I'd felt glad to mark my territory last night, but in the morning light, I regretted not having washed off my feet in the kitchen sink. At least I'd had the sagacity of soaking them in soap and ice-cold water before getting into bed.

After brushing my hair and teeth, I went into the living room to check on my uncle. Not only was he up, but he was having coffee with Nelson and August. I splayed my palm against the wall so I wouldn't keel over, which drove a smug smile to August's lips. How had I not heard our visitors? The apartment wasn't *that* big, and my werewolf hearing was supposed to be sharp.

I jerked my hand off the wall and took a tentative step, but grimaced. Could toes break from too much walking? Something definitely felt broken. And I wasn't even talking about the skin that had blistered and cracked in a multitude of places.

"I hope we didn't wake you," Nelson said, setting his mug down.

I took another slow, agonizing step.

"You okay, there, Ness?" August asked.

I pushed a smile onto my lips. "Yep. Great."

He leaned back in his chair and crossed his big arms like a spectator enjoying a show. Another step and I reached the small linoleum countertop that separated the living slash dining room from the kitchen.

The trail of blood I'd left behind the previous night had turned brownish, blending into the dark knots of the yellowed oak.

"Nelson and August stopped by because they were worried about our living arrangements," Jeb said, even though I hadn't asked. Not that I wasn't curious. I wondered what he thought about their concern. "And they brought us scones."

He pointed to the plate topped with golden triangles flecked with tendrils of lemon peel that scented the air, which was a feat considering how strongly August fragranced the space. I wondered if it was the mating link that intensified his aroma or if he didn't wash the soap off his skin after lathering up.

Keeping my hand on the countertop, I limped a couple inches closer to the small, round table.

"Yum," I said. About the scones. Not about August.

I mean he smelled good, but the scones smelled better. Good enough to eat. Unlike August, whom I had no desire to eat. Apparently incapable of doing two things at once, I stopped walking in order to shove away my cannibalistic deliberations.

"Are you sure you're all right?" Nelson asked.

"What?"

"You look like you're in pain." Nelson gestured to me.

Oh. "Just a Charlie horse." I looked down at my bare legs, regretting not having swapped my sleep shorts for something more concealing. I glanced toward my bedroom. *Nope.* Wasn't slogging back there. Besides I'd almost reached the free chair between Jeb and August.

One more step . . .

Cold sweat beaded on my upper lip as I finally dropped down into the chair with an audible oomph.

August, who was angled away from the table, crossed one foot over his opposite knee and grinned so wide I wanted to smack him.

"August suggested going for a hike," Jeb said. "And having a picnic."

"Nothing like sunshine and fresh air to clear the mind," August said.

I blanched a little at the idea of hiking.

"I could use a distraction." Jeb pinched the bridge of his nose. "And I wouldn't say no to physical exertion. Might help me sleep." He lifted his bruised blue eyes to me.

"What do you say?" August asked.

What do I say? Let me see . . . That you're sadistic, August Watt. Besides, I would need to be physically dragged along the trail considering the state of my body.

Obviously, I went with, "Um. I have an appointment to pass my driver's permit today." It wasn't a complete lie. If they could fit me in at the DMV, then I'd take the test. Could I just walk in?

The amused glint in August's eyes dimmed, and he grunted. "How convenient."

I lifted a scone off the plate and took a bite.

"We can leave after you're done," Nelson said. "What time's your appointment?"

The bite went down the wrong hole, and I coughed. August pushed a glass of water in front of me, and I downed it.

No rest for the injured.

What time was it now? I looked around the room for a clock. Found my answer inscribed on the cable box: 9:15. "Eleven-thirty."

"We're not in any hurry. We can leave straight after," August said.

Oh, goodie. I shot August a death glare, which put a glimmer back in his eyes.

"Great." I ripped off a large chunk of dense, flaky dough and stuffed it inside my mouth. Hopefully my werewolf gene would miraculously heal my aching bones and tattered skin within the next three hours. "Can't wait."

August cocked one of his thick eyebrows.

"I'll call Izzie to confirm the picnic." Nelson rose from his seat, cellphone already pressed to his ear.

Jeb laid his hand on my forearm and squeezed it. "Thanks for being such a good sport, Ness."

"Of course."

My uncle got up and brought his mug over to the sink. "I need to call the inn. I'll be right back."

I watched him make his way to his bedroom. Although his shoulders were hunched and his eyes puffy, he was far from the specter he'd been just a few days ago. It hadn't even been a week, I realized, yet it felt like it had been a month since the pledging ceremony. Time was a strange thing. Some days lasted seconds, and some days lasted weeks.

The heat of a hand on my knee made me look away from Jeb's closed bedroom door.

"I was just picking on you, Ness," August said quietly. "You don't have to come. Besides, you can't even walk, can you?"

August dragged his hand back to his thigh, the circumference of which equaled both my legs.

"I can hobble, and don't you dare say I told you so."

He raised both palms in the air.

"But maybe in three hours, I'll be better."

"Are you sure? You really don't have to come."

"It seemed to make Jeb happy that I was joining." I finished my scone, chewing on it thoughtfully. "If I really can't take it, I'll just sun myself until you guys are done traipsing through the woods." I wiped the crumbs off my palms. "Is your mom going to hike?"

He shook his head. "She's going to drive over. Actually, why don't you just hitch a ride with her and meet us at the lake?"

"That sounds incredibly more appealing."

Nelson came back toward us, stuffing his phone into the back pocket of his high-waisted jeans. "I need to stop by the warehouse. Christian wants to go over the blueprints of Mr. Sommerville's lodge. *Again.*"

August sighed and rose.

"Oh, you don't need to come with me, son. I can handle Christian."

"I don't mind. Besides, I'm sure Ness needs to study for her big exam."

"Why don't you help her study?"

Father and son exchanged a long look. Something passed between them. What, though, I couldn't tell, but I was most definitely going to find out the second Nelson walked out our front door.

The second it shut, I asked, "What was that about?"

"What was what about?"

"That look."

"What look?"

"Oh come on, August. I grew up with you guys."

August rubbed the back of his head sheepishly, glancing toward Jeb's door. "Dad doesn't want Jeb to be left alone. Not for the next week anyway. He's worried." August shrugged. "He's worried he might . . . " More neck rubbing. "Try to kill himself." Those last few words came out whispered.

"Oh." Goose bumps scattered all over me. "I'm here," I said finally.

"I know. *We* know."

"But you guys don't think I can handle him?"

"No. That's not it. My parents are also worried about *you.*"

My heart squeezed a little that anyone besides Evelyn cared how I was doing. "Tell them they don't have to worry."

He grunted as he sat down again and leaned back in his seat. I was a little afraid the rungs would snap right off, but the chair surprisingly held.

"Like that would ever happen," he said, picking up a knife that someone had placed on the table, probably to cut the scones in half, even though I had to wonder what self-respecting werewolf would eat only half a scone. He flipped the utensil, blade up, blade down. Over and over.

"So, does this mean we get breakfast delivered every morning? Because if that's the case, I'd like to put in some requests."

He glanced at me from underneath his dark lashes and let out a little grunt. I was starting to think grunting was August Watt's MO.

"Let me guess." He raised a finger. "Carrot cake muffins, preferably frosted." He flicked up another finger. "Chocolate-zucchini bread." A third finger came up. "Warm sourdough with salted butter." Another finger. "Cinnamon rolls with a hefty layer of icing." And then his pinkie leaped up. "Bacon—the thickly cut kind—with scrambled eggs."

I blinked at him, impressed by his memory. He'd just listed all of my favorite breakfast items. Not that I was the pickiest person, but I really did have a thing for cinnamon and fatty food. Discussing food brought me back to the meal I'd shared with Liam in his kitchen when he'd asked what I liked eating. August already knew all that about me. For some reason, this flustered me. I got up and hobbled to the kitchen to pour myself a mug of coffee.

With my back to him, I said, "Coffee. Just coffee. I don't really eat any of that stuff anymore." I wasn't sure why I was lying to August. Maybe it was because I didn't want him to think he had me all figured out. Even though he did.

I turned and leaned against the linoleum countertop. The edge bit into the sliver of skin on display between my crop top and my sleep shorts. Again, I thought about going to put on some more clothes, but I lived amongst wolves. They probably didn't even notice bare skin anymore.

August frowned at me, and then he frowned down at the white ceramic mug clutched between my fingers. I blew on the steam, watched it disperse and melt into the air.

Feeling like a jerk, I said, "If you really do have time, I'd appreciate some help with studying for my exam."

His gaze returned to my face. For a moment, I thought about confessing I'd lied, that he'd been right, that those were still all of my favorite things, but I couldn't get the words out. It was disarming to have someone know me so intimately. I hadn't eaten cinnamon rolls or carrot cake muffins in months, yet the mere mention of them made me salivate. It also brought back a whole slew of memories that included a table full of people—most of whom weren't part of this world anymore.

My mom had made the best cinnamon rolls.

And my father's usual Sunday activity—besides waltzing his wife around the house to a Roberta Flack song—was grating several pounds of carrots for her baking.

"Sure," August finally said. "Do you have the booklet?"

"No." I blew on my coffee again. No steam rose this time. "Can you pull up the questions on your phone?"

He nodded. As he quizzed me, his tone was so stiff that I knew I'd wounded him, yet I couldn't confess my deception. I might've been loyal to a fault, but I was one hell of a stubborn liar.

CHAPTER 25

I didn't end up hiking. But I did pass my driver's permit without making so much as a single mistake, and then I celebrated at the lakeside picnic with all of my favorite people—when Isobel had pulled up in front of the DMV, Evelyn was in the car.

I'd almost cried from how happy I was that Isobel had thought to invite Evelyn. Also, I was feeling pretty emotional from getting my permit on the first try. Now I only needed fifty hours of driving experience and a vision exam, and I'd be all set to cruise around Boulder— or around the country—on my own. I was drunk on the freedom that loomed at my fingertips.

Buoyed by the thoughts of all the places I would go, I walked to the lake's edge, slid off my sandals, and waded into the crisp water that felt delicious against my blistered feet. I picked up a stone and skipped it on the glassy surface just as Isobel's contagious laughter rang through the warm summer air.

This was a perfect day.

One of the most perfect days I'd had in a long time.

"Not bad." August stared at the ripples on the water as my rock sank to the bottom.

"You think you can do better, Watt?"

He answered me with a confident smile, the first one he'd given me since I'd shot him down earlier. With that smile, all was right in the world again.

His flat pebble leaped over the surface four times before plunging to its watery grave. "That was just a warm-up shot."

I snickered. "Uh-huh."

His freckles seemed to burn a little darker. He crouched and spent almost an entire minute scouring the rocky beach for just the right stone. I remembered making fun of him once for devoting half an afternoon searching a meadow for the most faultless red poppies to give Isobel one Mother's Day. I'd ripped up the first stalks I could find and squashed them into a bouquet, which wilted on the way to my house. Mom had still complimented their beauty and displayed them in a vase on her dresser.

Slowly, August unfurled his long body, the smallest and slimmest rock nestled in his palm, and walked over to the water's edge, crouched, all of the muscles in his body purling as he frisbeed the rock in one perfect sweep.

He pumped his fist in the air. "Take that, Dimples. Nine!"

I flung my gaze toward the water, which still undulated. I'd missed his exploit. For all I knew, the pebble had skipped twice before sinking, but I couldn't admit that, because then he'd know I'd been ogling him instead of the rock, and he'd wonder why.

I wondered why.

Perhaps it was the violently hot sun.

Or maybe it was the incessant cacophony of crickets.

"You win," I conceded, wading in deeper. Water snaked up my bare thighs. I should've worn a bathing suit but hadn't thought of it. My cut-offs and tank top would have to do. "I'm going for a swim."

A dragonfly skimmed the water's surface, its green pearlescent body adding to the lake's pulsing shimmer. I swept my hand toward the insect, and it dashed off the same way bunnies ran from me when I was in my other form.

"Want to join me?" I asked, looking over my shoulder at August.

He rubbed his chin as though debating, but then he lowered his pants and yanked off his tee. I turned my prying gaze away and submerged myself completely, staying under until I felt my blood cool down. When I popped back out, August was lying on his back next to me, floating like driftwood.

He looked peaceful.

Too peaceful.

Smiling deviously, I pressed both my palms into his abdomen and drove him downward. And then I laughed so hard that when he emerged and shoved me under, I snorted in an ungodly amount of lake water.

I propelled myself away from him like a squid. "Not fair," I said, laugh-snorting.

He grinned. When I saw him cut through the water toward me, probably to dunk me under again, I raced to the middle of the lake. Only then did I stop to take a breath. From the shore, I caught Evelyn shading her eyes. I waved to her to reassure her that I was okay just before I got dunked again.

When I broke free, I tossed my hair back. "Oh. You're going to regret that!"

August shot me a challenging grin. "Am I? What are you going to do, Dimples? Stick itching powder in my bed again?"

Ha! I'd forgotten about that. "Not a bad idea . . . " I racked my brain for something worse, though. When it finally came to me, I swam up to him and started tickling his sides. August was the most ticklish person in the history of ticklish people.

He roared with laughter until he managed to cuff my wrists. Then he tried to take revenge, but I wasn't ticklish. I'd never been. He must've remembered that fact at some point because he stopped prodding my ribcage and simply rested his palm against my waist. I wasn't cold, but my skin pebbled and my heart . . . it skipped a beat.

Possibly two.

Before he could detect my weirdness, I kicked away from him. "Nice try, big guy," I said, hoping my voice sounded normal. "Race you to the shore?"

His green eyes honed into the shore with the same intensity they'd honed into me a moment ago. August had never been competitive—not ever—and yet the way he looked at that shore made me wonder if he'd changed. Maybe, in the past, when we'd played backgammon or scaled a tree, he'd let me win, because I was so much younger.

"You're going to need a head start," he finally said.

"I'm all grown up now. I don't need any more head starts."

"You sure about that?"

"Yep."

"What do I get if I win?" He submerged his chin and mouth and blew out bubbles as he treaded water next to me.

"You want a prize for beating a girl?"

He popped his head back out of the water. "That's a low blow. How am I supposed to beat you now?"

I grinned at him, my dimples feeling like they were excavating my cheeks. "Ready?"

He grunted, which I took as a yes.

I propelled my limbs, wheeling them so fast they blurred, and my pulse skyrocketed. Unlike August, I had always been competitive. Which had been one of the reasons I'd entered the Alpha trials.

His body plundered the water parallel to mine. I didn't stop to check who was in the lead though, not until I reached the embankment. The minute my fingers grazed the shore, I shot out of the water and whipped my hair off my face. August touched the shore a couple seconds after me.

"Yes!" I smacked the water triumphantly, but then I noticed he was barely out of breath, and my triumph waned. "Did you let me win, August Watt?"

He pivoted and sat facing out. "Nope."

"Liar."

He side-eyed me, and there was something in his penetrating gaze that made my grin crumble like crushed chalk. It was as though he was saying, *that makes two of us*. Maybe I was reading too much into his expression. Maybe I was only seeing what I was feeling.

Whatever it was, I got out of the lake, cool water bleeding down my legs and between my breasts. When I reached the picnic blanket, I sat down and wrung out my hair. Isobel tendered me a towel, which I wrapped around myself.

"Remember those parties we used to throw down here, Jeb?" she said to my contemplative uncle.

His gaze was fixed to the pines swaying gently around the crystalline body of water. "I remember Nelson tossing me in one night with all my clothes on because I mentioned how pretty you looked."

Nelson chuckled, a tad sheepishly, whereas Isobel flushed but smiled as big as her son.

Keeping her gaze trained on August's back, on the caterpillar-like scar that extended the length of the waistband of his black briefs, she said, "Those were the days."

I didn't ask whether my parents had attended those lake parties. I sensed they had. They'd all grown up together. They'd all splashed around the lake together. They'd all kissed and gotten married and birthed babies together.

Shifters were a community, and like all communities, they'd been rattled by tragedy, but somehow, they'd all stuck around and lifted each other up when life had weighed them down. Until my father died.

Would our generation be supportive? Would I one day picnic with August and Matt and their respective wives and laugh about the good old days?

I hoped so. I hoped I would get what Isobel, Nelson, and Jeb had. I hoped I would get a real family again.

CHAPTER 26

The week following Everest's burial smeared into a long blur. Every day, someone from the pack would bring us breakfast and suggest an activity—a movie, a card game, a walk. At some point, Jeb started to turn people down, and then he stopped coming out of his room altogether, which meant I got to hang out with our visitors and prove I had everything under control.

And I did.

I ached, but my sadness was tempered by the fact that Everest had dug his own grave, even though I still didn't understand why he'd done all that he'd done, or why the Creeks had silenced him. Was it for the Sillin, or was there more?

When Matt dropped by at the end of the week, brandishing a bag of homemade blueberry muffins his mom had baked, I made him sit and tell me what was going on, because I was certain *a lot* was going on.

The blond bear of a man sank down onto the couch, palming the pale stubble on his square jaw. "Julian and Liam have contacted the Creek Alpha to ask for a meeting. She hasn't gotten back to them yet, so Robbie suggested heading out there to confront her." He sighed and sat back, hooking one arm around the back of the couch and dropping the other on the armrest.

I handed him a mug of the minty tea I'd just brewed and sat on the opposite end of the couch, folding my legs beneath me. "Do you think he was killed because of the drugs?"

"It's the likeliest scenario."

"Has anyone spoken to Aidan Michaels?"

"Aidan Michaels?" Both of his honeyed eyebrows shot up on his sun-reddened forehead. I guessed he'd been working outdoors this week. "Why would he know anything?"

"Because one, he had his own business dealings with Everest. And two, he's made it his mission to know everything there is to know about werewolves. Why would his interest in packs not extend over the Boulder town limits?"

Matt thought about this so hard his large forehead puckered. "True. I'll talk to Liam." He took a sip of his tea. "Or maybe you should?"

"No way."

"Why?"

I set my mug down before I could squeeze the tea right out of it. "Seriously, Matt? You're asking me why? You were there."

"I know, Ness, but we were all under pressure, and between the text and the voicemail—"

"He should've given me the benefit of the doubt. You *all* should've."

Matt chewed on his lower lip. "He hates himself for it, but you gotta understand, that's Liam. He's always been a little . . . *impulsive.*"

Impulsive? "So I'm supposed to forgive and forget?"

Matt went back to rubbing his jaw. "No. But I think you guys should talk. You don't have to get back together or anything, but he's real miserable, Ness. And his temper's gotten even shorter."

"Not my problem."

"He's your Alpha, so it sort of is your problem. It's all of our problem. If he flips a switch, he could do something that could endanger the pack."

"I'm not a shrink, Matt. Liam needs therapy. And I'm not saying that out of anger, but because his father really screwed him up. There's nothing I can say or do that can fix that sort of damage."

Matt screwed up his lips. "Tamara's sniffing around him again."

"Did she ever stop?"

"I guess not, but she's really coming on strong this time."

I stared out the window at the rolling mountains flecked with evergreens and grass. My heartbeat slowed as I pictured Liam's red-haired ex and the sneer she'd directed at me the night I'd gone out to Tracy's with the pack. The night she'd all but called me a hooker.

"She can have him," I said.

"Are you sure?"

I finally dragged my gaze back to Matt. "Yes."

He studied his dirt-flecked work boots. "Is it because of August?"

"August is like an older brother to me." One who'd stopped visiting since our lakeside picnic. Not that he'd promised to come every day, but it would've been nice to see his face or hear his voice.

"I heard you two are mates."

"Just because we're *supposed to be* mates doesn't mean we're attracted to each other."

Matt snorted, which made me bristle.

"What?" I asked.

"Nothing."

"Why did you snort?"

"Because you're hot, and August's a guy. And even if he might feel like a brother to you, the fact is, he isn't."

"So?"

"So he shot Sienna's advances down the other day. And then this waitress, who he used to hook up with before Sienna, asked if he wanted a nightcap, and he rejected her too."

I could see how him turning down girls could be misconstrued, but he was probably worried about his mother. Her surgery was on Monday. *I* was worried.

"He's got a lot going on, Matt."

"No unattached guy has *that* much going on that they turn down easy lays, Ness."

I sat up and placed my mug down on the glass coffee table. "I might have a theory."

"I'm listening."

This isn't going to be weird . . . Then again this entire conversation was weird. It was the sort of conversation I should be having with Sarah instead of Matt. Not that Sarah and I hadn't had it already.

Sarah had been picking me up most afternoons to give me driving lessons in her red Mini, so the subject had come up.

Jeb said she was probably trying to squeeze information about Everest and the Creeks out of me, but I doubted it. One, she could've gone to her uncle for information, and two, we didn't discuss pack dynamics all that much. We mostly listened to music while discussing UCB and the courses I should take. I hadn't gotten my acceptance letter yet. I imagined *it*, as well as my tuition, were contingent to a talk with Liam. I hadn't been ready to face him, but I was slowly getting there.

Next week perhaps . . .

"So?" Matt's voice broke me out of my daydream. "What's your theory?"

I dragged my hand through my hair. "The mating link makes our bodies unreceptive to people who aren't our mates."

He frowned.

"We can't be . . . um"—heat eddied through me—"intimate."

"Huh?"

"Oh come on, Matt." I yanked my hand through my hair again so hard this time I plucked out a few strands. "Don't make me draw you a diagram. This is embarrassing enough." So embarrassing that I kept my gaze locked on the blank TV screen in the corner.

"Whoa. You mean you can't have sex with a random person? *Whoa* . . . " He repeated *whoa* a couple more times. "Now I get why Liam tried to get August to leave town. *Whoa.*"

"Yeah. Sucks." For August more than me. I didn't know what I was missing.

"I don't get why August isn't hauling ass out of Boulder. I mean, I do get it. His mom being sick and all, but after that . . . " He rubbed his hands together. "After that, Ness, if he sticks around Boulder, he's sticking around for you."

I folded my fingers together. Not in prayer. Just to do something with them. This conversation had me feeling restless. Not to mention uncomfortable. Tremendously uncomfortable. I was antsy for Matt to leave.

As though he sensed it, he stood up.

"He'll leave," I said slowly. "There's no reason for him to stay. I won't act on the link. I don't want to be with someone because of some chemical or magical connection."

"Just because it's magical doesn't mean it's not real."

I cocked an eyebrow. "That's exactly what it means. Magic isn't real, Matt."

"We're magical, and we're real." He gestured between us. "How do you explain that, huh?"

"What would you do if you suddenly had a mate, and that girl wasn't Amanda?"

His features tensed. "You can't compare us. Amanda and I, we've been together for a long time. As far as I can see, neither you nor August are attached, so there's no real reason for staying away. Unless you're holding out for Liam. In which case—"

"I'm not."

He observed me a long minute before strolling to the front door. "Life's short, Ness." He drummed his thick fingers against the wall. "Shorter for some than for others. Just make sure you get to the end of it with more satisfaction than regrets. And yeah, I know not everyone needs a relationship or love or sex to feel happy, but avoiding it on principle is a sucky reason to stay single." He turned the knob and drew open the door. "And I know I've probably overstayed my welcome and doled out too much unwanted advice, but I know August. He's like a brother to me too, and even though he's quiet 'bout his feelings, he broke up with Sienna the minute you walked back into his life. And if I'm not mistaken, you guys weren't linked yet."

"Their breakup had nothing to do with me."

"If it makes you sleep better at night."

I wanted to tell him to butt out of my personal life.

"Remember when I caught you guys sexting after the first trial?"

I rolled my eyes. "We weren't sexting."

He side-eyed me. "If you say so, Little Wolf."

"I do say so. I can show you our messages. There wasn't anything remotely sexual about any of them."

"You guys have a connection."

"*Friends.* We're just friends."

"Uh-huh. Anyway, gotta hit the road. Wouldn't want *my boss* to fire me."

"Yeah. We wouldn't want that," I grumbled. I was feeling moody now because Matt had gotten under my skin.

So much so that once he shut the door, whistling loudly on his way down the steps, I retrieved my phone from the kitchen counter and began scrolling through my past conversations with August. Although not sexual, the tone of our back-and-forth texts was pretty personal.

As I scrolled up and up, our phone conversations started coming back to me, and my heart quickened. I couldn't possibly have a crush on August, or could I?

Ugh.

I worshipped him as a kid, because he was so sweet with me, so attentive. It felt wrong to crush on him today. I barely knew him anymore.

I was so wound up about this that I went for a long, *long* run. By the time I got home, I'd come to a conclusion that sounded extremely wise: I would stay away from him until he left town.

CHAPTER 27

I hadn't realized how nervous I was about Isobel's surgery until I woke up on Monday so early stars still blanketed the sky. I texted August, hoping he'd silenced his phone while he slept. I'd feel awful about waking him up.

ME: *Can you text me once the surgery's over so I can come and visit?*

His answer came barely a minute later. *Yes.*

ME: *Did I wake you?*

AUGUST: *No.*

From the time Mom was diagnosed till the very end, I hadn't slept through the night. I was about to ask him how he was feeling, if I could do anything, when a new text appeared on my screen.

AUGUST: *Sorry I haven't come by this week. It's been insanely busy at work. How are you and Jeb holding up?*

ME: *We're good. Don't worry about us. Besides, been busy here too. Almost everyone in the pack has dropped by.*

AUGUST: *Hope they've been bringing you good coffee.*

I bit my lip. I couldn't tell what the tone of his message was supposed to be: humorous or bitter?

ME: *No coffee. But I have enough confections to open a bakery.*

AUGUST:

Okay, so maybe August wasn't bitter. Maybe he truly was concerned about the quality of our coffee.

ME: *I should probably look into the bakery idea. I need a job. Ugh. Sorry to bore you with this.*

Dot dot dots bounced on my screen.

AUGUST: *We could use some help around the warehouse. Mom was taking care of the accounting, but she won't be doing that for a while. And Dad's planning on taking some time off to be with her.*

I read and reread his message, strange emotions eddying through me. I needed to say no. Being around August was not a good idea. But, hell, I really wanted to say yes. The business had been my father's, so I knew what it entailed. Although, considering the expansion, what the Watts did now probably differed from what Dad used to do.

AUGUST: *It would come with good pay of course. Anyway, think about it.*

It brought me back to one of our first conversations after my return to Boulder. He'd asked me if I wanted a job.

ME: *If I say yes, but I'm completely incompetent, do you promise not to keep me on because of guilt or pity?*

AUGUST: *Where did that come from?*

ME: *Just swear it to me.*

AUGUST: *OK. I swear it.*

It wouldn't have to be weird. It's not like we'd be working side by side. From what I'd understood, August was usually on the building sites.

AUGUST: *Why are YOU up so early?*

I looked out at the glittery expanse peeking behind my drawn curtains.

ME: *Just worried.*

AUGUST: *Everything's going to be fine.*

I sighed, wishing I could be so optimistic, but life had thrown me one too many curveballs. Still, I texted: *I know.* There was no point in infecting others with my skepticism.

AUGUST: *Get dressed.*

ME: *Why?*

AUGUST: *Because I can sense your stress all the way through the phone.*

AUGUST: *And wear comfortable shoes.*

I sat up in bed, fully awake now. After I washed my face and brushed my teeth, I tugged on black leggings, a black hoodie, and my sneakers, then went out to the kitchen and wrote Jeb a note in case he woke up and noticed my bed was empty. As I placed the paper on the dining table, I hesitated to text August that he didn't have to take care of me when he should be taking care of his mom, but a message popped onto my screen.

AUGUST: *I'm downstairs.*

I tied my hair up into a quick ponytail, grabbed my phone and keys, and left quietly so as not to wake up my uncle.

August looked pale, which was a feat considering his mixed origins. Then again, it could've been the effect of the light bouncing off his dashboard.

He smiled at me, but it didn't reach his eyes. "I think we're the two only people up in the whole of Boulder."

It was 4:30. My street was completely deserted, and every window we drove by was dark.

"Where are we going?" I asked as I strapped myself in.

"You'll see."

I wasn't the sort of person who liked to *see*, but I trusted August. As we drove, I played with the music, swapping his preferred jazz station with something a little more upbeat. And then I closed my eyes to rest them and drummed my fingers to the tempo of the music.

Up and up the mountain road we went. Finally, he pulled to a stop, grabbed a pack from the backseat, slung it over his shoulder, and we got out. We walked down a wooded trail that led to the sharp ridges of the Flatirons. The sight transported me back to the first trial, but I didn't tell August. Not even when some pebbles came loose under my feet and adrenaline spiked through my veins. I drove back my fear of the mountain raining down on me. The rockslide had been manmade—or rather *elder*made—just another part of the trials.

We came to a stop a couple yards from the lip of the steep cliff. I didn't have vertigo, but still, I didn't look down.

"You okay?" he asked as he unzipped his backpack.

"Yeah. Great."

He kept his gaze locked on mine as he tugged a blanket out of his pack, as though he didn't quite believe me. Could he sense my nerves through the link? He shook out the blanket and spread it onto the moon-bleached rock. "Want to tell me about it?"

I didn't, but at the same time I didn't want him to pin my nervousness on anything else. So I reminded him about the race, about the landslide. His entire body stiffened. He reached down and picked up the blanket, but I stepped on it.

"August, it's fine. I promise. Besides, like Mom used to say, best way to chase away a bad memory is to make a new one."

When he still hadn't let go of the blanket, I pried the edge out of his clenched fingers and let it flutter back to the stone floor. And then I sat, gathering my knees against me.

"I bet the sunrise is spectacular from here," I said, looking out at the ultraviolet darkness that stretched around us.

It took a while for August to shake off the tension in his body, but finally, he sat beside me. "Best in Boulder." He took a thermos out of his pack. "Here." When I raised an eyebrow, he said, "Coffee."

I twisted the top open, then took a sip of the scalding, bitter beverage before handing it back. "I didn't even think about bringing water. If I wasn't a shifter, and I was lost in the wilderness, I'd probably not make it out alive." I tucked my chin onto my knees. "You know, that show, *Naked and Afraid*?" I'd been watching a lot of TV recently. "They'd probably give me a survival rating of one-point-two."

August chuckled softly. "That's very specific. And incorrect, I'm sure."

"Maybe I should sign us up."

He glanced at me from the corner of his eye. "Don't we spend enough time *naked* and *afraid* as werewolves?"

"In my case, yes, but what are you afraid of?"

He passed me the thermos, gaze cast on the sky. "Helicopters."

"Helicopters? That's specific. Why helicopters?"

"Because I crashed in one."

My heart soared so high I felt it inside my throat. "When?"

"Three years ago." The darkness around us increased the shadows populating his face. "It's the reason I came back to Boulder."

I waited, not wanting to press him, but the stretch of time between that last sentence and the next lasted an eternity.

"My buddy was piloting it. I was in the backseat with two other guys from my squad when we caught enemy fire. One of them had been telling me how he planned on proposing to his girlfriend . . . " He stopped talking, and his lids came down hard. "Anyway, I made it. None of the others did. One of the medics kept saying how lucky I was. It made me so angry because how the hell was I the lucky one? I saw all of them die, Ness. All of them." He finally opened his eyes. They glinted. "And now I'm the one stuck with the memory every damn day."

I tightened my hold on my knees. I wanted to reach out to him, but then I remembered when Dad had been shot, how I'd hated the mere brush of a hand. Or the litany of *sorrys*. The only person I'd wanted to be around had been my mother. I'd even pushed August and Isobel away.

"You know what I thought when I was lying in that hospital bed?" He finally looked at me. "I thought about you. Of how brave you'd been at only eleven. I was in my twenties, and a freaking mess. It took me almost a year to stop having nightmares."

"I wasn't brave, August. I just shut myself off. I'm not even sure I've ever really turned myself back on. Not fully. A part of me died right alongside my father."

He blinked, but no tears slid out of his shiny eyes.

"How did you stomach enlisting again?" I asked after a long while.

"I thought it would help me get over what had happened." He grabbed the thermos of coffee and took a long swallow.

"Did it?"

He gave me a tight smile. "Nope. Just reminded me how much I hate helicopters."

I smiled, even though my heart bled. "You'd think that being magical creatures would give us the upper hand on death." I raised my face toward the absent moon. Although it hadn't birthed were-wolves, the traction of Earth's satellite influenced our magic. "Do you still want to go back into the military?"

He sighed. "I'm not sure what I want anymore."

A strange warmth pooled inside my stomach. Relief that he might not leave?

"But I might have to." He grabbed a loose rock and flung it through the quiet air as though he were trying to skip it on the sky.

My kneecaps dug into my cheek. "Why?"

He side-eyed me. "To make things . . . *easier*."

My heart sped up.

And up . . .

"On who?" I asked so softly I wasn't sure my words would carry to his ears.

"On both of us."

"Because of the link?"

Nodding, he rolled onto his back, cushioning his head with his palms. I glanced at him over my shoulder, hoping he couldn't feel all I was feeling, but I sensed he could. Hopefully, he'd chalk it up to the stress of the coming day.

"This is your home, August. You shouldn't have to leave it because of me."

His thick eyebrows slanted over his green eyes.

"Instead of going to UCB, I could attend college in some other state. I hear New England's nice."

Would the pack pay for a school that wasn't in Boulder, or did they only foot the bill when their wolves stayed on pack territory?

I gripped the thermos of coffee and tipped it up to my lips, then set it on the blanket and lay down next to August.

He hadn't opposed my decision to go to some faraway college, and my navel wasn't pulsing with any repressed emotion on his part. Whatever I was feeling for him was one-sided.

Could he sense *my* disappointment? I hoped not.

I balled my fingers into fists, then flexed them back out, damning Matt for planting ideas inside my head and damning myself for letting them take root.

CHAPTER 28

Isobel's surgery went smoothly, so I got to see her that very afternoon.

Although she was hooked to an EKG machine, and there were drainage tubes sticking out from underneath her powder-blue hospital gown, she was smiling and sported a way better complexion than I did. I kissed her forehead, nose prickling from the strong odor of antiseptic and infected blood, then sat in the chair August had occupied but freed up for me.

We talked about everything and nothing: the weather, college, doctors, even her work which I was supposed to take over the following day. Greg stopped by to see her at some point. Although the pack doctor hadn't been the one to operate on her, he'd been the one to choose the surgeon. Isobel laughed at something he told her, something I didn't catch because of who'd just walked into the room.

As our gazes collided, the room and all of the noise—the steady beeping of the heart monitor, Isobel's tinkling laughter, August and Nelson's quiet conversation—it all faded out for a moment. It had been eleven days since I'd seen Liam, but it felt like a month.

I jerked my gaze down to my lap, and then I jerked to my feet. "I'm going to grab something to eat from the cafeteria. Does anyone want anything?"

I was still looking at my feet when everyone answered *no*.

I walked around Isobel's bed and passed by Liam, sensing him everywhere. It was as though his *alpha-ness* had grown. Was that possible?

In the hospital hallway, I took a deep breath. The myriad of chemical smells and human diseases made my nose itch and my eyes water. Blinking repeatedly, I plucked a tissue from the box on the nurse's station to dab at the moisture.

The cafeteria was full of visitors, and the hubbub made my head throb. I needed sleep. A lot of it. Hopefully I wouldn't wake at the crack of dawn tomorrow morning. I bought an overpriced ham sandwich before returning to the wing where Isobel would spend the next two nights. As I ate my sandwich, a chill swept over my arms, and not from any AC vent; I sensed a presence. An unwelcome one. Through narrowed eyes, I took in every inch of the hallway, coming to a stop on a closed door. I strode over to it and squinted through the inset glass. The room was dark. I listened for a sound—a breath, a pulse— but was met with silence. Yet my uneasiness grew. I inhaled deeply, and layered over the unpleasant reek of the medical facility was a cloying, distinctive cologne: *Aidan Michaels's.*

I turned the doorknob and barged inside, hoping the reason I smelled him but didn't see him was because he lay dead in his hospital bed. No such luck. The bed was made with crisp, papery sheets, the adjustable overbed table wiped clean, and the blinds shut.

This must've been the room he'd recovered in.

As I turned to leave, I smacked into a large body. Heart battering, I lurched backward and flung my gaze up. Liam stared down at me, jaw set, eyes dark.

I clapped a palm over my frantic heart. "You just gave me a heart attack."

His expression softened the teeniest bit. "Good thing we're in a hospital then."

For a moment, neither of us spoke.

Then, Liam asked, "How have you been?" at the same time as I asked, "Did you find the owner of the yellow car?"

Liam pressed his lips together. "Straight to business."

He was right. That wasn't very nice. "I've been okay. And you?" The intensity with which he observed me dampened my palms. I wiped them on my leggings.

"I've been better."

Silence stretched between us.

"Cole matched it to a yellow Hummer. He saw the car on a traffic light monitor."

Cole had hacked into the city's traffic monitoring system?

Why was I surprised?

"Colorado license plates. CRK-590. Creek-owned, as I'm sure you got from the letters." He sighed. "No apology will undo how quick I was to blame you, but I'll say it again anyway." He took a step toward me. "I'll say it as many times as it takes for you to forgive me." He tilted his face down and dropped his voice to a murmur. "I. Am. Sorry."

And then he said it again through the mind link.

And again.

And with each apology, he moved closer to me, chipping at the defensive wall I'd erected around myself. He must've sensed he was getting through to me, because he didn't stop advancing until we were standing toe to toe.

I raised my hand and pressed my palm into his black T-shirt. "Stop."

I wasn't sure if he would, but he did.

He stopped.

Stopped speaking.

Stopped moving.

My hand tingled with his strong heartbeats, and my forehead prickled from his warm breaths. I lowered my gaze to his chin, smooth from a fresh shave.

His lips moved to form my name.

A slow burn traveled through my blood, concentrated in my navel, ignited there.

"I need you," he whispered.

"Don't say that. Please, don't say that."

My words had the adverse effect on him.

It untied his tongue, made him speak all the reasons he needed me—that I lent him strength, that I calmed him, that I made his life sweeter, brighter, better.

"Give me another chance, babe. Give *us* another chance. I won't screw it up this time. I understand what I stand to lose." His chocolate eyes glowed in the lines of sun spilling through the blinds. *I swear it on the pack.*

I hated his entire declaration, not because it was too little too late, but because it was too much too soon. "Don't swear on the pack," I whispered.

"On my life then. I swear it on my life."

Shaking my head, I let my palm drift off his T-shirt, off his heart. My eyes stung.

From Aidan's scent.

From Liam's.

"Liam, I can't."

For a moment, his expression shuttered up, turned into his firm Alpha mask, but a flush had risen to my cheeks. A chink in my armor. Even though he didn't lay a single finger on my body, his gaze traced the contours of my face. His earlier remorse and tentativeness were gone, replaced by something that all at once sharpened and softened all of his features.

Hope.

Even though I realized my grudge had faded, I also realized that giving Liam hope was unfair.

"Not now, Liam. Not until my mind and body clear of the mating link." Even though I appeared collected on the outside, chaos reigned inside of me. I was a mess of jumbled emotions and peculiar thoughts.

"I'll wait." He gave me a look that was so bruisingly ardent my heart fired like a rifle. "The same way your . . . "

His voice dimmed as I noticed the hulking figure darkening the open doorway. My stomach contracted. How long had August been standing there?

Liam exploited my moment of inattention to touch me. His fingers were suddenly on my face, pushing a lock of hair off my forehead.

I pranced backward.

He unhurriedly returned his hand to his side, seemingly unshaken by my reaction.

"What did you just say? The same way my what?" I repeated tersely.

"The same way your father waited for your mother."

"My father?" I frowned. "I don't understand." I glanced over his shoulder again, but the doorway was empty.

"Remember how I told you mates didn't always end up together the night of the pledging ceremony?"

Ice filled my veins. "My father had a mate?"

"No. *My* father had one."

What did Heath having a mate have to do with my father—

Oh . . .

Oh.

My hand climbed up to my mouth. "My mom was your dad's mate?"

He didn't nod. Didn't speak. Just looked at what his revelation was doing to me. At the thoughts detonating inside my skull.

My mother had been intended for Liam's father, not for my own.

Yet she'd picked my father.

She'd loved him, not her mate.

"It created quite the stir back in the day," Liam said, walking over to the bed to sit on it. The stiff mattress creased under him. "Your mom was sixteen and had already been dating your father for three years. And my father . . . Well, he wasn't looking to settle. But the mating link made tensions rise. I don't know the full story. Just bits and pieces. My father was an angry drunk, but a voluble one." Liam rubbed his hands up and down his thighs. "A month or two into the link, he decided he did want to be with your mother, so he tried to woo her away from your dad. But, Maggie, she was in love with your father." He studied one of the lines of sunshine that slashed the squeaky clean linoleum floor. "So you see, I don't put much stock in mating links, Ness."

He raised his gaze back to my face. Although I was no longer clasping my mouth, it still gaped. I wasn't sure whether it would ever close again.

My mother and Heath?

I shivered.

"Maybe the moon, or the wolf God, or whatever's up there"—he gestured noncommittally to the ceiling—"opens connections between people, but in the end, those people are still masters of their own destinies. Of their own hearts."

Dust motes spangled the air between us, coming in and out of focus.

Liam didn't speak for a long moment as though understanding that I needed time and silence to process this.

"You and August have history. And unlike my father, August is a good guy, so I understand if you're confused about how you feel about him—"

The chill that had enveloped my body was replaced by lava-hot heat. I palmed the back of my neck, hoping my cool hand would drive the heat back down.

"—but don't forget how you felt about me before he came into the picture."

How the hell did he know I felt conflicted about August?

Was it obvious?

I didn't want to have this conversation with Liam, the same way I hadn't wanted to have it with Matt.

Matt!

He must've talked to Liam. Shared our weird conversation.

I couldn't handle this right now. I blinked out of my daze and started toward the door, my strides hurried.

"And, Ness?" Liam called out.

I didn't stop. I just kept walking. I didn't want to hear anymore. I couldn't take anymore.

But his voice trailed after me, clanking inside my mind: **Remember that how you *felt* about me had nothing to do with magic.**

I clamped my hands over my ears—not that it could keep his voice out—and sped up, exiting the hospital.

THAT NIGHT, OVER DINNER, I ASKED JEB ABOUT WHAT LIAM HAD told me, because I'd begun to have doubts. Doubts that Liam had planted this story inside my mind to redirect me toward him. He knew how deeply I'd admired my parents' love, how deeply I wanted what they had.

Jeb raked his hand through his thinning hair. "How did you find out?"

"Liam told me."

I prodded the shrimp on my plate with the tines of my fork, just pushing it from one side to the other.

"It's true."

I whipped my gaze off the shrimp.

"Should've seen your father . . . " He got this faraway glint in his eyes. "Callum was terrified he would lose her, terrified she'd pick Heath, but Maggie never even spared Heath a glance. Your father was her first love. Her only one."

He inhaled a rickety breath and rocked onto his feet, gathering our plates without asking if I was done. He took them to the sink, scraped the rice and crustacean remnants into the bin, then hand washed both plates thoroughly.

"True love is rare, Ness. But Maggie and Callum, they had it," he added, wiping his hands on a towel.

"Did you have it too? With Lucy. Before . . . *everything*."

"I thought I did. Perhaps I did." He folded the towel, then refolded it. "To be honest, I don't know anymore." He set the plates on the drying rack before scrubbing down the sink and countertop.

My uncle was a surprisingly neat person. I wasn't sure why I'd assumed otherwise. Because he'd had a staff of cleaners?

Speaking of . . . "What's happening with the inn?"

Without removing his attention from the countertop, he said, "I'm trying to break the deal Everest—" His voice caught on his son's name. He swallowed, which made his Adam's apple joggle in his scruffy throat. "I'm trying to break the deal he struck with Aidan, trying to prove he wasn't in his right mind when he struck it. What with Becca's death . . . "

I hadn't thought of Becca in a long time. Was Everest with her now? Did people find each other again in the afterlife? *Was* there an afterlife? I scraped off a congealed splash of coconut-curry sauce from the dining table with my fingernail.

"My lawyer believes I have a real chance at dismantling the deal, but he warns me it might get pricey and could take a long time. He also warned me that he got a visit from a colleague yesterday who advised him to back off."

I felt my lids pull up real high. "He was threatened?"

"You're surprised? We *are* talking about Aidan Michaels, a man who shot his own wife."

My eyes widened further. Jeb knew about Evelyn? Had she told him or had Frank?

"Are you going to pursue it?" I asked.

"I built this inn on a parcel that's been in the family for generations. You can bet I'm going to fight for it." His tone made me jump. "Michaels has taken enough from this family, don't you think?"

I nodded. "I know Everest was probably killed by the Creeks, but do you think Aidan had a hand in it?"

"He owns a hotel on Creek territory. Is it so farfetched to think they owed him a favor, and he collected on it?"

No, it wasn't. It *absolutely* wasn't.

"Have you told Liam about your theory?" I asked, stretching my arms over my head and yawning.

"Yes. And he's looking into it."

I wondered if Liam had found out anything. Wouldn't he have called a pack gathering if he had, though?

That night, I dreamed of Liam. But suddenly, Liam morphed into another man.

One who looked so much like him.

Heath.

I woke up with a scream that had Jeb crashing through my bedroom door.

"Sorry," I rasped, trembling all over. "Just a nightmare."

Jeb's eyes, which had started glowing like his wolf's, dimmed. "Got plenty of those myself." He turned to go but paused. "Want to talk about it?"

I tucked my frigid hands under the pillow. "No."

I hadn't spoken about the night I'd posed as an escort to get access to Heath with anyone but Everest. I'd hoped that not speaking about it would somehow erase the memory, but it had simply repressed it.

"Wake me if you change your mind."

I closed my eyes, willing the nightmare to vanish when the sheets rustled. Jeb pulled the comforter over my shoulders and tucked it around me. And then he placed a palm on the top of my head.

"I hope better dreams find you. You deserve better dreams. You deserve better everything." His eyes shone like freshly buffed bone.

Once he left, I watched the wall that divided our bedrooms for a long time, finally understanding why my mother had listed him as the emergency contact on my school forms. She'd known that if I ever needed saving, he would come through for me.

CHAPTER 29

I was supposed to start at the Watts' the following day, but August texted me that it would be better if I began once his mother was released from the hospital. He'd have more time to show me the ropes.

So another day passed before I drove myself to my new job.

Jeb sat in the passenger seat. Where Sarah liked to tell me every little thing I could do better—she was annoying but thorough—he offered advice sparingly. Mostly he complimented my driving, which felt incredibly empowering, and then he told me Greg would come over that evening to give me an eye exam.

"Greg's an ophthalmologist?" I asked, sliding to a stop in front of the Watts' warehouse.

"No. But our eyes . . . our *eyesight* . . . it's not quite the same as humans."

My mouth rounded. And here I'd been ready to book an appointment with any old eye doctor. Good thing I hadn't.

Jeb got out of the Boulder Inn van and walked around the bumper. I took off my seatbelt and hopped out. As he took the seat I'd just vacated, he said, "You know, I could give you an allowance."

"And you know I would never accept it."

"Just as stubborn as Maggie."

Proud, not stubborn, although I would take any comparison to my mother.

"Call me when you're done," he said. "I'll come pick you up."

"Jeb?"

Although he clutched the handle, he didn't swing the car door shut. "Yes?"

"I'm happy I forgot to collect my high school diploma."

His forehead grooved, but then it smoothed, not entirely but a little; too much grief left indelible traces. "I'm happy you forgot too."

We smiled at each other a moment, then he tipped his head to the warehouse. "Scram, kiddo. You don't want to be late on your first day."

I backed away from the van and strode toward the warehouse. The second I set foot inside, memories of the last trial came pouring down over me. It was as though the semi-circle of men glaring down at me, the girl who'd challenged their boy, was still here. I looked away from the sawdust-covered floor and scanned the brightly lit space with its aisles upon aisles of tall metal shelving and its enormous worktables upon which carpenters were measuring slabs of wood or sanding them down.

I felt like a kid again, visiting my father at work. August would pick me up from school, then, after a pitstop at the ice cream parlor, he'd drive me over here. I wondered if the ice cream was as good as I remembered.

"Ness." A gravelly voice jerked my mind off the past.

August was standing by one of the aisles, an electronic tablet clutched beneath his arm. I walked over to him, garnering quite a few curious gazes from the employees.

"How's your mother?" I asked, tucking strands of loose hair behind my ears.

"Already on her feet when she shouldn't be." There was a startling gruffness to his tone, as though he was angry with his mother. "Let's get you set up in the office." He strode toward the glass enclosure at the back of the building without uttering a single word to me.

Once we reached the deserted office, I hooked my bag to the peg by the door.

"Dad jotted down some adjustments a client of ours requested. I need you to pull up the quote we gave that client, check what we're taking out, type in what we're adding, then look through our list of

suppliers, call them up, and find us the best and timeliest deals."
August handed me a stapled printout, turned on the office computer,
and pulled up a file that listed all the amendments that were to be
made.

I took my seat on the wheelie chair. "Do I factor in any commis-
sions to the prices I obtain?"

"No. We charge a rate on the overall project." He stared at the
huge beige printer in the corner as though it had wronged him.

"Are you okay?"

His green eyes flashed to mine, then to the computer keypad.
"Just tired," he said before returning to the door. With an almost
clinical detachment, he added, "Once you're done updating the
quote, email it to me. August@Watt.com."

And then he was gone, and I didn't see him the rest of the day.
But I did get an email from him with more things to do. Working
kept me busy and kept me from thinking about his crabbiness. The
warehouse grew silent as the hours ticked by, as I double-checked
spreadsheet after spreadsheet to make sure the money received corre-
sponded to the money owed.

I'd always liked numbers, so the job August had saddled me with
didn't feel like work at all. I'd even have called it fun, albeit a tad
disheartening. Disheartening because my access to the company's
finances showed me how it had thrived. Would my father have
managed to turn his carpentry business into the hundred million
dollar construction company it had become?

A knock snapped my gaze off the computer monitor.

"August told me to close the place down for the night," said a man
with an enlarged nose, teeming with burst blood vessels, and cheeks
that were slightly purple. He had a smear of wood stain across his
temple and a couple more on the top of his denim overalls.

"Oh. Okay." I saved the document before shutting down the
computer and grabbing my bag. As we walked through the deserted
warehouse, I sensed the man glancing my way repeatedly.

When I caught him at it, he reddened all over and said, "You look
exactly like your mom, but with Callum's dimples."

I blinked at him, sifting through my memories to place him.

He hooked his thumbs under the straps of his overalls. "Tom. I'm Tom."

"*Uncle Tom?*" I said so excitedly that he shot me a toothy grin.

The nickname had been given to him by my father who'd considered him family. Especially after Tom lost his wife, daughter, son-in-law, and grandkid one blustery Christmas Eve. He'd been behind the wheel when he hit a patch of black ice. The car ended up wrapped around a tree.

"I can't believe you still work here," I said.

He grimaced. "I'm old, I know."

"Oh, that wasn't why I said that!" *Aw, crap.* Now I felt awful. I hooked my bag higher up my shoulder. "I'm just surprised to see a familiar face, that's all."

His grimace finally receded. "The Watts are good people."

I smiled at him. "They are."

"How long—" He darted a glance at his scuffed work boots before looking at me from underneath stubby blond lashes. "How long will you be helping out? Rest of the summer? Or just until Isobel gets better?"

"That's not up to me."

He held the door of the warehouse open for me to step through. As he shut the heavy door, he asked, "Still carving little figurines?"

"No." I lifted my eyes to the star-strewn immensity over our head. "Haven't had a chance to do that in a long time." My father had taught me, but I wasn't ever good at it—not like August. Everything he carved looked so lifelike.

"I still have the wolf you made me," Tom said.

I lowered my gaze back to him. "You do?" Emotion robbed my voice of volume.

"On my fireplace mantle."

The high beams of a car turning into the lot momentarily blinded me. I hadn't called Jeb yet, so it couldn't be the van. Once my eyes adjusted to the darkness again, I noticed the make—a pickup.

"I'll see you in the morning, Ness." On his way to his parked car, he stopped to greet August.

I slid my cell phone out of my bag and texted Jeb that I was done, then watched August stride over, trying to gauge his current mood through the tether. *Tense.* He was tense.

He checked the lot. "How are you getting home?"

"Jeb's coming to pick me up." When he frowned, I added, "I only have a permit, remember?"

"Right." He looked over my shoulder at the warehouse wall. "I can give you a lift."

"I'm sure he's on his way already." I pulled my bag strap over my head so the leather cut across my chest instead of digging into my shoulder. "You still have a lot of work tonight?"

"No. I'm done for the day."

"Then why are you here?"

"I live here."

"In the warehouse?"

"No." He nodded toward a small building adjacent to it. "It's temporary. I bought a plot of land on the north side of that lake we swam in but haven't had time to develop anything."

"Can I see it?"

"What? The plot?"

"No. Your current lodging."

He rubbed his jaw, as though my request necessitated profound consideration.

"Forget it," I mumbled, a little hurt. What exactly did he think I would do? Trash his place or make disparaging comments about the decor?

He peered at the still-empty road before walking in the direction of his house.

Okay, just walk away from me. That's not weird at all.

He stopped and turned a little. "Are you coming?"

"No."

"But I thought you—" He turned completely this time, shoulders straining his gray T-shirt. A galaxy of stains speckled the cotton: glue smears, white paint, grease stains. "Why not?"

I felt both my eyebrows slant on my forehead. "You clearly didn't want to show it to me, August."

He loosed an exasperated sigh. "Ness . . . "

I tapped on my phone to seem busy. He grumbled something.

Because I couldn't leave well enough alone, I flung my gaze back onto him. "Did I do something?"

His jaw ticked. "I don't know. Did you?" His voice was so low that I wondered if I heard him correctly.

"You *are* mad at me!"

He just stood there, brooding and silent, cloaked in darkness, *oozing* darkness. He'd been mad at me before I came in to work, so whatever I'd *done* happened before today. But the last time we'd seen each other was at the hospital and—*Oh* . . .

Heat coursed through me as quick as the current in the Colorado River during snowmelt. Was August Watt jealous?

"Liam asked me when I was leaving," he finally said. "I'll get out of this goddamn place when I'm ready, not when someone tells me to, understood?"

My mouth fell open. *Not jealousy.*

My navel pulsed as though August's anger had somehow yanked on the tether between us. And then my heart began to pulsate in time with it. As fast as it had flooded me, the strange heat receded. I was mortified to have believed him jealous.

The darkness beyond August suddenly turned brighter, noisier. A van sped down the road, kicking up a pale cloud of dust. I kept my gaze locked on the approaching car because if I looked at August, I would either yell at him for thinking I was somehow complicit in trying to get him to leave Boulder, or I would start crying. I wasn't sure which was worse.

As I stalked toward the van, I tossed out over my shoulder, "I'll tell him to stop harassing you."

Had August concluded that Liam and I were a couple again after seeing us together in the hospital room or had Liam implied something?

As I took a seat next to Jeb and answered his questions about how my day had gone, I typed out a lengthy diatribe to Liam. In the end, I deleted all of it, sensing our Alpha would take it out on August.

So I simply sent: *I forgot to ask, do pack tuition loans extend to out-of-state colleges?*

Liam's answer came an hour later, while I was having dinner. *Why?*

ME: *Because I'm thinking of applying elsewhere.*

He called me then. Not sure I'd be able to control my tone, I declined the incoming call and texted: *Can't talk right now. But I can text.*

A couple seconds later, he sent me: *Your application's already being processed. You should be getting the welcome packet soon. And no, pack money and influence are only good on pack territory. We need to keep our wolves close.*

Then why are you trying to send August away?

I felt I knew the answer to that.

The doorbell rang then. I inhaled long and hard, expecting Liam's scent to hit me, but the smell was a mixture of antibacterial soap and ground coffee. Definitely not Liam's, unless he'd changed his soap to the hospital-grade kind and was jacked up on caffeine.

"That must be Greg," Jeb said, going to open the door.

Exhaling a relieved breath, I set my phone face down on the couch and stood up to get my eyes examined by the pack doctor, praying he wouldn't spot all the anger that brewed beneath my irises.

CHAPTER 30

The following day, Liam stopped by the warehouse to see me, seemingly none too happy that I hadn't picked up the two calls he'd made after his last text went unanswered.

When he strode into the office, I kept my gaze fastened to the computer monitor. I felt him at my back though, felt his body thrum and his scent invade the entire room.

"Why didn't you answer any of my calls?" he exclaimed.

"Because I was mad at you." I still didn't look at him even though he'd moved to stand in front of the desk.

"I got that. But why are you mad at me? What did I do now, Ness?"

I clicked on the keyboard, then moved the cursor to the next tab.

"Goddammit, don't ice me out."

I finally leaned back in the chair, crossed my arms over my chest, and stared up into Liam's narrowed eyes. "Did you ask August to leave town again?"

His pupils pulsed and pulsed, and then his eyes turned yellow as though his wolf was about to leap to the surface.

Finally, he shook his head. "I asked him *if* he was planning on leaving soon. I didn't ask him to leave. Excuse me for wanting to know what my wolves plan to do with their lives! Especially when so much is fucking happening around Boulder. Did you hear that some

Creeks pissed all over Julian's fucking hedges? Same wolves Lucas smelled around my house."

I blinked frenziedly, feeling suddenly petty for believing this had been about an amorous tryst.

"So no, I wasn't chasing your mate out of Boulder. I was trying to figure out if we could count on him if more Creeks arrived." Liam growled all of this, and his growl intensified the scudding of my heart.

"I'm—I'm sorry, Liam. I just assumed." I shivered, feeling as though someone had spun the AC to its lowest setting.

Liam didn't storm out like I was expecting him to. He just stood there, jaw clenching and unclenching, making me feel even more foolish.

I dropped my arms onto the armrests, then pushed myself up and walked toward him, laying a hand on his forearm, hoping he'd construe my gesture as a ceasefire. "What can I do to help?"

"We don't need your help," he bit out.

My hand slipped off his arm and landed on my waist. "But you need August's? You're not actually planning on making me watch from the sidelines, are you?"

"It could get dangerous." He rubbed his twitchy jaw.

"I'm not afraid."

He snorted. "You might not be, but I am."

Did he mean for me or for the pack?

"We have no clue what they're thinking, and their Alpha can't be bothered to pick up the damn phone. Robbie's dying to go to Beaver Creek to meet her, but Julian says to stay put. Like me, he's afraid it's a ploy to lure some of us to them." He stopped rubbing his face, but the hard lines of his posture didn't slacken, which told me he was still pissed. At me or at the Creeks?

"Maybe it *is* worth sending some of us to meet her."

His Adam's apple jerked in his throat. "Some of *us*? I hope you're not planning on volunteering, because my answer would be no."

"Why?" I exclaimed.

"Because you don't know the first thing about Creeks or diplomatic visits between packs."

"Then teach me."

"It can't be taught."

"Bullshit! Everything can be taught."

"I'm not sending you out there. I'm not sending any of my wolves out there. The Creeks want to talk, they come here. We are stronger on our turf than we are on theirs."

Slowly my hand slid off my waist and found purchase on the desk beside me. "What if they all come? All one thousand of them?"

"They wouldn't leave their territory unguarded."

"Even if half their pack came, they would grossly outnumber us."

"It's not always about numbers. They have many children and fe—" He stopped talking so suddenly that I sucked in a breath.

"I hope you weren't about to say females."

His pupils shrank before spreading back out.

I shook my head.

"Physically, Ness, we aren't the same, just like a child isn't built like an adult."

I fastened my gaze to the floorboards, glaring hard at the spaces between the planks.

I felt a finger crook my face up. I twisted free of Liam and stepped back. "Remind me how the Creek Alpha rose to power? Because the story I heard was that she defeated the Aspen Alpha in a duel."

"She was already an Alpha. Alphas are stronger. If she hadn't been—"

"Please just stop talking. It's making me unhappy."

"Look, I'm all for empowering females, but I'm not going to spout lies about corporeal equality when the hard facts are that we aren't built alike. How many firemen are women? They're even called fire*men*."

"No, they're called fire*fighters*."

He let out a molar-grinding growl and tossed his hands in the air. "*Ugh.* I can't win with you. I can never win!"

I crossed my arms. "Funny how illogical that is when you keep saying I have no chance of beating you."

His nostrils pulsed, and his fingers wrapped into fists. "Ness Clark, you fucking drive me crazy." And then he all but lunged toward me and cupped the back of my head, tilting my face up. "I must be one hell of a masochist for being turned on right now." His murmur skated over my lips, heightening the frantic pulse of my heart. "And just so we're clear, I don't find *you* inferior. You're too smart, persistent, and distractingly beautiful to be inferior. But that's how you'd win a battle. You might punch hard and at the right place, but your fists have nothing on"—his gaze fused to mine—"*you*."

When I felt the brush of his lips against mine, I backed away, put the desk between us. "I have work to do, Liam." I watched the door, hoping he'd take the hint and leave. I also watched it because I was afraid of looking at him.

Afraid he'd see how deeply he rattled me.

Damn Liam Kolane. The man was such a hot-tempered beast, everything I disliked about men, and yet, he got under my skin too. He slapped and then soothed the slaps with such care and tenderness.

Without uttering another word, he crossed the office toward the door and left. Unfortunately, his retreat did little to calm my nerves.

And then it got worse when I got an email from August that read: **Please keep your personal life out of the work place.**

I would've punched the monitor, but it would break, and the replacement cost would be taken out of my salary, whatever amount that was. Since I hadn't discussed specifics, I expected minimum wage.

Liam was wrong about me being smart. Smart people didn't find themselves saddled with debt, working for men whom they were physically linked to and infatuated with others who weren't especially kind.

It was time Ness Clark sharpened up and found a way out of her pit of misery. Which led me to send Sarah a message: *Can I come with you to The Den tonight?*

Clubbing wouldn't fix anything, but it would temporarily take my mind off the hole that needed plugging.

Sarah's answer came in the afternoon. *Ness Clark wants to par-tay?*
ME: *Yes.*
SARAH: *Should I be worried?*
ME: *About what?*
SARAH: *About you wanting to go out. You haven't been in the mood to have fun since, well, since the funeral.*

ME: *I'll tell you later.*

SARAH: *Counting on it. I'll be at your place at 8 with a hot dress.*

ME: *What's wrong with my dresses?*

SARAH: *Nothing. I just have the perfect one for you. Ciao.*

I was going clubbing, or at the very least I was going to sit in a DJ booth and watch people have fun and hope it would rub off on me.

When was the last time I'd had fun?

The music festival? Nah. Everest had ditched me for this Megan chick, and then Justin Summix had all but called me a whore.

The night I'd run with the pack after the trials? Actually, that night had been more meaningful than fun.

Swimming in the lake with August? His earlier message about not mixing business with pleasure nixed that afternoon, though.

What did he think I was doing in the office anyway? And had he been there, or had one of his employees ratted me out?

I sighed, realizing I hadn't had fun in a very long time.

CHAPTER 31

"Y ou want me to wear *that*? But it's . . . " I dangled the scrap of white fabric in front of me.

"Sexy."

"I was going to say slutty."

"Slutty *is* sexy." Like an impatient child, Sarah was bouncing on my bed, wearing a dress that wasn't much longer or looser than the one she'd brought me. "Besides, I was all out of denim overalls." She stopped bouncing. "Hey, you put me in charge of tonight, so put the damn dress on, Ness Clark."

Sigh-growling, I vanished into my bathroom to change into the white bandage. At least the material was opaque. I fluffed up my hair and twisted from side-to-side, checking my reflection. *Okay.* The dress was sexy and more covering than what I'd initially thought. Not that I would confess this to Sarah.

Sarah whistled when I came out. "Damn, girl. Maybe I should've dug up a pair of overalls. You're going to steal my limelight."

"No one can steal DJ Wolverine's limelight."

She leaped off the bed with the grace of a pole vaulter. "Now shoes—"

"Are we dancing?"

"Yes."

"Then flats. Heels kill me."

Sarah's lips hiked up in protest, but I slid my feet into my white sneakers before she could give me grief about it.

"I'm wearing the dress." I said this as though it were a great concession. Thank goodness I hadn't told her I liked it. I grabbed my bag, making sure I had my phone, keys, and wallet. But then I thought about my ID. "I don't have a fake ID!"

Sarah rolled her eyes so hard I didn't expect them to level back. "I work there, woman. Plus, you've got a killer bod and a *tolerably* attractive face."

I scowled, but I was smiling so my scowl lost a lot of its effect. "Tolerably attractive? Wow . . . *thanks.*"

She smirked. "Oh, come on. You know you're way too hot for your own good."

I dismissed her compliment with a flick of my hand. "Shut up."

"Can we get out of here already? My shift starts in an hour." She swept her mass of blonde curls off her shoulder.

When we walked out of my bedroom, we found Jeb sitting in the living room, watching a fishing show with Derek.

"Ciao, Mr. C.," Sarah called out.

"Bye, Sar—" His eyes all but bounded out of their sockets. "Um. You girls are going out dressed like that?"

I looked down at my dress, partly amused by his reaction and partly worried he might make me change.

"That's what kids wear these days," Derek said before pointing to the screen. "Jeb, check out that monster bass."

Jeb glanced at the TV, but then his gaze returned to us. "What time will you be home?"

"I'll have her back here by one," Sarah said.

"One?" he all but sputtered.

"I'm seventeen, Jeb," I said quietly. Since when was he worried what time I got home? It wasn't as though he'd cared much back when I was living at the inn.

He rubbed his bearded chin. "Okay." He hadn't shaved since Everest's funeral, as though marking the terrible day by the length of his facial hair. "And, Sarah, if you're driving, don't drink. But if you do drink, call me, and I'll pick you girls up."

"We're wolves, Mr. C. Can't die in car crashes."

We could, though.

A flash of pain illuminated Jeb's face.

Sarah winced. "*Shit.* I'm so sorry."

He wrung his fingers together in his lap and studied them. "Just be careful, all right?" he croaked. Before we could leave, he added, "Are any of the boys going to be at The Den tonight?"

"They're *always* there."

Not that we need boys, I wanted to add, but put a lid on that thought. If the presence of males appeased my uncle, then who was I to rattle his peace of mind?

Once we were tucked inside Sarah's Mini, she said, "I really put my foot in my mouth back there."

"It's fine."

She shook her head and sighed. After a beat, she said, "It's sort of sweet how protective he's become of you."

I stabbed my seatbelt into the buckle. "It's sort of weird. He wasn't like this before." I stared at the squares of light in our downstairs neighbor's place, an ancient woman who only ever came out of her house to water the patch of grass and flowers she called a back yard. "It's as though I'm his replacement kid."

"You are. Just like he's your replacement dad. It's not a bad thing to have someone care for you like that."

"I have Evelyn."

"But she's not living with you anymore, is she?"

"That wasn't by choice."

"Hey." She tapped my knuckles. "You have two people who would lay down their lives for yours. That's a shitload more than most people."

I sighed deeply before side-eyeing her. "What you're saying is that you wouldn't lay down your life for me?"

"To salvage my dress, possibly."

I grinned and smacked her upper arm, which was firm with lean muscle. I knew she never hit the gym and ate more than the average human guy, so I imagined she shifted into her wolf form often.

At the thought of shifting, my body thrummed. "Want to run together sometime?"

"I don't own sneakers." She cast a disgruntled look at my feet as though my shoes had somehow wronged her.

I shifted them out of sight. "I meant in wolf form."

"Sure. I'll even slow my pace so you can keep up."

I snorted, even though I didn't doubt she could beat me. After all, she had years of training on me. She slowed at a red light, and a bunch of pedestrians crossed the street. Excitement that it was almost the weekend wafted off most. One girl didn't seem as thrilled as the rest. She kept darting looks around her as though worried someone was following her. I checked the sidewalks but didn't notice any stalker.

As she passed in front of the Mini our eyes locked, and recognition hit me dead-center.

Megan.

Everest's Megan.

I powered my window down and called out her name.

"You know this girl?" Sarah asked me.

Megan quickened her pace.

I unstrapped myself and leaped out just as a motorcycle swerved into the lane next to ours, almost bowling me over.

The biker yelled at me, but I didn't respond. I just took off running after Megan.

"Megan! Wait up!"

She didn't wait up. Instead she *sped* up.

So I did too. She turned a corner. Why wasn't she stopping? When I rounded the corner, I found myself face-to-face with a giant wooden cross.

"Don't come any closer!" she screeched. "Or I'll call the cops."

I backed up, frowning at the wood and the girl beyond it.

"I know what you are!" she yelled.

Obviously she didn't if she thought a wooden cross could keep me away. But I let her think she had me figured out.

"You don't go to UCB," I said, getting to the heart of the matter. "Everest told me you were a student there, but you're not. Why'd you lie about it?"

"I never claimed I was a student at UCB." She pushed her shoulder-length dirty-blonde hair behind her ear, fingers trembling. "Your cousin's a liar."

"*Was.*"

"Huh?"

"He's dead."

The cross came down an inch, then another, as though it suddenly weighed too heavily in her hand.

"Yes, and I'm sorry if I startled you back there."

A car squealed to a stop next to me. And then Sarah flung open her door and stalked toward me. "Ness?"

Megan's knuckles whitened on the wooden cross. "You're that . . . that socialite deejay."

"And you are?" Sarah sniffed the air.

"No one." Megan took a step back. "I'm no one."

Sarah cocked an eyebrow. "What's up with the giant cross?"

Megan didn't answer. She just kept backing away, gaze bouncing from me to Sarah. "I'm sorry for your loss, even though I'm not surprised. Everest was a creep."

"What do you mean?" I asked.

"He tried to recruit me for his escort agency." She made a grimace that contorted her heart-shaped face.

"*His* escort agency?"

"He said I wouldn't have to sleep with anyone, just gather information."

I must not have blinked in a while, because my eyes started to prickle.

She kept backing away. "Was he killed?" Her voice was barely above a whisper. "Wouldn't surprise me if he was."

I couldn't get my mouth to close or open. It just gaped like that striped bass Derek had been ogling.

"Anyway, leave me alone. I was serious about calling the cops." When she reached the end of the street, she spun on her heels and took off running.

"Well, that was weird," Sarah said after a beat.

A car honked so shrilly I jumped.

"Chill out, dude!"

At first I thought Sarah was saying this to me, but she was staring daggers at the driver in the car behind hers.

She grabbed my arm to unglue me from the pavement. "Come on."

The driver honked twice more. Sarah flipped him the finger.

Once inside the car, she drove out of the small street and pulled onto a delivery parking spot. "What the hell was that about?"

I told her everything. Every sordid detail.

"Your cousin was a pimp who used girls to spy? Fuckin' a. No wonder he's dead."

I realized then that perhaps it wasn't the Sillin that had gotten him killed. Perhaps it was the espionage.

"What was he up to?" Sarah asked.

"I don't know, but at least I understand *why* he's dead." Or I assumed I'd come a little closer to understanding.

He must've spied on the wrong Creek.

"But what about the Sillin? How does that fit into the equation?" she asked.

I squeezed my bare knees with my clammy hands. "Maybe it was a security measure. Maybe he needed some to give to the girls he hired." I'd used my own stock on Heath.

"Why would he drug human girls with it?"

"No. He gave it to them to use on the customers." The same way he'd told me to dose Heath's drink.

"So he was spying exclusively on the shifter community?"

Sarah and I stared at each other a long moment. And then she whispered, "Fuck," which pretty much summed up the situation.

"Sarah, I think I need to talk to my Alpha. And I think you need to talk to Julian."

CHAPTER 32

Two cars, besides Liam's black SUV, were parked in front of the sleek cabin: Matt's Dodge silver sedan and a little blue BMW. I was sort of relieved Matt would be here. Even though I'd come to discuss a serious matter, a buffer was welcomed.

As I got out of the Mini, I tugged on the hem of my white dress. "I'm sorry about the way tonight turned out," I told Sarah.

She shook her head. "Babe, I'm just sorry for what that calculating fucker put you through."

I shivered. Ever since my run-in with Megan, I couldn't get my body to warm up.

"You want me to wait for you?" Sarah asked.

"No. I'll be okay."

"Talk tomorrow?"

I nodded, then closed the car door but heard the window power down. "By the way, why the hell did that girl have a wooden cross?"

I smirked. "Because she knew what I was apparently."

"Apparently? Where'd she get her info from? *Twilight?*"

I chuckled. "I guess." But then, as Sarah backed out of Liam's driveway, I stopped laughing. Whatever supernatural she thought I was, she deemed me dangerous. I now had my answer to how the world would react if word got out.

"Ness?"

I whirled around.

Matt was standing by the front door. "What are you doing here?"

Even though the door was only open a crack, a heady beat was pouring out through it.

I circled around the cars. "I need to speak with Liam."

"Um." He palmed his buzzed blond hair. "Yeah. Um." His skin was getting increasingly red. "Why don't you wait out here? I'll go get him."

"You're seriously going to make me wait outside?" I asked, a little peeved.

Okay, *very* peeved.

"I'm chilly. And not in the mood to wait outside." I pressed past him. Or at least, I tried to.

Matt barred my way with his forearm.

"What the hell, Hulk? I don't fucking care if you're having an orgy right now. I need to speak with Liam. This is a pack matter."

I pressed on his big arm. Matt sighed and finally let me through.

They weren't having an orgy. Just a small get-together that seemed very PG.

"Ness!" Amanda squeaked from her spot on the couch next to Sienna. "Hey."

"Hi, Ness." Sienna offered me a wispy smile that flickered off her pale face almost as quickly as it had appeared.

Lucas was here too, as well as two other guys from the pack. One was definitely named Dexter—it was the sort of name that had stuck with me—but I wasn't sure what the other one's name was. Michael, maybe? They were sitting around a table in the corner of the living room, playing a card game. I guessed poker from the stacks of chips.

"Nice dress," Dexter said, leering a little.

I wasn't sure if he was making fun of me or paying me a compliment. I didn't really care, though. "Where's Liam?"

Lucas tipped his chin into his neck and started distributing cards.

No one spoke for so long that I asked, "Did no one hear me?"

Lucas placed the deck on the table, evening it out until no card stuck out. "Matt, why don't you grab Ness a beer from the kitchen? I'll go get Liam."

"I don't want beer. I just want—"

Liam walked out of his bedroom then, buttoning up his shirt, hair tousled as though he'd just taken a nap. When his gaze landed on mine, he froze.

And so did everything and everyone in the room. Even the air seemed to congeal into one thick, unbreathable mass.

Liam shot Matt a look, and something passed between them— probably an order spoken through the mind link. Matt all but leaped toward his Alpha, skirting around him and into the bedroom. He shut the door so fast I guessed Liam had someone in there he didn't want me to see.

I pressed my lips together and swallowed. I had no right to be jealous, and yet . . . and yet I was. Or maybe I was just disappointed by how quickly I'd been replaced, especially after he'd told me he would wait for me.

That I was worth waiting for.

Apparently not.

I swallowed again, but the lump grew larger and more jagged. *Crap.* I closed my eyes and breathed in through my nose. *Crap.* Why did it have to hurt?

I didn't want back in his arms. I didn't want back in his bed.

So why did it have to hurt so damn much?

His voice crashed into my mind: ***It didn't mean anything to me.***

But, to *me*, it did.

It meant that for all my insistence to the contrary, I'd still been hung up on Liam.

I felt a hand cup my shoulder and then I smelled him—mint and musk—but I also smelled her.

Whoever *her* was.

I hoped Matt would keep her inside, because I didn't want to see the girl's face.

"Ness?" This time Liam spoke out loud.

His voice was like wind. It gusted over my skin, making goose bumps rise, making my heart shudder. I stepped back and opened my eyes. I was afraid to speak. Afraid of what my voice would sound like. But I did it anyway.

"I need to—" I was right to be afraid. I sounded like I'd just spent the evening shouting at the top of my lungs. I swallowed again. "I need to talk to you about"—I glanced at the girls sitting on the couch, both of them jiggling their folded legs—"about something I found out tonight."

Liam followed my line of sight. "Hey, Amanda, can you and Sienna go into the kitchen a minute?"

Amanda's lips opened as though she were about to protest, but she must've sensed it wasn't a suggestion. She got up and, towing Sienna, vanished into Liam's kitchen.

"What is it?" he asked, tracing the shape of my face with his dark eyes.

"I ran into Everest's ex-girlfriend." I glanced at Lucas. "That Megan girl."

Lucas's blue eyes flashed in interest.

"She's not a UCB student, and she's not an escort, but Everest apparently tried to recruit her." I crossed my arms over my chest and hugged my torso tight so I would stop trembling. "She claimed *he* ran the agency. Apparently he was using the girls to spy. I think—" I gulped, and my saliva went down like a dulled knife blade. "I think he must've spied on a Creek."

Dexter speared his fingers through his spiky brown hair. "Everest was a pimp?"

Michael—or whatever his name was—placed his cards face down on the table.

"My guess is Everest stole the Sillin to use on the people . . . on the *wolves* he sent the girls to," I said.

Lucas frowned. "Aidan Michaels keeping tabs on us is one thing— he's a shifter-hater. But Everest? He's . . . he *was* one of us."

"I know. Look, I think we should try to locate the woman he was working with." I unknotted my arms to dig through my handbag for my phone. My fingers trembled so hard the slick device almost slipped out. "Uh. I'll forward the Red Creek Escort contact to you."

"You already sent it to me, remember?" Lucas reminded me.

Neither Dexter nor the other shifter asked what I was doing with the number of an escort agency, so I assumed they'd heard.

I supposed all of Boulder had heard.

It didn't matter.

Just like Liam sleeping with another girl didn't matter.

Who was I kidding? It *did* matter. So damn much.

After I'd managed the impossible task of putting away my phone, I told them about Megan's wooden cross. "I know we're not a complete secret around these parts, but I just thought you'd want a head's up."

"Were you alone when this happened?" Dexter asked, gaze running over my legs.

I wished I'd had a pair of tights on. I felt so exposed in this dress.

He winced suddenly, dropping his gaze to the poker chips. Liam was glaring at him. Had the Alpha barked at Dexter through the mind link?

"I was with Sarah Matz. We were on our way to The Den." I yanked on the hem of my dress. "She went to inform Julian about our run-in. Maybe you should call him, Liam."

Liam just stared at me, seemingly lost in thought. Was he thinking about his father? About Everest? About Julian? Or was he thinking about me?

"Um, Lucas, can you give me a ride back to my place? I don't really feel like walking."

"I'll give you a ride home," Dexter offered, already rising.

"I'll take her," Liam snapped.

"No," I said softly but firmly. I couldn't ride in a car with Liam. Not when he still smelled like *her*. Not when I was feeling so emotional. "No."

His Adam's apple joggled in his throat. "Ness, please."

"No. Lucas?" I blinked. My eyes felt so hot, but the rest of me felt cold. It was as though every ounce of heat in my body had converged into my lids.

Chair legs scraped, and then Lucas was next to me. "Let's go."

I nodded and turned away from Liam, trailing Lucas out. I prayed my tears wouldn't tumble out until I got home, but my prayers went unanswered, as my prayers usually did.

"I thought you guys were over," Lucas said after a long beat.

"We are," I whispered raucously. "Still hurts."

He touched my forearm. Briefly, but long enough to make me blink. "It sucks to walk in on someone."

My brow furrowed.

"That's what happened with Taryn. I found her with a Pine." His blue eyes flashed to mine. "Justin Summix of all people."

My mouth rounded, and for a moment, I forgot how deeply my heart ached, because Liam and I, we hadn't even been together when I caught him rolling out of bed. Lucas and Taryn though, they'd been a couple. I'd misjudged him, I realized. I'd thought he'd wronged Taryn.

"I really hate those Pines," Lucas murmured.

I didn't try to argue that they weren't all bad, didn't try to console him either. Silence grew between us, a quiet, easygoing silence that bonded us in our misery.

Once he slid the car in front of my house, I thanked him. He nodded but kept his eyes on the darkened street.

"Just remember it takes half the time you were together to get over a person," he said.

I paused with my fingers on the door. Liam and I, we'd been together for all of four days. If Lucas's logic was accurate, my grieving period should already have been over.

"How long were you with Taryn?"

Gaze sunk on the obscurity, he muttered, "Too long."

My heart went out to him. Which was crazy because I didn't think my heart would ever have gone out to Lucas Mason. Then again, I never thought my cousin was a pimp, or that Liam would lead a girl to his bed so soon after almost kissing me.

On my way up the staircase, keys jingling in my trembling fist, I worked on coming up with a good lie as to the reason I was home early. I hated deceiving my uncle, but I couldn't share what I'd just learned with him. It would shatter what little good memories he had of his son. I palmed away my tears and stepped inside.

CHAPTER 33

The next day, I went to work and pretended everything was great when I felt completely broken on the inside. August and I didn't cross paths at least, so there was that.

I spent Saturday in bed. On Sunday though, Evelyn called and said she was expecting us for brunch. Jeb made me drive to Frank's house, and I did so without a single glitch, even though I hadn't slept well and my eyes felt gummy. I'd believed my heart couldn't possibly shatter more than it already had back at Tracy's, but I'd been wrong. The shards had simply been crushed into finer ones. Just like the vase I'd knocked over in my house one of the first times I'd shifted. The glass had fragmented on our pine floor, and then the pieces had been ground to a powder under my father's boots as he'd tried to corral me into his arms to calm me down.

"I phoned up the DMV and set an appointment for a driving test tomorrow," Jeb said, whipping me out of my thoughts.

"I thought I needed a year before I could pass it?"

"The woman who runs the place, she owed me a favor."

I glanced at Jeb.

He indulged my curiosity. "Her husband was using the inn to shack up with his mistress." He shot me a jaunty smile. "I wouldn't have tattled had the guy been an upstanding citizen, but he was a jerk, who at some point tried to get with Lucy." His glee dampened a little at the mention of his wife's—ex-wife's?—name.

"Is she still locked up in Eric's basement?"

He stared at the winding mountain road. "No. She's back at the inn."

"She's working for Aidan?"

"She's packing up and arranging the handover."

I almost swerved off the road. "I thought you were going to fight for the place!"

Jeb clutched the grab handle. "My lawyer suddenly changed his tune. He said the contract was airtight and it would be a waste of my resources to try and nullify it. And now I can't find a single lawyer in our zip code willing to represent me. Aidan Michaels's money is burning holes in too many pockets."

Not for the first time I wished the hunter dead.

I thought of Megan and her cross. Once people knew us, once they realized we weren't all out for blood, maybe their fear would subside. "Do you really think that if knowledge of us spread it would be so bad?"

Jeb scrubbed his beard, and it made a chafing sound. "That's a tough one. Some people have a romanticized idea of werewolves, but finding out we exist . . . I'm not sure their awe would outweigh their fear."

"Do you think we'd get hunted down?"

"Remember what they did to people they claimed used witchcraft back in Salem?"

I shuddered.

"And they weren't even witches. So, to answer you, Ness, I'd rather not find out." He reached over. I thought he was going to adjust my hold on the steering wheel, but instead, he laid his hand on top of mine. "Aidan Michaels is old, Ness. He'll die soon enough."

Unless he died tonight, it wouldn't be soon enough. "Did you at least recover the payment for the inn?"

"Yes. But it's being held in escrow until the divorce is finalized. Hopefully, that'll be soon." After a beat, he added, "Lucy's being a little . . . *difficult*."

I didn't ask what that was supposed to mean. If Jeb wanted to tell me more, he would.

"I like the apartment, Jeb, but I was thinking, if you have any money set aside with which you could fix up Mom and Dad's old house"—I shrugged—"at least the windows and front door, we could move in there?"

"The place needs more than new windows and a door." Jeb removed his hand from mine.

"I know, but I thought I could do the rest myself. I know how to sand and oil a floor, courtesy of Dad. I could borrow the material from the Watts. And then we'd just need to buy some paint for the walls."

"It needs an electrical overhaul and probably new plumbing."

I batted my eyelashes, trying to whisk away the disappointment that clung there.

"Derek's son is an electrician. I could ask him about rewiring the system. And we had some plumbers back at the inn. I'll get us some quotes."

I blinked at Jeb. "So yes?"

"Why not?" He smiled, but I smiled wider. "You sure you want me living there with you, kiddo? You sure you don't want to sell the parcel?"

"Sell it?" I croaked. I hadn't even considered selling it. "I just got it back. Thanks to you."

Jeb sighed. "I never should've made your mom sell it, but all our money was tied up in the inn—"

This time, I was the one who placed my hand on Jeb's. "You got it back. That's all that matters," I said just as we reached Frank's house.

There was another car parked next to Frank's—a familiar forest-green Land Rover.

"Are Nelson and Isobel here?" I asked, getting out of the car.

"Guess so." Jeb grabbed the bottle of red wine we'd bought on the way over.

A second after we rang the doorbell, I was swept into a pair of warm arms and peppered with kisses. I instinctively closed my eyes, which was smart considering some of Evelyn's kisses landed on my puffy lids.

"Oh, how I have missed you, *querida*." My ear got a loud peck, which momentarily made it ring.

"I'm glad to see you too, Evelyn."

She finally pressed me back, running her thumbs under my eyes. "You have been crying." She shot my uncle a disgruntled look that made him stick his hands in the air.

"No. Just not sleeping enough. That's all. Nothing to worry about."

She harrumphed. "I hope you are hungry. I have made all of your favorites. Cheese quesadillas, candied bacon, chocolate-zucchini bread, and Isobel is glazing the cinnamon rolls I baked this morning."

I peeked around Evelyn and caught sight of Isobel. If it wasn't for her pallor and slightly hunched shoulders, it would've been impossible to tell she'd been operated on six days ago.

Next to her, her son was wiping his hands on a kitchen towel. "Huh. I thought you weren't a fan of all that stuff anymore." He plucked one of the rolls off the cooling tray and chomped on it, while his mother chided him for not waiting until we were seated.

Evelyn cocked one of her penciled-in black eyebrows that made a flush creep up my neck.

I decided to avoid August's taunt and Evelyn's pointed gaze. "I can't believe you're already up and doing things, Isobel."

August grunted, while Evelyn said, "I do not think Isobel knows how to be still."

Isobel smiled. "I'll be still when I'm dead." But then she must've remembered we were in the presence of a man who'd just lost his son, because she bit her colorless lip. "Sorry, Jeb."

He shrugged.

She gave him a rueful smile and handed her son a dish. "Can you take those to the table?"

August scooped up the plate with one hand, and then Evelyn clapped, and we all took our seats around the table—me, between Evelyn and Jeb. August sat across from me. Unfortunately the table wasn't wide, and as he adjusted his legs, his feet knocked into mine.

Frank's grandson came out of the bedroom I'd slept in the night Everest died, bleary-eyed and messy-haired, and made his way over to the seat beside August. They fist-bumped.

The wine was uncorked and poured.

"Want some, Ness?" Nelson asked.

"She's underage," August said.

I rolled my eyes but said I was good with water.

Nelson tutted as he served Jeb. "You were drinking way before you were twenty-one, son."

"Doesn't make it legal," August said, to which I shook my head.

What was up with his hoity-toity behavior? It was so unlike him . . .

After Evelyn said grace, we all tucked in. The food was delicious, and the company, besides Mr. Broody in front of me, was delightful.

"Were you at The Den on Thursday night, August?" Jeb asked.

"No. Why? Were you?"

Jeb smirked. "Me? I'm way too old to hang out in a place like that. Ness went, but they turned her away at the door."

I took a swig from my ice-cold water, and it went down the wrong hole. I coughed so hard Evelyn rubbed me between the shoulders. The lie I'd told Jeb was that the bouncer hadn't allowed me inside, thus embarrassing me. Thus making me cry. I would never have cried about it, but Jeb ate it up.

"I told her she should've phoned one of the boys. That they would've gotten her in."

August narrowed his eyes. "That place is full of college kids. Besides, doesn't that friend of yours dee—"

I kicked his shin under the table. He couldn't blow my cover.

One of his eyebrows arched high. "I guess they're stricter in the summer."

I stabbed a piece of quesadilla. The golden shell crackled from the impact of my fork.

"Any more Creek spottings?" I asked Frank before I stuck the morsel inside my mouth. I was desperate to change the subject, but I also thought that if anyone was up to date on pack information, it would be the elder.

"It's been quiet." Frank darted a worried glance at Jeb, who was concentrated on his plate.

Perhaps me bringing up his son's murderers had been indelicate. "Is Liam going to send anyone to Beaver Creek?"

A small, vertical groove appeared between August's eyebrows.

Frank took a sip of wine. "I was thinking of going out there myself. I know Morgan. I know the way she thinks."

Evelyn went whiter than the glaze atop the cinnamon rolls. "Frank . . . *no*."

He took her hand in his and gave it a firm squeeze. "I'll be fine."

"I could go," I volunteered. "Maybe the Alpha would take well to a girl."

August's freckles darkened. "Ness, that would be completely—"

"*No, no, y no.*" Evelyn squeezed my wrist so hard she cut off my blood circulation.

"Some women feel less threatened by members of the same sex," I said.

Frank scratched his wrinkled neck. "I don't think it would be wise. The Creeks are . . . well, they're very in tune with their other nature, which doesn't make them very *civilized*."

"They killed Everest, Ness," Jeb whispered. "I won't lose you too."

I pressed my lips together. For Jeb's sake, I stopped fighting.

No one spoke of pack politics after that. They talked summer Olympics and tax reforms. When Little J left to meet up with his friends and the men started talking politics over cigars and whiskey, I cleared the table. Evelyn and Isobel tried to help, but I told them to go sit down, that I was happy to move after all the food I'd ingested.

"Honey, help Ness," Isobel told her son as she went to take a seat on the sofa.

August pushed off one the wooden beams and reluctantly made his way to the kitchen.

"I don't need your help," I said, slotting plates into the dishwasher.

But I got it anyway.

We didn't talk as we cleaned up the kitchen, didn't even look at each other.

At some point, he asked, "Why do you look like you cried all night?"

I licked my lips. There was no point in denying something that was so blatantly visible. "Because I did."

"Why?"

"A couple days ago, you send me a harsh email, and now you're concerned about why I cried?"

He frowned. "Harsh email?"

"Not to mix business with pleasure. For your information, I didn't ask Liam to come over, just like I didn't ask him to make you leave Boulder, just like I'm not *dating* Liam, okay? So there was nothing personal or remotely pleasurable about his visit." I poured in the dishwasher powder, then smacked the door shut. "Besides, you must've misunderstood him, because apparently he didn't ask you to leave. He asked *if* you'd be leaving."

August grunted.

"Can you stop grunting all the time? Seriously, you're twenty-seven. Even Little J doesn't grunt as much as you do."

He blinked at me, and then he crossed his arms and leaned his hip against the kitchen counter. "Any other compliments you want to lob my way?"

"I'm sure I can think of more if you give me a few minutes."

He had the audacity to smirk, which just infuriated me because he was obviously not taking our conversation seriously. "You get very flushed when you're angry."

"And that's funny?"

"When you were a kid, you'd get beet-red when things didn't go your way."

"Still don't see why that's funny." I washed my hands, then dried them on the kitchen towel and started covering the leftovers.

August pressed off the counter and took the Saran-wrapped dishes to the fridge. "Want to tell me why you lied about not liking zucchini bread and cinnamon rolls and all that other stuff?"

"Because I don't like people assuming they have me all figured out."

"Since when am I *people*?" There was a twinge of hurt in his tone.

I looked up from the platter topped with scraps of smoked salmon. "You think you know me because I get red when I'm angry, or because I still eat all that stuff I pretended not to like, but I'm not that little girl you ferried around in your truck and brought to the ice cream parlor for a scoop, okay?"

His frown deepened, brought out lines on other places of his face.

"You're ten years older than me. You'll always be ten years older. That's never going to change, but every time you call me Dimples, I feel like I'm six. I don't think you mean to make me feel like a kid, but that's the way it comes out. I'm tired of people thinking I'm childish. Or expendable."

"*Expendable?*" August's eyes were the vivid green of the leaves dotting the tree outside the kitchen window. "When did I make you feel expendable?"

"That wasn't—You didn't." I dragged my damp hands through my hair. "I'm really beat, August." I tried to pass by him, but he held out his arm to bar my path.

"Who made you feel expendable?"

"No one. I don't know even know why I said that."

"Ness—"

"It doesn't matter. Not anymore."

"If it didn't matter anymore, then you wouldn't look like you were about to have a meltdown." He didn't lower his arm. "You might've changed, but I haven't. I'm still a great listener."

My lips quirked into the smallest of smiles. "I appreciate the offer, but I'd rather gnaw off my arm then have a heart-to-heart with you about boys. No offense, but it would just be weird. And not because of the link, but because you're a guy."

He still didn't lower his arm.

"Fine. Want to tell me why you broke up with Sienna?" I asked, trying to prove a point, not because I wanted to discuss his ex.

The memory of the other night twisted in my gut like a dagger. Once the initial shock of finding Liam with another woman had worn off, I'd realized that something else had hurt even more: the fact that he'd done this with so many people present. It was tacky. Again, though, he hadn't cheated on me. I had to stop seeing this as a betrayal. He'd betrayed no one.

"No," August said.

It took me a second to remember what question he was answering. "See?"

He finally lowered his arm to let me through. I walked over to Evelyn and Isobel and talked exclusively with them for the next two hours. The skin on the back of my neck prickled more than once. At some point, I turned around to see if I was going crazy or if someone was watching me. I caught August staring.

At least I wasn't going crazy.

I squeezed a smile onto my lips, feeling as though our talk had somehow dismantled some of the tension between us. If only a talk could also dismantle our link.

Five more months.

What was five more months?

CHAPTER 34

There was a knock on the office's glass door. I looked away from the three tabs I'd opened on the desktop to check who'd arrived.

"Hey, August."

He walked toward me, hands in the pockets of a pair of olive-green cargo pants that had a couple small tears in them, as though they'd gotten snagged on the construction site.

"I bought cake for one of the guys. It's his birthday. Want some?"

"Um. Sure." I started to wheel myself away from the desk when I caught the time on the upper right hand corner of the screen. "Actually, I'm going to have to take a raincheck on that cake." I gathered up my stuff and wedged it inside my bag.

"Going somewhere?"

"Driving test. I sent your dad an email that I'd be taking off for an hour."

"Oh." He thumbed the seam of his lips.

"Was I supposed to inform you, too?"

He dropped his hand from his face and shook his head. "Break a leg, or should I say a side mirror?"

I smiled. "I think that if I break a side mirror, I won't get my license."

His thick lips crooked into a smile. "Yeah. Try to avoid that."

"Will you be here when I come back?"

He nodded. "I'm working from the warehouse today."

"Good. Because I found some discrepancies on invoices from this one lumber company. Anyway I'll tell you all about it as soon as I come back." I dashed through the warehouse just as my phone started ringing.

"I'm outside," Jeb said.

I stepped through the wide-open loading dock entrance. "Me too."

I RETURNED TO THE WATTS' WAREHOUSE AN HOUR AND A HALF later, clutching a piece of paper so hard I'd wrinkled the crap out of it.

August and Uncle Tom were bent over a thick plank coated in a palette of stains. August must've sensed me approach through our little tether, because he looked up.

"Did you get it?" he asked.

I thought it would be obvious by my shit-eating grin, but apparently it was too subtle for August.

"Did you have any doubts I would?"

He smiled. "Well done, Dim—Ness."

"*Dimness*? That's a new one."

"I meant, Ness. Just Ness."

"I know. I was just teasing."

August scratched the base of his neck. "Hey, Tom, does your nephew still work at KPR?"

Uncle Tom tweaked the button of his overalls and gave a quick nod.

"Can you tell him to warn drivers about a blonde at the wheel of a big black van?"

I stuck my tongue out at August. "That's very mature."

Uncle Tom grinned, which made his candied-apple cheeks puff out.

I raised my chin in the air. "I'll have you know I'm an excellent driver."

August chuckled.

"The guy who gave me the exam said I was a natural." He'd then asked if I wanted to have dinner with him sometime, but I left that part out. I'd just smiled pleasantly even though I'd found it a little icky. He was a good two decades older than I was and missing a tooth, and not a molar. I wouldn't have noticed a missing molar.

"I didn't know driving instructors doled out compliments. I certainly never got one."

"Maybe because you weren't all that impressive behind the wheel of a car." I shot him a teasing smile.

"August's pretty impressive anywhere he goes," Uncle Tom said very seriously. "When I was young, even though it might seem hard to believe, I was pretty impressive myself."

That *was* hard to believe, but I said, "I don't doubt it." Yes, it was a lie, but it was a kind one. Kind lies were acceptable. Right?

The rest of Uncle Tom's face went red.

"You had something to discuss with me?" August asked.

I returned my gaze to him. "Oh. Yeah."

Together we walked to the office. I shook the computer mouse to awaken the monitor, then clicked all the tabs back open and showed him how several timber delivery slips didn't match the warehouse stocks.

"Either they're not delivering the amount listed, or someone's been stealing supplies from the warehouse." Some being a benign amount, but still noticeable. Like a missing molar. Not an incisor. I then showed him how the pattern went back almost three years.

"Shit." August perused all the highlighted numbers.

"Look, it's probably the timber company. I mean it's always the same one. If one of your employees were skimming, he'd probably do it on every order, not just on Black Timber's."

Unless the person was smart. I truly hoped it was the timber corporation and not an individual.

"How did Mom miss this? That's thousands of dollars of loss!"

"$17,533."

August blinked at me.

I shrugged. "I'll print everything out so you can double-check my number."

August stood up straighter. "I trust your calculations, but yeah, print it out so I can show Dad."

I hit control P on various documents, which made the mammoth printer roar to life in the corner.

August walked over and plucked the papers from the tray before crossing the office, but then he paused in the doorway. "Can you keep this between us? Until I find out what's going on?"

"Of course." I mimicked zipping up my lips.

He stepped out but doubled back. "And congrats again on your license. That's a heck of a milestone."

I smiled stupidly at him.

With the hand not clutching all the printouts, he tapped the doorframe. "Don't leave before I get back, okay?"

I nodded, imagining he'd want to debrief after meeting with Nelson. "I drove here, so I'm totally independent."

A butterfly performed a backflip inside my stomach.

Independent.

How I'd longed for this day.

CHAPTER 35

The sun was setting, and everyone had left, yet August still wasn't back. I'd been done with my workload for almost an hour and had been poring over the three-dimensional elevations of a luxury lodge. I could almost smell the oiled pine floors and the tall evergreens that had been digitally added beyond the bay windows.

"What do you think?" A warm breath licked up the column of my neck.

I startled, and the 3D printouts scattered on the dusty floor. I slapped a palm across my chest, trying to ease my galloping heart. "August! You scared me."

His gaze set on my midriff. "You didn't *feel* me approach? Because I can sense you from miles away."

I lowered my palm to my stomach where the phantom thread throbbed, where it had been pulsing for a while, but I'd dismissed it as hunger pangs. "I thought I was just really hungry."

He smiled as he dropped into a crouch to gather the papers. "And? Are you hungry?"

"I don't know." August's proximity confused the heck out of my body.

He set all the papers back on the desk and nodded to them. "What do you think?"

"I'd want to live there."

"I thought your dream house was a glass cube centered around a courtyard."

"A glass cube?"

"You sketched it on a paper napkin when we went for ice cream once and made me swear I'd build it for you someday."

"Oh. I don't remember." I twisted my hair into a rope and wound it into a high bun, looping the ends through the coiled mass to make it hold. "I was quite a demanding kid, huh?"

"You even picked the sort of tree that would go in the courtyard."

I concentrated on my memories but couldn't locate the one in question. "What tree did I want?"

"A palm."

I grinned, dropping my hands from my hair. "Seriously? How *tropical* of me."

"It would thrive in Colorado."

I wrinkled my nose. "But it would probably be an eyesore."

"It'd be original, that's for sure." He tilted his head to the side. "A little like a girl in an all-male pack."

"Hmm." When he put it that way . . . Maybe a disruptive tree would do this place some good.

"You also wanted a loose floorboard in your bedroom. Like the one you had at the foot of your bed."

That, I remembered. When I was six or seven, Everest and I had pried a wooden slat loose from my floor with one of my father's work tools, and then we'd lined the shallow hollow with burlap. I stowed my diary inside, along with a treasured collection of Polaroid pictures—my Dad in his wolf form, a few silly selfies of Everest and me, one of my parents dancing in our living room, and several close-ups of August. I remembered this one shot of him, with the sun on his face and this faraway glint in his eyes. I'd labeled it *The Dreamer*.

When I'd first moved to LA, I'd look at it every night, but at some point, the sight of August just made me sad, so I'd shoved the Polaroid inside a shoe box along with the rest of my keepsakes. The next time I'd lifted the lid on that box was about three years later. A leak in our apartment had filled my box with dirty water, ruining the few mementos I'd carried from Boulder.

I blinked out of the memory. "How did the talk go with your dad?"

"I'd rather not discuss it in here."

Did he think the place was bugged? I didn't ask.

August gestured to the door of the building, and I followed him out. He turned off all the lights before setting the alarm. I thought he'd tell me about his conversation outside, but he tipped his head toward the side of the warehouse.

"Ooh." I was sure my eyes lit up. "I get to see your man cave?" I rubbed my palms together like a little kid.

"Man cave?" He grunted.

I flicked his arm.

"Ouch. What was that for?"

"Every time you grunt, I'm flicking you."

"Are you now?" he muttered.

"Uh-huh. It'll make you take notice of how often you do it."

He shook his head a little, but a smile softened his expression. "Should I remind you that inflicting bodily harm on your boss is majorly frowned upon?"

"Bodily harm?" I snorted. "I don't think I could inflict much harm on that *impressive* body of yours." I winked at him.

He flicked my ribs.

"What was that for?" I said, rubbing the spot. "It wasn't a dig. Besides, I didn't even come up with the descriptive term. That was all Uncle Tom."

"You grunted," he said matter-of-factly.

"I did not."

"You did."

I shook my head but matched his smile with one of my own.

August unlocked his front door with a digital keypad and then tapped another keypad inside, and a dozen different lights flared to life.

I tilted my head up and took in the narrow, but dizzyingly high-ceilinged space. "Wow."

The walls were brushed concrete, and the floors were gunmetal-tinged wood, and over the kitchen, there was a giant mezzanine topped with a king-sized bed.

"Total man cave," I declared.

August walked to the kitchen and tugged open the fridge that was stocked with beer, milk, and more beer.

"Don't eat here often, huh?" I ran my fingers over the knots in the giant slice of trunk that made up his kitchen island. "This is beautiful." The sides were uneven but smooth, almost like ruffles. "I want an island like this in my glass cube." I took a seat at the island as he pulled out two beers which he uncapped with his fist. I tipped an eyebrow up. "I thought I was underage."

He smiled. "I was trying to irritate you." He handed me one of the bottles, then held out his own. "To milestones."

We clinked, and then I took a small sip.

"I probably shouldn't drink and drive. Especially not on an empty stomach."

"I was going to order pizza."

My spine straightened a little. "You don't have to feed me."

"Cole's coming over soon. He requested an extra-large pie."

I took another sip. "You guys hang out often?"

"Well, we work together, but yeah, we hang out every day."

They were the same age, or maybe a year apart. "I don't remember you guys being such good friends before I left town."

"Those last few weeks you were around, we were on the outs over a girl. He hooked up with her right after I broke up with her."

"And that was a violation of the *bro-code* or something?"

He snorted.

I leaned over and flicked his wrist.

"Hey." He rubbed it, eyes glinting with a smile.

I tipped my bottle to my lips, relishing the cool fizz of the beer as it hit my tongue, as it hit my veins. "So what happened after that?"

"He ended up going out with her for four years."

"And you didn't talk the entire time?"

"Nah. We patched things up pretty quick."

I thought of the girl inside Liam's room. I still didn't know who she was, but I couldn't imagine wanting to hang out with her. Then again, Cole and August had been friends before a girl had come between them. I had no girlfriends in Boulder, besides Sarah, but Sarah had obviously not been the one behind that wall.

Would I have forgiven her if she had been?

"Ness?"

"Yeah?" I blinked out of my glum thoughts.

"Want some pizza?"

"Sure."

As he phoned up the delivery place, I went back to thinking about the girl in Liam's room. Went through my entire beer dwelling on *her*.

I really needed to get my mind off it. "So what did your dad say?" I asked once August was done placing the order.

"He said he knew. Mom caught the discrepancy."

"And?"

"And you don't need to concern yourself with it."

I crossed my legs. "You're really going to leave me hanging like that?"

He studied the label on his beer bottle, as though checking the ingredients, studied it so hard a small groove appeared between his eyebrows. Finally, he sighed. "Tom's been skimming. His nephew—the one who works at the radio station—well, his ex-wife had a shopping addiction. She emptied their bank account and left town, but she'd racked up an insane amount of debt and stuck him with it."

Debt. I knew a thing or two about that.

He peeled off a corner of his label and stripped it off the green glass. "Tom was just trying to help his nephew out."

"Why didn't he just come to you and ask for a loan?"

"I suppose he was afraid he'd be turned down, and then turned out." August leaned his forearms on the counter, folding the label up and up until it resembled a miniature accordion. "We never discussed your salary, by the way. I imagine this is just a summer job for you."

"If you need me for longer, I could temp during the fall."

He rubbed the pleated label between his fingertips, and the sticky paper disintegrated into flecks.

"But only if you find me competent—"

"We find you competent." He finished reducing the label to a mound of rice-sized pellets. "Too much so."

I blinked up at him. Was there such a thing as too competent?

"Would twenty bucks an hour be acceptable?"

"Twenty bucks?" I choked out. I'd made eleven and change back in California. "That's really generous."

He grabbed my empty beer bottle, scooped up his little mess, then dropped both in the bin underneath his sink. "Do you have money trouble?"

"Huh?" What led him to ask me that? Did I give off some starved vibe? I tried to blank out my expression. "No."

"Then why did you take that escort job?"

"To confront Heath."

"I'm not talking about that one. I'm talking about the second one."

I wrinkled my nose. "How do you know about the second one?"

"Cole was there."

Ugh. "I was promised three grand to go to dinner with Aidan. I didn't know who he was. I wouldn't have gone if I'd known."

August stared at me so long that I felt the heat seep higher than just my neck.

"Look, I'm really not proud of it, but it was three grand *just* for dinner."

"I'm not judging you, Ness."

"Everyone else did," I mumbled.

He covered one of my hands with one of his. Even though I was still a little tanned, the contrast between our skin colors was jarring—light brown against golden ivory.

"But I do want an honest answer out of you about your money situation. I know your uncle's in a bind waiting on the payment from the inn to clear, and I know what medical bills cost."

I swallowed hard, praying August couldn't feel the clamminess of my skin. "I was a minor, so after Mom . . . after she died, I wasn't responsible for her medical bills. I just needed to pay day-to-day stuff and a couple extras, you know, rent, food, her"—I slid my bottom lip between my teeth—"her funeral." I kept my gaze on our hands. "So to answer your question, I need a job, not a loan."

The doorbell rang then. The scent of melted cheese and tangy tomato had my stomach rumbling. Unhurriedly, he removed his hand and walked to the door. He relieved the delivery boy of three cardboard boxes and tipped him generously, before ferrying the food back to the island. He flipped the lids up on two of the boxes but kept the third one shut—probably Cole's extra-large pie.

"Can you give me your bank details?" he asked, taking out plates and handing me one. "So we can deposit your salary straight into it at the end of the month."

"I'll email it to you later." I eased a perfect triangle out of the box and bit off the pointy tip.

Silence fell between us as we ate. It was interrupted by a sharp knock on the door, followed by beeping.

"Yo," Cole said, walking in. He stopped when he saw me. Although Cole tried to hide his surprise, it was all over his face.

"Ness got her driver's license," August informed him. "We were celebrating with beer and pizza."

I patted my lips with a paper napkin, grabbed the bag I'd flung on the seat next to me, and hopped off the barstool. "I was just leaving. Don't want to crash your date."

As I walked toward the door, Cole squeezed my shoulder.

His fingers smelled like cigarettes. "Matt told me what happened."

Don't say it out loud. Don't say it out loud. I didn't want to relive it.

"It was a dick move," he added, lowering his hand, "but it's his loss."

I studied the floor beneath his sneakers. "He didn't do anything wrong. We weren't together," I said softly. And then I tried to smile but failed miserably. It had been five days, and yet my heart still shuddered every time someone mentioned Liam. "Good-night, boys," I mumbled, stepping out into the cobalt darkness.

I watched the stars as I made my way toward the van. And then I watched them some more while I drove myself home, wishing I could feel happier, because today had been a good day.

I thought of my dream house as I drove past the road that led to my old one, and then I rammed my foot on the brake.

Oh.

My.

God.

I blinked in the direction of my childhood home, Everest's last message trickling into my mind, then gunned the car up the drive.

CHAPTER 36

I parked the van and raced around the house toward my old bedroom. The window that I'd busted when I'd sprang through it to rescue Evelyn was still gaping wide. I'd thought about boarding it up, but then, with everything that had happened, it had slipped my mind. Never was I gladder to be forgetful.

Shards of glass remained in the frame. I grabbed a rock from the ground, the largest I could find, and ran it around the frame, knocking out any sharp remnant. Palms and chest tingling with my rapid pulse, I heaved myself up and through the dark hole.

I must not have gotten all the glass, because beads of blood appeared on one of my palms. As I wiped them on my T-shirt, I traced the dusty floor until I located the slab. I dropped into a crouch and coaxed the floorboard up, heart rate sprinting, filling my mouth with the taste of metal. I wasn't sure what I was more afraid of: finding something or finding nothing?

Without a sound, the slat lifted.

I stared into the dark hatch but didn't reach into it. I carefully set the floorboard aside, took my phone out of my pocket, and called the one person I didn't want to speak to.

Ten minutes later, a car rumbled up my driveway. I stepped out of my bedroom and walked to the front door to unlock it. Liam and Lucas got out of the black SUV and then trailed me through my old home.

I pointed to the hatch. "I didn't touch anything."

Liam shone the light from his phone into the hole, catching the metallic glint of the stack of packages my cousin had crammed inside. With no refrigeration, was the Sillin even salvageable? I didn't ask. I didn't care. The only thing I cared about was that Liam and Lucas didn't assume I'd had a hand in hiding the Boulders' drugs.

Liam scooped the foil packets out and dropped them on the dusty floor.

"Are they all there?" Lucas asked.

Liam counted them out slowly. "There's one missing."

One out of thirty or so. Twenty-four pills to a packet.

When Liam raised his gaze to mine, I tensed up. "I didn't take it."

An emotion flared in his eyes. Pain? Regret? I averted my gaze, the ache of being in his presence still too raw.

"Ness, I wasn't insinuating that you had." He straightened up and tentatively stepped toward me. "Thank you for finding these. And for reporting them."

I nodded, gaze on the hodgepodge of Sillin.

He touched my cheek, and I jerked backward.

"I should go." I turned and started through the house, not looking at anything but the floor. I was afraid that my heart, which already felt enlarged with grief, would balloon right out of my chest if I caught sight of something that reminded me of my parents.

I got back into the car, and under the canopy of stars, with tears dripping and drying on my cheeks, I left my dark home and the stash of drugs that had caused so much harm to pass.

CHAPTER 37

F reshly brewed coffee was waiting on my desk when I got in the next morning. I wondered if the drink was for me, and when no one came to claim it, I sipped it. I'd slept fitfully, so caffeine was extremely welcomed.

After I'd left, Liam looped in the whole pack about the recovered drugs. He didn't mention specifics, like where they'd been found and by whom, but I bet people phoned him to find out. News traveled fast through the pack.

I took another much-needed sip of the scalding beverage. It was deliciously aromatic, almost like it had been steeped with caramel and cinnamon.

Since August wasn't working from the warehouse, I sent him a text: *Do I have you to thank for the coffee?*

His answer came much later. *Was it good?*

ME: *Amazing. You'll have to tell me what brand it was.*

AUGUST: *Glad you liked it.*

AUGUST: *How are you feeling?*

I rubbed my brow.

AUGUST: *Ness?*

ME: *Fine.*

AUGUST: ...

ME: *What is ... supposed to mean?*

AUGUST: *It was me grunting.*

Smiling, I scoured my list of emojis until I found one that looked like a flick. I sent it.

AUGUST: *OK?*

ME: *That was me flicking you.*

August sent me a smiley face. Then: *Shouldn't you be working?*

Yeah. I should've been. Plus I needed to get my mind off the previous night, so I placed my phone face down on the table and didn't so much as glance its way the remainder of the day.

Just as I was getting up to go, someone filled the office's doorframe.

"Did I offend you with my last text?" August asked, leaning his broad shoulder into the door frame.

"Huh?" I strapped my bag across my body, then lifted my hair to free it from the strap.

"You never answered me after I told you that you should be working."

Oh. I smiled. "I didn't answer you because I took your advice to heart. *I worked.*" I grabbed the travel mug I'd cleaned earlier and carried it over to him. "Thanks again for the coffee."

"Same one tomorrow morning?"

"You don't need to make me coffee every morning, August."

"I live next door. Besides, I make a pot for myself. Pouring it into a mug and dropping it off isn't too hard."

"Well then, sure." I extended the mug, and he took it, our fingers brushing.

A little jolt went through my hand.

Static.

Or maybe it was the link.

I stuck both my hands into the back pockets of my jeans.

"Got any plans tonight?" His voice sounded a little rough.

The blood pounding against my eardrums probably created this distortion, because his expression was entirely normal.

"I'm having dinner with a UCB jock. What about you?"

"A UCB jock?" He straightened up, which seemed to give him an extra inch. "You're serious?"

"As a heart attack."

He grunted.

I flicked his pec. He didn't rub the spot I'd flicked.

Instead, he crossed his arms, tendons pinching underneath the skin. "What's the guy's name?"

"Why?"

"Just wondering if I know him."

I smiled a little. "You know him."

His pupils pulsed. "Really? Is it David?"

"David? Who's David?"

"Dexter's cousin. The kid with the birthmark under the eye. He plays football at UCB. He's a junior."

"Oh. No." *If David's a junior, thus two years older than I am, and you think he's a kid, what does that make me?* "My date's actually the former running back for the Colorado Buffaloes."

August's gaze narrowed.

"Might've heard of him. Jeb Clark?" I winked at him, and his eyes went wide. Then I added, "No dating for me in the near future. I'm taking some time off men. Like a year, or a decade." I slid past August. "Anyway, I promised Jeb I'd eat with him tonight since I stood him up yesterday." I stopped halfway through the warehouse and spun around. "Want to come?"

He studied the lid of the mug. "No. I'll get some more work done."

I was a little surprised he preferred staying in the office over a warm meal with family friends. But then I realized something. "You don't have to worry about me, August. I'm not depressed or anything."

He glanced up from the mug, brow knitted as though I'd misconstrued his concern. He opened his mouth to speak just as a shrill howl pierced the night, and then another and another. My chest tightened, and my skin bristled, the fine hairs thickening. I'd never heard it before yet knew it was my Alpha's call. The insistence of it had me gaping at August.

"You're going to have to postpone that dinner of yours," he said, setting the travel mug down and yanking off his shirt.

The urgency of the moment was momentarily supplanted by the sight of August's bare chest which gave new meaning to the term washboard abs—you could most probably do laundry against his abdomen.

"Ness? Three howls means something serious has happened."

I snapped out of my daze. Had the Sillin been stolen again? Or maybe they were dummy tablets? I lowered my gaze to the swirls of sawdust beneath my feet and swallowed, my throat feeling as dry as those corn husks Evelyn filled with masa dough.

August strode over to me and cranked my chin up. "You'll be okay. I'll be there."

I nodded, fumbling to remove my bag. When the strap caught in my hair, August assisted me in hoisting it up and off. Flustered by his proximity and nakedness, I backed away. My hands trembled as I dragged off my necklace and then my T-shirt, and then my navel pulsed chaotically when August's eyes, which were on me, began to gleam brighter.

He turned away, Adam's apple working in his throat.

A howl tore through the night, seemingly nearer. Was the pack headed here? I ducked behind one of the work desks, and, keeping my back to August, I unclipped my bra and pushed down my jeans.

Claws clicked nearby, and it made my own claws jolt out of my cuticles. Making sure I wasn't in August's line of sight, I scraped off my underwear before my tail could shred it. My bones shifted and my muscles swelled, and I fell onto my knees, back arched as the rest of the change rippled through me.

When it was done, August bumped his wet muzzle into my shoulder.

Ready? he asked.

I dipped my head in assent. At least I'd face Liam in fur tonight. I felt less vulnerable in fur than I felt in skin, as though my thick white pelt could somehow shield me better than my pale hide.

Another howl stirred the air.

We trotted to the door. With his mouth, August jerked the handle, then shoved the door open with his shoulder. For a moment, I wondered how we would find the pack, but then I felt the tug of something in my chest. Like the tether that bound me to August, there was another tether inside me.

One that tied me to Liam.

One that led me straight to him.

CHAPTER 38

I n a part of the forest where the trees grew as dense as the underbrush, the pack had assembled. Most were in wolf form, but a few had stayed in skin—the few being the elders. The moon wouldn't be full for another week, so I imagined they hadn't been able to shift. And yet they'd still come. They wouldn't understand what was being said, unless Liam spoke to them through the mind link.

Could he, in wolf form?

I saw Jeb, or rather I recognized the gray-blond fur, the light-blue eyes, and the lemony scent of his body. I walked over to him, squeezing my scrawny self between him and Frank's grandson, who was as big as me in fur. Not in skin, though. I wondered why that was. But then I pressed that contemplation away.

I felt Liam's glowing amber eyes on me, but I kept mine trained on the squashed pine needles beneath his giant paws. His lupine body had grown in bulk and breadth since he'd become Alpha.

A nose pressed against my haunches, shifting me a little more toward Jeb, and then another large body sidled in next to me, lining up between Little J and me. *August.*

Liam's gaze moved to my neighbor's. For a moment, they just observed each other. Then August took another step forward, and his pelt bristled, ostensibly making him seem bigger. It was an illusion.

He hadn't actually grown, but he was sending Liam a message not to look at me.

I nudged my friend's flank to tell him I was okay. That he didn't have to make such an aggressive show. God only knew how the others would interpret it.

He didn't back down, but his fur smoothed, and Liam pivoted to face another part of the circle.

The Creek Alpha finally made contact, he said. *She will be coming to Boulder with a delegation of Creeks tomorrow. She says she's coming in peace and will be staying at the inn.*

Aidan Michaels is allowing that? someone asked, interrupting Liam.

He probably doesn't know they're shifters, one of the men said.

Aidan Michaels knows, Lucas growled out. *He has fucking files on the entire werewolf community, but I guess he isn't above taking money from our kind.*

I glanced at my uncle. His stare was unflinching, but I could hear his heart beating a little more strongly than the rest of the hearts around me. I rubbed his shoulder with my cheek in a show of affection and support. He turned his head and rested his own cheek against my forehead a moment.

What do they want? August's deep voice quieted the whisperings that had kindled like wildfire around us.

To meet with the Alphas and their packs. She is convening us to a meeting at the inn tomorrow night at sundown, Liam answered. *I want you all to be there.*

I peeked around the large brown wolf and met Liam's hardened gaze.

We need to present a united front, Liam said, and I swear I felt that comment was directed only at me.

Will the Pines be there? someone asked.

The Pines will be there, Liam answered.

This is a trap. We shouldn't go, someone barked.

We caught the owner of the yellow Hummer—Everest's murderer, Liam said.

I stiffened and emitted a barely audible whimper.

Liam shifted his gaze to my uncle, who stiffened next to me. *And we've identified him as Morgan's son. She knows we have him. That's one of the reasons she's coming. To retrieve him. Whether he lives or dies depends entirely on how she behaves.*

I nosed out from behind August. *He might walk away with his life?* He killed *Everest. Is this becoming a thing? Murderers get to kill without retribution?*

He's worth more to us alive than dead, Liam said. *Besides, Everest was dead either way. Morgan's son just spared me from exacting justice myself.*

Jeb's strangled moan made goose bumps flourish beneath my fur.

I'm sorry, Jeb, Liam said, *I understand this is still not easy for you to hear.*

Whining, Jeb folded his ears and scrambled backward and away from the pack. I started to go after him when Liam called out my name.

Ness, this meeting isn't over.

His voice held so much authority it had me lowering my head and turning around. It was as though my body and mind were two separate entities—where my mind wanted to go after my distraught uncle, my body obeyed my Alpha's command.

The Creek Alpha insisted that you come earlier with me.

Me? Why?

Apparently she's heard a lot about you.

I waited for snickers to erupt from the males whose gazes were all trained on me now. No one snickered.

So be ready at seven, Liam said.

Then he proceeded to give us orders about the night ahead, urging us not to ingest any drink or food offered at the inn in case they were doused with the missing Sillin.

I thought we recovered it all, someone said.

Almost all. But this doesn't mean the Creeks don't have their own stock, Liam barked.

He doled out more precautions, but his voice faded into white noise as I pondered why Morgan, the great and feared Alpha of the Creeks, had asked to meet *me* beforehand.

Was she looking for an ally in my pack?

CHAPTER 39

I went in to work the next day with a mix of excitement and dread bubbling deep in the pit of my stomach. August exacerbated the dread part of my mood. His concern was so heavy that I asked him if I could leave early. Before I could drive away, he asked if I wanted him to come at seven too. When I turned down his offer—because I feared Morgan wouldn't appreciate me bringing a bodyguard—his eyes darkened like the evergreens on a moonless night.

I hadn't meant to hurt his feelings and almost backpedaled, but he'd be there shortly after me. Besides, I wasn't frightened. Well, not overly frightened.

Especially after Sarah dropped by, chattering nonstop about the meeting. She swung three dresses onto my bed. Even though I insisted on wearing something of mine, she told me this was a *soirée*. A soirée apparently called for fancy attire.

"I'm not looking to seduce any Creeks," I muttered to Sarah as I reluctantly tried dress number two.

"One of the first things Julian taught me was that the way you present yourself, the way you hold yourself, the way you speak affects the perception people will have of you. By walking in looking like a thousand dollars—I think that one was actually two—you'll stand out, because everyone, be they wolf or human, has a vested interest in beauty and riches."

She fingered the black tulle of the midi skirt while I blanched. I'd never asked how much the red dress I'd worn to her brother's wedding cost, nor the little white number that still hung in my closet.

I smoothed down the stiff bustier top that shoved my breasts together. Considering mine were way smaller than Sarah's, I asked, "Can you even fit into this thing?"

"Nope. Internet order I was too lazy to return. It's yours."

For a second, I pondered reselling it, but it would probably hurt Sarah's feelings. Plus it was really nice *and* black, so probably easy to wear to other occasions.

I finally turned away from the floor-length mirror glued to the back of my bedroom door. "You're like a fairy godmother. Except instead of little wings and a gray bun, you have sharp claws that can shred a man's throat, and a sharper attitude that can shred his ego."

She slashed through the air, manicured nails curving.

My lips quirked into a smile that tumbled off when a car honked.

Sarah lurched off the bed and peered out my window. "Liam's here. Are you gonna be okay?"

"Yeah," I lied, going into my bathroom and fishing my mascara from the glass in which I kept my toothbrush and eyeliner. Even though my hands trembled, I managed to apply a thin coat of makeup to my lashes without incident. I left the rest of my face bare. The dress was loud enough. I fluffed out my hair which had dried a bit wavy and fit my feet into my black heels.

"Let's pray tonight doesn't turn into something out of a slasher film," Sarah said, running her hand along her hair, which she'd had professionally flattened. It made her look like a different person— less wild and more refined.

I gasped. "Why would you say that?"

"I was just kidding."

"Well, it wasn't funny," I muttered.

Sarah did something very un-Sarah-like. She gave me a hug. "She has no reason to murder us. She probably came to beg for her son's life. And maybe offer us an alliance." She squeezed me tight, her flowery perfume prickling my nostrils like rose thorns. "Or maybe she wants to marry you off to her son."

I pulled away. "What?"

Sarah shrugged. "I was just speculating."

"Well don't speculate about something so . . . so awful."

"You're mated. Just use that excuse if she tries to marry you off."

As I wrenched my bedroom door open, I caught my reflection in the mirror. My face was as wraith-like as Isobel's had been back at the hospital.

Liam honked again.

"Better go before he comes upstairs and hauls your ass into his big car."

My heartbeats snagged behind my compressed ribs. "I'm not ready," I whispered, panicked.

She strode up to me and tucked a piece of hair behind my ear. "I'll come early." When I still hadn't moved, she said, "Everything'll be fine."

Oh no, no, no. Why'd she have to say that? To use those exact words?

Chilled to my bones, I finally walked out. Liam neither greeted me when I climbed into his car, nor did he spare me a passing glance. He wore his usual black V-neck and blue jeans but had added a black dinner jacket.

"Am I overdressed? I let Sarah pick my clothes . . . "

His gaze didn't budge from his windshield, but a nerve ticked in his jaw. "Are you fishing for a compliment?"

"What? No! I was just asking if I should go change before we leave."

He pressed on the gas pedal, and the car lurched forward. I hurried to strap myself in.

"Too late now," he snapped. "I'm sure August will appreciate your little princess dress."

That stunned me into silence. But only for a minute. "Don't be a jerk, Liam."

He side-eyed me. "Me? A jerk?" He barked out a dark laugh. "I think you got me and your mate mixed up." He pronounced the word *mate* as though it were something rotten.

Anger welled up behind my breastbone. "How is August the jerk? He's not the one who said I backst—"

"He challenged my authority in front of the pack! I can't even put

him back in his place verbally or physically, because he's your *mate*."
He narrowed his eyes. "Tell me, are you and him a thing now?"

I shook my head, not as an answer, but because he was acting crazy.

"If you and him fuck, that's it for you. You're stuck with him for life, and from what Sienna says, he's a boring lay."

I blanched, and then I flushed with anger and glared at the low buildings smearing past our window, wondering why Liam had to be so crude and petty. I wasn't the one who'd jumped into bed with someone else the second I was unattached.

He jerked the car to a stop at a red light. "The crazy thing is how much shit I'm getting from my buddies about this. It's not like I strayed, yet I'm the bad guy."

I was gripping the tulle as though it were a stress ball. Didn't do squat for my stress level. "I know you're hurt—"

"I'm not hurt! I am *fucking* furious!" He slapped his steering wheel. "You toss me to the curb at the first mistake I make. I'm not perfect. No one is! Not even you."

My knuckles whitened, and my eyesight sharpened, but I pushed back my wolf before she could rip through my *little princess* dress.

"I slept with Tammy because she stroked the ego you'd crushed." The volume of his voice had dropped, but it still rang too loudly in the car.

Tammy. Tamara. Why was I not surprised?

Had he ever stopped seeing her? Why was I torturing myself with this? It didn't matter.

She didn't matter.

What they *did* didn't matter.

"How am I supposed to be Alpha if I'm made to feel like a piece of shit?" he asked.

I didn't make a sound. I barely breathed. My spine tingled, and again, I shoved my wolf back.

The light turned green, and Liam flattened the gas pedal, weaving between cars like a Formula 1 pilot.

"She was just a means to an end," he added, so low I almost missed his words.

I still didn't say anything.

He pulled to another violent stop, this time on the side of the road that led up to the inn. "Say something," he yelled. "Shout at me! Do something! Tell me what a prick I am, slap me, tell me what a bitch Tamara is!" His violent words were limned with desperation.

Is that why he'd taken her to his bed? To test my affection? Or was it to stroke his ego like he'd said two minutes ago?

He reached over and clasped my shoulders, pivoting me toward him. "Aren't you even a little jealous? Don't you care about me?" he whispered, his powerful voice faltering.

"You broke my heart, Liam." I was incredibly calm, and it wasn't even an act. I didn't feel vindictive. "I let you in, and you wrecked me. Is that what you want to hear?" I licked my lips that felt as dry as my eyes.

His hands slid down my arms, gripped my biceps as though to keep me from falling away from him. But I'd already fallen away from him.

"Are you and August—"

"There is no me and August."

Liam's eyes flashed with something—hope. Like a lit match, it spread and made the air inside the car crackle.

"But there is also no me and you, Liam." One-by-one, I pried his fingers off my arms. "You have to let me go," I said softly. "You have to let me go."

Red handprints remained where he'd squeezed.

"I will obey you like I vowed, but don't ask me to love you."

He scrubbed a hand through his gelled hair. A hardened lock fell into his shiny eyes. "Ness . . . "

"Please, Liam, let me go," I murmured.

I touched his cheek, smooth from a fresh shave, the only soft part on his body. The rest of him was all hard lines. He swallowed, and his jaw muscles juddered under my palm. He covered my hand with his and kept both anchored to his face as we sat on the side of the road, the inn just out of reach but already in sight.

"Let's get tonight over with," I said, slipping my palm out from underneath his.

He lowered his eyelids, then lifted them back up, drawing in a long breath through his nostrils. Or maybe he was drawing in a lungful of courage. The Creeks' reputation was so dire that I worked hard on quieting my own nerves as we slowly made our way up the hill toward them.

CHAPTER 40

L iam parked up front, behind a compact row of cars that ranged in fanciness, from gleaming Cayennes to rusted Civics. The sight of rust reassured me I wasn't out of my depths, that I'd be able to relate to some of these shifters.

We walked toward the inn side by side, the earlier tension between us diffused. We were in no way relaxed, but that had nothing to do with our row and everything to do with the den of wolves we were about to enter.

"Why do you think she asked to meet me specifically?" I asked.

"You're Everest's cousin. You worked as an escort. Maybe she thinks you spied on a Creek or two." Liam's neck was a rigid column on the unyielding mantle of his shoulders.

I must've gone slack-jawed, because Liam ran a knuckle under my chin as though to shut my mouth.

"You didn't, right?"

I removed my chin from his fingers. "Spy on Creeks? *No.*"

Car doors slammed shut, making me jump. Liam and I both turned to scan the lot. Lucas, Matt, August, and Cole were walking up from where they'd parked the pickup.

Was it eight already? Had Liam and I spent an hour in his car? The sky was streaked with oranges and pinks, which told me they were early.

"We didn't feel right about you two going in without protection,"

Matt said as he approached in a pair of black jeans and a long-sleeved T-shirt, both fitting snugly over his broad, ropy limbs.

He'd made even less of an effort to dress up than Liam, which confirmed my earlier worries that I was way overdressed. The boys were like evergreens, and I was like that palm tree I apparently wanted in my dream house. I gripped the tulle, wishing I could transform it into a pair of jeans and a tank top.

Lucas's blue-eyed gaze skipped between Liam and me, as though trying to gauge from our postures where we ranked on the scale of love and hate. The shaggy-haired shifter must've noticed that only billowing smoke remained from our spat, because his features relaxed. Had he been expecting to have to pry my claws out of his Alpha's skin?

August's face was a blank mask, but through the link, I felt his body thrumming with something, something that made him cross his arms, straining the fabric of the dark-olive Henley that matched his eyes.

"Shall we go see what the great Creek Alpha wants?" Lucas gestured to the inn.

Liam turned back toward the revolving doors, but Matt shoved him aside.

"I'll go in first," the blond giant said.

The doors spun, tossing the familiar scent of chimney smoke and potpourri at us, as well as the scent of musky sweat and damp fur. It smelled like the Creek delegation had traveled by paw instead of by foot and tire. Perhaps some had.

Liam went in after Matt, then Lucas. Cole gestured for me to go, so I pressed my fingertips into the cool glass and pushed. I expected noise but was greeted with silence. The place was eerily quiet. No one stood behind the bell desk. No one roamed the hallways. No footfalls echoed on the buffed pine floors.

I'd stopped just outside the revolving doors, so when Cole stepped through, I felt his hand on my back, pressing me a couple of inches to the side so he could fit into the inn without toppling me over. The tether tautened when August came in. I dropped my hand to my navel instinctively, not because it itched, but because touching it seemed to lend me strength. Unlike Cole who'd gone to stand next to his brother, August remained standing at my back, his steady heat pulsing against my bare shoulder blades, battling the goose bumps swarming over my skin.

"This doesn't feel right," Cole said.

The silence rattled my bones.

Lucas sniffed the air. "The place reeks of them."

"I sense heartbeats," Liam said. "Human and—"

There was pounding, scratching, then two wolves lurched out of the living room. Not wolves—*dogs*. Huge black and tawny ones with droopy faces. They stopped in front of the six of us, teeth bared, drool spilling over their floppy jowls.

I backed up, smacking into August's chest. His hands settled on my arms at the exact same place where Liam's had been not too long ago. Instead of bruising like Liam's, August's grip on me was gentle but firm—velvet instead of steel.

I relaxed when I noticed the dogs were hooked onto leashes, leashes that were stretched tight. Footsteps sounded on the hard-wood floors, and then a silver-haired man came through the living room doors.

Aidan Michaels.

He reeled in the leashes. "I hope you'll abstain from slaying my new Bloodhounds. I only received them a week ago."

While Cole inched closer to me, Matt and Lucas positioned themselves in front of Liam. August didn't move. Didn't let go of my arms that had started to shake. Not with fear but with pure, unadulterated hatred.

I had no interest in killing the dogs, but their owner . . . I was sure interested in sectioning off one of his arteries and watching him bleed out.

"He can't hurt you," August murmured.

I wasn't afraid of him hurting me. Quite the opposite.

"What are you doing here?" Liam's tone was as cutting as a chainsaw.

"I was just visiting my new acquisition. It's a tad shabby, but the view is splendid. Best thing about the place." His bespectacled navy eyes sought mine through the wall of male bodies.

"Where are your *guests*?" Lucas bit out.

"They went out for a little exercise. Lovely bunch. Very educated and forward-thinking. A nice change from the citizens of Boulder."

"All of them?" Liam asked.

"They're not all sharp as tacks, but—"

Matt cut in. "Liam meant, are all of them out running?"

"Oh, yes. They all went. Even the young'uns." Aidan scratched one of his hounds between the ears. "If you'll follow me, I'll lead you to the festivities."

"You're staying?" Lucas asked.

"Why not? This place is mine now, isn't it?" Aidan swept his gaze over the high-ceilinged foyer.

Tendons shifted in the back of Liam's neck. "Does Mrs. Morgan know you'll be staying?"

Mrs. Morgan? Wasn't Morgan her first name?

Aidan smiled that oily smile of his. "Oh, she does. Now come this way." He gestured toward the living room. "After you."

"You go on ahead, Aidan," Liam said. It was the first time I'd heard him address the old man by his first name. "*We'll* follow *you.*"

The hunter's lips curled higher. "I've no rifle on me, Kolane."

"Unless you want me to snap your dogs' necks, you'll walk in front of us," Liam said.

Aidan tapped the flank of the bigger of the two Bloodhounds affectionately. "These two boys could be your cousins."

"We aren't related to dogs," Liam gritted out.

Liam's rising anger was fueling Aidan Michaels's perverted glee.

The old man yanked on the leashes and then turned, leading the way into the living room. Liam turned toward me as though about to say something. His eyes glowed amber with bloodlust, the color intensifying when he caught August's hands on me.

I'd been so absorbed by the sight of Aidan that I'd forgotten August was even holding on to me. I eased out of his grip. No one spoke, making the already uncomfortable moment all the more awkward.

"I can't believe the bastards are out running," Matt finally said.

"It's nothing more than a negotiating technique," Liam muttered. His eyes were slowly shifting back to their normal human hue. Only the rings around his irises remained lit like flames.

I crossed my arms, rubbing my pebbled skin. They'd turned the AC units to their full power.

"Is turning this place into an icebox also a negotiating technique?" I asked.

"Anything that creates discomfort is a technique." He unbuttoned his jacket, as though to offer it to me.

Before he could, I walked off, heels clicking on the hardwood floors. "We'll wait for them on the terrace then."

Matt caught up to me, matching my brusque pace. "Don't separate yourself from the group, Ness."

A new chill swept up my spine at his warning, and then another locked my knees when I stepped into the two-storied living room. Standing right beside the entrance was Lucy, flaming hair coiffed in neat waves, pert smile slicked with red lipstick. She was dressed in a black shift that accentuated all of her curves and the milky paleness of her freckled skin. She proffered a silver platter topped with shot glasses.

"Welcome," she said, the ashen stink of her breath grating me almost as much as her presence.

"Mrs. Clark," Matt said.

"Oh. Just Lucy now. Haven't you heard? As of this afternoon, I am no longer a Clark. The dirt over my son's grave has barely settled, and already, I'm cast out of the family I gave twenty years of my life to." She turned the full power of her icy smile on me. "The Clarks are a fickle bunch."

"Why are you serving at this party, Lucy?" Liam's question shifted my aunt's attention on him.

"Aidan Michaels has just made me director of the inn."

"You accepted a job from your son's killer?" Lucas said. "That's sick."

Aidan, who'd stepped onto the terrace, came back inside, dog-free. Had he set them loose or tied them to the balustrade?

"Now now, Lucas, *I* didn't kill Everest. But you know that since the killer's in your custody, is he not?"

Aidan Michaels's knowledge of us was truly chilling.

"Just because you didn't get your hands dirty, old man, doesn't mean they aren't filthy as fuck," Lucas shot back.

"It's a real shame you were raised by a pack of wolves, Lucas. An education would've done your speech wonders."

Lucas reeled his arm back, but Cole caught it before Lucas could let his fist fly into Aidan's jaw.

"Jumpy tonight, aren't we?" Aidan nodded to the platter before lifting one of the diminutive glasses. "Why don't you try our welcome drink? It's lovely. Lucy made it herself with rose water distilled from her prized roses."

Just the scent wafting from the glasses had my eyes stinging.

"And what else did you put in there again, my dear?" Aidan asked, tapping his index finger to the flared rim of his shot glass.

"Sillin?" Matt supplied under his breath.

"Vodka and sugar syrup," Lucy said brightly.

"Sillin?" Aidan's eyebrows rose, crinkling his forehead. "Now why would she have used Sillin? It wouldn't have added any flavor to this exquisite drink."

"How do you know the flavor of Sillin?" Liam asked, narrowing his gaze on the hunter.

Aidan thumbed his ear, then pressed his wire-rimmed glasses back up the bridge of his nose even though they hadn't slid down. "When I research something, Liam, I do so thoroughly," he finally said. He raised his glass and waited, but none of us followed his lead. "Your loss." He knocked the clear drink back, then smacked his lips. "Absolutely delightful, just like the woman who concocted it."

Was Aidan Michaels hitting on my aunt—*former* aunt? *Yuck.*

When two spots of color rose to her cheeks, I gagged. I must've done so audibly, because she glared at me, smile gone.

Voices suddenly rose in the foyer.

"I believe more guests have arrived. Shall we go out to greet them, Lucy?"

Aidan took the platter from her hands and offered Lucy his arm. And she took it.

"More guests, and still no host," Matt said, gaze sunk on the darkening forest that swayed beyond the overhanging porch like wet paintbrushes.

Liam tipped his chin toward the terrace, and the boys followed him out. I was still too stunned by what I'd just witnessed to move.

"Ness?" August's voice pierced the gray fog of my thoughts.

I released my elbows, letting my hands drop into the fluffy, itchy tulle. "Jeb can't come. He'll—He'll . . . " I patted my skirt as though to locate a pocket, but I had no pocket just like I had no bag. I hadn't thought I would need to bring anything since my uncle was coming. "Can you call him, August? Tell him not to come." My voice was shrill with nerves. "I don't want him to . . . to see what we just witnessed."

August fished his phone out of his pants pocket and pressed on the screen before lifting it to his ear. As he spoke, I caught sight of a familiar blonde and expelled a breath of relief.

Sarah walked over to me in a shimmery gown that made her look more goddess than wolf. "I heard the Creeks were late."

"You didn't drink the shots, did you?" I whispered urgently.

She nocked a crooked grin onto her glossy lips. "Wouldn't dream of ingesting anything Creep-made." Winking, she threaded her arm through mine and pulled me toward the terrace, but I dug my heels in.

"Did you get him on the phone?" I asked August.

"I did. He'll stay home."

A trickle of relief dripped through me, too little to do away with my gnawing anxiety. "I have such a bad feeling," I murmured to Sarah as we joined the others on the deck.

She squeezed my arm. "It'll be fine."

Even though her voice didn't waver, her optimism did little to reassure me. Perhaps it was because Liam looked as though he was about to snap someone's head off and Lucas hadn't taken a jab at Sarah's appearance as he usually did, even though he'd stared her up and down a couple times. Or perhaps it was because of the matching grim expressions August and the two Rogers brothers wore.

Whatever it was, I braced myself for utter chaos. Better to be pleasantly surprised than surprisingly disappointed.

CHAPTER 41

Julian Matz strolled through the living room as though he owned the place, his sister, Nora, hanging from his arm.

"Is your father here?" I asked Sarah.

Surprise, or was it shock, puckered her brow. "My father had a falling-out with my uncle some years ago. He's no longer welcomed to pack gatherings."

"Your parents are divorced?"

"No, but they lead separate lives."

"Oh."

Julian advanced toward us. "Miss Clark, it has been too long." He let go of his sister and picked up my hand, bringing it to his pouty lips, the diamond on his pinky ring glittering wildly. "Much too long." His breath, like his kiss, skated over my knuckles.

I snatched my hand away. I wasn't afraid of Julian, but he still unsettled me. "Good evening, Mr. Matz. Mrs . . . " What was I supposed to call her?

"Matz," Nora supplied. She offered me a smile that gleamed as brightly as the sapphire hoops speared through her earlobes. "Ooh, Robbie and Margaux have arrived. I'll be right back."

She tottered in her sky-high heels toward her son and his wife. Both were dapperly dressed. Unlike my pack. I resembled a Pine more than a Boulder tonight, and that didn't feel right, but it wasn't

Sarah's fault. She couldn't have guessed my pack would make no effort.

Once Julian had gone off to greet some more arrivals, I asked, "Why is your mom's last name Matz?"

"Because Dad's not a wolf," Sarah said, as though it were obvious. "Last names are pack names. If you ever married outside the pack, you keep your wolf name, and your kids get your last name. It makes tracing bloodlines easier."

I raised a brow. "Huh."

She rolled her kohl-lined eyes. "Babe, you're such a newb."

Lucas, who was standing beside us, smirked.

"What are you smirking about, Mason?" Sarah shot him a little glare. It was more playful than vicious though. She was probably stockpiling the vicious ones for when the Creeks arrived.

"Your hair. What's wrong with it?"

Color rose to her cheeks. "I straightened it."

I became distracted by Julian and Liam walking toward one end of the terrace, heads bent in conversation, two burly Pines in tow. Matt and Cole strode closer too, dividing their attention between Liam and Julian's bodyguards. I watched the two Alphas for a long moment, wondering what they could be discussing, hoping they had a strategy to get us out of here safely if the Creeks attacked or set fire to the inn.

My heart juddered. Where had that contemplation even come from? From the logs burning in the massive stone fireplace beyond the sliding glass doors? I glanced toward the staircase at the side of the terrace. It was wide, but if everyone suddenly started running for it, it would clog up. I peered over the railing. I'd survive the two-story fall, but it would surely break some of my bones.

"What are you thinking about?" August asked, stealing me out of my dire musings.

He'd gone over to see his father and the elders but had come back without my noticing and was now standing with his hip propped against the wooden handrail and his arms crossed. I needed to be more aware of my surroundings.

"Fire," I whispered, gripping the smooth log.

He cocked up a dark brow.

"What if they're not here because they want to set fire to the inn?" I murmured.

I wanted August to tell me that was crazy-talk, that they'd come in peace, but he didn't.

"We'll jump and make a run for it," he said.

I swallowed.

"I won't let anything happen to you, kid." He tendered me a strained smile.

Kid? I'd take Dimples over kid any day. I clutched my elbows and turned to face the forest.

"Ness?" August asked.

Why did it even bother me that he thought of me as a kid? I made no sense to myself. It was the link. The link was screwing with my emotions.

I didn't say anything, just concentrated on the woods.

And that's when I heard them.

The distant sound of hearts pounding in unison, of paws stamping the earth.

August had sensed them, too. "They're here," he whispered.

Every single Pine and Boulder had sensed them because every face turned toward the woods.

CHAPTER 42

The Creeks came, pounding our land underneath their giant paws, breaking our blades of grass, ploughing our soil with their claws, stealing our air and lacing it with the scent of their damp, furred bodies. They raced toward us, moving like columns of soldiers with a wolf larger than all the others up front.

Their Alpha.

Morgan.

The light-brown wolf led her wolves toward us with a determination that made me step back from the railing, that made many of us retreat from the balustrade.

Silly since there was no way her shifters could leap onto it.

When she stopped and let out a long howl, the fine hair on my arms thickened.

No one shift, Liam ordered.

My skin felt uncomfortably tight, but I reined my wolf back.

Julian must've given the same order to his pack, because everyone stayed in skin.

On the great expanse of grass below us, the Creeks began to rise onto two legs, their fur vanishing into human pores, their pointed ears migrating to the sides of their faces, their muzzles shrinking into noses. Breasts developed on certain bodies, and chest hair on others. The smaller bodies had no body hair and no breasts.

I moved my attention off the sea of naked bodies and onto the woman at the helm. Her hair was short like a man's, but her face was thin and feminine, just like the rest of her body. She had muscle, but nothing like the bulk of some of the wolves crowding her. I kept my gaze fixed to their faces, or attempted to. It was a feat when appendages swung each time someone so much as twitched. Clearly, the Creeks weren't prudes . . .

I wondered if anyone else was bothered by their nudity. Some Pines were grimacing, but I didn't think it was for the same reason. I checked Liam's face. What was he thinking? How I wished he would speak to us through the mind link, because I wasn't sure how to take the display beneath the balustrade. His features were hard-set, his gaze amber and glowing, his shoulders pulled tight.

Julian spoke, breaking the thick silence, "You have accomplished a great feat tonight, dearest Cassandra."

So Morgan was her last name.

Small wrinkles bracketed the Alpha's pale eyes as she carefully examined the rows of faces looking down at her.

"You have accomplished the feat of making me feel overdressed." Julian guffawed, and so did many other Pines.

With bated breath, I scrutinized Cassandra's face, waiting on her reaction to Julian's comments. When her lips bent with a smile, a collective exhale of breaths whooshed around me.

"I apologize, Julian," she said, her voice making me blink and blink.

She skimmed the row of faces again until she found mine.

Until her eyes settled on *mine*.

"I've heard great things about the woods in these parts." She smiled, baring shiny teeth that overlapped.

Heart hurtling against my ribs, I backed up, and one of my heels caught. I windmilled my arms. Lucas caught me before I could fall.

After steadying me, he muttered, "Can you let a Pine wipe out first?"

Don't show fear, Ness, Liam said through our mind link.

How could I not show fear?

I gaped at him, and then I gaped at all of the Pines and Boulders who'd turned to look at me, and then finally I gaped back down at the Creek Alpha.

Aidan Michaels crossed the lawn, coming to a stop next to her, and then, like her, he smiled up at me.

CHAPTER 43

"W hat is it?" August asked, the only person who was still staring at me.

Everyone else was peering downward as Cassandra pressed her cheek into Aidan Michaels's, as though marking him, as though he were a wolf instead of a hunter.

August stepped in front of me, blocking my view of the Creeks so I would focus on him. "Ness? Why are you so freaked out?"

I blinked up at him. "Cassandra . . . she's . . . I . . . "

He placed a hand on my shoulder, leaking warmth into my frozen skin, not enough to thaw me out of my stupor though. "What is Cassandra?"

"Her voice," I whispered.

"What about her voice?"

"*IknowitIknowher*." I whipped the words out so fast they blended into one another.

He frowned. "How?"

"She's . . . she's the woman who . . . who operates . . . Red Creek Escorts. Called herself . . . Sandra." I slammed the back of my hand over my mouth. "Oh my God. I'm going to be sick."

"Shh." He pulled me into his chest while I dry-heaved.

Thankfully my lunch didn't come up. Just my anxieties. They rose and rose like steam from a pressure cooker. I was going to blow. I pressed away from August and rushed back to the guardrail.

"You!" I yelled at her, at Aidan, my voice ringing through the night, quieting all the others.

Gasps arose.

"Hi, Candy."

"Candy?" Sarah echoed.

"Probably some Creek-way of saying sweetie," the girl next to her said.

For a long moment, the woman I'd come to know as Sandra stared at me, and I stared back at her, and the rest of the world faded around us.

Had she manipulated Everest into working for her the same way she'd manipulated me into going on a date with Aidan? I turned my searing gaze onto Aidan, who was thumbing his ear. What connection existed between the hunter and the Alpha?

"Get dressed!" the Creek Alpha bellowed, shattering the silence.

"What was that about?" Liam asked me.

I was still too rattled to talk, so I let August explain.

The Creeks poured past her, trickling into the inn by the doors beneath the terrace, the ones that led to the pool. A moment later, the first clothed ones reemerged. One of them, a young girl with hair the color of Cassandra's fur, returned toward the Creek Alpha, brandishing a light-blue shift, which Cassandra pulled over her head. It settled shapelessly above the Alpha's ankles.

"Thank you, Lori."

Lori craned her neck to look at us. Her face was thin like Cassandra's, eyebrows thick and curved like the Alpha's. I bet they were related. Mother and daughter perhaps? I wished I'd studied the Creeks. It would've spared me the shock of finding out that I'd been casually conversing with their Alpha.

Cassandra Morgan. I shivered.

She'd barely even bothered to disguise her identity. Had she wanted me to figure it out? Both women and Aidan started toward the terrace stairs, making their unhurried way onto the deck.

Liam and Julian waded through the throng of Pines and Boulders, positioning themselves in front of their packs.

"Cassandra," Julian said.

"Julian." She didn't smile at him. She turned toward Liam, looked him up and down as though sizing him up. She was slightly shorter than he was, but that could've been because she was barefoot, whereas he wore boots. "Your resemblance to Heath is simply alarming." She didn't smile at him either.

Tendons shifted like windblown branches in the back of Liam's neck, the only part of him I could see from my vantage point.

Lori, who was standing just behind her Alpha, regarded Liam, but unlike her Alpha, she seemed to like what she saw because her pink lips lilted into a seductive smile.

"Aidan Michaels abhors wolves, Cassandra," Julian said, just as more of her pack walked up the porch steps, creating a thick wall behind Cassandra.

"You must be mistaken," she said, wrapping one of her hands around Aidan's wrist. "Aidan's a great animal lover."

"He might love dogs and his fellow rats, but he has no love for wolves," Liam said.

"Aidan!" She released his wrist to clap a hand over her chest. "What am I hearin'?"

A smile tugged at Aidan's thin lips. A matching one clung to the lips of many a Creek.

I stepped around Sarah and the girl from her pack to better see the Alphas, but something tugged on me, stopping me from moving any closer. I looked around me, wondering who'd grabbed onto my dress, but no one had. When I met August's green gaze, I realized it wasn't a hand that had held me back, but a tether. He shook his head, as though warning me from going closer. I bit my lip, turning back toward the Alphas.

"Grandma's bones must be rattlin' around in her grave," Cassandra said.

I frowned.

"Why would your grandmother's bones be *rattlin*?" Julian asked, accenting the last word to match her diction.

Cassandra smiled. "'Cause Grandma was staunchly opposed to wolves hatin' their own."

I inhaled so fast white dots danced on the edge of my vision. Was she saying Aidan Michaels was a . . . a—

Julian gasped. "Aidan Michaels is a wolf?"

"Yes." Cassandra cast Aidan an affectionate glance. "My cousin."

No one spoke, but a couple of the Creeks snickered.

"He doesn't smell like a wolf," Liam said.

She stuck her nose in the crook of Aidan's neck. "It's slight, I'll admit. The Sillin he's been ingestin' during all the years he's lived amongst you has weakened his scent."

Aidan Michaels is one of us.

It made absolutely no sense. Why would he threaten to reveal the existence of werewolves to the public if he was one himself?

Everyone turned to me, and I realized I'd spoken this out loud. I was so shocked I didn't even flinch from the onslaught of attention.

"It enhanced my cover story," Aidan said.

"So you don't have files on us?" I asked.

"Oh, I have files on each one of you, or rather Sandy does."

"But not your lawyers?"

He took off his wire-rimmed glasses and cleaned them on the hem of his blue dress shirt, then placed them back on his nose and peered at me through them. "I know what you're getting at, Miss Clark. You're thinking nothing's standing in your way of killing me."

I held his gaze. "Isn't *a life for a life* the law of all packs? Or do the Creeks play by different rules?"

Cassandra was the one to answer me. "We play by the same rules, Ness, but I strongly discourage you from killin' my cousin."

"Why is that, Mrs. Morgan?"

"'Cause then this whole terrace would turn into a bloodbath, and we honest to goodness came in peace."

"But he killed my father."

"And Julian Matz killed mine!" Her voice rang out shrilly over the terrace. "Yet you don't see me lungin' for his neck. We've all lost people, Ness. Which is the reason I'm here. Because I think it's time we unite instead of fight. But first, I'd really appreciate seein' my son."

"He's indisposed tonight, but you'll see him in the morning," Liam said.

She glared at him a long moment. "He better be alive and well, Kolane."

"He's alive." Liam said nothing about his condition.

She turned her attention to her cousin. "Aidan, you said there would be food."

Aidan clapped, looking through the crowd until his gaze set on Lucy's. He nodded to her, and she scurried inside. I didn't have time to see her expression, see if she shared my shock in learning that the hunter was a wolf. Did anyone have suspicions about him, or had he really flown underneath every single Boulder and Pine's radar?

CHAPTER 44

S ervers spilled onto the terrace, as well as music. I recognized Emmy and Skylar but not the others. They weaved through the mismatched crowd, platters bobbing from their fingertips. Had they heard anything that had been said? Did they know what we were? Emmy caught my eye, but then her gaze lowered to the tray of mini sandwiches in her hands, her face uncharacteristically pale.

She'd heard.

She knew.

Would they tell more people? Or had Aidan Michaels somehow bought their silence?

"What a fucking fuck-fest," Lucas muttered behind me.

"Couldn't agree with you more, Mason," Sarah said.

"*You're* agreeing with *me*? Shit, can I get that in writing?"

"Shut the hell up."

Their banter unfortunately didn't ease my stress. I wondered if it eased theirs?

When Cassandra started toward me, I stood my ground even though I wanted to leap over the railing and run far away from the inn, from Boulder, from this woman who was a stranger, and yet who wasn't.

But I wanted answers. And I sensed she had many of them.

Stay calm, Liam whispered through the mind link, making his way back to me. ***Whatever she says, stay calm.***

That was easy for him to say, harder for me to do. She'd *manipulated* me. I liked being manipulated as much as I liked slicing my finger on a kitchen knife.

Suddenly, Cassandra was standing right in front of me. She was so tall that even in my heels I had to tip my head up. I hated having to tip my head up to her.

"I understand why your pack's been going through such an upheaval since your return."

I disregarded her bizarre compliment. If that's what it was. "Was it you who hacked my phone?"

"Not me personally."

"But someone from your pack?"

"We tried to warn Everest ourselves, but he didn't believe us. We were just trying to help him."

"You mean, get him off your land before the Boulders arrived and realized your connection to him."

When her gaze grinded into mine, I realized I'd struck a nerve. Well, I was about to strike a whole bunch more, because I wasn't done with her.

"Whose idea was the escort agency, *Sandra?*" My voice was as tight as my spine. "Everest's or yours?"

She cocked her head to the side, lips pursed. She was older than I'd assumed. Fifty, sixty perhaps. Tiny wrinkles ringed her mouth. What held my attention, though, was the odd bluish tinge to her lips —a recent bruise or a strange birthmark? Or maybe she was chilly. The nippiness in the air definitely made me regret not having taken a jacket.

"It was my idea," she said.

I blew out a relieved breath. "Why?"

"To get insight into other packs."

"To spy, then?"

She wrinkled her pert nose. "I'm not a fan of the word *spy*."

"Would you rather I say *snoop?*" My voice crackled with animosity.

She snapped her head straight. "Aren't you a little spitfire?"

"How did you reel Everest into your opportunistic scheme?"

"I didn't. Becca did. The silly girl fell in love." She took the glass of water someone tendered her way—Lori.

I gave the tall woman beside Cassandra a cursory once-over. All of her was thin and narrow, from her face to her body.

"Thank you, sweet thing." Cassandra wrapped fingers topped with lacquered burgundy nails filed to a dull point around the glass and tipped it to her bluish lips. "Where was I?"

"Becca and Everest fell in love," I supplied curtly.

"Right. Becca convinced me Everest was unhappy with the Boulders." She slanted her eyes to Liam. "That he could be an asset. So we talked, and I brought him on."

Liam's body had hardened next to mine as though he were made entirely of bones.

"Everest wanted to have Heath demoted and asked if I had anythin' on him he could use. Even though Aidan had supplied me with somethin' your cousin could've used"—her gaze slid back to me—"my goal wasn't to instigate a war between the packs. I told him I'd let him use the girls to dig up his own dirt."

Even though Liam didn't react verbally or physically, I sensed the frenzied beat of his heart inside of mine. All of the pack seemed to sense it, because suddenly Frank was wrapping his fingers around Liam's wrist, and Lucas had squeezed in between Liam and me.

Lori handed Cassandra a plate laden with food and took away her glass of water.

"And whose idea was it to use me as an escort?" I asked.

Cassandra devoured a pig-in-a-blanket in a single bite, then made another vanish just as swiftly. "His. But I seconded it. You were vengeful and desirous of closure. I believed meetin' with Heath would bring you closure."

In a way, it had, but I would never ever admit this. I kept my expression blank. The air was so rife with tension that I expected some of the Boulders to shift, but everyone remained in skin.

"Why did you send me to meet Aidan?" He wasn't by her side and he wasn't in the crowd. "So I could get closure for my father's death?"

"No. I did that so that *he* could get closure. Killing your father was a mistake. A terrible one. He'd been aimin' for Heath, but I believe you already know that."

"Doesn't erase what he did."

"No, it doesn't. Except he was tryin' to help your father, Ness."

"What are you talking about?"

"I'm talkin' about something your Alpha should explain."

She started to turn away, but I called her back. "Mrs. Morgan, why did you have Everest killed?"

"I didn't have Everest killed. I had him followed."

"Having him followed got him killed."

"Extorting money from my pack got him killed," she lobbed back. "Your cousin was a thief. He said he had access to Sillin, made us pay a substantial deposit for it, and then he never delivered."

My heart was beating double-time. "What did you need Sillin for?"

She made a sort of guttural sound, halfway between a growl and a sigh. "For injuries. For travel. For my cousin—although now he won't be needin' it anymore. And before you go on assumin' anything, we had *no* intention of using it as a weapon."

Like I'd ever believe that . . .

She shook her head. "An Alpha's responsibility is to protect the pack at any costs. At least, that's what an Alpha *should* do. May I suggest that before you go judgin' me and mine, you take a good look at your own Alpha."

Liam's eyes glowed as bright as the flames I'd imagined licking up the sides of the inn.

With a skein of Creeks trailing her, she finally took off toward the living room but paused by the sliding door, her blue sheath flapping in the gentle breeze. "Oh, and, Candy, I'll be here for several days. We still have so much to discuss, you and I, so don't be a stranger." She flicked her fingers in a little wave, then went to take a seat on one of the couches inside.

Her wolves milled around her, quietly ferrying plates to and from the buffet, gazes roving over us in both curiosity and caution.

The hush that draped over all three packs raised the hairs on the nape of my neck.

"Liam?" I whispered.

He looked everywhere but at my face.

My stomach felt as though a swarm of moths were flapping their little wings against its lining.

"What was Morgan talking about, Kolane?" August asked.

"None of your fucking business, Watt," Liam snapped.

"If it has to do with Ness, it is my fucking business."

Without turning around, I said, "No, August. I know you consider me like a sister, but I'm not. So it's not your business. This is between Liam and me."

My words stung August. I sensed it in the tremor that crossed through the tether. As he backed away, it vibrated like a flicked clothes string. He didn't leave the inn, just put distance between us. A lot of it.

I accorded Liam my full attention. "I'm listening."

A nerve ticked in his temple and another in his jaw.

When he still didn't speak, I asked, "Would you rather I ask Aidan Michaels to enlighten me?"

"A couple days before he was shot, your father challenged mine for Alpha," Liam said roughly. "My father said he would kill him, and Aidan caught it with one of the many bugs he'd planted in our homes. After Callum died, when we came for Aidan, the bastard played back the recording. Said he'd play it for the entire pack. Even though Dad didn't shoot Callum, it made him look guilty. That's why your father's death wasn't avenged."

The music stopped, replaced by a screechy recording. A voice risen from the dead boomed across the terrace.

"The nerve of Clark! He already stole my mate. And now he wants my pack?" Heath sounded crazed. *"The fucking nerve of him."*

Something shattered. Heath had probably lobbed one of his crystal highballs into a wall. I could just imagine the whiskey dripping down the wooden pillar in his cushy home.

"Why do you think he challenged you?" Liam's fifteen-year-old voice rang across the deathly quiet porch.

"To bring his bastard child into the pack. He doesn't get that she's not his kid. That she can't fucking be his kid. Boulders don't have girls!" Heath bellowed a couple expletives that had Frank shutting his eyes. *"The Clarks are parasites, Liam. They suck up the resources of the pack and bring nothing but fucking problems in return."*

For a moment, no sound came out of the speakers, and I thought Aidan or whoever was broadcasting the recording had pressed pause.

I looked at Liam, but he stared at the weathered teak slats beneath our feet.

"I just had a fucking fantastic idea." Heath's voice exploded over the terrace. *"I'll kill him before he publicly challenges me."*

A pause, then: *"If you make it look like a hunting accident"*—Liam sounded so cool and collected, the complete antithesis of his dad— *"you can blame that creepy-ass hunter so we can finally get rid of him."*

There was a click. It was probably the recording, but it felt like my heart. Like an explosion had detonated in the marrow of my bones, surged into my muscles, and vibrated through my flesh, coating every inch of me in goose bumps. They cascaded over my skin in icy waves.

"I didn't even know my father wanted to be Alpha," I whispered, even though that was far *far* from the worst part of what I'd just heard. Of what everyone had just heard.

Liam lifted his face, pain etched inside each one of his features.

I rolled my fingers into such tight fists that my nails carved up my palms. I had a strong urge to hit him. In the heart. Instead, I wiped my mouth on my forearm in an attempt to erase every kiss we'd ever shared.

He dragged a hand through his dark hair, and a lock flopped into his eyes. "I was fifteen, Ness. A kid. I had no idea what I was saying."

"Is that really your excuse?" My voice rang inside my ears.

"I just wanted Aidan gone. Not your father—"

"And yet you didn't tell your father not to kill mine."

Sarah tried to touch my arm, but I whipped it out of her reach and stepped back until my tailbone smacked into the guardrail.

"Ness . . . " Liam started.

I'd pledged myself to a man who'd been on board with eliminating my father. "You are Heath's son."

Liam shut his eyes as though I'd taken a swing at him.

"I don't want you as my Alpha." I gripped the handrail behind my back for support. "How do I break our link?"

His eyes snapped open, then grew wide.

"You can't break the Alpha link," Frank said, forehead grooved with so many wrinkles that it seemed as though the evening had added years to his face. "The only thing you can do is move away until you don't feel the pull of the pack."

I stared at the elder, then at the shifters surrounding us, at the Creek Alpha who was sitting with her wolves in the living room, watching me through the open glass doors, at Sarah whose mouth gaped, at Lucas and Matt and Cole who all wore matching looks of regret, and finally at August. He was the only one who didn't stare back. His eyes were like twin rifles set on the back of Liam's head.

"I'll leave, then." I pressed off the balustrade and walked past Liam, who put his hand on my arm. "Don't you *dare* touch me." I snatched my arm away, my icy shock replaced by a searing wrath.

"I'm sorry," he murmured as I passed by him.

I whirled. "No, you're not. You're just sorry I found out."

Liam shook his head. "They were just words. We never ended up hurting him. Aidan pulled that trigger. We didn't."

"Lucky for you, huh? Lucky for you he made a mistake!" I backed away before stalking off, speeding through the living room in my stupid heels, clutching my stupid dress. I walked toward the bell desk to phone my uncle.

As I dialed his number, Aidan strolled out of the back office, a USB key in his hand—probably the vessel containing the malicious conversation. I dropped the phone, and it clattered at my feet, the battery flying out of the handheld device.

"Should've heeded my note," he said.

"What note?" I pressed a hand against my chest as though to keep my heart from dropping like the phone.

"The one I tied to the bicycle, which I had delivered to the inn."

"You shot my father and your ex-wife. You really thought I would stop by for tea?"

"I'm not a fan of tea. I'd have served something fizzy . . . "

I arced my hand in the air in frustration. "Oh, you know what I mean!"

He squeezed an oily smile onto his lips.

I crouched to grab the phone and then attempted to fit the battery back inside, but my hands were shaking.

"Want some help?" He extended his hand.

"No." After several botched attempts, I jammed the battery back in. While the phone powered up, I said, "I know killing my father was a mistake, that you were aiming for Heath. Why?"

"I had my own vendetta toward him. He took something I loved."

I hadn't considered Aidan Michaels capable of love, but I also hadn't considered he could be a werewolf.

"The recording came in handy when Heath came to avenge your father's death. Should've seen how astonished he was when I played it back for him." He flashed me a smile that made my skin crawl.

Aidan Michaels was a monster. Just like Heath Kolane. Where Heath raped women, Aidan shot them.

"Even though you didn't mean to kill my father, it was still your finger on that trigger."

"Is that a threat, little girl?"

"Maybe it is."

"I'd be very careful doling out threats. You might be an orphan, but there are still people you care about . . . "

My stomach curled onto itself at his menace. I backed away from him, clutching the phone to my chest. Keeping one eye on the Creek wolf, I tried to dial Jeb's number from memory, but an automated message kept telling me I'd entered the wrong number. *Ugh.*

"Need a ride home, Ness?" Aidan asked.

"Like I'd ever let you drive me anywhere."

"Oh, I would've phoned up my driver. I have better things to do with my evening. Better yet, you could use the bicycle I sent back. Here, let me get you the key to the garage."

Footsteps pounded the foyer floor, and then a gruff voice said, "She won't be needing that key."

CHAPTER 45

"Y ou don't need to take me home, August," I said.

"You're right. I don't, but I was leaving. If you don't want a ride, by all means, make your own way home." He paused by the entrance of the inn, waiting for me to decide.

I all but flung the phone at Aidan Michaels and raced to the revolving doors As soon as we were outside, I said, "I'll kill that man someday."

August glanced at me, eyes bathed in shadows, shadows I'd put there. Not all of them, perhaps, but some. We didn't talk as we walked to his pickup, and we didn't talk as he drove me back home. When we reached my street, August finally spoke.

"You're not serious about leaving Boulder, are you?"

"I am."

"You're still a minor."

I stared up at the darkened apartment. Was my uncle already sleeping?

"Jeb will understand that I can't stay in Boulder. He'll understand that I can't obey a man I . . . I can't trust."

"You don't have to leave. Liam won't harm you."

"I know Liam isn't that spiteful fifteen-year-old boy, but every time I'll look at him, I'll remember that he was complicit in killing my father." I touched the door handle. "Besides, my leaving will benefit you."

"How?" he asked sharply. "How will it benefit me?"

I quirked an eyebrow. "Um. Did tonight's gathering make you forget about the mating link?"

"The mating link doesn't bother me, Ness."

"How can it not?"

"Does it bother you?"

"No, but I've sworn off men." I raised a smile I wasn't really feeling. Mom used to say that if you smiled in spite of being down, your emotions would eventually catch up with your face. "Anyway, August Watt, I promise I'll write this time."

He stared fixedly ahead of him. I was tempted to lean over and plant a kiss on his cheek but chickened out. I got out of the car and shut the door, then climbed the steps. The pickup didn't pull away. August was probably waiting for me to go inside. A gentleman till the very end . . .

I rang the doorbell. Seconds passed. When a minute went by, I rang the doorbell again but heard no footsteps. Was my uncle not home?

Frowning, I went back down the stairs and knuckled the passenger window. August powered it down. His phone was already ringing, and then my uncle's voice came on the speakerphone.

"Yes, August?"

"Ness was trying to get home, but she doesn't have her keys."

"I'm at Headquarters, watching over our asset with Derek and his son. If you swing by, I can give you the key."

I bit my lip. "What time will you be home?"

"I won't. I don't want to risk those bastard Creeks freeing Everest's murderer." His desire for vengeance palpitated through the phone.

"Okay, we'll figure something out," August said.

When he hung up, I said, "I can—" I had been about to say drive myself there and back, but Jeb had taken the van. *Shoot.* I was stranded. "Actually, do you mind giving me a ride?"

He nodded, and I got back inside.

Pulling away from the curb, he said, "I don't like the idea of you sleeping here all by yourself. Not with the Creeks in town."

"I lived six months on my own in a real crappy neighborhood."

"You weren't on my watch then."

"I'm not on your watch now either."

"Ness," he sighed. "Please give me a break tonight."

I nibbled on my lip and relented. "What did you have in mind?"

"You can stay with me tonight."

"Um." The seatbelt felt like it was cutting off my breath. I hooked my thumbs underneath the taut fabric and tugged.

"I'll sleep on the couch," he said.

Yeah. But his place was one big open space. Taking the couch wouldn't give either of us much privacy. "I could go to Frank's—"

"He might not get home until late." He'd already started driving toward the warehouse.

I sensed reminding him that Evelyn would be there would do little to change the course of my evening. "Fine, but I'll take the couch."

"The bed's more comfortable."

"It's your bed."

"It's also my couch."

A ghost of a smile made its way to my lips.

"Do you know how many girls would love to be in your shoes right now?"

"My shoes are starting to hurt my feet, so I don't think many."

He side-eyed me, and although there wasn't much light, his eyes seemed greener. "There's the Ness Clark I know and adore."

"Shut up."

He chuckled softly, and it smoothed the spiny ridges of this strange night.

CHAPTER 46

After feasting on leftover lasagna, I showered and changed into one of his T-shirts that smelled so strongly of him it made my head spin. Did I also smell like sandalwood and sawdust now? Or did August smell like me? Or maybe our scents had mixed and created a completely different aroma.

I asked him as I helped him pull a sheet over the couch.

His freckles seemed to darken at my question, which of course prompted me to ask, "What?"

He spent an extra-long time tucking the sheet under the seat cushions before straightening up and rubbing the back of his neck. "They meant that we smelled like we"—he snatched the coverlet from the coffee table and unfolded it—"like we'd had sex."

"Oh." I wrinkled my nose. "So . . . sweaty?"

A bark of laughter burst out of him.

I tossed the pillow I'd been stuffing in a pillowcase at him. He caught it and finished my half-ass job.

"What did I say now?" I asked, arching an eyebrow.

"What sort of strenuous sex have you been having?" He was still grinning.

I dragged my hand through my hair. "I, um . . . haven't."

"Never?" His grin settled into a faint smile.

I was certain I was beet-red.

He simply said, "Huh," which was really worse than not saying anything at all. "I didn't mean to make you feel embarrassed."

"You didn't. It's just a really weird conversation to be having." I straightened the coverlet he'd tossed over the couch. "On the upside, I don't know what I'm missing." I sat down, the T-shirt with the small Watt logo riding up. I tugged on the hem. "I know you said you got used to the mating link, but you know what you're missing, so it must suck."

His Adam's apple bobbed. "I've had so much on my mind lately between Mom and the pack and work that I haven't had much time to dwell on it."

"Apparently men think about sex every seven seconds."

He snorted. "Is that so?"

I leaned over and flicked his arm.

He shook his head, but his grin increased. "You're really going to keep that up?"

"Until I leave."

That zapped the smile right off his face. He sat down next to me, his weight dipping the couch. "You shouldn't have to leave again. It's not good for your body."

"It wouldn't be good for my mind to stick around. The day Liam's no longer Alpha—"

"Could be decades from now."

"—I'll come back." I stuck my hands between my knees and squeezed them.

"Ness . . . "

"Let's not talk about it anymore, okay? I'm really tired."

Sighing, he wrapped an arm around my shoulders, dragged me into his body, and kissed my temple. I closed my eyes, enjoying the proximity of him, the smell of him. Enjoying it too much.

Another reason I needed to leave . . .

I had feelings that weren't sisterly at all toward August, and that would just make things weird between us in the coming months.

I ducked out from underneath his arm. "Mind if I turn off the lights?"

"Go right ahead."

I got up from the couch and walked over to his front door. I touched the little panel and then returned to the couch. Moonlight filtered in through the open window, but even without moonlight, I could see well in the dark. Probably not as sharply as a real wolf, but more sharply than a human. This was how I saw the great lump sprawled on the couch.

"Take the bed, Ness."

"But it's your bed."

"Didn't we just have this conversation?"

"Fine." I padded toward the ladder and climbed up to the mezzanine, then crawled over the giant bed and slipped underneath the thick comforter. I wasn't sure I'd be able to sleep. Every time I closed my eyes, I heard the recording again.

And again.

If you make it look like a hunting accident, you can blame the hunter.

I kept my eyes open until the darkness turned a bit brighter.

A bit greener.

A bit bluer.

And I was running.

Next to a big black wolf with smiling silver eyes. *You think you can catch that squirrel, baby girl?*

I darted after the fluffy rodent that spiraled up the trunk of a pine and snatched it right off the tree. *Too easy, Dad.*

Snap his neck quick. You don't want it to suffer.

A second later, the squirrel stopped moving. We feasted on the squirrel, blood and gore dripping from our noses. Well, mostly from mine.

My father was watching on, eyes shining with pride. Suddenly, he whipped his head to the side, ears pricked up, and whirled around, muscles coiled to leap. *Ness, run!*

We didn't have time to run.

A bullet whizzed through the inert air and buried itself into his pelt with a pop. He faltered and tumbled, and blood sprayed out of him, covering my face, mixing with the squirrel's blood.

I whimpered and whimpered, my lament disseminating through the woods like torn dandelion florets.

Suddenly, a heavy weight pinned me to the supple ground, and I flailed, clawing my attacker, trying to get him off me, snarling.

"Ness, wake up! It's just me."

My lids flew open. August was straddling me, my wrists cuffed in his hands. A line of blood seeped out of a thin gash right beneath his eye.

I gasped. "Your face!"

"My face is fine."

"You're bleeding." I struggled to free my wrists from the vice of his hands. He let go, and I hovered my fingertips over the strip of skin I'd removed. I didn't think touching the cut would staunch the reddened flow, so I wiggled out from underneath him, and then once I was sitting up, I tugged the hem of my T-shirt up to the wound.

"Shoot. I'm so sorry."

"It's okay." He shut his eye as I applied pressure.

The blood reminded me of my father's. Except there had been so much more in that forest.

I shuddered and shut my lids.

Large, warm hands clamped my cold cheeks. "Look at me."

I did.

"It was a nightmare. You're awake now. You're safe."

I pulled my bottom lip into my mouth as I lowered the fabric to peer at the torn flesh. The hairline cut was already sealing. "I didn't get you anywhere else, did I?"

He smiled. "Not for lack of trying." He sat back on his heels, his smile flickering as his gaze dropped to the inches of bare skin between the band of my black underwear and the bunched-up cotton T-shirt I was still holding.

I released the hem, and it fluttered back down.

Palming his cropped hair, August turned to get off the bed, but I reached out and caught his elbow.

"Can you stay with me? Please?" I felt incredibly childish for asking. "Just until I fall back asleep?"

Several seconds slipped by before he gave a nod so heavy it almost made me regret asking. I lay back down and tucked my hands underneath the pillow.

"I'll try not to attack you again," I said, pressing my cheek into the creased fabric that was damp with tears or sweat—perhaps both.

I watched as August attempted to get comfortable beside me. He didn't venture under the comforter. His long legs ensconced in a pair of gray sweats spanned the entire length of the mattress.

"Did I steal your side of the bed?" I asked as he threw one of his arms over his head.

He was sprawled on his back, his T-shirt riding up, revealing taut brown skin dusted with a trail of dark hair. I snapped my eyes closed, but the image was already seared behind my retinas and was doing strange things to my stomach . . . And lower. I squeezed my thighs and flipped over.

"I usually take up the entire thing," he said.

I slid to the edge of the mattress to make myself smaller.

"What are you doing?"

"Trying to give you more space."

And myself.

I needed more space.

He grunted.

I didn't flick him; I didn't dare touch him. But he touched me. He dragged me back toward the center of the bed. Except his hands were nowhere near my body.

"How did you do that?" I asked, part enthralled, part freaked out. Controlling another person's movements without touching them resided in a realm of magic I just couldn't wrap my mind around. *And yes, I know . . . I could transform into a werewolf.*

"I pulled on the rope connecting us."

My navel still pulsated. "Can you teach me how to do it?" Not that I'd have much use for the ability once I was gone . . .

"You have to focus your mind on that rope. Visualize it. For me it's blue and shiny. Once you can *see* it, you contract your stomach, and it reels it in. That's how I do it, anyway. Maybe for you it's different."

"Can I try?"

He nodded.

My brow puckered as I concentrated. I saw the rope. It wasn't blue but it was shiny. I wrapped my mind around it and sucked in my stomach. I felt a tightening, but August's body didn't even budge an inch.

"I'm bigger and heavier than you."

I tried again. Failed again. "Can you feel it at least?"

"Yes." He smiled. "It tickles."

"You can haul my body over several feet, but when I do it, it tickles? Damn. That's unfair."

He turned up the force of his smile but winced when it tugged on the flesh I'd clawed. I reached out and ran my thumb over the cut, and his breath caught.

"Does it sting?" I asked.

"I'm fine, Ness." He dragged my hand away from his face.

Our heads were so close I could see the shape of each one of his freckles. I remembered trying to map out constellations on his skin when I was a kid. I remembered succeeding, although I didn't remember the names of the ones I'd found.

"What are you thinking about?" His voice was a gravelly whisper.

"I was trying to remember which constellations I'd matched to your freckles."

"Cassiopeia. You were convinced this"—he took the index finger of the hand he was still holding, set the tip of it on his injured cheek, and dragged it down, then straight, then down again, and finally up—"was Cassiopeia."

His warm breaths hit my nose, and yet it was my stomach that felt warmer, not my face. I dropped my eyes to his mouth, wondering what it would feel like to kiss him. His breathing hitched as though he could read my train of thoughts, as though he could sense it through our link. Perhaps he could.

I slid the finger he still gripped out of his hold and glided the tip across the hard plane of his cheek, over the dark stubble of his jaw, down the side of his strong neck. I watched my index's path as I traced the edge of his body, as my finger rounded his broad shoulder and dipped along his carved bicep. When my finger met bare skin, his flesh pebbled.

I kept waiting for him to put a stop to my exploration. I kept waiting for him to ask me what had gotten into me, but he stayed silent, allowing me access to his sinful form. I outlined the sharp edge of his elbow, then drew a straight line down the inside of his forearm, where the skin was the softest, stopping when I reached the center of his palm.

Only then did I dare look up into those mossy eyes that had enchanted me my entire childhood. His pupils pulsed, devoured his irises. I inched closer to him until my lips were aligned with the trail of dried blood on his cheek. I pressed my mouth to his skin and darted my tongue out to lick away the coppery smear. Never in a million years would I have imagined licking August's face. Perhaps in fur, but not in skin. In fur, the act would've been deemed playful, affectionate. In skin, it was intimate.

August, who'd lain perfectly still, finally stirred to life. The hand I was still touching clamped over mine, cocooning my fingers, and his other hand snaked underneath my head and threaded through my hair. Gently, he tugged on it to unfasten my mouth from his cheek.

"Ness . . . " My name felt like a gust of night wind, the sort that made fir needles shiver and sway. "If you kiss me, then you can't leave," he murmured.

It took me a moment to make sense of his words. "Why not?"

"Because you can't feed a starving man, then take away his food." If his voice hadn't been so low and raucous, I might've poked fun at him for that metaphor, but his timbre told me he was serious.

"You'll find better food," I finally said, heart fluttering the gray cotton that had coiled around my torso.

The fingers cupping the back of my head relaxed, slid to the nape of my neck, then back up. "How long?"

I thought he was asking me how long I was planning on staying, and I said until the morning.

"No, Ness. How long have you felt this way about me?"

Oh.

Oh . . .

I lowered my eyelashes, heat snaking up my chest like a warm current. "For a while now. Since the lake. But this link . . . it confuses me. Every time you touch me . . . even when you do it by mistake—"

"I never do anything by mistake."

I jerked my attention back to his face, the warm current spreading and heating up *every* part of me. "Well, when it happens, it does things to me, August. Things I don't think I should be feeling. Things I don't think I should be telling you about."

But here I was, confessing my deepest, darkest secrets.

"Is that why you got mad at me for calling you Dimples or kid? Because you thought it meant I only saw you as a little girl?"

I nodded, and the audacity that had taken ahold of me began to slip through my fingers like crumbling rock.

He stayed quiet so long that I said, "If you don't say something soon, I'm going to die of embarrassment."

His fingers spiraled up the column of my neck and stilled on the back of my scalp again, tipping it infinitesimally upward. "What would you like me to say?"

I twisted up my lips before mumbling, "That you feel a little bit of the same things I do."

"But if I said that, I'd be lying."

My heart squeezed in humiliation, and then my lids clinched.

"I'd be lying because whatever you feel, I feel it tenfold. But I've been feeling this way since you walked into that living room with that chin held so high. Since before this link snapped into place between us, which makes me reticent of letting this kiss happen at all."

I opened my eyes, humiliation replaced by something else entirely. Something that made the tether between us thrum. "Why?"

"Because once you're far from Boulder, far from me and our link, you'll stop wanting me, but I won't stop wanting you."

"You don't know that."

"That I won't stop wanting you? Yeah. I do. I was in—" He licked his lush lips, making them glisten. "There was an ocean separating us, and I couldn't get you out of my mind, Ness. And it screwed me up real bad. I wasn't focused on the team, on the mission. All I could think of was you and what the pack was putting you through, and what you were feeling. And then when Cole told me Liam—"

He rolled onto his back, releasing my hand but curling the other around my shoulders. I laid my head in the crook of his shoulder, my hair fanning over his arm. He wove his fingers through it, making my scalp tingle, making all of me tingle.

"When Cole told me Liam made a move on you, I was blinded by such jealousy that I made a grave tactical error that put one of my buddies at risk. It was bad, Ness." He shuddered and closed his eyes a long second.

I placed my palm over his beating heart, trapping its brisk rhythm with my fingertips. "I'm sorry."

"It's not your fault, sweetheart. I left you. Not the other way around."

And now I was the one talking about leaving. What if he did find *better food?* The mere thought of that waitress or Sienna resting where I lay had me gritting my teeth.

"I lied," I said, trying to ease the tension in my jaw. I kept my gaze on the palm flattened against his chest. "I've had a crush on you since I was a kid. A *real* kid. Which I know is disturbing. But you were everything to me. You *meant* everything to me. Remember the day you let me tag along on that movie date of yours with Betsy, or whatever her name was?" Her face flashed behind my lids. "I hated that she had curves and brown hair, and that I was as flat as a board and blonde. I hated that you kept touching her hair. Her hand. I hated it so much that I faked a stomachache so you'd take me home. So that you'd stay with *me.* So that you'd touch *my* hair."

He didn't say anything for a little while, as though trying to locate the memory. Or maybe he was rethinking what he'd told me, about liking me after my declaration.

"Her name was Carrie."

Oh, goodie. He remembered her. Worse, he smiled as he reminisced. A punch in the ribs would've hurt less.

He looped the ends of my hair around his fingers. "She broke up with me that night, because I chose you over her." His smile grew a little broader. "I knew you had a crush on me, but—"

"It really wasn't a crush; it was an infatuation." I grimaced. "And I honestly have no idea why I'm telling you all this."

"I think I know."

"Really?"

He rolled onto his side. "Because you're trying to test my willpower." He stared into my eyes. "Or break it . . . "

"Is it working?"

"When have you ever failed at anything?"

I smiled, but then I didn't. Then, in a rush of boldness—or foolishness—I closed the distance between our mouths, fitting mine on top of his.

A groan rumbled out of his chest, and he skated his mouth off mine. "Are you staying?" His chest rose and fell.

"I don't think I can—"

He winced.

"Let me finish my sentence. You didn't let me finish my sentence."

His gaze tripped over my face. "Finish your sentence."

Heart palpitating against my jaw, my lips, my chin, my forehead, I repeated what I'd said, but added the final word, the one that would change everything.

For him.

For me.

For us.

"I don't think I can *leave*."

I didn't want to answer to Liam, and I wasn't sure how I would get around this if I stayed, but I wasn't ready to abandon August, Evelyn, or Jeb. I didn't want to lose the ability to transform into a powerful beast, nor leave the home I'd just gotten back.

August clasped my chin with heartbreaking tenderness. "I need you to be perfectly certain about this."

"*This?*"

"Staying. Being with me." He ran his thumb over my lower lip. "I want you as my mate, Ness. Not tonight. Not tomorrow, but before the Winter Solstice. I need to know if you want this too. Because this isn't a simple crush. At least, not for me."

He was talking about *forever*. Forever scared the hell out of me. "I've never even been in a relationship, August."

"So you're not ready?"

"Because you are?"

"I've been with other people. I know what's out there, and I understand how precious what I've been given is. How precious *you* are." He caressed my cheek.

"I want to be with you, August—only you—and I *have* seen what's out there. I'm not settling for you because you happen to be around and magically connected to me. But I don't want to promise you forever, because that scares me." I moistened my dry lips with the tip of my tongue. "If that's not enough for you—"

His hand scooped up the back of my head and pressed my face

closer to his, interrupting the flow of my thoughts and words. Against my lips, he whispered, "*Only me*."

"Only you," I murmured to the man lying beside me, so familiar and yet a complete stranger.

He crushed his mouth to mine, and the rope that bound us drew me nearer and nearer. I didn't know if he'd reeled me in or if I'd done that. All I knew was that each one of our bones aligned; each inch of our flesh molded together to the point where it was impossible to distinguish where one of us began and the other ended.

And that—fitting so perfectly with someone—scared me more than anything, because if we ended, it would tear up more than just our hearts. It would tear up our very bodies.

CHAPTER 47

S leep fell over me as quietly as dawn crept over the horizon and kept me in its arms the same way August kept me in his. I felt safe and calm and sated in a way I hadn't felt in a long time. All we'd done was kiss, our fingers not venturing across the acres of skin that were now ours to explore. I sensed August was worried of frightening me by going too fast.

I appreciated the slowness. Everything with Liam had been rushed. We'd kissed as though we were out of time, and in a way, we had been, even though neither of us had known it then.

As the sun crested higher into the sky, I stroked August's long fingers splayed on my stomach, keeping me pinned to him, thinking of the awful recording, dwelling on how low men could sink to keep what they believed was theirs, and then I thought of my father wanting to be Alpha.

I found it strange that he'd coveted leadership. Had he desired this to bring me into the pack like Heath insinuated, or had it been a life goal? Had my mother known his intentions?

My mother who'd been another man's mate . . .

As I lay with the one who was supposed to be mine, I wondered if resisting the pull had been difficult. Perhaps it hadn't been such a feat considering her mate was neither gentle nor sweet. The fact that she'd managed, though, reassured me that I hadn't ended up in

August's bed because of any magic. If August had been a violent narcissist, I would've kept my distance.

As though he'd felt me thinking of him, he stirred behind me, and the fingers I was caressing crimped my T-shirt and hoisted me a little higher up his body. I smiled, knowing the reason he'd readjusted me . . . having *felt* the reason against my tailbone. His lips connected with my shoulder blade and laid the warmest and softest kiss that penetrated through the barrier of cotton and skin, and then those lips moved to the slope of my neck and pressed a tantalizing kiss there, and then he nipped his way higher, to the sensitive place right behind my earlobe.

Still smiling, I spun in his arms to face him.

He returned my smile, a hesitant version of it, though, that had my heart beating double-time.

"No regrets?" he finally asked.

"No."

He ran a knuckle down my cheek, dipping it into my dimple before curving it around my jaw.

"What about you?" I asked.

"My only regret is that morning has come."

"Are you worried I'll turn into a pumpkin?"

He laughed, and then he pressed that beautiful, laughing mouth of his against mine and spilled the deep notes of his joy inside me. As the kiss deepened, the shape of his mouth changed, uncurled, opened. He pulled me into him, all of me, from my tongue to my body. When the bulge that strained his sweatpants pushed against my thighs, he disconnected our mouths and pressed me slightly away as though afraid to bruise me.

He studied my face, tucking a piece of hair behind my ear. "I'm going to be saving lots on water heating."

I studied him back. From his pupils ringed with brown that melted into the brightest green flecked with gold, to the scattering of chocolate freckles on his light-brown skin, to the dark auburn stubble on his oblong jaw, to the faint scar left over from my nighttime attack.

"I'll make up for your cold showers by taking extra hot ones," I said.

His pupils dilated, and his nose flicked mine. "Planning on showering here again, huh?"

Heat engulfed me. What in the world had prompted me to say that? "No. Um. Only if I get stranded—"

"I hope you'll get stranded often then." He smiled while I tried to rein back the rising heat. "I might even arrange for it to happen." He deposited a brief and searing kiss on my mouth that did absolutely nothing to cool me off.

"I'm going to need a cold shower too," I mumbled.

"I'd suggest taking one together, but that would defeat the purpose."

"It really would."

He combed another lock off my face, lifted my hair, then released it, watching as each strand fluttered down. "Do you think it might be real gold?"

I gave a very unladylike snort. "I wouldn't be riddled with debt if it were."

His gaze turned guarded. "You said you didn't—"

"It's nothing." I bit my lower lip. "Nothing I can't handle."

"How much?"

"Not telling you."

"Why not?"

"Because, it's personal."

"So are we. How much?"

"Please, leave it alone."

He rolled into a sitting position. "Fine. I'll leave it alone."

My lips fell open at how swiftly he'd relented. "Thank you."

"Mm-hmm." He scooted to the foot of the bed, then swung himself around and latched onto the ladder. "Going to take that much needed shower now. And I'll put a pot of coffee on."

I propped myself onto my elbows. "Hey, can you text Jeb to find out if he's home? I need to get back into the apartment."

"Will do."

I lay back down for a moment and watched the play of light and shadows on the concrete ceiling, wondering what I was supposed to do with myself now that I was staying—not professionally-speaking, but pack-speaking. Would I have to attend gatherings? How had yesterday's ended? If only I had my phone, I'd call Sarah. I was never leaving the house without *it* or my keys from now on, or my wallet for that matter. I prided myself on being street smart, but if I truly had been, I'd have taken my bag with me last night. I pressed my fingers into the still-warm duvet, watching the indent they left behind. Then again, if I'd taken my bag, I wouldn't have slept on this cloud of a bed, cocooned against a sexy shifter. The mere thought of the night had my body murring—the wolf's version of a purr.

When the percolator began gurgling, I got out of bed and stretched, before climbing down the ladder. The hardwood floor was cool beneath my feet, but the air was delightfully warm. I spied my dress on one of the kitchen barstools and debated whether to put the itchy thing back on but elected to keep August's T-shirt. It was comfier than tulle and long enough to cover my ass.

I padded into the kitchen and looked through cupboards until I found the one with mugs. No two recipients were alike. I shuffled them around, smiling at some of the slogans printed on them. I sucked in a breath when my gaze settled on a thick muck-green mug. I took it out and just stared at it.

Ceramic wasn't magical—unlike stinky wooden fossils—and yet this particular mug held magic. It made time reverse. I was sitting behind a pottery wheel, my hair in two long braids. Unlike most of the other kids who were making something for their parents, I'd decided to craft something for August. I stroked the glazed handle, the same way August had touched it when I'd given it to him seven years ago.

I set the mug down reverently, then filled it with coffee, the first sip of which had me moaning softly.

Something beeped, and then a door swept open. I froze, mug clutched in midair.

"Auggie, I brought—" Cole stopped talking when he spotted me.

We blinked at each other, and then another door groaned, and August strolled into the kitchen, a towel wrapped casually around his hips, the scent of his sandalwood soap almost choking me. Or maybe my increased heartbeats were choking me.

As August banged around behind me, probably getting himself a mug for the coffee, I considered ducking behind the island in the hopes that Cole would *unsee* me.

"It's not what it looks like," I blurted out.

But then I felt the heat of August's still damp body against my back. "It's exactly what it looks like."

Oh . . . God, strike me down. Because *He* didn't, I elbowed August gently and stepped to the side so that he wasn't glued so conspicuously to my backside.

A shit-eating grin rose to Cole's lips as he walked over to us. "Damn."

I tried to reason it could've been worse. It could've been Nelson or Isobel who'd come through that door instead of Cole.

"Mom sends muffins." He dropped a plastic container on the island. "I send my congratulations."

Had someone turned up the heat? Because I was pretty certain I'd started perspiring. I set my mug down. Holding hot coffee wasn't helping my sweating situation. Self-consciously, I tugged on the hem of my T-shirt. Not that Cole could see my legs with an island between us. I really wished it were a real island—palm trees and sand dunes and all.

Holy crap. I really did have a thing for palm trees apparently.

"Um." I pivoted around. "August, can we talk a second?" *In private,* I mouthed.

His gaze left Cole's and set back on me. The power of it, combined with the smug smile gracing his lips, sent me into cardiac arrest zone.

"Sure thing." He tipped his head toward the bathroom door.

I all but raced toward it.

"I can leave if you guys want," Cole said while taking a seat on one of the barstools.

"We'll only be a minute," I reassured him.

"One minute?" Cole gave an amused snort. "All those weeks of sexual frustration taking a toll, huh?"

August flipped him off as he trailed me. I shut the door and locked it, even though it was ridiculous. It wasn't as though Cole would barge in. I unlocked it.

"Let me guess, you want me to change the door code?"

"What? No. I mean . . . maybe." I dragged my hand through my hair. "But that's not what I wanted to discuss."

He crossed his arms in front of his broad, broad chest. I tweaked the inside of my wrist to refocus myself, but a glimpse into the foggy mirror nulled the effect of the pinch. The glass was clearing, so I could see August's V-shaped back which was frankly just as alluring as his front.

"You okay, sweetheart?"

I twisted my hair into a long rope to lift it from my neck before my skin could scorch it right off. "Um. Yes, but . . . "

"You don't want people finding out about us?"

I nodded a little maniacally.

"Why?"

"Because. Liam and I, we just broke up—"

"Happened three weeks ago."

Had it already been three weeks? Okay, good. At least I wasn't a total tramp. "Can we still keep it on the down-low for now? Just a couple weeks . . . "

August leaned back against the white enamel sink top, one eyebrow cocked up. "Why?"

"Because . . . "

"Because what?"

Ugh. Why couldn't he just go with it? "Because I'm afraid to hurt Liam's feelings."

"He wasn't afraid to hurt yours."

"I walked in on him. It wasn't like he flaunted his hookup in my face—"

"I wasn't talking about the *hookup.* I was talking about what went down at Tracy's." There was a jagged edge to his deep voice. "Ness, do you still have feelings for him?"

"What?" I blinked. "No."

"You sure?"

"Of course I'm sure."

His Adam's apple bobbed once, twice. Then he sighed, pushed off the sink top, and took a step toward me. His arms came loose before wrapping around my waist.

I tipped my head up. "Why would you think that?"

"Because I'm jealous, and it'll probably get worse, although I'm not sure how that would work considering I already want to wring the neck of anyone who so much as looks your way." He tipped his head to the door. "Cole included."

"You don't have to be jealous. I promise. I'm just nervous. What if your parents are horrified?"

"My parents already love you like a daughter."

"Exactly."

"Exactly what?"

"They might find it weird that you and I . . . you know . . ."

He smiled down at me.

"You're enjoying how nervous this is making me?"

"A little. You're cute when you blush."

"Puppies are cute. And I don't blush."

"You do. And fine, you're drop-dead gorgeous, and I'm the luckiest bastard in the entire world."

I rolled my eyes. "You don't have to overdo it."

"That was me stating a hard fact, Ness. You *are* the most beautiful girl, and I *am* the luckiest guy." He leaned in and stole a kiss. "But I don't think we'll be able to hide this for weeks. Days, possibly."

I nodded. "Days are good."

He kissed me again, dragging my mouth open, deepening the kiss until the tiles beneath my feet vanished. And they really did, because he lifted me and pressed me into the warm wall. Before I could fall, I wrapped my legs around his waist and got so carried away with our make-out session that my brain turned blissfully blank.

But then a phone rang, and Cole's voice resonated outside the door, and I landed with a thump back into the present. August set me down gently, the stiff swell tenting his towel brushing along the insides of my thighs. Dizzy with lust, I leaned back against the wall to even out my scattered heartbeats.

August bracketed my head with his palms, breathing in the air I panted out. "I might have to take another shower." His gravelly voice intensified my lust-induced daze.

There was a knock on the door. "Guys, sorry to interrupt, but there's been a development, so if you two don't mind taking a little break from—"

I opened the door so fast Cole almost stumbled inside the bathroom. "What development?"

"Julian just challenged Cassandra Morgan."

I frowned. "Challenged her to do what?"

"A potato-sack race," Cole said, just as August whispered, "No way . . ."

"Yes, way." Cole spun his phone between his fingers. "And I was kidding about the race."

"He challenged her for leadership of the Creeks?" I blurted out. "What did she say?"

He inhaled a long breath. "When an Alpha challenges another Alpha, Ness, there are two solutions. You either relinquish your territory and scram, or you accept to duel and hope you'll catch the challenger on a bad day."

"She'd have to give up Beaver Creek?" I asked.

"And the inn. And any other land that belongs to them. It's the law of the packs . . . the law of the fittest."

"That's a ballsy move on Julian's part," August said.

Cole stopped twirling his phone. "He'll either go down a legend or an imbecile, that's for sure."

"Do you think he'll challenge Liam next?" I asked.

"Julian would've done it before now if he'd wanted our pack's land," August said.

"Julian was probably frightened of doing it before," Cole said, "what with the whisperings of the pack being so *evolutionary*."

"Evolutionary?" I asked.

"All-male," Cole said. "And before you rip me a new one, I neither came up with the term, nor did I believe we were more evolved. I was simply guessing at a reason Julian never challenged Heath."

"But what if he *does* challenge Liam?" I asked. "Or *she* . . . ?" Dismissing Cassandra was foolish, considering she'd already defeated an Alpha.

"If either of them challenge Liam to a duel, my guess is he'll fight them," Cole said.

My heart skipped into my throat and expanded there until I had so much trouble breathing that August sketched small circles on my lower back.

"We'll be okay," he said.

Black dots danced at the edge of my vision.

"*He'll* be okay," he added in a weighty whisper, sensing I needed reassurance that Liam's life wasn't in peril. August stopped circling his palm, drawing me into his side instead, and then he kissed my forehead and repeated, "He'll be okay."

I clutched the hand wrapped around my waist as though it were the only thing keeping me from tipping over.

"Hey, Cole," August said, heart thudding steadily against my shoulder blade, "keep what you saw this morning to yourself."

Cole nodded. "Course, man." He pressed off the doorjamb. "Anyone want a muffin?"

My throat had closed up so tight that I didn't even think coffee would go down. "I need . . . clothes. I need clothes. Jeb—" I whispered raucously.

"He's home. Let me get dressed, and I'll take you."

"Okay," I breathed.

August unwrapped his arm from around me but threaded his fingers through mine and towed me back into the kitchen. I climbed onto a barstool, while he went through a passageway next to his bathroom—I assumed his closet.

After pouring himself a cup of coffee, Cole watched me from beneath his blond eyelashes. "I'm surprised you still care about him after last night. You looked angry enough to murder him."

Huh? Him? Oh . . . Liam. "The only person I wish dead is Aidan Michaels."

Cole leaned his forearms into the island. "Can I ask you something?"

I pressed my lips together warily.

"What are your intentions?" he asked.

"That's really none of your business, Cole."

"I just want to know if you're serious about him. That's all. He's been through a lot. And before you growl at me, I know you have too, but he's . . . well, he's—" He ping-ponged his phone between his hands. His fingers were as thick as Matt's and dotted with the same blond hairs. "I guess what I'm trying to say is I hope this isn't a rebound."

Even though I didn't appreciate his mistrust, I couldn't help but admire the consideration he had for August, which was the only reason I answered, "It's not a rebound."

"Cole," August said sharply, emerging from the closet dressed in army fatigues and a cream thermal tee molded to his torso.

Cole straightened up, raising both palms in the air. "Just watching out for you, man."

"Thanks, but stay out of it."

Cole's jaw set tightly. "Sorry."

As August leaned over me and nuzzled my neck, I said, "August?"

"Yeah, sweetheart?"

I pivoted to face him, forcing him to stop making my skin tingle. "This right here"—I pointed to Cole—"what he just asked . . . That's the reason why I don't want people to find out. The others will have the same reaction. It doesn't matter that Liam and I broke up three weeks ago, or that he's already slept with someone else; I'll be seen as *that* girl."

August's gaze tightened before glowing greener. "If anyone so much as insinuates—"

I pressed my finger against his mouth to calm his rising wolf. His hair had begun to lengthen and thicken. "Let's not discuss this anymore. Not with everything that's happening."

He dragged in a long, long breath, and I lowered my hand. "Fine. But if anyone says something—"

"I'll clock him over the head with the hammer from that state-of-the-art toolbox you got me last Christmas," Cole offered.

"Thank you," August said, rising up to his full height.

"You'd do the same for me."

"I would." August grabbed a muffin, bit into it, swallowed, bit into it again, swallowed again. Two more bites, and he was rubbing his hands together to get the clingy crumbs off. "Ready to go?"

I got down from the barstool. "If you don't mind me keeping the shirt, then yes. If not, I can put the dress—"

"Keep the shirt."

He pocketed his car keys, wallet, and phone from a hand-carved wooden bowl on the island, while I stuck my feet back into my heels and grabbed my dress. When I drew the front door open, brightness flooded the loft-like space.

Sunny days heralded good things.

Today would be a good day.

Julian would take out Cassandra.

It struck me that he would inherit her pack. Would all of them move to Boulder? I hoped not because a thousand more werewolves in the area would not only clutter our woods but also instigate territorial skirmishes. I turned away from the bright sky to see what was holding up August. I imagined it was Cole, but both of them were staring at me.

I shifted a little. "Are you coming?"

August smacked his buddy's chest, tossed him a murderous look, then walked over to me. He wrapped his arm around my waist and ushered me out. The warehouse parking lot was full of cars and trucks, so I stepped out of his reach.

His eyes, that hadn't lost their homicidal glint, swept over me. He didn't say anything, but I felt a tug deep in my stomach, and the tug had me sidling back up to him.

"August—" I gasped, tripping on my heels.

He reached out to steady me. "What?" His tone was innocent, but his expression wasn't.

"You know exactly what," I grumbled, quickly scanning the lot.

Thankfully no one was outside.

When we reached the pickup, he opened the door. "Ness, I have a physical need to keep you close to me. It's beyond my control."

I shook my head. "Says the man with the greatest amount of self-control."

"Not when it comes to you."

He dipped his chin into his neck, and then the hand that wasn't holding the door brushed my waist before opening like a flower in front of me. Sighing, I slipped my hand into his proffered one and climbed into the truck.

Once he was settled behind the wheel, and we'd pulled out of the lot, I scooted closer to him and rested my head on his shoulder. His arm came around my waist and held me against him.

"Do you think Julian will win?" I asked.

August sighed, and his sigh fluttered pieces of my uncombed hair. "We'll know soon enough."

"This fight-to-the-death tradition is so barbaric."

August pulled away to look down at me. "Says the girl who signed up for the Alpha trials."

"I didn't know that was going to be the ultimate test. The elders just said I would have to leave if I lost. They didn't mention dying."

He stopped in the middle of the road. Thankfully there were two lanes, so although we got honked at, the cars went around us.

"I thought you were aware of the final trial."

"No."

"Would you have signed up had you known?"

Before I could answer, Liam's voice filled my mind. *The fight will take place at noon on the lawn of the inn. I hope to see you all there to support our allies, the Pines.*

I checked the time on the car's dashboard. "That's in—in one hour."

August's fingers cinched around the steering wheel. "I don't want you to go, Ness. These fights . . . they can escalate. Spark other fights."

"And you don't think I can hold my own?"

"Of course I think you can, but do I want to risk it? No."

"I appreciate your desire to keep me safe, but I'm never going to be the girl who'll stay at home and wait by the phone. That's not in my DNA."

A couple different emotions slotted over his face—surprise, frustration, alarm. "Fine," he finally said, "but you'll be at my side the entire time. Hope you'll be okay with that."

"August . . . "

"Not up for discussion."

I growled a little.

"Indulge me, sweetheart. You've never attended a duel. These things are ugly. Even if the wolf you're rooting for wins, they're ugly."

I *had* attended one, but not as a spectator. I didn't think bringing up my own trials again would help ease August's mood, so I kept quiet. Besides, I didn't hate the idea of being at his side.

CHAPTER 48

We drove to the inn in August's truck. I let Jeb sit up front, content to have the backseat to myself. As we rolled up the road to the inn, I intermittently texted Sarah and stared out the window at the sun-soaked mountains. She was confident her uncle would demolish the Creek Alpha. I hoped she was right.

"I've never seen so many cars." Jeb stared at the ocean of parked cars unfurling like a multi-colored wave down the sloping driveway.

Even though he was hyper—probably jacked-up on coffee and stress—I worried coming here would be tough on him. Especially if his ex-wife was in the vicinity, fawning over Aidan Michaels. I really hoped Lucy wouldn't show her face. For Jeb's sake, and for mine. Could she not see what a vile man Aidan was? Could she not spy the dried blood of her son underneath the hunter's—the Creek's—buffed fingernails? Sure, he hadn't confessed to Everest's murder, but I sensed with every fiber of my being that Aidan had had a hand in it. After all, the inn would still be Clark-owned if Everest were alive. Which would've been a heck of lot less convenient to host Aidan's extended family.

"You heard Aidan Michaels is a wolf," I told Jeb as I got out of the car.

"I heard. I still can't believe it. The quantity of Sillin he must've ingested to keep his scent in check . . . " He shook his head, which ruffled his already mussed-up blond-gray hair. I'd never seen him so unkempt.

August came around the car, hands in his pockets, probably to keep them off my body. Even though I'd promised to stay close, I'd begged him not to touch me. Touching would give us away. Maybe our scents already did.

My uncle's red-tinged gaze kept flitting from place to place without ever settling. "He probably can't shift anymore. Or if he can, he must be one hell of an ugly bastard. One of those *halfwolves*. The only good part about him being a wolf is that now you can end him."

August came to an abrupt halt. "End him?"

One of Jeb's eyebrows shot up while the other slanted downward. "Don't you want Callum's murder avenged, August?"

"Of course I do."

My uncle dropped his voice to a mere whisper. "Ness should use the duel as a diversion to slit his throat."

"Do you care about your niece?" August barked, jerking on the tether to bring me closer to him.

"Excuse me?" Jeb asked.

"If you cared about her, you wouldn't incite her to do something so incredibly reckless."

"Reckless?" Jeb blurted out. "Blood killings are allowed! Encouraged, even."

"Perhaps, but advising her to attack the man during an Alpha duel? You and I both know how that could finish." August was growling now.

"It could finish with my brother getting peace, that's how it could finish." A vein ticked hectically in my uncle's temple.

"Why don't you slit the asshole's throat yourself, then?" August bit out.

Ping.

"Because I plan on slitting another man's throat today."

"Whose?" I asked.

"Alex Morgan's."

"Cassandra's son?" I asked.

He nodded. "I spent the better half of last night contemplating the little shifter's face through the silver grate. If Eric hadn't kept me in check, the boy would be dead this morning." On top of looking like he was hopped-up on drugs, my uncle sounded like it.

"Is Alex here?" I gestured to the inn.

"He'll be here later." Jeb dropped his voice and took a step closer to us. "Liam's bringing him to barter in case . . . in case Julian isn't successful."

"Barter against what?" August asked.

"The Creeks's immediate departure from Boulder," he whispered loudly. "If she doesn't accept Liam's terms, then I get to kill the son-of-a-bitch." Waves of anger and bloodlust pulsed off my uncle.

I glanced up at August, worried today would turn into absolute carnage, and his expression mirrored mine.

Jeb checked his wristwatch. "Twenty minutes to go." His eyes sparked. "Twenty minutes." He rubbed his palms together gleefully before prancing ahead of us. "I'm going to go find myself a front row seat."

For a while, neither August nor I spoke. We just watched my uncle's form vanish into the entrails of his former inn.

"Well, well, well. What do we have here?" came a voice I hadn't heard in a long time. A voice I hadn't missed at all.

August inspected my face slowly before he turned around even slower. He stepped in front of me, barring me from Justin Summix's view.

"If it isn't G.I. Watt." Justin was chewing on a piece of gum, which made him look more bovine than lupine. Like at the music festival, he was flanked by his two cronies. "Heard you were dishonorably discharged."

"Is there a reason you're trying to provoke me, Justin, or do you simply get a kick out of being a world-class prick?" August asked, his voice stretched as taut as a rubber band.

Justin smiled before starting back up on his loud mastication. He craned his neck to the side to look at me. I wasn't hiding behind August. I just had no desire to look at the sleazy Pine.

"Guess I had you pegged right the first time we met, huh?" Justin blew out a bubble that smacked against his crooked mouth.

"Choke on your gum, Justin," I spat out.

He smirked, and so did his two friends. One of them cracked his knuckles while the other just leered at me.

"How does it work?" Justin continued. "Do you take them one at time or all at once?"

That was it. I lunged around August, but he tugged so hard on the tether I flailed backward, whacking against his chest. A second later, Justin was dangling in midair, sputtering. Either August was squeezing his neck too tight or the gum had gone down the wrong hole.

"Apologize. Now," August growled.

"Landon," Justin wheezed, his face beginning to turn purple.

Did that mean *I'm sorry* in some weird werewolf tongue?

His friend, the one with the matching wifebeater and buzz cut, shot his arm out. I guessed Landon was a name.

August dodged the fist flying at his face, then backhanded Landon in the jaw so suddenly that he blinked and stumbled backward before toppling onto the ground. I charged the other friend just as he raised his foot to kick August between the legs. August would've probably blocked the hit, but I didn't wait to find out. I slammed my foot against the boy's rising leg, flinging it away, then grabbed his shoulders and kneed him so hard in the groin he let out a high-pitched shriek before bending over and panting in pain.

Adrenaline coursed through me, sharpening all of my senses. I could feel the cluster of raw energy on the lawn of the inn and the din of voices. I could hear the whisper of the smile growing on August's lips and the steady thumps of his heart as he gazed down at me.

"Fuck . . . you . . . both," Justin hissed, snapping August's attention back onto him.

"That didn't sound like an apology," August said.

Justin's nails curved and sharpened, and then he clawed at August's hand.

August tossed him almost as far as the rock he'd skipped on the lake. "If any of you so much as look at Ness again, I will shred you like the vermin you are."

I grabbed onto his hand. Blood trickled out of the puncture wounds, ribboning down his wrist and soaking the cuff of his cream cotton shirt. I pushed his sleeve up, then dug a tissue from my handbag and pressed it against the four small wounds.

"You're a fucking lunatic, Watt, just like all the Boulders. All fucking inbred degenerates," Justin rasped, rubbing his reddened throat. "First thing Julian'll do when he wins the duel is kick your pack off our land for good."

"We aren't on your land," I said, still tending to August's wounds.

"He'd have to win first," August added matter-of-factly. I didn't think for a second he hoped for another outcome, but the taunt made Justin purple with rage.

"Like that bitch has a chance in hell," Landon muttered.

"She beat the Aspen Alpha," I reminded him.

"I see where your loyalties lie." Justin tugged on the hem of his white wifebeater to lower it over his baggy jeans. "Is it because she's a bitch like you?"

"Stop referring to my gender like that." I lifted the bloodied tissue and balled it up in my fist. The torn flesh had stopped bleeding and was already knitting together.

The fight begins in five minutes.

Both August and I craned our necks in the direction of the lawn at the sound of Liam's call.

"Let's go." August snaked his arm around my waist and towed me up the driveway.

No one was inside the inn—no housekeepers, no perfidious aunt. I stretched my hearing to check if I sensed human heartbeats, but all the hearts that pounded were not the least bit human.

Before we walked into the living room, August said, "You were remarkable out there."

I rolled my eyes.

He stopped and pulled me against him, stroking my cheek. "I'm serious. In case you forgot, I was at the receiving end of a punch once."

I frowned.

"The day I startled you at the gym . . . "

The day I'd decided to enter the trials. That day felt like eons ago.

He dipped his head. Before he could kiss me, I pulled out of his arms.

"August . . . " I whispered.

Thankfully no one was around. Justin and his friends must've circled the inn walls.

August rubbed his mouth. "Right."

I knew it was silly to worry about being caught, considering what was happening outside the inn walls, but I couldn't help it. I was a ball of nerves—because of August, but also because of the impending duel.

We crossed the living room toward the wall of bodies lining the deck's railing. I slid in next to Cole, scanning the grounds for Sarah. She stood between her brother and another girl—a short redhead.

Although the Matzs were too far below for me to gauge their expressions, the set of their shoulders told me Julian's family was on edge. The rest of his pack seemed slightly more relaxed. They formed a loose web behind Julian, who was discarding his clothes. He was down to a white undershirt and a pair of tight white briefs.

His sister was circling Cassandra, whose body was already bared, shoulders held back, large breasts hanging low. Did the Creeks walk around naked all the time? Nudity was really the last thing I should be wondering about at this moment.

"What is Nora Matz doing?" I asked.

"She's Julian's Second," August said, just as Lori broke away from the Creek Pack and crossed the field toward Julian.

"What's a Second?" I asked.

Cole leaned his hip against the railing, one eyebrow raised.

"Don't look at me like that, Cole. My werewolf education was cut short when my dad died, and although I've learned a couple things recently, I know there are still a lot of gaps in my shifter knowledge."

"Alphas can't duel without Seconds. It's a human tradition that the packs adopted and have used since the first recorded Alpha duel in the Appalachians." It was August who answered. "Like in human duels, Seconds are in charge of making sure there's no foul play. They'll also watch the duel up close—like referees of sorts. If any rules are broken, they can separate the parties. The duel is then either postponed if both parties desire a rematch or canceled altogether. If that happens, then each pack has an obligation to return to their territories and the Alphas are no longer allowed to challenge each other during the rest of their lifetime. However, if one of the packs sees a new Alpha rise, then that new Alpha may challenge the reigning Alpha of the enemy pack."

"What if the Seconds can't stop the duel in time and one of the challengers dies as a result of a broken rule?"

"Then the Second of the fallen Alpha can challenge the victor instantly, without waiting a full moon cycle." August was focused on Lori who was circling Julian's now entirely naked form, stopping to grab his hand and look beneath his fingernails. She then tilted his head up and stuck her finger inside his mouth.

"She's checking for concealed weapons and illegal substances implanted in the enamel," Cole explained, angling his big body back toward the lawn.

If anything, I was more confused now. "I don't understand how fighting right away benefits the Seconds," I said, returning to the rules of dueling.

"The victor expends a lot of energy during a fight. Especially in an Alpha battle. Considering the Second isn't an Alpha, their odds of winning against one are usually nil." August's eyes were on me now. "Let's say Julian beats Cassandra, but somehow Lori notices that he used foul play to do so—a trap on the ground, or a staged commotion in his ranks, or he somehow turned a stick into a weapon—Lori has the right to challenge him on the spot. She'll have the advantage of being fresh *and* her body won't go through an inspection, so technically she could have a concealed weapon. You can bet both Lori and Nora are prepped to counteract. Of course, it doesn't mean they can beat an Alpha. They won't have the body mass or training of an Alpha. Most of the times, Seconds forfeit to save their hides."

"I've never heard of a Second challenging a victorious Alpha," Cole said.

The Creek Pack shaped a compact arc behind Cassandra. I guessed from the sheer swell of unfamiliar faces that all the Creeks had arrived for the event. The mass of bodies made the hundred Pines standing behind Julian seem measly. The Seconds met in the center of the field. After they exchanged quiet words, they both nodded and traipsed back toward their respective families, ridding their bodies of clothes before shifting into fur.

You stayed. Liam's voice inside my mind was so jarring that my heart leaped.

I placed a palm against my chest before looking for him in the row of Boulders lining the railing. I'd imagined he was standing somewhere below, holding Cassandra's son in some death vice, but Liam was right there amongst his men and me, no Alex in sight.

I'm truly sorry, Ness. And not that you found out. I'm sorry for having wanted your father dead. I'm sorry that I kept it from you, that I hurt you . . . that I disappointed you . . . again. I hope in time you'll be able to forgive me.

I bit my lip, whisking my lashes down to counter the surging slickness. I darted my gaze back to the field, Julian's and Cassandra's naked forms coming in and out of focus. Next to me, I felt August's fingers graze my hip. I moved away from him, bumping into Cole.

From the corner of my eye, I caught Cole exchanging a look with August. Sadly, I knew what that look was about. Cole oozed wariness. It wafted off him like the stench of his cigarettes. He was wrong to be wary. Not wanting August to touch me had nothing to do with harboring secret romantic feelings for Liam. I simply didn't want attention from the pack—be it from Liam or from any other Boulder.

August gripped the railing as though ready to splinter the wood he and our fathers had sanded down years ago, tendons pinching in his hands, making the dried blood that still stained his skin crackle.

A low howl pierced the bright-blue sky, and then a second howl answered.

"And so it begins," Cole whispered under his breath.

CHAPTER 49

My hands joined the many other sets gripping the deck railing. The fight had started about ten minutes ago, and although the light-brown fur on Cassandra's back was tinged red from where Julian had sank his teeth into her, she was still on all fours. She moved slowly, as though the pain in her rear was taking a toll on her body. Considering he'd bit her at the start of the fight, she should've begun to heal.

Julian waited for Cassandra to creep closer before jumping on her. She flattened against the grass, then rolled over onto her back. I expected she'd keep rolling, but no . . . she stopped moving, as though waiting for Julian to land on her. The second his body came within limb-length of hers, she slashed his belly with her claws, then whirled around beneath him and bucked him off her injured back.

Julian landed with a heavy thump a couple feet away from her. For a moment, he didn't move.

I held my breath.

Everyone held their breath.

Cole said, "He's going to end her."

Julian pressed back onto his paws like a mountain rising from tectonic plates and lunged toward Cassandra again, dark muzzle wet with her blood, fangs bared. He gripped her thigh in his mouth and shook his head as though trying to dismember her. Her leg stayed attached, but she toppled over. He dragged her a couple feet, but then she bucked, and Julian sputtered, emitting a great choking sound as though he'd gotten a mouthful of fur. The moment he let her go, she crawled away from him, belly to the ground.

But he was still wheezing, batting one of his legs across his muzzle as though trying to brush off Cassandra's blood. He retched.

Voices began to rise, shouts, jeers, cheers. Like spectators at a sports match, the crowd was becoming boisterous. Although they kept a safe distance from the wolves, Nora and Lori orbited around their Alphas.

At the sound of Julian vomiting, Cassandra flipped around, positioned herself in a crouch, and, with a keening moan, heaved herself up. Her momentum was so sluggish it looked as though she were moving in slow-motion and yet she managed to tip Julian over. Both wolves crashed down in a mix of bloodied brown fur, bodies writhing and jerking.

A snarl echoed against the tawny trunks of the swaying pine trees and ricocheted like the blaring sunlight on the tall glass façade of the inn.

A whimper ensued.

And then the wet snap of an overextended vein.

My skin broke out in goose bumps as one Alpha stole the life of another.

CHAPTER 50

Julian had fallen.

The upset created a ripple of cries and outbursts down below but also on the deck. Every Boulder body tightened and straightened, every set of eyes strained, and every mouth pursed. No one spoke beside me, not even Liam through the mind link. We all just stood shoulder to shoulder, solemn in our shock and grief.

Yes, *grief* . . .

Even though I hadn't much liked the Pine Alpha, I liked Cassandra even less.

A sharp cry tore through the field as Nora rushed to Julian's mangled, inert form. Robbie sprang away from his pack and caught his mother before she could throw herself atop her brother. She whimpered and whined and snarled at her son, while he spoke quietly into her ear. After a long moment, she stopped snarling and slid back into skin. Shaking with sobs that were so shrill they could probably be heard in the middle of town, she burrowed her head against Robbie's chest.

My gaze skated over the strange scene below. People had begun pouring onto the field to felicitate their Alpha, who was still in fur. On the other side of the field, Sarah had crumpled to her knees. I started to go toward her when August caught my wrist and shook his head.

"No," he said, his tone brooking no argument.

"But Sarah—"

"Sarah will be taken care of." His grip was all at once loose but firm, as though he was fighting his urge to hold me tighter. "Stay up here."

Margaux and a redheaded girl had kneeled next to Sarah, but still I itched to go to her. What decided me to stay away was the pulse of terror throbbing through the link. My already clenching stomach roiled and contracted with August's fear.

I returned to the railing, and he let go of my wrist. Although he didn't put his hands on me again, he held on to me through the tether as though he didn't trust me not to sprint down those stairs.

"I won't go," I reassured him, but it did little to loosen his invisible grip.

I turned my attention back to the ground below. For the final time, the fur receded into Julian's pores, his muzzle retracted, and his limbs twisted back into his human ones.

"Do you wish to contest the fairness of the fight and challenge the Alpha today?" Lori hollered, back in skin and clothes, her voice thundering over all the others.

Along with every shifter present, I watched Nora. Watched as she turned in her son's arm. Watched as her lips trembled. Watched as her head shook, first with a shudder, then with an answer.

No.

"Do you wish to challenge the Alpha in one moon cycle from now?" Lori asked, voice loud and clear.

Again, Julian's sister shook her head. Robbie plucked the blonde hair sticking to his mother's pale forehead and cheeks. Margaux tossed a sort of cape over her mother-in-law's shoulders, and then Robbie wrapped an arm around her and helped her off the field. A cry ripped from her throat, and then another, her grief echoing against the Flatirons and the farthest and tallest mountain peaks.

"Alpha of the Creeks!" Lori turned to her mother who was still in fur. "The fallen's heart is yours for the taking, and with it, the fallen's pack."

The fallen's heart?

I wasn't sure if I asked this out loud or if August read the confusion etched on my face, but he said, "The victor eats the heart of the loser, thus acquiring a link to the dead Alpha's pack."

A lump of bile shot up my throat.

August stepped in front of me and tucked me into his chest. "I told you it was brutal."

I didn't look, but I heard the watery tear of flesh, the placid crunch of bones, and the bloody squelch of what had once fueled life into a man and would now fuel magic into a woman.

Even though I was probably imagining it, I felt as though I heard the blood drip off Cassandra's muzzle and mix into the tear-and-vomit-soaked soil.

At long last, triumphant howls ripped through the summer sky, announcing that an Alpha had fallen and another had taken its place.

I thought back to the last trial I'd had to endure against Liam— the test of strength. Was what I'd just witnessed what the elders had in mind? Had they hoped Liam would tear open my breastbone and eat my heart?

I shuddered, which made August squeeze me tighter, and I let him. I didn't care who spotted me in his arms. I still had a heart beating inside my chest. I wouldn't force it to be quiet to avoid criticism or stares, just like I wouldn't force August to keep his distance. I needed him. I wanted him.

If today had taught me anything, it was that life was too short to worry about what others thought. I wrapped my arms around August's waist and burrowed closer, hoping that his scent and warmth would help dull the terrible images and sounds that kept replaying in my skull.

CHAPTER 51

Voices grew louder around us. Ambient conversations began to penetrate my buzzing mind.

"What do you think he swallowed that made him throw up?" Matt was asking his brother.

"Fur, or maybe a chunk of flesh. That'll make anyone gag."

At the mention of gagging, bile rose anew in my throat. "You were right. I shouldn't have come," I murmured against August's chest.

He tucked a strand of hair behind my ear. "At least now you know." His mouth brushed the top of my head while his fingers brushed down my spine. If anyone had lingering suspicions as to whether he and I had crossed the line between friendship and more, I imagined our present proximity obliterated them.

"You should take her away from here, son," I heard Nelson say.

I peeled myself off August so fast I must've left a couple eyelashes behind.

Nelson's mouth was pressed into a grim line. "That was awful, wasn't it?"

"Y-yes," I stammered.

I forced myself to meet Nelson's deep-brown eyes, dreading the disgust I expected, but there was no disgust. Just wariness. I tried not to wonder if his wariness stemmed from what had unfolded down below or from what had unfolded up on the deck between August and me.

I pushed the bra strap that had slipped down my arm back under my tank top. "What's going to happen now?"

Several Boulders were speaking in hushed tones behind Nelson. I heard the words: *Cassandra, duel, Liam.* I feared that those words might belong in the same sentence.

"Now"—August's father inhaled a grave breath—"the Creeks will probably extend their trip in Boulder. The time it takes to acclimate the newest members of their pack."

James, the blond with impeccably coiffed hair, came up behind August. "It'll be good for business."

"You can cut and style their hair all you want, but we won't be doing business with the Creeks," August said.

"We lived alongside the Pines for almost a century and we did business with *them*. Why wouldn't we take Creek money?"

August's jaw hardened, as though he were holding back a biting retort.

Nelson touched his son's forearm. "Let's see what happens. There's no point forecasting what we will and will not do until we understand what it is they want."

"What they want is to take our land," Rodrigo said, coming to stand by James's side, "and our men."

I didn't even bother sticking my hand up to remind him that I wasn't a man. It was really beside the point.

"How do you know that, Rodrigo? Did you have yourself a little chat with Cassandra before the duel?" Nelson asked. I'd never heard him be so short with anyone. I didn't even know he was capable of such curtness.

"No, Nelson, I didn't," Rodrigo bit out. "But why else would they have all come? Why else did they have Aidan observe us for so many years? Liam said there was a missing packet of Sillin. I bet they got some pills in Julian—"

"He wouldn't have been able to shift. Besides, he didn't drink or eat anything last night," James said.

"How do you know? Were you with him all night, Jamie?" Under his breath, he added, "*Again.*"

James backed away, shaking his head. "You can be a real ass sometimes." He turned and headed toward another group of Boulders.

"Liam told Robbie they should have Julian's blood analyzed for Sillin." The dark-haired, dark-tempered firefighter tipped his head toward the lawn where Liam was talking with Robbie. "But Julian's body belongs to the Creeks now that Nora refused to fight. If they so much as allow him a burial, I'd be surprised."

"Will Robbie challenge Cassandra now?"

"Possibly," Rodrigo said, "but his odds of winning against an Alpha would be shit." He slanted his dark eyes on me. "You have to have a screw loose to challenge an Alpha."

I recoiled, because that last part felt personal.

Nelson's fingers tightened around August's arm. "That was out of line, Rodrigo."

"My father could've won," I murmured.

"Odds are—"

"Enough!" Nelson said, still gripping August's arm. "That's enough."

Rodrigo pinched his thick pink lips closed.

"It takes courage to fight for what you want," Nelson said. "What takes no courage is denigrating others."

Rodrigo lowered his eyes, chastised by Nelson, but too proud to apologize for having insulted my family.

"August, we need your help with something." Cole cocked his head toward Matt and Dexter.

When Nelson released his son's arm, August turned toward me as though worried to leave me alone.

I flexed my lips into a smile I wasn't feeling. "Go."

Reluctantly, he left with the three other Boulders.

I stepped a little farther from Nelson, who was still giving Rodrigo a tongue-lashing. I tried to glimpse Sarah down below. If Liam was down there, it was probably safe—

"You and August a thing now?" Lucas asked.

He stood next to me, forearms propped on the railing, gaze sunk on the field below, or rather on the crumpled girl with the lustrous blonde hair. Margaux placed a kiss on the top of Sarah's head, then, cradling her abdomen, she stood and walked over to an older man—her father perhaps.

"Yes," I finally said.

Lucas pivoted toward me, leaning against the balustrade. "Is it serious?"

Margaux made her way over to Robbie next. Although he was still deep in conversation with Liam, Robbie tugged his pregnant mate against him.

I sighed. "I stayed."

"You were really going to skip town?"

"Yeah."

"Where would you have gone?"

I shrugged. "Maybe back to LA. I couldn't feel the pack's pull out there." The idea of returning to Los Angeles made my stomach churn. LA reminded me too much of Mom. "Or maybe I would've tried my luck on the East Coast."

"You know he feels like shit about everything, don't you? The recording. Tammy."

I returned my gaze to Sarah, who was alone now. "I'm sure he does, but it's not really my problem anymore, is it?"

"He's our Alpha, Ness."

"What are you saying?"

"A conflicted Alpha can get sloppy, and that can impact the entire pack."

I crossed my arms. "So what? Are you suggesting I go down there and give him a big old hug and tell him I forgive him for breaking my heart?"

"Did he?"

"Break my heart? Yeah, he did."

Although the tinny scent of death stained the air, most of the bloody patches on the lawn were hidden behind clusters of shifters—some in mourning, some in celebration. Someone had covered Julian with a white sheet from which only his feet and head protruded. Blood bloomed on the white, so much of it that I didn't think any amount of meat tenderizer would be able to get it out.

"You cared that much about him?"

"I did."

"He still cares about you."

"He'll get over it."

"What if he doesn't?"

"Did you get over Taryn?"

He watched Sarah as she rose and craned her neck to stare into the sun. Maybe she was hoping its blazing heat would dry her tears.

"I don't miss her anymore," he said.

She squinted toward the inn. When she caught sight of us, she headed for the porch steps, treading fast, as though in a hurry to get away from her new pack, ironed hair glinting like a swath of gold. When she reached the deck, she lurched toward me. I just had time to open my arms before she sprang into them.

"We told him not to challenge her." Her tears soaked the collar of my tank. "We begged him not to do it."

I rubbed the top of her spine.

"He's gone. And now we're . . . we're . . . Creeks." Her voice cracked on that last word. "It's her voice I'll hear in my mind. She'll be the one to tell us what to do." She pulled away from me, fixing me with her shiny brown eyes. "I. Hate. Her," she bit out, trembling all over. "I hate all of them." She glared at a small group of Creeks passing below us.

There were five of them, not much older than us. Where two of the boys and one of the girls stared at us with restraint, the other two —a boy and girl, who looked so much alike I assumed they were siblings—watched us with unabashed interest.

"They can't all be bad," I whispered to her, trying to soothe her.

"I still hate them," she muttered.

"I know." I smoothed her hair back.

She pressed away from me and shot her red-tinged gaze toward Lucas. "Liam has to challenge her. He has to take the packs back. You guys have to tell him to challenge her."

The blood drained from Lucas's face, turning his complexion as white as the scar that slashed his black eyebrow. "No way. If she doesn't challenge him, then we're advising him to stay out of it."

"I'm sure she cheated, Lucas. I don't know how she did it, but I'm sure of it. Julian wasn't throwing up *fur balls* out there. I bet she poisoned him."

"If she had"—I wrinkled my nose for what I was about to say—"she couldn't have eaten his *heart* without it poisoning her."

"Ness is right, Sarah."

Sarah scrubbed her eyes with the heels of her hands. "But she did something. She must've. Maybe she managed to slip him Sillin. It would've weakened him."

My brow puckered. "How would she have done that?"

"I don't know, but—"

Lucas interrupted Sarah. "Wouldn't Sillin have made him shift back into his human form?"

Would it? "It keeps us from shifting when we're in skin," I said, remembering what it had done to me, "but I'm not sure what it does when we're in fur."

"It'll show up on his tox screen," Lucas said.

The same way it had shown up on Heath's . . .

"If we're even allowed to run one," Sarah muttered.

"If she doesn't allow you to run one, it'll be as much of an answer. It'll prove she has something to hide."

Cassandra had finally shifted back. Her body was bruised and bloodied, yet pride squared her shoulders and her jaw. A man was wrapping a bandage around her thigh that was still weeping blood.

"What if it's in her blood?" I whispered.

"What if what's in her blood?"

"The Sillin. What if it's in her blood?" I kept my voice so low that both Lucas and Sarah strained toward me. "Her wound should've sealed up by now."

"But she managed to shift into a wolf," Sarah said.

"She must've swallowed it while in wolf form," I said, scanning the makeshift dueling ring for what—white pills, a crushed foil packet?

"Mom would've seen her eat something and signaled it."

"Maybe your mom missed it?" I suggested.

Sarah inhaled a swift breath. "You know what this means, though? That she's weaker now. That if Liam challenged her, he might very well win."

"Unless she poisons him, too," I murmured.

Color had returned to Lucas's face. "If the Sillin's in her system, there's no way she can shift back into fur. Not for a couple hours. Possibly days, depending on the dose."

"Could they duel in skin?" I asked.

"Would be atypical, but why the hell not?" Lucas sounded pumped.

I didn't like his enthusiasm. *Feared* it. Feared it might incite Liam to act recklessly. Before I could quiet him, Lucas shouted, "Great Alpha Morgan, shift back!"

Everyone turned to stare at him, and I mean, *everyone*.

"Excuse me?" Cassandra said.

Lucas had his arms crossed in front of his chest. "Shift. Back."

"Why, Mr. Mason?" I was impressed she knew his name. Then again, she must've spent decades studying all the files her cousin had sent her.

Her cousin, who was standing next to her, looking like the cat who ate the canary. How I despised Aidan Michaels.

"To satisfy my curiosity," he said.

"I bet you, she won't do it," Sarah whispered.

"Very well," Cassandra said.

Keeping her gaze locked on Lucas, brown fur poured from her pores, and then her eyes flashed with an inhuman glow, and she landed on all fours, trampling our Sillin-theory the same way she trampled the broken blades of grass underneath her paws.

CHAPTER 52

A whoosh of breath lurched from Lucas's mouth. "How?" he whispered.

Sarah blinked hard at the wolf that was slowly turning back into a woman.

Once Cassandra was in skin, she craned her neck to look up at us, pulling the bandage that had slid down her thigh back up. "Have I satisfied your curiosity, Mr. Mason?"

Lucas's lips were still parted, but no sound came out of him.

Could she have applied a cream to her body that would've made Julian sick?

"Was Julian allergic to anything?" I asked Sarah.

She shook her head, eyes so wide there was white around her irises.

"Fuck," Lucas finally said, just as heavy footsteps pounded the terrace floor.

We all turned toward the disturbance.

Gripped between August and Cole stood a boy no older than I was. Was this the infamous Alex Morgan? Everest's killer?

Alex had the blond curls of a cherub, a boyish jaw that had yet to be chiseled by life even though it was riddled with fading bruises that matched the violet shade of his eyes. He was more pretty-boy than cold-blooded killer.

"Damn, she's way hotter in real," he said, gaze raking over me.

August smacked his elbow into the side of Alex's head.

"Ow. What was that for?" Alex carped, trying to raise his hand to cradle his head, but both Cole and August clamped down on his wrists, pinning them behind his lanky body.

Alex really didn't look like he needed two mammoth shifters to keep him in check. Then again, there was something slippery about him, as though he were more eel than wolf.

"*He* killed Everest?" Sarah asked.

"I know, right," Lucas grumbled.

Alex smirked at Sarah, or rather at her rack. "The region's good to its females."

"Shut the fuck up," Lucas growled.

Alex grinned, seemingly getting off on irritating everyone. He stared beyond us then, at the lawn. "Hey, Ma, I'm home!"

A couple muffled laughs rose from the Creek pack.

"You said you wouldn't hurt him," Cassandra snarled at Liam.

"No. We said we wouldn't kill him. And we didn't." Liam sounded chillingly calm.

Cassandra gave him a hard stare. "Your terms. What are they?"

"You take your pack and leave Boulder immediately."

Sarah gasped.

I put a hand on her arm. "He surely doesn't mean you," I murmured reassuringly.

"I doubt my new pledges—" Cassandra began.

"Pledges?" Sarah's fingers curled into fists. "We didn't pledge ourselves to you. We would *never*!"

Cassandra flicked her gray gaze onto my friend. "My new *compatriots* . . . Does the term suit you better, Miss Matz?"

Sarah scowled.

"I doubt they want to abandon their land," Cassandra continued, returning her attention to Liam. "Technically, *my* land."

"So you don't accept my terms?"

"I do not accept your terms," Cassandra said calmly.

I snuck a glance over my shoulder at Alex. He was no longer grinning, but he was also not peeing his pants.

"Technically, Kolane, Everest was already a dead man, was he not?" she continued.

"We're not in a court of law. Your son isn't getting off on a technicality. This is pack law, and pack law forbids inter-pack murders," Liam said, a pointed edge to his voice. "We have proof your son deliberately ran him off the road. We found yellow paint on Everest's Jeep. Yellow paint that rubbed off from your son's Hummer."

"Paint? That's your proof?" Cassandra's lips puckered. "When Everest took off from our property, he back-ended my son's car. That's why—"

"Just before the crash, he called me!" My voice fired across the field, leaving a trail of billowing silence. "He said he was being chased." I swallowed hard. "So don't you *dare* claim he crashed into that ditch by accident!"

Cassandra's eyebrows quirked in surprise. She licked the blood off her lips that seemed bluer in the sunlight.

Fingers twined with my own. Slender fingers. Sarah's. She squeezed my palm tight.

"Look, Kolane," Cassandra said, "if you give me back my son, I swear in front of every Creek and Boulder that I'll *never* challenge you to a duel." She tapped the spot over her heart as though to prove her sincerity. "I'll let your pack go on. I'm willin' to sign a treaty with you this very minute."

A spark of hope ignited within me . . . within Liam. I felt the speeding up of his heart inside my own chest.

"I didn't come here to challenge Alphas," Cassandra said. "I came here to create alliances."

"Says the wolf who just murdered a man," Robbie interjected.

"I didn't challenge your uncle!" Cassandra's temper exploded all over her haggard face. She took a few steps back, a noticeable limp in her right leg. "He challenged me! And he *lost.*" She stopped backing up and jerked her arm toward Julian's remains. "That's what hubris does to men. It makes them feel like gods but act like fools."

Liam studied her for a long moment. I prayed he was considering her terms.

"Take her deal," I whispered, not that he could hear me. "Take it."

Sarah glanced at me, conflict written all over her face.

"No!" Liam's answer was like an explosion—terrifying. "You fight me right here. Right now."

My blood became ice.

"Liam!" Lucas rushed the handrail so fast I worried he would break right through it.

Cassandra scrutinized Liam. "Trying to take advantage of my injuries, Kolane?"

"Do you accept?" Liam asked.

"Liam, no!" I yelled.

"Do. You. Accept?"

"Didn't you listen to a word I just said about *hubris?*" she asked calmly.

"Are you afraid to face me?" Liam asked.

I willed her not to accept.

"You'll need a Second," she finally said.

Liam wheeled toward us and craned his neck. "Lucas—"

"Don't fucking ask me to do this, man." Lucas shook his head so fiercely his black hair flogged his sheet-white jaw. Liam must've said something else to him, this time through the mind link, because Lucas growled a loud, unflinching, "Absolutely not!"

Liam flung his gaze on Matt.

Matt jerked, and then, like Lucas, shook his head. "No."

Liam's eyes narrowed.

A smile lilted Lori's lips. "Your pack doesn't seem very confident in your abilities—"

"Rodrigo?" Annoyance chafed Liam's tone.

Rodrigo's face glistened with perspiration. "Take her deal, Liam."

Have faith in me! His voice raged inside my skull.

I clapped my hands against my ears. I wasn't alone in doing this.

I can defeat her! She is weak. I can do this! But I have to do it NOW.

A whimper escaped me.

Liam fastened his eyes on mine for a long moment. So much passed between us then. Regret, resentment, disappointment, affection.

Don't do it, I mouthed.

Finally he spun back around. "I challenge you without a Second."

EPILOGUE

Cassandra drummed her fingers against the bloodied bandage on her thigh. "Dueling without a Second is unheard of."

"Unheard of but not unlawful," Liam said, his voice taut with determination. "Besides, it puts me at a disadvantage. You should be jumping at the opportunity."

Cassandra studied Liam. "I don't *jump*. I calculate risks."

I frantically scanned the faces of the Boulders surrounding me. Some had gone ghostly pale.

August's gaze struck mine. "Liam—"

"Don't even think about giving me advice, Watt," Liam barked.

I sucked in air, but it seemed devoid of oxygen. I pulled in another breath, and it went down the wrong pipe. I began to cough so hard I thought I would hack out one of my lungs.

Perhaps Liam could defeat Cassandra, but what if he couldn't?

Then . . . then she'd . . . she'd eat his heart.

Not for the first time today, bile shot up my throat. I was about to spin back around when my gaze landed on Alex's. He was smiling as though he could taste his freedom, as though he sensed his mother wouldn't walk away from the challenge, as though he knew she'd be victorious.

I flipped back around. Cassandra was stroking her narrow, bloody chin. Next to her, Lori and Aidan stood side by side, both relaxed and smiling as easily as Alex.

"I volunteer," I shouted suddenly. "I'll be his Second!"

"What?" Lucas roared, at the same time as August yelled, "Out of the question!"

Before anyone could stop me, I flew down the stairs and raced toward Liam.

His dark eyes were wide with shock.

"But since I'm the Second, I get a say in when the duel happens."

"Ness—" Liam started.

"Right?" I all but screeched, my throat on fire.

"No. Only the challenged party gets a say in when and where it happens," Lori said. "And we'd—"

"Release my son, and you'll get to decide when and where the duel takes place."

"Like hell we're setting him loose," Liam said.

"My son won't harm anyone. I'll give you my word."

"Your word means shit."

"Then let's fight now." She was limping and bleeding, and yet she was willing to go back into the ring?

"Liam." I jutted my head toward the indoor pool.

Jaw set tight, he headed for the inn, slid open the glass door, and after we'd both stepped inside, he shut it so hard the glass rattled in its frame. Before I could talk, he exclaimed, "Are you trying to screw me over?"

"Screw you over? No, Liam. I wouldn't have signed up for this if I were trying to *screw you over*."

His pupils pulsed and pulsed.

I glanced through the glass at Cassandra, who was rubbing her body down with a wet towel to get rid of the blood and gore, and then around the pool room to check for surveillance equipment.

I didn't see any cameras, but it didn't mean the place wasn't bugged, so I dropped my voice to a hissing whisper. "She did something to Julian, and I plan on figuring out what that is, so it isn't your heart she eats next."

"Why do you care what happens to my heart?"

I dragged my hand through my hair, my fingers snagging on some strands. "Beats me. I just do."

"You chose August."

I squashed my lips together. This was so not the moment to have this discussion. Then again, there would never be a good time to have this discussion.

"You spent the night with him." It wasn't a question.

"It's none of your business."

"You're my wolves. It is my—"

"No, Liam. What happens between August and me only concerns *him* and *me*."

A nerve ticked in his clenched jaw. For a long moment, he simply stared at me.

"Look, I know you don't want to release Alex, but it'll buy us time. We *need* time." When that didn't extinguish the bloodlust lighting up his irises, I tossed my hands in the air. "You know what, if you don't give a shit about dying, then by all means, be your usual hotheaded self and go fight her now, but you'll be doing it alone, because I won't stand by to see you get gutted!"

Doubt finally smudged his eyes. "Fine. *Fine*, I'll wait."

"Good."

"But I'll only take you on as a Second on one condition."

"No conditions. You either take me on or you don't. But if you don't, you'll lose."

"Maybe I won't lose."

I growled with annoyance. "Liam. Come on. This isn't some joke. This is your life! Don't you care about seeing another night? Another year?"

"My condition is simple. All I'm asking is—"

"I said I wasn't negotiating with you."

"—that you don't date August until after the duel."

"What?"

"I want you focused on *me*. If you're consolidating a mating link, your mind and body will be too preoccupied with him to worry about me."

"Liam . . . " I breathed. "That's ridiculous."

"If I'm going to put my life in your hands, I need your hands not to be busy rubbing down some other man's body."

Heat smacked my cheeks. "Liam!"

"I don't see the problem with what I'm asking. The guy's so infatuated with you, he'll wait. It's not like I'm asking you to stay unmated until the Winter Solstice. Just until my duel."

I blinked at him in disbelief. "Which we haven't even set a date for. It could take months."

"Better find out quick how she cheated then."

This was ridiculous. *He* was being ridiculous.

"Look, my condition isn't a way to win you back. It's just a ground rule to avoid distractions that could cost me my life."

"A life you were willing to sacrifice a moment ago."

He stared long and hard at me. "Do you accept?"

He was being completely unfair. Dating August wouldn't impair my focus. Sure we were mates, but I'd be able to concentrate on other things . . . on other people.

My nostrils flared with annoyed breaths. "What if something happens?"

"If *something happens*, then *I'll* pick the duel date."

"You do realize how stupid that is, right? You're blackmailing me with your own fate."

"By accepting you as my Second, I'm putting my fate in your hands. I'm choosing to give you the benefit of the doubt. Truthfully, I still think I should go fight her right this second." His gaze shifted to Cassandra's before settling back on me. "So? Do you accept?"

I hated what he was asking of me. "I'll still work for him and his dad."

"No. I'll pay you from now on."

I opened my mouth to object.

"Prepping me for the duel will become your job."

I still hadn't shut my mouth.

"Your *only* job. Understood?"

August would be pissed. I could already sense through the pulsating tautness in the tether that my volunteering to be Liam's Second was eating at him.

"You reeked of him this morning, so don't think for a second I won't know if you spend *time* with him."

"I'm not even allowed to spend time with him now?"

"Not alone, and not in close quarters."

"What about college? Do I get to go to college, or is that off the table too?"

"You can attend classes, but as soon as they let out, you're with me." He extended his hand. "Do we have a deal?"

"I hate you," I said, giving him my hand.

"If you hated me, then you would've let me fight today." His smile grew, not wider, just wickeder. "We're going to have fun working together."

"Fun? This'll be a lot of things, but not fun."

Our hearts were both on the line; our lives both suspended.

He lifted my fingers to his lips and kissed my knuckles.

I snatched my hand away and rubbed it against my cut-offs. "This is just some game to you, isn't it?"

"In a way, it is. If I play my hand well, I stand to win *everything* I've ever coveted." His gaze stroked my face. "What do you say we become the characters of the bedtime stories shifters will tell their children for generations to come, Ness Clark?"

"I say, let's save your damn life so I can go back to living mine."

His eyes gleamed with the same stealthy smile that adorned his lips. He nodded toward the lawn, slid the door open, and ushered me out of the shadows and back into the sunshine.

AFTERWORD

Dive right into
A PACK OF LOVE AND HATE.

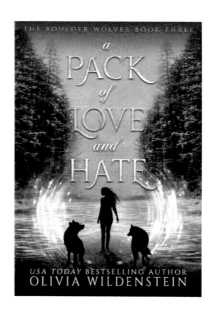

Be sure to sign up for my newsletter to stay up to date on all of my future releases.

Sign up on www.oliviawildenstein.com

ACKNOWLEDGMENTS

The Boulder Wolves has been praised and criticized since its release back in April 2019, because it didn't shy away from major triggers. Mainly in the love department.

I do not sanction "bully-love," which might be the best way to describe how Liam handles his attraction to Ness at the end of this book, but I do realize it exists. And because it exists, I'm going to bring it up.

If my mother taught me one thing (she taught me way more than one thing, but listing them all will lead to a whole other book . . .), it's that talking about things—even negative ones—is healthier than keeping silent.

Relationships are complicated, and made even more so when people have baggage. Liam is a complicated person. Not fundamentally bad, but he has a bad way of going about getting what he wants. *Spoiler alert* . . . he will be redeemed in the last book but will have to fight long and hard against his demons.

Now onto August . . .

Yes, he's ten years older than Ness.

Yes, she's only seventeen (almost eighteen).

I know all of this and yet still decided to write their love story. Growing up, I was convinced my husband would be ten years older than me. Why? Because my parents have a ten-year gap, and their love is so wonderful that I yearned for the same one.

As I grew older, I realized that love isn't determined by years and numbers, but by how well you click with someone. My husband didn't turn out to be ten years older—only five—but my brother's wife turned out to be a decade younger than him, so there . . . one of us emulated our parents.

All this to say that I hope you'll end up loving Ness and August as much as I do.

Thank you, dear reader, for traipsing along on this lupine adventure.

Thank you to my publisher and to my wonderful team—Krystal, Monika, Katie, Theresea, Vanessa, and Astrid—for helping me bring the Boulder pack to life.

Thank you to my mother for her boundless wisdom, and to my father for his unwavering support.

Thank you to my husband for always being my rock.

And last but not least, thank you to my three extraordinary children for being the greatest and *loudest* cheerleaders.

Be sure to visit http://oliviawildenstein.com to stay up to date on all the happenings.

ALSO BY OLIVIA WILDENSTEIN

YA PARANORMAL ROMANCE

The Lost Clan series
ROSE PETAL GRAVES
ROWAN WOOD LEGENDS
RISING SILVER MIST
RAGING RIVAL HEARTS
RECKLESS CRUEL HEIRS

The Boulder Wolves series
A PACK OF BLOOD AND LIES
A PACK OF VOWS AND TEARS
A PACK OF LOVE AND HATE
A PACK OF STORMS AND STARS

Angels of Elysium series
FEATHER
CELESTIAL
STARLIGHT

The Quatrefoil Chronicles series
OF WICKED BLOOD
OF TAINTED HEART

YA ROMANTIC SUSPENSE

Masterful series

THE MASTERKEY
THE MASTERPIECERS
THE MASTERMINDS

YA ROMANCE STANDALONES

GHOSTBOY, CHAMELEON & THE DUKE OF GRAFFITI
NOT ANOTHER LOVE SONG

ABOUT THE AUTHOR

USA TODAY bestselling author Olivia Wildenstein grew up in New York City, the daughter of a French father with a great sense of humor, and a Swedish mother whom she speaks to at least three times a day. She chose Brown University to complete her undergraduate studies and earned a bachelor's in comparative literature. After designing jewelry for a few years, Wildenstein traded in her tools for a laptop computer and a very comfortable chair. This line of work made more sense, considering her college degree.

When she's not writing, she's psychoanalyzing everyone she meets (Yes. Everyone), eavesdropping on conversations to gather material for her next book, baking up a storm (that she actually eats), going to the gym (because she eats), and attempting not to be late at her children's school (like she is 4 out of 5 mornings, on good weeks).

oliviawildenstein.com
olivia@wildenstein.com

Printed by BoD™in Norderstedt, Germany

9 781948 463171